We the States

We the States

AN ALTERNATE HISTORY NOVEL

ADAM SIVITZ

Palmetto Publishing Group
Charleston, SC

First Edition

Printed in the United States

ISBN-13: 978-1-64111-075-4
ISBN-10: 1-64111-075-9

Book One

UNITED STATES ASUNDER

Chapter I

1788

George Washington wore flannel pajamas, faded and tight against his skin. He preferred undergarments to his military blues, weighted with medals and shining armor. The miraculous hero of an adulating nation had risked his life in battle, returned home from his journey, and now, dressed in jammies, stood in the center of his damp horse stable, inhaling the pungent odor of manure and leather that collided with a summer breeze from the dung repository outside. The thick odor lingered like the smell of hot iron and gunpowder from cannonballs that had surrounded him for so many years. Hard smells of hard labor remained from the enslaved men and women who tended the horses all day. It all blended together in the cozy aroma of home. Washington retired to bed every evening at nine o'clock, but lately, he'd had trouble sleeping, kept awake by a thunderstorm raging in his head and by an unsettling evening sky that threatened to erupt in chaos over his Mount Vernon mansion. As of yet, it had only leaked a faint drizzle.

Washington's brick stable at Mount Vernon was sturdier and more spacious than most houses in Virginia, and for good reason: It sheltered a true hero of the American Revolution. Nelson stood over five feet tall and was more muscular than a Greek god, even more muscular than Washington. Massive strength burst from the horse's legs and physique, covered in a chestnut coating that shone like a Virginia sunrise over the Potomac River. His coat blazed through the black night and turned iridescent by the fire of Washington's lantern. Nelson had survived the most arduous days of the Revolutionary War alongside his master, including the treacherous winter

3

at Valley Forge. He had charged more redcoats and dodged more bullets and arrows than any soldier on either side of the war.

Washington always admired Nelson's calm and assertive demeanor. He would never forget how impressive the warhorse had handled himself at Yorktown. As the British surrendered, the gallant stallion stood his ground during tense negotiations and stared down General Cornwallis through a set of piercing, black eyes with a silent fixation that said, *Now and forever, lay down your guns, you son of a bitch.* He was heroic, he'd done his duty, and now he lived peacefully in retirement, a quality that Washington envied most.

General Washington bowed forward as Nelson lifted his long, white face to greet his master with some gentle nudges on the shoulder. A steady and subtle vibration fluttered from the horse's neck and reverberated down Washington's spine. Nelson, unlike any other horse, purred in tranquil moments like this one. The general never told anyone of this anomaly—not friends, colleagues, or even his wife. Only a fool would claim that horses purred like kittens. But Nelson did, in fact, purr. It was louder than a nicker and softer than a snort—a consistent drumroll from the horse's internal engine that Washington imagined was its soul.

Only two other people knew Nelson's secret: Peter, the enslaved horse breeder at Mount Vernon, who knew Nelson almost as well as Washington did, and Alexander Hamilton, the general's aide-de-camp during the war. Over the course of fighting a revolution and serving at the Constitutional Convention, Hamilton had become like a son to the childless Washington. They discussed animal behavior often. Washington insisted Nelson's purring displayed deep emotion. He recalled a dreary night in New York when the two had debated the subject with great passion. Hamilton pointed his finger in a stabbing motion as he spoke: "Animals have no emotional life, and what we perceive as emotion is merely a biological reaction, no different from a sneeze." Washington disagreed, but he appreciated an aide with the audacity to argue with a general on topics like animals or agriculture. Although, when it came to matters of war, Hamilton modeled an unyielding loyalty that Washington demanded from all his soldiers. Hamilton could only be faulted for possessing too much revolutionary fervor. At times, Washington thought his young aide too ambitious for his own good.

He sometimes accused Hamilton of overzealousness and a dangerous appetite for battle and glory.

The general thought of Hamilton often during these nighttime consultations with Nelson. George Washington was uncomfortable depending on others, but since his return from the Constitutional Convention in September, it was all he could do—have faith in the political talents of others. "It's out of my hands now," he said to Nelson. "I need nine states. Nine states to ratify. Madison and Hamilton possess the two most patriotic and brilliant minds on this continent. Their political instincts are far greater than mine. Surely, they will secure ratification—and if they don't, then a retired farmer I shall be."

Washington served as president of the Constitutional Convention in Philadelphia, where he led America's preeminent politicians in writing a new constitution to replace the ineffective Articles of Confederation. Adoption of the United States Constitution required ratification by nine of the thirteen state governments, and this could not be guaranteed by any stretch of the imagination. It had been an uphill battle from the start, and he agonized more and more as opposition to the US Constitution mounted in Virginia. George Washington symbolized the United States, and he symbolized its proposed constitution. Its failure would be *his* failure.

As he stroked Nelson's reddish-brown hair, a crashing noise outside startled them both and jolted the stable as if a meteor had fallen. On instinct, Washington reached for his sword, but found none in his pajama bottoms. Nelson's head hurtled toward the stable entrance. His purring came to an abrupt stop. Like a rising tidal wave, a monstrous shadow overpowered the flickering candlelight while a man rose from the ground, trying to salvage what was left of an oversized piece of cake, balancing it on a dinner plate.

"Reveal yourself!" demanded Washington.

"Sorry, Mastuh Washton. Didn't know you was still up," said the shaking voice. "Looked like Peter left the stable door open." His heavy, green eyes glimmered through the evening air that concealed his dark-brown skin.

Washington glared at his enslaved cook, Hercules, who had no business being outside this late in the evening. Caught red-handed with dessert, the cook rubbed his tongue in and out of the wide gap between his bottom front teeth where he was missing an incisor—a nervous habit. Washington considered scolding Hercules for startling him. He could have questioned why the slave was outside so late and nowhere near the slave quarters. He could have reproached him for the cake, which was no doubt stolen from the kitchen. But, in a rare void of emotion in response to a breach of routine, Washington replied, "It appears to be quite a storm on the way. You'd be best to stay inside, now."

"Yes, suh, Mastuh Washton," Hercules said, looking surprised to find his master in the stable. "Suh, would you like somethin' to eat first? Plum puddin' or some tea? It'd be no trouble at all, suh."

"No, I'm afraid you've filled my stomach quite enough for one evening. Though I will expect corn beef hash in the morning. Now, you get yourself inside," Washington commanded his cook.

"Yes, suh. I'll be goin' right now, suh."

Washington detected the puzzled look on his slave's face. He had even surprised himself for not losing his temper and pronouncing some harsh punishment. Washington treated his slaves better than most plantation owners but would never tolerate insubordination, and no enslaved man or woman at Mount Vernon was ever immune to the whip of an overseer. The general had earned a similar reputation on the battlefield. He treated the young boys under his command with decency, though any disorder resulted in swift punishment and deserters would always be shot. Perhaps he would change his mind and punish Hercules in the morning.

Before Hercules could exit, Nelson fired off a menacing stare. His head nodded in a circular motion, and he let loose an angry growl, jealous and annoyed that the slave had interrupted his time with the master. Hercules guarded the cake close to his muscular body, turned back to the entrance, and continued into the night, toward Mount Vernon's slave quarters, known as the Family House.

"I should probably heed my own advice and return inside, Old Nelson."

Still in deep thought, Washington began a slow pace across the moist ground of his estate. In the distance, he saw his cook hurrying around the back of the mansion toward the Family House. The drizzle had stopped for a moment, but the heavens still seemed ready to unleash an inferno of a storm.

Martha Washington lay sound asleep, stiff as a board beneath a single linen sheet. George stood at attention in the bedroom doorway for a moment before entering. He thought of how fragile she had become since they'd married, the sacrifices she'd made, the losses she'd suffered, and what a burden it must have become to be the wife of George Washington.

"My apologies," he whispered.

Tumultuous winds swept through the window and rattled a few picture frames that decorated the walls. Martha's four children from her first marriage looked soft and innocent in the dangling portraits. All of her children had died too young, and George heard their voices whistling in the wind, calling out to him, "Protect Mother. Be good to Mother."

He entered the bedroom, which was adorned in Martha's unassuming style. The space flaunted nothing exceedingly majestic. It was her sanctuary, which included a Sheraton-style bed; a squeaky, wooden chair; the family portraits; and her beloved Holy Bible, read so much that the battered, leather binding struggled to contain its dog-eared pages that fell out of the sides.

A small burst of heat escaped from underneath the sheet as George positioned himself beside his wife. He ruffled the pillows in an attempt to wake her, and she moaned to acknowledge his presence.

"You're still awake, my lady?"

"No, darling, *you* are still awake. And you are in need of solace, yes?" She yawned and unclenched her body, then curled into a fetal position facing her husband.

"I'm afraid I will need you to convince me again why it is me, among so many brilliant men, why it is me, the axis around which this nation's progress revolves."

Martha inched toward him with an exaggerated sigh, unafraid to express her frustration at the prospect of having this conversation again.

George continued, "Why is Hercules not the undisputed leader of this new nation?"

"Oh, darling," she said as her head fell fast to his shoulder. Her eyes squinted through thinning white hair. "You've been spending too many hours in the horse stable. Has all that manure tampered with your mental faculties?"

He was surprised to learn that she knew of his nights in the stable, but ignored it.

"I've posed a legitimate query. Why not Hercules? If physical prowess is the reason men follow my lead, then Hercules is stronger and broader than I. He has the strength of three men, yet he lives out his days a slave. Hercules has the courage to steal cake from our home to feed his people. I've reached the age of fifty-six, and he is in the prime of his youth. Why does not every American man, woman, and child put their faith in *him* to create a new government?"

Martha's voice was gentle and steady. "My dear, Hercules lives out his days a slave because Hercules is a slave." She had a unique way of communicating both patience and annoyance in a single tone of her voice. "You live out your days a leader of men because you are a leader of men. Leaders lead, and slaves slave. This is the intention of nature."

"The intention of nature? And what of the very principles of our revolution?"

She spoke a bit louder now. "All men are *created* equal, yes, but after creation, God doth have a way of sorting out the shepherd from the sheep."

George shook his head. "I may once have agreed with you on this topic, my lady, but years of warfare and bearing witness to the worst of human nature have changed my views considerably. I can tell you this: After creation, a bullet to the head kills a soldier as fast as a slave. All men aren't just created equal. All men die equal, helpless and destitute of all earthly things. All men will stand as equals before the Almighty."

Martha sat up straight and looked her husband in the eye. "I am no stranger to your capacity for exaggeration, George Washington, and I will not pity your philosophical dilemma. We both know it is not principles that trouble you. It is the work of one man, and it should take a greater man than Patrick Henry to bring about such torment in you."

George flinched at the mention of Patrick Henry, his political enemy who led a coalition of influential Virginians in opposition to the Constitution. Henry spoke in every tavern and wrote to every newspaper in Virginia. The champion of "Give me liberty or give me death," persuasive as ever, generated impassioned support everywhere he spoke. Washington depended on Alexander Hamilton and James Madison, the two leading federalists, to thwart Henry.

George leaned back on his pillow and took a deep breath, as if to exhale a diatribe against his rival, but said nothing.

Martha crawled on top of him. "Listen to me, darling. This man who you allow to cause such anguish merely sits around in taverns and talks. Talk, talk, talk. Oh, how Patrick Henry loves to hear himself talk. Slaves slave, talkers talk, and leaders lead. You, my dear, take action, and there is more honor in action than in words. You have demonstrated more honor through your actions than any man in this country, and *that*, George, is why the people have placed their trust in you. A man like Patrick Henry has an ego that dwarfs his sense of duty. His only concern is personal aggrandizement." Martha paused. "And besides, you are obviously the one indispensable American who can unite this nation. I would have married no one less."

George cracked a smile for the first time in days.

All heroes have their insecurities; in fact, they have more insecurities than ordinary women and men. Yet a strong, devoted spouse convinces them to distrust their suspicions.

⚯

"It is tyranny defined!" he roared from the podium.

Patrick Henry boiled in a raging crescendo that captivated every delegate in the sweltering Richmond Theatre. He had not attended the Constitutional Convention, but Henry seethed with anger after reading the document it produced. He could never consent to a central government with such enormous power, and he cringed at the thought of a government controlled by northern interests, including the interests of miniature, overrepresented New England states.

"I would sooner submit to King George again than to obey a consolidated government that would render the state governments powerless!"

At the Virginia Ratifying Convention, he would convince the other 167 men to reject the United States Constitution or he would keel over and die trying.

Henry stood a gaunt six feet, and he waved his arms in the air like a man on fire. The temperature rose a few degrees when he spoke. A flame burned in his belly, and it ignited with every word he shouted through the convention hall. His tattered jacket smelled of burning logs, tobacco, and gun smoke from his last fox hunt. He clawed at the red-and-silver, rust-colored stubble that littered his sunburned face and the endless wrinkles that crisscrossed his brow, which gave him the appearance of a man much older than his fifty-two years. Unpolished for sure, he took pride in being different from most men in the room. He took pride in the fact that no American could match the oratory skill that he intended to display throughout the month of June in Richmond.

"Aristocracy! That wretched little paper before you gives birth to an American aristocracy that, in its infancy, will rob the people of our natural rights. And how presumptuous of the authors to write on behalf of *We the people*. We the people will not be enfranchised to elect this tyrant called *president* with unlimited terms. An electoral college of the most privileged elite in America will collude with the president and secure their fortunes by making him ruler for life. Aristocracy, gentlemen! The House of Representatives will include just one representative for every thirty thousand people, and the Senate is smaller. A mere twenty-six senators—twenty-six unelected aristocrats—will conspire to make all treaties and appoint all federal judges."

Only Patrick Henry could get away with admonishing aristocracy in a room full of aristocrats. His audience included an exclusive club of Virginia landowners, the most well-established aristocracy in America. A large majority of the delegates were wealthy landowners who had inherited their riches, and many were related to one another, either by blood or by marriage. None of these facts could extinguish Henry's fire. He preyed on their arrogance. These men sat comfortably atop Virginia's social and political food chain, and a new federal government threatened to gnaw away at their privilege, to bump them down a link.

"Even worse, these judges will not be bound by the Constitution to respect the right of trial by jury!"

Patrick Henry and other anti-federalists never missed an opportunity to remind the convention of trial by jury and other sacred rights that the United States Constitution ignored. Even many federalists felt apprehensive to support a constitution that lacked a bill of rights. The room shook as delegates pounded their tables and stomped their canes in ovation.

Henry stared down James Madison, who listened in the center of the room, sweating like a hot spring underneath his pristine powdered wig. When Madison could finally tolerate no more, he rose from his chair in perfect posture. He stood half a foot shorter than Henry, and he spoke in a rapid, nasally whimper that some delegates found inaudible.

"Our Virginia Declaration of Rights, of which you boast with such arrogance, guarantees the right to trial by jury and every other right that you so jealously guard," Madison confirmed. "There is nothing in the United States Constitution that would prevent a state government from protecting the rights of its own citizens."

No man at the Philadelphia Convention had played a greater role in shaping the proposed constitution than James Madison. He was instrumental in proposing ideas, serving on committees, and working out compromises. He thought he had endured the sharpest criticisms of the plan in Philadelphia, but Virginia produced some heavy-hitting politicians, and many of them opposed the young prodigy. In addition to his formidable opponents, Madison battled the most severe stomach acid, ulcers, diarrhea, and every other stomach ailment known to man.

In excruciating pain, Madison approached the podium and stole the floor. "Thirteen state governments will remain stable and intact. I will remind the gentleman that the twenty-six senators he calls an aristocracy are to be chosen by those very state governments and may be removed from office every six years. Furthermore, presidential electors who make up the electoral college may be chosen by the people if that is the wish of our state. Now, if there was ever a democratically elected aristocracy in the history of the world, then I've never heard of it."

"You have heard of it now, Mr. Madison, for in all of your genius, you have engineered it! And the Constitution will most assuredly prevent state governments from protecting citizens, by declaring itself the *supreme law of the land.*"

Hoots and hollers pushed through the thick humidity.

Of all the heavyweights packed into the convention hall, Henry and Madison were the undisputed champs. Some of the delegates attended the convention just to witness the two political giants square off against each other. At thirty-seven years old, Madison understood the United States Constitution better than anyone, and he was, without question, the most intelligent man in the Richmond Theatre. However, Patrick Henry was the most charismatic and the loudest man in the room. It was a debate for the ages.

Henry continued his tirade: "Did we not just throw off a king in grievance of unfair taxation? Did we not march in the streets chanting 'no taxation without representation'? All of you did so with revelry. Yet now you are asked to ratify a constitution that would allow Congress to directly tax you. Think of it: representatives of Massachusetts, Pennsylvania, and that madman from New York, Alexander Hamilton, directly taxing the good citizens of Virginia. Our Declaration of Independence is clear on the matter, and should Thomas Jefferson have attended this convention, he would decry every word of the assault on our liberties."

Madison fumed at the last statement, so much that he raised his voice in defiance of the stabbing pain in his abdomen. "For shame! For shame on you indeed, Mr. H.! Your tongue drips with the poison of disunion!" Until now, Henry had simply espoused bad ideas. Now he made matters personal, and even worse, offended the character of Madison's friends who were absent and unable to defend themselves. Hamilton, whom many others called a madman, was fighting the same political battles in New York's ratifying convention. Jefferson served as an American ambassador in France and had been gone since before the Constitutional Convention.

The entire convention hall now heard Madison loud and clear. "I should hope for your own sake that your last comment will be stricken from the record. To even mention the names of such brave patriots in their absence, and then presume to speak on their behalf, is nothing less than a disgrace! I happen to know, through private correspondence, that Mr. Jefferson pledges his full support for the US Constitution; but it is quite within reason that you disagree with him, because you, sir, you are no Thomas Jefferson!"

A solemn silence filled the air for a brief moment. Thomas Jefferson enjoyed a reputation second only to Washington as the quintessential Virginian. His name evoked great emotion in every delegate.

"Very well, Mr. Madison," Henry acquiesced. "Let the statement be stricken from the record, but let also my arguments for a people's republic remain and forever erase the stain of tyranny."

The debate continued without an end in sight.

George paced in circles around the bedroom, waiting for Martha to finish preparations for their guest. The floorboards creaked as if they were about to split apart and send him crashing down to the first-floor study.

"He shall arrive any minute, my lady, and you know I can't do this sort of thing without your grace and experience."

George was not always thrilled to accommodate every plantation owner, aspiring politician, or war buddy that visited Mount Vernon as if his mansion was a cheap boarding house. But Martha never failed to set her husband's mind at ease. Nobody demonstrated Southern hospitality or offered a more amiable welcome to her home than Martha Washington. Here she was in her element, and she'd taught George the ropes. The art of politics demanded this type of formality. George relied on Martha's talent to help transition him from military leader to politician. She coached him in the game of stroking the egos of America's gentry.

"My dear, your dress is exquisite in its simplicity and beauty. Now may we please adjourn to the parlor for our guest's imminent arrival?"

Martha waved a hand in front of his face, a familiar gesture that said,

"Shut up, George. I'll be ready when I'm ready. It needs to be perfect."

"He should be here already," George said, badgering her.

"Sire! If you would like the Carolinians to ratify your little Constitution, then the proper dressing of my hair is the best chance you've got." She turned to Ona Judge, her personal slave. "The feather is too high, the bonnet is too flat, and my hair, much too rough! Now brush it more. Softly. More!"

My wife, the drill sergeant, George thought. At times, he'd seen Martha treat Ona with kindness reserved for family. However, when preparing to entertain the most well-bred, illustrious families in America and from all around the world, Martha behaved as haughty as her guests.

She continued to bark out orders at Ona. "I shall wear rubies this afternoon. Our guest of honor is a highly distinguished statesman, so nothing too small that would insult him, yet nothing too ostentatious either. He is important, but he's no Benjamin Franklin."

In her search for the appropriate rubies, young Ona opened a porcelain jewelry box containing her mistress's diamonds. Martha slapped the young slave's wrist, producing a cracking sound that echoed off the ceiling.

"Slaves do not handle my diamonds, Ona. You know this." She shook her head in disappointment. "The porcelain box is usually hidden from the help for this very reason. I've demoted body servants to field labor for such carelessness. Now, I expect you to be more prudent."

"Yes, mistress." Ona obeyed. "Didn't know they was diamonds, ma'am."

George sank his head. Martha had become an old, cranky taskmaster. Her consternation came from a reluctant acceptance of old age. At sixteen years old, Ona and her example of vibrant youth didn't help matters.

When their company arrived, Martha shed her hostility and projected a magnanimous charisma, as usual. She dressed in the most colorful, flowered, silk gowns—purples and pinks, an armor of lavender, as colorful as her charming etiquette, which she'd perfected with age. She fashioned an elegant but not too extravagant residence, and she beamed with merriment in the company of friends. Every visitor departed Mount Vernon under the impression that Martha wanted them to stay longer.

At the mansion's entrance, George greeted Charles Cotesworth

Pinckney of South Carolina. Washington's warm smile revealed his false, ivory teeth.

"Mr. Pinckney, what a pleasure to have you in our home."

"Your servant." Pinckney bowed to the general.

Washington responded in kind. "Of course, you remember my wife, Martha."

Pinckney bowed a second time to kiss Martha's outstretched hand. "How could I ever forget such an embodiment of grandeur? And what a splendid bonnet, Your Grace."

Martha raised her brow sarcastically at George. She held Pinckney's hand between her palms and lowered her voice. "George and I were devastated to hear the news of Sarah's passing. I know well, the pain of a widow. The Lord will heal your pain, sir."

He nodded with gratitude.

Charles Cotesworth Pinckney served in the Continental Army and showed more promise than any other rising star in political circles. In a unique brotherhood, he and General Washington shared a bond only understood by those who had fought together in battle. Each man had demonstrated his willingness to die for the other. Regardless of their differences, political or otherwise, regardless of status and the competition among statesmen, the Continental Army reduced their judgements of one another to one simple adage, that their lives were equally fragile and they were equally dependent on the other during the darkest days of war.

Over dinner, Pinckney assured Washington that the South Carolina Ratifying Convention would support the Constitution—one soldier's word to another.

"I give you my word, General. South Carolina will ratify, and then set an example for North Carolina, although North Carolinians have about as much interest in a federal government as the savage Indians have for our Lord, Jesus Christ."

Martha's eyes lit up at the mention of her savior. Unlike Martha, though, George preferred keeping religion a private affair.

"I hope the opposition in South Carolina is not half as vicious as Virginia's," he said, getting the conversation back on track.

Pinckney continued in a slow, sophisticated drawl: "There are some concerns, of course, about the future of Southern property. But most of the men hold firm to the belief that ratification would secure our unique economy. After all, slaves today will be slaves tomorrow. The opposing faction finds more trouble with the simple majority required to pass legislation. It boils down to basic mathematics, really. The Northern states outnumber the Southern states, and Northern interests will always prevail in a majority vote. Some of the delegates still push for the two-thirds vote. Rest assured, though, they represent the minority. South Carolina will ratify."

Pinckney's demeanor quelled Washington's fears. The man was genteel, self-assured, and he never sweat a drop under the scorching sun. George tapped Martha's foot under the table, signaling for her to take over the conversation from there.

Traffic slowed to a manageable pace in the weeks after Pinckney's visit, and the house slaves appreciated some peace and quiet around the mansion. On a balmy summer evening, with no company expected, Hercules cleaned up the dining room and prepared the piazza, which overlooked the Potomac River. Here, his masters took their tea in the evenings. With reluctance, he accepted the help of Ona Judge, Martha's body servant. Hercules towered over her petite figure like a giant ogre. When he flexed his arm muscles through the sleeves of his livery, the cook's bicep grew almost the size of Ona's waist. Her light, caramel skin was soft, attractive, and typical for house slaves, so as not to offend distinguished guests. In stark contrast, Hercules's immense size and dark skin, nearly black as night, made him quite the unusual house slave.

The cook peered down at Ona's freckled cheeks. He spoke in deep tones to establish his authority. "If you gonna help, you follow my rules. Now set the teacups."

She giggled just enough to get under his skin. "How come you work inside? You too big to work inside. You should work the fields with *big* slaves."

"I work the kitchen 'cause I'm the best cook on this here plantation.

Best cook in Virginia. I ain't jus' some dumb slave. I'm a cook," he answered, well aware that his talent in the kitchen was all that kept a slave of his size out of the fields.

"How come you so dark?" she continued to nag. In her aloof chuckle, she almost dropped a cup from Lady Washington's china collection. "You look like one a them saltwater Negroes, straight from the boat. Africa black." Her giggles turned to slight convulsions. "And how you get that hole in your teeth? You funny-lookin', Mr. Hercules."

Hercules stopped polishing a honey jar. He raised his brow and squinted his eyelids in a stare that could hush anyone. Resisting the strong urge to shout back at her, he clenched his teeth. *Africa black!* he thought. *You wanna talk skin? How come you so spotted? You look like a damn spotted owl.* He knew Ona despised her freckles. It was her greatest insecurity, but Hercules chose to keep a still tongue. He had vivid memories of childhood, overweight like some strange monster, twice as large as the young boys on the neighboring plantation from which he was sold to George Washington. Ona's freckles must have haunted her just the same. He said nothing. His angry grimace got the job done.

Hercules never expressed it outright, but he felt insulted, having to work in the mansion with such a young girl. It cheapened his talent. He had prepared meals for the most prominent men in America, yet still had to clean up alongside little freckle face—and quite an attractive face with high cheekbones and tiny dimples that distracted him from his work.

Ona stopped her teasing. "I'm gonna get good gossip tonight. Leave the staircase alone. I'll clean it later." She gave him a conniving smirk.

Hercules shook his head in disapproval. "Little girl, you gonna get a whippin', and I ain't gonna save you."

"I'll whip *you*, you big—big cook."

They both smiled, and Hercules swelled with pride. "That's right. I'm a cook."

He disapproved of Ona's eavesdropping. When no guests cluttered the mansion hallways, George and Martha, like clockwork, retired to the parlor after their tea to read newspapers and other mail. George enjoyed reading the papers aloud to his wife, and Ona took advantage. She could not read, nor could any slave at Mount Vernon, so she spied like an alley cat when George discussed the news of the day. Ona acquired the most information by leaving work undone in the parlor's adjoining rooms until it came time to read the papers. Then she cleaned the large dining room and the stairway in the central entrance, all the while snooping for information.

The slaves at Mount Vernon constructed a secret network of free-flowing information. Field slaves got news from neighboring plantations. Some slaves brought news back from Williamsburg or Baltimore after running errands or being hired out. Many got news at the Sunday market in Alexandria. House slaves collected the most reliable information straight from the papers or from the visiting politicians in their own words.

Ona, and almost three hundred other slaves at Mount Vernon, spent many nights gossiping in their quarters. Field slaves shared stories in their cramped, square shacks on the outlying farms. The house slaves, as many as seventy at a time, squeezed like sardines into the Family House. They shared what they knew and what they imagined about Massachusetts and Pennsylvania. Massachusetts had banned slavery, and Pennsylvania had passed a gradual emancipation law. They wondered, would the new constitution kill slavery for good? Ona knew it would not, but she kept that to herself. If Charles Cotesworth Pinckney, a South Carolina slave driver, endorsed it, then it did not bode well for enslaved people. Pinckney was a frequent visitor to the mansion. On more than one occasion, Ona overheard his rehearsed homily on the virtues of the slave system. "Slavery is indeed God's intention. Slavery has existed since biblical times." If Charles Pinckney was correct, then to hell with God, and to hell with the Constitution.

Nonetheless, Ona felt a craving for some news tonight because Master Washington had been pacing around the mansion with more anxiety than usual. She finished laying out the papers in a neat assortment as George and Martha entered the parlor. George enjoyed the *Virginia Gazette* and *The Pennsylvania Gazette* in particular. On occasion, he received the *Massachusetts Centinel* and the *New York Journal*. As debate over the Constitution raged in the press, Washington devoured the papers, especially the anti-federalist articles that criticized the Constitution.

George hurried to open the *Virginia Gazette* and skimmed an article on Indian relations in the Ohio Country. He cleared his throat to speak in a clear voice for Martha. "'Hostilities inevitable as American settlers continue to expand into territory inhabited by a confederation of Indian tribes, including the Shawnee, Delaware, and Miami. Chief Blue Jacket of the Shawnee has petitioned the Continental Congress in New York to uphold its land treaties, and has vowed to defend Indian lands in the Ohio Valley by use of force, if necessary.'"

Ona frowned on her way out, hoping to hear more substantive information. She left the parlor and took position by the stairwell to continue eavesdropping.

George sighed and vented his frustration to Martha. "Once again, the United States Government is powerless to defend itself against savage tribes. If ratified, the Constitution would allow the federal government to raise an army and coerce every tribe west to eternity. But heaven forbid we have an actual army. We may offend Mr. Henry's sensibilities."

Martha nodded in agreement. "I dare say, not many Pennsylvania militiamen will volunteer to defend territory that is not even theirs to defend."

George continued shuffling through the mail until he came across a letter from Charleston.

"Why was this not brought immediately to my attention?" He looked for a slave to reprimand, but to no avail. He hurried to tear open the letter and read its contents from Thomas Pinckney, President of the South Carolina Ratifying Convention and younger brother of Charles Cotesworth Pinckney. "My dear, Mr. Pinckney has done it! He has done it!" George jumped up in excitement, almost knocking over the chair beneath him. "Charles has done it!"

"And you doubted him?" Martha replied.

"Not for a second, my lady." He began reading aloud: "'The South Carolina Ratifying Convention has voted one hundred forty-nine to seventy-three in the affirmative on ratification of the United States Constitution as proposed by the Federal Convention in Philadelphia. South Carolina takes great pride in being the eighth state of the required nine for formal ratification.'"

"You see, George," Martha chimed in. "In due time. Your ninth state—most likely Virginia—will ratify in due time."

George clenched a fist in approval and continued reading. "'Brother Charles led the federalists in convention. Consent was not unanimous for the proposed plan of government, but a vast majority agreed that the Constitution is the first step toward putting the United States on a path to prosperity.'" George continued reading Pinckney's praise for his brother. "'After a ninth state ratifies, Charles would even make a splendid president of these United States, if not for the—'" He stopped short. An awkward silence sucked the air out of the room, and Martha closed her eyes, hanging her head a bit lower as if to conceal her exasperation from George.

She could have finished the sentence herself: "If not for the inevitable election of Your Highness, George Washington, the first president of the United States of America."

It was the most feared topic of discussion ever to haunt the parlor room. They made every effort to avoid speaking of it. Perhaps the one thing scarier than the Constitution's failure was its success. Nobody in America doubted that George would be elected the first president by unanimous consent, even though he vowed to remain in retirement after the war. Only one question remained unanswered: would he accept? For as much as George volleyed the question around in his head, and for as many late-night hours he spent with Nelson, Martha never doubted the answer. He would serve. His devotion to country, his duty, would again outweigh his devotion to family. Martha could not bear the thought of leaving Mount Vernon to take up residency in Philadelphia, or even worse, New York, the likely choices for a capital city.

"President Charles Cotesworth Pinckney. It sure could happen," George said. It sounded so unnatural, he couldn't even fake an expression to accompany it. "Eight have ratified. Just one more state, my lady. One more state."

Martha opened her eyes and forced the best smile she could piece together. A single teardrop fought its way back under her eyelid. "Virginia will follow, George. They can't let you down now."

Five states remained undecided, with one more needed to adopt the

Constitution. George pondered the possibilities, still unsure. "You can forget Rhode Island. They refuse to even hold a convention in the face of such rabid opposition. New Hampshire has adjourned without voting, and North Carolina's convention will not take place for months. They will most likely follow Virginia's lead. So, it is left to New York and Virginia. I'll take them both," he said in an inspired voice.

The absence of consent from either New York or Virginia would be devastating to the fledgling country. Virginia, the most populated state, had produced an A-list roster of revolutionary heroes that included Washington, Jefferson, Henry, and Madison. New York was already transforming into the fulcrum of America's economic activity. Washington needed the blessing of both states for the United States Constitution to succeed.

⌇

Martha sat on the edge of her bed to read a chapter of her Bible, as she did each night before going to sleep. She could no longer hold back the steady stream of tears from flowing down her puffy cheeks. By the time she looked up, it was too late to hide her emotion from Ona, who had been preparing the bedroom.

"How much longer must I share the man I love with every person in America?" Martha whimpered through heavy tears and her sniffling nose. "His body is here, but his mind is everywhere else—in Richmond, in New York, South Carolina. I want my husband here. I want all of him here." She slapped her open hand down to the bed, and her eyes gave way to another wave of tears like a broken levy.

"The loneliness is unimaginable. All of my children have passed on." She paused and looked up again to Ona. "It's as if my husband has, too. I feel like a widow again."

Ona stood in complete silence before summoning up the safest possible response—"Yes, ma'am"—and even that, in a whisper. It could be the wrong answer to such an unprecedented cry for consolation from slave owner to slave.

Without wiping her eyes, Martha gazed back down to the bed and quoted the Book of Isaiah from memory: "'Fear not, for I am with you; be not dismayed, for I am your God; I will strengthen you, I will help you, I will uphold you with my righteous right hand.' The Lord will not forsake us, Ona. He shall guide us, and he shall not depart. And should his pillar of strength lead us to Philadelphia, then *we* shall not depart from *him*."

Hesitant, Ona tried to straighten the picture frames on the wall, but before she could turn, Martha embraced the young slave girl. She threw her arms around Ona's boney waist and pulled her closer, down to the bed. "And you shall follow the Lord with us. You shall come to Philadelphia when the time arrives."

Ona stiffened her body in utter shock, uncomfortable with Martha's outburst of piety and affection. She had touched Lady Washington before, but in the course of her work, putting on clothing or dressing her hair. Neither woman had ever confided in the other until this moment. Ona caught her breath to repeat the only words her flat voice could find: "Yes, ma'am."

Chapter 2

"There's just too damn many of them. We're outnumbered." He moaned. After a long day of debate and frustration, Alexander Hamilton struggled to hold his head up above the splintered table at the Van Kleeck Tavern in Poughkeepsie, New York.

"I served under Washington and represented this state in Philadelphia. Madison and I practically wrote the Constitution. And yet somehow, I cannot convince a group of backwoods, New York nincompoops to ratify the most well-founded document in the history of the world."

John Jay, another New York lawyer, sat across from Hamilton and listened to his rant. They took turns yawning, exhausted from suffering through the first week of the New York Ratifying Convention.

"Uninspired, uneducated nincompoops, I tell you." Hamilton made no attempt to conceal his antipathy.

He was young, handsome, brilliant, and absolutely nothing could go his way. Of the sixty-five delegates elected to New York's convention, forty-five of them had already declared their opposition to the Constitution. It was beginning to feel like an exercise in futility, but Alexander Hamilton would never give up. Always the most ambitious man in the room, his impassioned yearning for liberty would drive him onward, destined for greatness.

"Does it not even matter that we win on merit? We win every debate and tear the arguments of lesser men to shreds. There are simply more of them than us, and they refuse to hear perfectly reasoned political theory."

John Jay looked up from his glass of porter. "It is not that they refuse to hear. They listen to you speak all day, Alex. The more you speak, the more you turn them off."

"Even when I speak the truth?" Hamilton fired back.

"Especially when you speak the truth." John Jay had analyzed the situation with a much clearer head than the compulsive Hamilton. "These are simple people, Alex. They see a young, hotshot lawyer from the city giving grand discourse on reasoned political theory and warning them of dire consequences, when all they want to do is feed their families and be left alone."

"Damn it, John! They can't feed their families *now!*" He punched the table and knocked his glass of rum off the edge. The rattling sent a pool of candle wax rushing from a rebellious flame.

"True. But they will refuse hearing it from you. To them, Alexander Hamilton is just some power-hungry, immoral adulterer."

Hamilton furrowed his brow.

"Your reputation with the ladies is no secret around here."

"Drink your beer." Hamilton smirked. "You're not exactly a pilgrim either, you know."

Although John Jay had in fact earned the closest reputation to that of a pilgrim among New York politicians. He attended Trinity Church on Broadway, and he conducted himself with the utmost moral character, though he did enjoy a good brew at the tavern. Jay surprised everyone by befriending someone like Alexander Hamilton, a brazen, loudmouthed philanderer. But, Hamilton knew right from wrong, and he loved liberty as much as the next American.

"I'm on your side," Jay said. "You and I represent the merchants on Wall Street. To these countryside delegates, we may as well represent the moon—and to the Poughkeepsie spectators, we may as well speak in a foreign tongue."

The ratifying convention had been held in Poughkeepsie by no coincidence. The New York legislature, controlled by anti-federalists who opposed the Constitution, made sure that the decision on ratification would be made outside of New York City and far away from every major federalist newspaper.

An experienced diplomat, John Jay made every attempt to find common ground. "I do agree with them on one point: Why should the Southern states be rewarded with more representation for the barbarity of slavery? Counting three-fifths of their slaves in population only serves to inflate their numbers in Congress. They wish to treat slaves like cattle, yet count them as men. They can't have it both ways."

Hamilton's patience expired. "Good God, man, you know as well as anyone that the Southern delegates would have walked out of Philadelphia faster than Dr. Franklin's lightning bolt if we hadn't made certain concessions on slavery. I deplore every clause on the subject—three-fifths, the slave trade, and capturing runaways. I condemn every word of it. But the fact remains that our purpose is to unite a nation, and that nation includes slaveholders—myself included. And you, too, I might add—Mr. Pilgrim."

"Mr. Hamilton, watch your tongue." Hamilton had struck a nerve, and Jay let him know it. "I inherited my slaves from my father, and have already emancipated some. You won't find a more fervent proponent of abolition anywhere in New York."

Hamilton threw up his arms in disinterest, not wanting to reopen beleaguered debates from the past. He pivoted the conversation to strategy. "I will write Mr. Madison tonight. Virginia must close the deal. I still believe we can convince this delegation to move with the tide, but not until after the ninth state has ratified. These New York gentlemen are not leaders—but they will make fine followers."

"Madison must hurry," Jay added. "We can only delay so long before they vote us down. If we fail in New York, it would give more momentum to the naysayers in Virginia."

Hamilton scowled. "In the meantime, we continue writing the press in defense of the Constitution. I'd say it's also in our best interest to write some lengthy speeches. You think I bore them now? Wait until I give them a treatise on the history of republican government in antiquity. That should buy Madison plenty of time in Virginia."

Jay scratched his chin. "I fear you underestimate the opposition in Virginia. At least your enemies here in New York respect your talents and treat you—a thirty-three-year-old kid—with the honor that a statesman commands. Virginia has set aside all such pleasantries. They express fundamental disagreement over the very purpose of the United States Government. They do not haggle over small differences of opinion. The old hounds of

Virginia may very well swallow up a young pup like James Madison."

Hamilton brushed off the comment with a shrug. "Nonsense. You underestimate the value of superiority. Madison is superior in character and in intellect compared to all of these self-righteous Virginian boobs. He will win the day, and then our New York boobs will join forces with their Southern counterparts."

The barkeeper poured another spruce beer for an elderly Native American sitting alone in the tavern. Irked by the man's presence, the barkeep heckled him through a mountain of facial hair. "Hey, Injun, tell your buddy Blue Jacket to knock it off out there in Ohio. The war's over."

The old man stared straight ahead without making eye contact. "Blue Jacket is Shawnee. I am Kanienkeh, what you call Mohawk. I know him like you know the chief of France."

Harassment of the natives had grown more acceptable since the War of Independence, because most tribes had fought for the British. Blue Jacket's resistance to white settlement in Ohio heightened the tension. The press made matters worse by depicting the small alliance of tribes defending their ancestral lands as an uncivilized group of murderers on the loose, hunting innocent Americans for sport. Blue Jacket's battles drew special attention from the newspapers because his firm alliance of Shawnee, Delaware, and Miami Indians had decimated the white settlers and small militias who attempted to drive them off the land. Americans were unfamiliar with losing Indian wars.

The bartender scrubbed an empty beer glass as he spoke. "If the king of France slaughtered white settlers like your pal Blue Jacket, I wouldn't be afraid to knock him out. That's what we do in this land. We bring down chiefs."

The morose old man spoke in a choppy grunt. "What you do on this land will forever remain a mystery to my people."

Most tribes in New York had migrated to Canada after the war. The ones who had stayed negotiated bad land agreements with the new

American government and were pushed away to the West. With the exception of Seneca Indians, New York's native population was declining at an accelerating rate. The Mohawk man at the tavern had refused to leave his homeland and, like so many others who stayed, fell victim to alcoholism.

Hamilton overheard the conversation about land and continued to address Jay: "Our impotent government trying to manage the land of this great continent is like a domestic cat trying to rule the jungle. It will take great power in government to administer this land. We must be lions."

Nearby, the drunken Mohawk stood and stumbled over his chair in the direction of Hamilton. The chair screeched across the floor through puddles of tobacco spit and performed a balancing act before landing on its four legs again. He attempted to stand up straight, despite a total loss of coordination.

"I will sell you a cloud." He burped in the direction of Hamilton.

"I'm afraid I don't understand, man." Hamilton's smooth complexion formed the flawless smile of a disingenuous public servant playing to the audience.

"I have a cloud to sell you."

"And why should I purchase such a cloud, old man?"

"I do not know why," he slurred. "But if you are interested in buying land, then perhaps you are interested in buying a cloud. Or maybe you'll buy the wind. It is just as stupid." He then laughed in an uproar, showering Alexander Hamilton's face with the fumes of alcohol. Hamilton sat back and sipped his fifth glass of rum.

"This cloud will bring shade to protect you and rain to cool you. Great power and prosperity it will bring," the Mohawk explained. "You will rule an empire."

Half amused, though wanting some privacy, Hamilton took the man up on his offer. "I will buy your cloud, old man." He tossed a Spanish coin toward the native. It fell to the ground, and the man stumbled, sinking his fingernails into an inch of filth atop the floorboards to retrieve it.

"Good evening and good luck," Hamilton said.

"Why encourage the man's defects?" Jay asked as the native stumbled away. "You just bought that man another drink, which he unquestionably does not need."

Hamilton let out a playful smile. "You misunderstand, my good man. Our new government will issue a strong currency and create a national bank. That Spanish coin will soon be worthless. Meanwhile, I come out of the deal with a perfectly good cloud."

Through his fit of laughter, Hamilton ordered the glass of rum that would push him past the edge of sobriety and into a drunken state of free and uncontrollable expression, not unlike the old native. John Jay had become quite familiar with this unique state of consciousness, in which Hamilton revealed some of his deepest secrets: his sexual dalliances, his love of all things British, and his personal disdain for many of America's most beloved statesmen. Jay ordered another porter to enjoy while listening to whatever wild revelation Hamilton would let loose this evening. It didn't take long.

"We carry the flag, Mr. Jay. We carry the flag. Of course those other delegates attack us from all angles because we are carrying the flag across the battlefield. And you know as well as I that the soldier carrying the flag has the biggest target on his uniform. Fire at the flag, boys!"

Jay tilted his head down and smiled. *This ought to be a good one.*

"You know, I should be dead," Hamilton slurred, his words just clear enough to be understood through his inebriation.

"Come again, Alex. Dead?"

"D-E-A-D. You should be looking at a dead man. My bones should be buried at Germantown. Shouldn't even be here." He paused for a second of reflection, considering the story he was about to tell. His conscience screamed from inside, pleading with him to stop speaking, but the message drowned in a sea of rum that churned in his belly. His voice grew sullen, still slurred. "I watched a boy go down at Germantown, couldn't have been more than sixteen. I'll never know why a kid that young carried the flag straight into British regulars. He put up one hell of a fight, waved Old Glory, and then got his life shot right out of him, right in front of me. Flag fell to the ground, blanketed his corpse." He paused again.

"A sad tale, indeed. But I hardly think you should be dead," Jay suggested.

"I turned my back and ran the other way. A soldier's duty is to pick up that flag and charge forward. But, you know, the soldier carrying the flag has the biggest target on his uniform. Fire at the flag, boys. I watched that flag fall to the ground, and I left it there. I'm sure someone picked it up. And I'm sure that person's dead. It should've been me."

The background noise of chattering townsmen at the bar filled the heavy silence created by Hamilton's story. Jay remained speechless. Ashamed, Alexander Hamilton stood and exited the bar with his head down. Tomorrow would be a new day of debate, and he would never remember his last conversation of this evening.

Straw-filled, wooden bunks lined the inside of the Family House. Washington's house slaves either crammed into these bunks at night or they slept on the slightly more spacious dirt floor. They took no pleasure in the fact that any vitality regenerated overnight would be given up to their masters first thing in the morning. Even their sleep belonged to Washington. The one consolation was that nobody got whipped in their dreams—nobody except Ona. Curious, she often dreamed of being whipped. Like very few slaves, Ona had never felt the brutal lash of an overseer, and at age sixteen, her initiation was overdue. In the depths of her consciousness, she felt the whip from Master Washington, Lady Washington, the overseers, even other slaves—even Hercules—but awake, Ona somehow stayed immune to the taskmaster's weapon of choice.

She sometimes heard chilling echoes in the distance, the echoes of cries that soared out from under the whip on outlying farms. She had seen the scars on the backs of others, both men and women, young and old. As a young child, she had witnessed a field hand strung up by John Fairfax, the worst of the overseers. Ona often daydreamed and replayed the bloody episode in her mind, as if it was happening right in front of her again. Motionless, she stood by to watch, and after just a few cracks of the whip, the helpless victim made eye contact with her and his voice roared out like a grizzly bear: "Run, girl! Run on outta here!" His voice frightened her as much as the whip. At age five, when this occurred, Ona had sprinted to the mansion, away from the horror. On that particular occasion, the man's offense had been falling down on the job, resting in a tobacco field, suffering from dehydration. Ona couldn't remember the man's face, but the bear's voice echoed in her memory: "Run, girl! Run on outta here!"

On the night of Martha Washington's bizarre affection, Ona had dreamed up another whipping. It took place in Lady Washington's bedroom. Martha stripped Ona naked and tied her arms to the tall bedpost that held up its drapery. An overseer cracked the heavy cowskin from behind her, raising the ridges from her soft skin. Martha walked out of the room, saying, "You'll be a woman, Ona. You'll be a woman someday." Each lash sent a stream of blood down Ona's backside and legs. "You'll be a woman."

Ona made no expression. She didn't cry out. She felt no pain. She endured the cruel whip, and focused her eyes on Hercules, who stood in the corner of the bedroom with his arms outstretched to hold her when it was all over. He smiled at her, and she smiled back. The overseer threw the bloody lash upon her, harder and harder, so forceful that she suddenly awoke. Catching her breath, she laid her head back down to the bunk, and the overseer commenced where he left off.

Hercules arrived at the mansion every morning by 4:00 a.m. to stock the kitchen and begin preparations for breakfast. Others filtered in, appearing out of the darkness, so by the time the Washingtons rolled out of bed just prior to sunrise, the estate would be operating like a well-oiled machine.

Hercules enjoyed the first few hours of serenity each morning, before the house bustled with servants, before the kitchen help arrived, and before orders came shouting out from the masters and their guests. He worked alone and listened to the sounds of a small symphony of birds, honeybees, and horses, accompanied by a cool breeze off the Potomac River. It hadn't stopped drizzling for days, and the slow raindrops gave a nice rhythm to the sounds of nature.

He stepped out of the kitchen, closed his eyes, and tilted his head back to taste the cold rain. Darkness began to fade, and when Hercules opened his eyes, he could still see the pale moon resting on a bed of lavender clouds.

Nelson walked freely through the paddock just outside the stable. He interrupted Hercules's meditation with a deep, penetrating growl that came through the log fence nearby. Hercules ignored the horse and entered the smokehouse to choose a ham, one of which he cooked daily on direct orders from Martha.

"Mighty hot in hell this mornin'," Hercules observed. He called the smokehouse "hell" because it contained an ungodly fire pit dug into the earth, which heated the scores of dead animals hanging from the ceiling. Hercules used iron utensils to choose the first ham he could reach. He then exited the gates of hell to avoid the burns on his flesh that would result from overstaying his welcome. As the chef shuffled back to the kitchen, Nelson whinnied even louder and stood up on his hind legs. Startled, Hercules stuttered his step and strained his lower back, trying to balance himself and the ham in his arms.

"Damn that horse," Hercules muttered. "Damn that horse to hell. Wouldn't mind hangin' you from that roof, right next to the swine and cattle."

He scrambled back to the kitchen and then returned to the outdoor entrance of the basement for some extra jars of honey. George Washington's sweet tooth devoured honey with most meals, and Hercules struggled to keep it in stock.

Nelson became more agitated with each trip Hercules made outside. He howled like a wolf until Peter, the enslaved stableman, intervened.

"Ho, Nelson, ho, now. Is that you out there, Uncle Herc?"

Hercules had acquired the nickname "Uncle" as a course of Virginia custom. It would be improper to address a slave, especially one as dark-skinned as Hercules, as "sir." But, Hercules exercised a certain amount of autonomy around the mansion, so "uncle" replaced the title of "sir."

"Uncle Herc, what kinda spell you put on that hoss? Acts up every time you near." Peter smiled, reluctant to raise his voice so early in the morning.

"Ain't no spell. You shut that horse right up!" Hercules shouted over to the stable. "I got work to do. Hoecakes and honey, and corned beef mush for breakfast today. I got work."

Each morning, Peter groomed the horses in preparation of Master Washington's ride to the outlying farms after breakfast. As a former field hand, he had been worked to the bone and was now more useful in the stable. Patches of curled, salt-and-pepper facial hair decorated his wrinkled face. To the best of his knowledge, Peter was about sixty years old.

Hercules noticed the old man moseying toward him with a slight hunch in his back.

"You know mastuh don't like when Nelson outta sorts," Peter said. "That's his favorite. Man's got a favorite hoss, imagine that. I got no favorite hoss here. You gotta favorite hoss, Uncle Herc?" Peter liked to make friendly small talk.

"Jus' take him back in, Pete. That damn horse chase me to work every day. Worse than a white man."

It was very much out of character for George Washington to have a favorite anything. He had crafted a golden reputation of impartiality by avoiding favorites. He favored no soldier, no slave, no politician, no friend, no relative. Nelson was the one exception. Nelson was, without question, Washington's favorite steed.

Peter smiled and changed the subject. "Look at that moon up high. Hangin' round. Sun come up, but that moon jus' won't go away. Imagine that. Say, why you think the moon never leave this place?" Peter often obsessed over why he could see the moon in the daytime.

"Jus' stubborn, I guess," Hercules said, having no interest in the conversation. He did feel sorry for Peter, though. It must be a lonely man indeed who craved such meaningless banter about the moon and horse shit.

"Hey, we gotta visit them beehives soon," Hercules remembered. "Runnin' low on honey again. Gotta steal from them bees out in the poplars when the rain stops." Hercules possessed a true passion for cooking, but he loathed retrieving honey, the most challenging part of his job.

"Man sho' does love honey, mastuh does," Peter opined. "Honey's okay, I reckon. Me? I likes molasses. I likes coffee, too. Imagine that. You likes coffee, Uncle Herc?"

"I like it fine. But mastuh, he needs honey. Mastuh's teeth get real weak now. Got jus' a few real teeth left. Gotta have soft food, and next shipment don't come in till next month."

"Them bees gonna sting you real good again." Peter laughed. "You get, what? Ten, eleven stings last time? Whole beehive fell right on ya head. I ain't never heard you scream like that, no suh. Bees don't bother me none, though. Nibble on you all day, but don't mind me none. Imagine that." Peter hunched over to ninety degrees and slapped his knee in riotous laughter.

"Yeah. You wouldn't be laughin' if you felt them stingers, Pete. Must be nice."

For as much as Peter annoyed Hercules, the cook relied on the old man's assistance in gathering honey because, for some odd reason, the bees displayed no attraction to Peter. He never received a single beesting.

"How come you ain't use them boxes no more, Uncle Herc? Soothe them bees, jus' like I do with the hosses."

Hercules hated being reminded of his failed attempts to domesticate bees. "Already told you, fool. Can't tame these bees, here. I tried makin' my own hives. Made one outa wooden box, and one outa straw. Them bees jus' won't come. One time they did, I lost the queen. Man up in Alexandria told me, 'You lose the queen bee, and the whole colony fall apart.' So, if you want honey, them bees ain't gonna help you out none. You want honey, you gotta take it. That's why we harvest honey in the wild."

They located hives underneath rocks and inside hollowed tree trunks. Hercules attempted several different methods to retrieve the honey. For a while, he preferred dumping boiling water over the hive to scare the bees away, at which point Peter could swipe the honeycomb. Always the perfectionist, though, he grew unsatisfied with the runny, waterlogged texture of the honey. To improve the texture and taste, Hercules now smoked the bees out by starting a fire underneath the hive. It had the same effect on the bees and gave a smoked flavor to the honey once it was extracted.

Their next honey quest would have to wait for another day. The swarming storm clouds broke at last, and a hard rain blitzed down with authority, making it certain that Master Washington would not be going on a horse ride either. Peter led Nelson back inside. Hercules prepared his specialty breakfast of corned beef mush. He was an innovator in the culinary arts, just as George Washington was to agriculture. The two men shared much in common, though neither would ever acknowledge it.

As part of the morning routine, Hercules brewed a pot of coffee for John Fairfax, overseer of the house farm and expert with the whip. Hercules usually left the pot with a few cups sitting on the front doorstep of Fairfax's quarters, but the rain shot down in buckets. He knocked on the door and waited in the pouring rain to deliver the coffee in person.

"Just a moment, General! I'll be right there, sir," Fairfax said, assuming it was George Washington. The frantic sound of clanging glass bottles came from inside. When he finally opened the door, a foul odor of stale beer and urine escaped the room. He stumbled forward. His infamous whip hung from the back of the door, like a thick snake climbing the walls. Fairfax let out a sigh of relief at the sight of Hercules.

No worries, Hercules thought. *You ain't leave Mastuh Washton standin' in the rain.*

"Well, what the hell do you want?"

"Coffee, mastuh. Didn't wanna leave it out in the rain. Hot and fresh, the way you like, mastuh."

"That's very thoughtful of you, nigger." He adjusted his suspenders and cracked his neck before reaching out to accept the delivery.

Knowing not to look a white man in the eye, Hercules waited with his head down, a stream of rain gushing over his neck down the back of his shirt.

Fairfax gazed up at the never-ending armada of black storm clouds. "On account of the rain, I reckon I'll be taking breakfast in the mansion this morning. I'll have a waffle with berries. Crisp."

"Yes, mastuh. Crisp."

Waffles were a favorite at Mount Vernon since Hercules had conceived and designed his own waffle iron, a crowning achievement in which he took great pride. George Washington preferred his waffles a bit undercooked, soft for his aching gums, but the cook's little invention could also prepare them as crisp as John Fairfax demanded.

"Now get out of this rain and go make my breakfast, nigger. Run."

"Yes, mastuh. Crisp." Hercules obeyed and ran back to the kitchen.

Cold rain crashed hard on the tattered roof of the Family House. Storm clouds blocked an emerging sun over the river. Inside, Ona Judge lay tangled with two other female slaves across the highest bunk, her arms dangling over the edge. She had survived the evening's imaginary whipping, and now, half awake, she reflected on Martha's abnormal display of vulnerability the night before. Ona would be expected in the mansion soon, although Martha may have slept in due to the rain. She contemplated the meaning of Martha's embrace. Was it a one-time fluke to be disregarded? Or had Ona's relationship with her mistress taken a momentous turn? If it had, was this turn for the better or worse? Would an emotional attachment become a heavy burden? She knew of white men having sexual relations with their slaves but had never heard of a mistress having any sort of friendship or emotional bond with her property. Ona decided to tell nobody of her concerns until she could figure them out for herself.

A voice startled her from the bunk below: "Ona, why you still here?" The voice was Charlotte's, followed by the whimpers of her crying baby, Eliza. The commotion woke everyone in the slave quarters. "Shut up, little thing," Charlotte reprimanded the newborn. "Godforsaken child never stops cryin'."

A thin ray of sunlight found its way between the rain, through the small window, and into Ona's eyes. She jolted out of her trance and fell off the top bunk, taking a nasty fall to the floor. Her left leg struck Charlotte's arm on her way down, and Eliza began to wail even louder.

"So sorry, Char. So sorry, Char," she said. The baby screamed through what sounded like the lungs of a coyote. "Was an accident, Char." Ona reached out her arms to hug Charlotte's leg from the floor.

"Ona, what's got into you?" Charlotte pushed Ona away and tended to the infant that she'd tossed onto the bottom bunk. "You shut that mouth, little devil," she said. "She's fine now, jus' scared. You hit my arm, that's all."

Ona sat on the ground and cringed at the pain shooting through her ankle. "Was an accident, Char," she said, gasping for air and squeezing her foot.

"It's okay, dear. I know you ain't mean to. Sun is up now. You should be in the mansion."

Ona realized how late the hour had become. She hobbled up, favoring her right leg, and reached for her stockings and cream-colored petticoat hanging on the wall. Her frizzy, black hair scrunched up and twisted in every direction, but there was no time to brush it. Charlotte helped slip on stockings and shoes over Ona's tiny feet. She pushed Ona out the door and rocked her daughter back to sleep. Ona limped into the hammering rain.

A racket of thunder and lightning joined the downpour outside. Ona tried to jog through her limp to escape the elements. It was a short distance to the house, but cold rain battered her from above, and it splashed up from the cobblestone walkway that flooded beneath her. The rain attacked from all directions and hurt her skin on impact, each drop sending a cold, resonant pulse through her body.

Endless thunder roared from the black clouds, causing Ona's heart to skip a beat. In a flash, a thick, white aspen tree from the side yard of the mansion split through the middle as if someone had taken an ax to it. The tree sparked in an instant. Half of its trunk bolted toward Ona and thrashed her across the upper back. The burning tree trunk plowed her straight to the wet pavement, and a dissonant ring in her ears paralyzed her senses. She was numb, but lucky to be alive.

Ona struggled not to cry. She grunted. But when the pain enveloped her body, she wailed as loud as the sonic blasts falling from the sky. The storm washed away her tears and overpowered her cries so that no one could hear. It was dangerous business for a slave to cry, but at this moment, Ona could get away with it. She screamed out in pain as long as no one listened.

Ona sprawled out flat on her chest, helpless for fifteen minutes before the sobbing let up. Her uniform could no longer absorb the heavy rain, which began to bounce off of her. When the numbness in her back subsided, she pulled herself up to her knees, shivering in spasms, and crawled the last fifty yards through excruciating pain to the piazza in back of the mansion. The rain pounded on the roof so hard that it blocked out any noise she made entering the house. Once inside, she stood and leaned against the wall, taking the weight off of her injured ankle. She would need to look presentable before seeing Lady Washington. It was no use. The ground had scuffed her face red; her hair knotted up in clumps; and a waterfall rushed from her clothes, leaving puddles all over the floors of the entryway. Blood trickled around her neck, staining her collar red.

Ona planned to find Hercules before anyone else discovered her. He would maybe have an extra shirt or an apron in the kitchen; he could dry her with a tablecloth, a hand towel, a napkin—anything. The pain still fired down her back as she improvised a hunched-over tiptoe through the house. It smelled of fresh flowers, as if she had entered a different world.

Before she could escape the entryway, Ona looked up and saw her mistress. Martha gazed over the railing from high above the stairwell. Her voice echoed throughout the mansion. "There's the little wench! You've decided to grace us with your presence."

She waited for Martha to come closer. Surely, her mistress would understand what had transpired and would allow Ona to clean up. She touched the cut on her cheek to release a drop of blood so Martha could see.

"You know, slave girl, coffee does not serve itself. A bedroom does not clean up after itself, and my papers do not organize themselves by magic." She descended the stairs to the third step, where she still stood a few feet higher than Ona.

The derision did not bother Ona, but Martha had never called her *slave girl* before.

Surprised, she tried to interject. "I apologize, mistress. I tried—"

"Do not presume to interrupt my speech, young thing! You are to be available for service when I awake. This is an indispensable requirement of your labor, and I do hope you understand the alternatives, should I find your performance unsatisfactory."

Ona hushed. She waited to explain what had happened, and she made sure to speak with the proper diction of a house slave. "Lady Washington, the storm outside has become quite strong. A tree knocked me to the ground." She began to cry again. "I would—"

"I shall tolerate no excuse from a slave girl!" Martha interrupted, having lost her patience. "If some misgiving may result in your tardiness, then I should expect you early to avoid it. I have entrusted you with certain responsibilities. It is a privilege to be my bondwoman, but I fear you do not appreciate this fact."

Ona was losing patience as well. Only hours ago, she'd held her mistress in her arms and had dried Martha's tears, consoling her. Martha now behaved as if none of it had happened.

"Mistress, Baby Eliza was injured and needed care. I injured my foot and my—"

Martha took one more step down to eye level, wound up her arm, and slapped Ona across her face, which had already been bleeding.

"Your job is to worry about *my* injuries! My injuries, and not some other nigger's! And you will not dare talk back to me in this manner again. As for feigning injury, George and I will tolerate it no longer. Injury and illness so conveniently afflict our slaves who've gotten lazy and wish not to work, and they've been punished for it."

Ona dropped her head and said nothing. A fresh stream of tears warmed her face.

"Now, you will move out to the laundry house and put on suitable attire," Martha fumed.

Ona felt a burning in her chest, as if the spark from that lightning had caught fire in her heart. She stared at the wet floor. "Yes, Lady Washington." She turned and walked away, still with a slight limp.

Martha sighed and closed her eyes as soon as Ona disappeared. Her outburst was not just a reaction to Ona being late. She needed to reestablish her authority after the moment of weakness she'd displayed the previous night.

The two women went about the rest of the day without speaking a word to each other. A slave owner could never display frailty, nor could a slave openly express anger.

As the evening turned black, a dim candlelight rose from the middle of the floor inside the Family House. Ona sat against the crooked wall with her arms wrapped tight around her knees, pulling them into her chest. She craved Charlotte's sympathy, but would never ask for it.

"Too much rain, too much mud. No market tomorrow," Charlotte said. "I's gonna get Eliza a toy, too."

"Marketplace a big waste a time, if you ask me." Ona pouted. "I got no money and nothin' to trade. I ain't gonna go to market jus' to watch you sell dresses and Hercules buy fancy shoes."

Enslaved workers sometimes visited the market in Alexandria on their Sundays off. Charlotte attended often. She had become quite adept at bartering the clothes she sewed in what little spare time was afforded at Mount Vernon. She used scrap fabric and blankets to make surplus clothing. Washington provided his slaves with one blanket every year, but Charlotte made a habit of sleeping with no blanket because the fabric could be turned into profit.

"You a seamstress, and you trade clothes. Hercules a cook, and he trades food. What do I do? I serve that old witch lady every day. I wish I could drag her to Alexandria and trade her. Cheap, too. I'd jus' take a teapot for her."

Charlotte laughed while she burped Baby Eliza over her shoulder. She was a plump woman, and she put one hand on her hip as she spoke with authority. "No, no. You gotta be better at business. I'd get you the nicest dress from Europe for the old hag."

Ona didn't attend the market often, and when she did, it was to socialize and gossip. For the past few months, everybody in Alexandria had buzzed about Pennsylvania. Ona loved listening to the stories, even though she knew much of it was exaggerated. *No more slaves. I heard they give everyone a farm. They have whole towns of freedmen.* She listened and compared what she heard to the information she'd acquired from snooping in the mansion. She deduced that Pennsylvania had at least begun a gradual abolition of slavery and that Pennsylvania wasn't too far away.

The women hushed as a hard knock rumbled over the door. Charlotte opened the door halfway and poked her head out. "Get out the rain, dummy," she said, pulling Hercules inside. "Ain't you go down the farms tonight?" Hercules had three children who lived on the farms of Mount Vernon.

"No, ma'am, not yet. I wanna check on Ona first. You okay, Li'l Miss?"

Ona pulled her legs in closer to her body. "Ain't never okay, Herc. That witch'll make sure I ain't never okay." She sniffled. "You gonna buy a nice outfit tomorrow?" She tried to change the subject. "Silk shirt, leather shoes?"

Hercules was one of the best-dressed slaves in Virginia. He sometimes stole extra food from the mansion and traded it for the finest clothes in Alexandria. He took pride in looking as dapper as any white man. Washington sometimes allowed Hercules to sell extra food for cash, a privilege known to very few slaves at Mount Vernon. Tonight, Hercules didn't care to discuss it. He didn't let Ona off the hook.

"You be careful, Ona. I seen mistress send people out to the fields. Or worse, sell 'em to Georgia or the West Indies. Sent my own son Richmond off to field labor."

"What'd he do?" she asked, peeking up from under her arms, her eyes wet.

"Stole money from the mansion. Got hisself a fine whippin' on the way out, too. I never seen Mastuh Washton so angry. Dumb kid, had it comin'."

"How old was he when mastuh whip him?"

"Jus' a boy, Ona. Younger than you. Maybe fourteen. Mastuh didn't whip 'em hisself. Mastuh Fairfax hit 'em—hit 'em hard. I wanted to whip that man right back. Mastuh Washton stood right by, so's I didn't. Boy had it comin'. I gotta admit. Mastuh Washton is a fair man. Boy had it comin'."

Charlotte hissed at the words "fair man."

"Don't you start up now, woman," Hercules chided. He and Charlotte had debated this topic before. "Mastuh *is* a fair man. Jus' look at me. I work harder than any man on this plantation, and mastuh treat me fair. I cook extra food, make some money. Why you think you never seen a slave dress like I do? Hmm? And you jus' watch. Someday, when I work hard enough, I'm gonna buy my freedom from mastuh and leave this place."

Charlotte widened her eyes. "You so naïve. Buy your freedom? That's the funniest thing I heard in a long time, Uncle Herc. Buy your freedom." She laughed in a frantic fit, mocking Hercules's dream.

"You laugh now, but mastuh is a fair man," he insisted.

"Don't you get it?" Charlotte's hand fell back to her hip. "Mastuh can be the fairest man alive, and it don't matter none. 'Cause it's the *world* that ain't fair. Ona's jus' startin' to learn that, and you'd be best to learn it, too. The world ain't a fair place."

Hercules wagged his finger. "You'll see."

Ona loosened her grip around her legs and lifted her head. "Sometimes I wish she would do it—send me off. Sell me to Georgia. She a fake old woman. Treats me like a daughter one day and a dog the next. It'd be kinder to treat me like a dog always and stop toyin' with me. Stupid me, I thought the witch had feelin's. She ain't got no feelin' but greed." Ona began to weep again.

Charlotte handed Baby Eliza to Hercules. She sat tight next to Ona on the floor. "You listen to me, child. Lady Washton don't use the whip on body servants. You get sent to workin' fields—them overseers, they use the whip." Charlotte's massive hand took Ona's face in its palm, forcing Ona to look her deep in the eyes. She spoke in a raspy whisper. "I done felt the whip, child. You don't never wanna feel that whip. You hear me? You hear me, girl?"

Ona wept louder. "Yes," she said, surrendering.

Unsatisfied, Charlotte turned and lifted the back of her shirt, exposing the black ridges tattooed up and down her back. "That's what it look like, and it feels like you been set on fire. That's from a hickory stick, and I ain't never work the fields. Those scars come right here at the mansion, but them field slaves get it worse. We up here talkin' 'bout feelin's and such. Them field hands ain't got no use for feelin's. You jus' be happy you know *how* to feel anything."

The room went silent until Eliza began crying through Hercules's mangled embrace.

"Oh, Lawd, here we go." Charlotte shook her head. "This damn child won't go five minutes without howlin' to the moon." She reached for her daughter and patted her bottom, harder until it became a spank.

Ona looked on, confused. "Charlotte, how come you so mean to her? She jus' a baby. Try singin' her a lullaby." Ona laughed out loud at the thought of Charlotte singing in a soothing voice. Hercules laughed too, and even Charlotte laughed at herself.

"No lullabies," Charlotte said. "Truth is, Eliza gonna be sent off to the fields as soon as she gets to workin' age. Lady Washton got no use for infants in the mansion no more. All her children dead. Grandchildren growin' up. I got no time to get close to this one. So why am I mean? 'Cause the world ain't fair, remember? Never too young to learn that," she asserted. "Uncle Herc, you talk some sense in to this one," nodding toward Ona. She wrapped the infant in an old shirt and whispered some baby talk.

Hercules stood high above Ona. "She's right, Ona. We gotta be happy with what we got." He helped her up to the bottom bunk. "You best go back to work with all smiles come Monday mornin'."

Ona's voice trembled. She hated being weak, a weak little girl, a girl that needed constant comfort and pampering, like Charlotte's infant. She wiped her face hard with her fists, trying to scrub the childish freckles off her skin.

"Oh, I'll go back and smile," she said, "but I won't be happy 'bout nothin'."

Ona's short haircut accentuated the smooth skin on her neck, which shone in the candlelight. A few beads of sweat raced down to her torso. She noticed Hercules staring before he flinched his head away.

"You seen my new shoes yet?" He tried to draw attention to his fancy clothes.

"Herc, what you know 'bout Philadelphia?"

He looked uncomfortable with the topic. "I heard of it, like you. Mastuh been there a lot. Some place up north."

"You know they ain't got slaves there no more?"

Hercules looked over his shoulder toward the door. "Shhhh. You can't be talkin' like that. I know what you talkin' 'bout, and it's dangerous—

dangerous talk. Ain't even Philadelphia anyways. It's Pennsahvania you thinkin' of, and we ain't even know where that is." His tongue quivered inside the gap in his front teeth.

"So, you do know. Philadelphia's *in* Pennsylvania—"

"And that got nothin' to do with us. Nothin'." His forehead glimmered with bubbles of perspiration.

"It does, Hercules. Now you listen to *me*." Her eyes lit up, and she spoke with confidence. "Mastuh ain't jus' been to Philadelphia. He goin' back. He goin' back with the whole family to live this time, and they gonna need help."

Hercules rolled his eyes.

"I ain't sayin' we run to Philadelphia. I'm sayin' we go with them. You and me, we obey like always, and when mastuh move to Philadelphia, he take us with him. *Then* we run. We escape in Philadelphia, and we free."

Hercules shook his head. "You talkin' crazy now. You obey, that's fine, but anything else is jus' crazy talk." Frustrated, he turned to exit. "Jus' get some sleep, Li'l Miss." Hercules took a slow walk back to the mansion in deep thought. He would spend the evening alone in his room above the kitchen, shining the buckles on his fancy leather shoes.

James Madison sat confined in the disgusting outhouse of the Richmond Theatre with his head hunched over between his knees. It was all he could do to slow down the spinning in his head. Stabbing pain pushed deeper and deeper into his abdomen as floor debates wrapped up inside the convention hall. He always suffered from a weak stomach, but the anxiety and stress brought on at the ratifying convention produced a poison in his gut that he'd never experienced before. Cold sweats and diarrhea had plagued him from the day he'd arrived in Richmond. His head pounded in a fevered temperature of over one hundred degrees for days. Madison wanted to participate more in the debates, but his poor health prevented it.

From the outhouse, Madison listened to Patrick Henry shouting down the convention with his oratory—every word amplified—echoing in his ears like the Liberty Bell. Madison's mind churned out rebuttals that would silence the loudmouth, if only his stomach would allow him to stand straight. His body ached more with each argument that he would never get the chance to present.

Henry took full advantage of this opportunity to fire off his most salacious rhetoric in the absence of the bespectacled philosopher who would correct every fine point.

"You will sit by and watch as New England and New York vote to strip you of your rights to navigate the Mississippi River, or the right to expand west at all, for that matter. It is the inevitable result of allowing just one president and a small Senate to ratify treaties in the west. They will conspire to crush Southern interests under a hammer of federal power—federal power which you, gentlemen, now have the opportunity to reject once and for all, for the good of our confederation!"

Madison could no longer sit in the stench of his own shit and listen to Henry's guile. He finished his business and ran, hunched over, through the thunderstorm, which now brought high winds, hail, and random bolts of lightning that illuminated the sky like it had caught fire.

Madison burst through the door and threw himself at a desk next to Federalist George Wythe, who was dressed in all gray and black. Henry didn't miss a beat, continuing his obnoxious speech through the disruption.

"Are you hearing this blasphemy?" asked Wythe.

"All of Virginia can hear," Madison responded as he wiped the rain and perspiration from his pale face.

"He's absolutely brilliant," Wythe said. "This entire charade about the Mississippi is all to scare ten feeble men from western Virginia into voting nay—and I fear it's working."

Madison rose to interrupt Henry, ignoring the debate rules. "Mr. Henry, you rant and rave about the North forcing the South into submission. The almighty North and the anemic South. What you fail to understand is that the North *is* the South! The South *is* the North! We are uniting *one* nation, not two. So why, in heaven's name, would the North cut off trade in the South? Would they cut off their own arms? I think not, sir!" He fell back to his seat, exasperated, coughing deep from inside his lungs. Red blotches began to patch up his pale, haggard face. Wythe poured him a glass of water.

Henry grinned from the podium. "In fact, this monster of a government would cut off two of its arms, for the Constitution grants it the power of a thousand arms! And that, gentlemen, is why this convention must vote to chop off its head!"

The theatre erupted in applause from spectators in the gallery and jeers from federalists on the floor. George Wythe's aging eyes squinted at Madison with an incredulous expression, accentuating all of his wrinkles. These were the two strongest advocates of the Constitution in Virginia's convention: an elderly bald man past his prime and a rookie politician with explosive diarrhea. They felt the absence of Washington and Jefferson more than ever. On the other side of the aisle, Henry allied himself with a powerhouse lineup of influential anti-federalists, including James Monroe, William Grayson, and the legendary George Mason. Also in attendance was Virginia's governor, Edmund Randolph, who had attended the Constitutional Convention but refused to sign the document in protest.

Henry knew that the large applause was an appropriate time to step down from the podium. He yielded the floor to George Mason, who launched into an attack on the Constitution's biggest flaw.

"The right to trial by jury, the right to a free press, the right of free worship and to free thought—the list goes on and on, of rights to which this constitution denies acknowledgement." Mason didn't come close to matching Henry's theatrics, but his reputation on the subject was immaculate.

"Twelve years ago, I authored the Virginia Declaration of Rights to guarantee that certain inalienable rights never be molested, be it by a British government or by an American one. Yet here we find ourselves, some of us willing to sign away those sacred rights with the stroke of a pen."

Mason was sixty-two years old, the same age as George Wythe, but he spoke with a passion and enthusiasm that surpassed most of the younger delegates. He wore a silk, yellow waistcoat with knee breeches and high stockings that emphasized his bulging calf muscles. A flowing white wig topped off the perfect image of a Southern gentleman, pleasant as a dandelion. Any symptoms of age were hidden by his soothing brown eyes, which commanded attention when he spoke.

"Without a similar bill of rights, this monstrous constitution must be rejected—rejected in a powerful voice of not just a simple majority, but with a resounding nay from an overwhelming coalition of Virginians. Nay now, and nay for all of nature's eternity against any plan of government that would fail to secure our most consecrated and undeniable liberties."

Another round of thunderous applause gave Madison the uneasy feeling, for the first time, that he was losing the debate. The storm outside blew open a window, letting in powerful gusts of wind and cold rain. For Madison, the breeze brought a delightful relief before the window was shut and his fever persisted.

The volume of George Mason's voice increased to compete with the heavy winds. "Now, I shall address the most egregious passages in the entire constitution. I call your attention to article one, section eight in the document before you." He waited for the delegates to find it.

"Not one of you, for a second, should be so naïve to assume that a government would not abuse the power of assembling a standing army. And here it is, in plain language. This proposed government may 'raise and support armies,' and not just for war. There is no language whatsoever to prevent keeping an army during peacetime. It further dictates that control of your state militia shall be given up to Congress. And for what? Section eight goes on to define the use of said military 'to execute laws of the union.' Not just to defend our shores, but to execute laws, this army will be enacted against you. And what laws would an army enforce? Well, again section eight reveals, whichever laws 'shall be necessary and proper.' Gentlemen, please! How could we, in good conscience, ratify a constitution that grants a federal government the power to legislate on anything they find necessary, enforce the so-called necessity with an army, and then deny you a jury trial when accused of violating the necessity?"

Shrieks and howls echoed throughout the convention hall before Mason even finished. The room grew so loud that it was pointless for him to even attempt speaking over the noise. The shouting came from everyone present except for Patrick Henry and James Monroe, who huddled together in conference in the back corner of the theatre.

Edmund Pendleton, the chairman of the convention, banged his gavel at the front of the hall to no end. "Order! Order!"

The ruckus continued another minute until Pendleton could quiet the room.

James Monroe stepped forward and announced in a bold voice, "I move to end debate and call the question of ratification."

Before the federalists' eruption overtook the hall, Patrick Henry screamed, "Second!" A penetrating roar shook the room. Tables and chairs vibrated, and delegates now directed their screams at one another. No one present expected to take a vote until at least the following week.

James Madison and George Wythe panicked.

"We cannot vote now!" Madison cried. The momentum had completely swung to their opponents' side. Madison shouted over the pandemonium, "Postponement! I move for a postponement!"

It was no use. Nobody would tolerate a postponement in such a heated uproar. In this same situation, the federalists in New Hampshire adjourned before taking a vote. That was not an option this late in the game.

Pendleton again banged the gavel to demand order. "The question has been called and seconded." The delegates' shouting killed any chance of further coherent discussion. Pendleton allowed the noise for a few minutes before standing on a table to announce, "All in favor of ending debate, say aye."

"Aye!" shouted Henry and his followers in unison.

"All opposed!"

"Nay!" The federalists strained their voices.

"The ayes have it!" Pendleton shouted as the federalists hollered out in anger. He waited a moment for the chaos to subside.

George Wythe bent over the crooked table in front of him to make a motion. "Mr. Chairman, I move that the final vote on ratification be taken by secret ballot." He turned to Madison. "It's our last chance, James." Hopefully, enough delegates could vote for ratification without the pressure of Patrick Henry staring them down.

Edmund Randolph seconded the motion, drawing an evil eye from Henry. An uneasy silence overtook the hall. Political conventions did not often vote by secret ballot in the American colonies. If a man cast a vote, he was expected to cast it in public, for all to see, without being a coward. Had the motion come from anyone else, the other delegates may have laughed in hysteria at the idea of voting in secret. However, George Wythe commanded a certain respect from the convention. He was the elder statesman, Virginia's version of Benjamin Franklin. Some of the younger delegates studied under him in law school.

Patrick Henry shook his head and threw up his arms out of frustration. He just wanted to strike while the iron was hot. He needed a vote taken as soon as possible.

Wythe explained his reasoning further. "The entire Constitutional Convention was held in secret, to avoid outside pressure on the delegates. The same principal applies here. No man's vote should be influenced by anything other than his own conscience—certainly not on a vote as consequential as this one. The final decision on ratification must be determined by secret ballot."

Pendleton led the convention through another tumultuous debate and vote, and the delegates agreed to vote by secret ballot, mostly out of reverence for George Wythe. They scrambled for paper and ink, and within minutes, the delegates began approaching the chairman, one by one, to cast the most important vote they would ever cast. Their vote would either confirm James Madison's life work or reject it in favor of the unbridled passions of Patrick Henry.

The next hour was the most arduous of James Madison's life. He spent most of it defecating in the outhouse, and he vomited twice before reentering the Richmond Theatre. The hailstorm continued, so the delegates had little else to do but wait inside. They spoke very little. Most of them felt a weight lifted off their shoulders simply for having voted.

After counting the votes with a few witnesses, Chairman Pendleton slapped down the gavel one final time. The delegates and spectators crammed in the building to hear the final vote. Total silence overtook the hall, and tension could be felt in the sticky air.

"Done in convention this twentieth day of June, one thousand seven hundred and eighty-eight. We, the delegates of the people of Virginia, by vote of eighty-five to eighty-three, reject the federal convention's proposed United States Constitution."

Chapter 3

George Washington attended regular, nighttime therapy sessions with Nelson, to calm his nerves. He arrived a bit earlier, before sundown, and stayed further into the night. On a luminous evening, a full moon glowed through the stable, and the rains subsided for the first time in days. Nelson purred up a storm while George contemplated an uncertain future. Earlier in the day, he had received a letter from New York that injected some doubt in his convictions:

Poughkeepsie, New York
June 21, 1788

Dear Sir,

I trust this letter finds you well, though I regret to inform you of the current machinations working against us in convention at Poughkeepsie. No vote has been taken, but the delegates find little utility in strong, federal government and conspire to defeat the measures at hand by large majorities. The political climate may change once adoption of our Constitution has been secured. Dissention may dissipate, for no New Yorker wishes in sincerity to stand against the progress of a new nation. Should Virginia ratify and thus consolidate the states, New York's disposition may transform to one more agreeable. I shall continue to argue the rightness of our cause with great fervor and devotion. Please extend my warmest regards to your lovely wife—and also to your vibrating horse.

Your most obedient servant,
A. Hamilton

Washington read the message with great trepidation, but not much surprise. "It makes sense that the most politically mature—the noblest state—Virginia, should cast the ninth and deciding vote." He looked Nelson in the eye, as if the horse could comprehend what he said. "We are on the precipice."

Nelson's face reached out in a gentle head butt to Washington. When a strange, ruffling sound came from the yard, George yanked his body away from Nelson and marched outside in a combative posture. He could usually control his temper, but when he lost it, those serving under him knew to steer clear.

"Hercules! Enough of these games!" Washington's eyes searched through the darkness but saw only shadows under the full moon. He snorted like Nelson, and his blood pressure climbed to a dangerous level, overheating his body early in the hunt. "Hercules!" He snarled again.

Washington turned toward the river and saw the profile of a man walking alongside a horse. He jogged downhill toward the shadow, but cramped up with shortened breath. He approached the figure and could discern that whoever this ghost was, it was not Hercules. The man's frame appeared much too scrawny. Perhaps a runaway slave—maybe one of his own, maybe from a nearby plantation.

Washington stopped running to ease the pain in his side, but continued walking forward in a brisk pace, never losing control of the situation.

"Come forward! Now! Release the horse!"

The figure stood so short that Washington considered, for a moment, that it may be a child. A young man with bronze skin came into plain sight and froze, looking petrified of the large, fuming behemoth that pursued him, getting closer and closer.

Washington didn't slow his pace. As he advanced, his gigantic forearm swung like a tree branch in a violent, downward motion and struck the man on the head. The intruder fell straight to the ground and then rolled downhill a few yards. Washington may have lost some speed over the years, but his strength was difficult to match.

"Explain yourself!" Washington shouted. He hovered over the uninvited guest and then walloped him over the head a second time. "Speak, man!" The turmoil sent fear through the man's horse, who began chasing his tail in circles.

The frightened young man could not get a word out.

"Mmm, ma . . . j-j-j-j . . . mad," he tried, panting between each syllable. "Mmm, ma . . . j-j-j-j . . . mad."

Washington knelt to the ground with his arm raised high, threatening to strike a third blow if the man didn't start speaking.

"Jay–Mada"—he locked his eyes shut, then took a deep breath and belted it out—"James Madison sent me!" He coughed and reached into his pocket. "Here," he said, holding out a handwritten note from Madison. Washington seized the paper, almost ripping the courier's hand off with it.

Out of the darkness, Hercules came sprinting toward the commotion. It puzzled George Washington to see his cook again, afterhours. Why did he continue to encounter Hercules so late in the evening, and outside? Hercules could never have heard the scuffle from the Family House, or even from the quarters above the kitchen. More concerned with the letter in his hand, Washington ignored the anomaly.

He dashed toward the river, where the moon's reflection off the water allowed him to read the letter. He ignored the horse and the two men behind him. Holding the letter close to his face, he knelt back down to the ground and whispered the words as he read: "'Dear Sir, with my deepest apologies, I have failed you.'" Washington panted. "No." He continued reading.

Our opponents have forced an early vote, and they have prevailed. Virginia has rejected the Constitution with eighty-five votes. I shall arrive at Mount Vernon soon to discuss matters further.

With my deepest regrets,
J. Madison.

Washington sat motionless with a blank stare into the Potomac, his back toward the mansion.

Hercules's voice called out for his master's attention. "Mastuh Washton?! Mastuh, I take 'em to Servants' Hall, suh?!"

Washington's body remained rooted into the hillside; his white hair blew in the wind, but his body stayed stiff as a statue.

Hercules calmed the horse and then lifted the stranger to his feet and brushed off the cakes of mud and grass clippings. He tossed the little man around like a rag doll. In the process, Hercules noticed the man's expensive jacket, waistcoat, and high stockings made of silk fabric, unlike the linen and cotton ones worn at Mount Vernon. The jacket was blue instead of the black-and-white garments with which Hercules was more familiar.

Before they departed for the guests' quarters, Madison's servant ran back to Washington.

Hercules reached out to restrain him but missed. "Boy, you crazy?" Hercules asked. *A man must be insane to take a beating from George Washington and then run back for more*, he thought.

The strange visitor stood behind Washington, keeping about ten feet between them. He spoke in a sincere, composed voice. "Sir, Mr. Madison is in need of a doctor. He is not well."

Washington remained rigid as a stone. The servant turned away, ready for Hercules to show him to his quarters.

Hercules escorted the newcomer toward the mansion at a quick pace.

"Thank you for your help, sir," the man said, struggling to keep up. "I go by Jonathan." A drop of blood crawled across the top of his nose from the gash that Washington had planted on his forehead.

"Hercules," was the cold response. He continued forward, but again, the stranger fell off the pace. Hercules turned and watched Jonathan vomit onto the trunk of a magnolia tree. A horrible stench from an acidic stomach, combined with the foul-smelling weeds that lined the garden, became intolerable. Whatever stomach bug assailed James Madison had spread to his slave, though the slave never requested a doctor for himself. It would be imprudent.

"I don't know what you been fed, but I make you somethin' real fine. I'm the cook around here," Hercules said. It was the first display of compassion he'd made since helping the man out of the mud. In return, he just wanted to know one thing: "Where you get them clothes?"

Jonathan looked surprised at the question. "Philadelphia. New York. All over, really," he said, wiping off his face. "I just came from Richmond tonight."

"You a free man?" Hercules assumed the man's freedom, not just due to his travels, but also his fine clothing and demeanor. He walked with the posture and confidence of a white man, and Hercules couldn't contain his jealousy.

"Oh, no," said Jonathan. "I am the property of Mr. James Madison. Mr. Madison should arrive tomorrow, God willing. He has come down with a terrible illness that I pray is not apoplexy."

Hercules didn't feel any better knowing that the man was enslaved; in fact, he grew more unsettled. What kind of slave called their master "Mr."? And who talked like that? What on earth was "apoplexy"? He probed a little more. "So what kinda slave goes around all dressed up, town to town, without no mastuh?"

"Mr. Madison travels frequently, and I accompany him. On an occasion such as this, I serve as a messenger, and Mr. Madison follows behind in the carriage—just a small gig. Tonight's message required urgent delivery. As for my dress, I assure you, my clothing resembles nothing unusual in New York." He continued to brush off his jacket, having had no luck in removing the grass stains.

Hercules lost his train of thought, wondering who would have hell to pay for this man's puke in the marigolds.

"But you jus' a young man," Hercules said. "He let you travel alone?"

Washington's slaves traveled the few miles to Alexandria, but never as far as Richmond, and never out of Virginia.

Jonathan smiled. "I do believe I am twenty-five years of age. I've assisted Mr. Madison for over one year now. He set his last assistant free."

"He done *what*, now?" Hercules was certain he'd misheard the last statement.

Jonathan smiled and nodded. "Yessum, that man is free today."

Hercules had never met a free black man. He knew that some black people were born free in the North, and he'd heard stories of slave owners granting freedom, but he'd considered them just tall, hopeful tales. No, the surest path to freedom was to buy it, which Hercules planned to do with the money he'd saved from selling leftover food. The great George Washington would have to reward Hercules's loyalty, and if George Washington wouldn't, then nobody would.

He spoke with a befuddled look on his face. "Why would mastuh—Mr.—free someone like that?" he asked.

"Well, not exactly *set* free—more like stopped looking for him. Mr. Madison grew attached to Billy. He had been a body servant for many years, from the time they were both young boys. Billy tried to escape so many times as an adult that Mr. Madison eventually just let him go." Jonathan sighed, as if he thought the man was much worse off for having fled. "He's in Philadelphia now," he continued, shaking his head. "Say, what happened to your tooth, there?' Jonathan pointed at the cook's missing incisor.

"Jus' missin' one, that's all," Hercules snapped.

"So, you're a cook without a sweet tooth. Isn't that something?" Jonathan laughed.

"Listen, sometimes you gotta do what you gotta do. Ain't happy 'bout it, but you gotta sacrifice. Got it?"

"Uh, yes, of course." Johnathan apologized. "I mean no offense, honestly."

"Ya know, some of us don't get to ride around Richmond, New York—wherever you go. Some of us got real work to do. Every day, sacrifice. And sacrifice gets rewarded in the long run."

"Again, my apologies, sir."

Hercules's head quaked with tension by the time they reached Servants' Hall. He tied the black horse to a tree outside and before showing Jonathan the bunks, stopped short at the door, causing their bodies to collide. Jonathan bounced off of Hercules.

Pointing to an adjacent building, Hercules said, "Now, if you need to use the necessary, the outhouse is over there."

Jonathan squeezed his host's thick hand with both of his own. "Much obliged, Hercules."

Ona had spied on her master enough to know that James Madison was a significant government official. She'd heard his name mentioned more than any other name in Washington's private correspondence and in the newspapers. When he arrived at Mount Vernon, the illustrious young Madison looked like an old pauper searching for his deathbed. All color had escaped his face, and his breath stunk like the pits of hell from the acid that burned a hole in his stomach.

Ona stood close to Martha as they watched the family physician, Dr. James Craik, extract ten ounces of blood from Madison's arm. The doctor also prescribed a liquid diet to be administered for a few days. Hercules rushed to the kitchen and got straight to work on the doctor's orders.

Madison repented to Washington for his political failure while the doctor poked and prodded at him.

"I have fallen short, sir. All of America will suffer the consequences of my shortcomings. Should I be worthy of your forgiveness, it is only by the hand of providence," he rambled, like a small child that had misbehaved and had embarrassed his father—although he would have rather disappointed his own father than George Washington.

"It is not your failure alone, but a shared one," Washington observed. "I have lost far more battles than I have won, yet not a single missive has ever eclipsed the fruits of victory. We will prevail. Somehow, we will prevail."

George and Martha sat at Madison's bedside in the first-floor bedroom of the mansion. Dr. Craik handed Ona a bowl, overflowing with Madison's blood, which splashed over the edge and dripped down the side of the curved porcelain. Martha ordered her to discard it, then to continue her work in the mansion. She ran the bloody porcelain to the necessary and carried the dirty bowl back to the house. A few drops of Madison's blood inched down her arm and on to Ona's wrist without her knowing.

When she reached the mansion again, Ona scuttled up the stairs to scrub the floors of the second story. She entered the guest room, above the makeshift hospital for Madison. Both rooms contained a corner fireplace, and the conversation below could be heard through the connecting chimney. Ona stood near the portal, but struggling to make out the conversation, she decided to cram her entire body inside the fireplace to eavesdrop. Her injured back and ankle still hurt, but it was worth tolerating the pain to hear what transpired downstairs.

"Mr. Henry's mischief has only just begun." Madison's soft voice turned guttural with illness, making it easier for Ona to hear through the sooty shaft. "As we speak, he is in North Carolina, scheming to create a Southern confederacy. North Carolina will now call a convention, and on its first day, reject the Constitution, at which point Virginia and North Carolina will begin the alliance."

"Such egregious faction." Ona could hear the disbelief in Washington's voice. "But South Carolina has already ratified. Mr. Pinckney and his allies would never consent to such a plot. Georgia has ratified, as well."

Dr. Craik exited the room, and Madison propped himself up in bed.

"Henry is quite assured that Virginia's rejection will lead to New York's rejection, and New Hampshire's, too," he said. "After ratification fails, the Southern legislatures will, one by one, secede from the United States and join the new confederacy—Maryland, too. George Mason is already hard at work writing a new constitution."

"And Hamilton's news from New York brings no encouragement." Washington lowered his voice in despair, a depressed tone that Ona had never heard from her master. She heard the rustling sound of Martha rubbing George's shirtsleeves to relax him.

As Ona adjusted her position in the cramped cubbyhole, she inhaled a whiff of ashes and coughed out loud. The voices below went silent. She held her mouth, forcing back the coughing fit.

Washington eventually broke the stubborn silence, instructing Martha: "My dear, perhaps you should leave us." His voice still sounded crestfallen.

Madison continued his assessment of the disastrous turn of events. "One thing is for sure: This new Southern confederacy—whatever political form it may take—will secure our human property. The slave trade will continue uninterrupted, and the institution will expand west. I assume that statesmen of the North—at least the most radical among them—will push for emancipation. I pray that war can be avoided over the matter."

Washington's tone turned serious again as he said, "My dear friend, I have fought my last war. I served this nation to the best of my ability. I fought to defend man's sacred obligation to the advancement of liberty. But to the prospect of waging war in attempt to proliferate human bondage and suffering, I say to you again, I have fought my last war."

Ona's heart sank as she listened to the prediction of slavery extending its influence. Black soot colored her cheeks, and dribbles of sweat drew vertical lines down her face. She needed time to digest the new information. If Virginia was now in a new country, would they be moving to Philadelphia? Would they be moving at all? She feared the worst.

The sound of Martha's footsteps from the stairwell interrupted Ona's deep thought. She crawled out of the fireplace, reaching for a wet rag to scrub the floor. She knew it was Martha coming from the sound. Ona could identify the sound and rhythm of anyone who walked the squeaky, wooden floors of the mansion. George was the easiest to recognize because he sounded like a ton of bricks approaching. Hercules made a similar sound, except most of the time he carried some sort of prop—clanging pots and pans, or the chime of sharp knives and fine china. Martha trumpeted a slow, graceful stroll, easy to pinpoint. She sounded like a wheel rolling down the hallway, always at a steady tempo, never slowing down or speeding up.

Ona kept her back to the door and her head down to hide her charred face from Martha.

"The floors look marvelous. Just marvelous," Martha proclaimed, not even glancing down to notice that they had not yet been touched.

Ona peeked over her shoulder through the corner of her eye and saw Martha's giddy smile. The porcelain bowl, stained with the blood of James Madison, still sat against the wall. Ona stiffened, hoping it would go unnoticed.

"I do hope all of that Philadelphia talk didn't frighten you, Ona. We are safe here at home, and perhaps Philadelphia can wait. You'd like that better now, wouldn't you?"

"Yes, ma'am." Ona stayed close to the floor.

"The Lord will guide us, my dear." Martha's joy beamed from her voice and from her body, draped in a radiant lilac gown. "'Behold, I am with you always, until the end of the age.'" She only quoted the Bible in her most emotional states, so even if she saw the bloodstained bowl, she probably wouldn't even recognize it.

Ona understood that such pleasure in her mistress would deliver sorrow in the souls of Mount Vernon's slaves. They would not be moving to Philadelphia. No other prospect could turn Martha's misery into bliss in one fell swoop.

Martha hummed a pleasant tune and strolled to her bedroom to write a letter. Of course, George could never know that the biggest failure of his career delivered an overwhelming elation to his wife's heart. She would finally share her life with the man she loved—a life from which circumstances had deprived them for so long—she would share her life with him and nobody else in America—a life of togetherness, in which their only passions and loyalties were for each other—and if a Southern confederacy was necessary for that life, so be it.

Plumes of steam rose from the boiling cauldron of medicine, making the kitchen look like a misty morning on the plantation. Hercules heard footsteps approaching but couldn't make out his visitor through the thick fog.

"Knock, knock, Hercules. Anybody home?" He recognized Dr. Craik's voice in an instant.

"Yes, suh, doc. Jus' mixin' up the roots you prescribed for Mastuh Madison. You be careful in here. Everything's hot."

Dr. Craik stepped into the kitchen with caution. "Damn shame about Madison. I've seen very few people *that* dehydrated. But I have no doubt of his recovery. He's in good hands now."

"Good hands indeed, suh. Good hands, indeed. I've cooked up potions for every sick man, woman, and child at this here mansion," Hercules said. "How can I help you, suh? Somethin' to eat maybe? Vanilla puddin'?"

"Oh, no, not for me. I've come to check on *your* health, Hercules. How have you felt since our little, uh, operation?"

"Oh, jus' fine, I guess. Pain gone away. Gums don't look black no more." Hercules pulled down his lower lip and smiled wide, exposing the large gap in his teeth, where Dr. Craik had removed an incisor.

"Well, that looks to be healed pretty well, I'd say. Infection is all gone. You just be sure to keep it clean. Any problems eating?"

"No, suh. No problems like that. It's jus', uh—no problems."

"No, no. Go on. Speak. Do you experience any pain whatsoever?"

Hercules stopped mixing and looked down to the floor. "People notice." He paused, embarrassed to be complaining. "I can't never get rid of this big hole in my face. And these damn beestings leave welts and scars all over me. I feel like a damn beast. Like one a them hams hangin' in the smokehouse. A beast from hell."

"Well, you make up for it with all those fancy clothes of yours."

Hercules failed to find humor in the doctor's joke.

"Listen, I know you endured unimaginable pain, and pain like that will leave its mark. It reminds us of the sacrifice. And you made quite the sacrifice. General Washington's dentures are a true work of art. Just think of the ungodly beast *he* looked like with just two or three teeth! You should be proud. You've contributed a tooth to the dentures that help nourish the most important man in America."

Hercules was not convinced.

"It had to be you, Hercules. You know that. No other slave matches the physical form of General Washington better than you."

"Now that's some horse shit!" Hercules stopped short, guilty of raising his voice to a white man. "Sorry, suh." He softened his tone. "But it ain't need to be me. I know now. Mastuh got horse teeth in them dentures. My tooth sits side by side with horse teeth. But not jus' any horse. You think Nelson's teeth in them dentures? You think mastuh would think of puttin' Nelson through the pain he put me? I'm worth less than a ridin' horse. Sacrifice? I sacrificed my wife, my kids, my tooth, everything I have. For what?

So Mastuh Washton can taste a little honey on his bread. Now, how much a man gotta sacrifice, doc? How much before he get somethin' for it?"

Craik lifted his hand to his patient's shoulder. "I'm no doctor of theology, but I've always felt that when we meet our maker, it will be better to have sacrificed too much than too little." He empathized with slaves more than most white people. "I will tell you this, Hercules: As a physician, I've worked on countless patients. Royalty, like the Washingtons; ordinary farmers; and slaves like you. And biologically speaking, there's not a damn difference between any of them. Not a one. That's not something I can express at the dinner table, and if you repeat it, I'll deny it. But it's the truth. Not one biological difference between a free man and a slave. The general using your tooth is just one small example."

Hercules appreciated the doctor's candor and felt comfortable pressing him further. "Doc, you think Mastuh Washton a fair man?"

"He is the fairest man I've ever met, and probably ever will. That's God's honest truth."

"Yes, I reckon that's true. So, you think a fair man like Mastuh Washton would let me buy my own freedom? Someone like me who sacrificed?"

"Oh, Hercules. You are of such great value to the general. I venture to say almost indispensable. Who could match your skills in the kitchen? Or your knowledge of Mount Vernon and the health of its occupants? You would command such a high price, I doubt an arrangement like that would be affordable for you, or any buyer for that matter. You should take that as a compliment."

"So Mastuh Washton the fairest man in the world, but life jus' ain't fair? You believe that?"

"Is life fair?" Dr. Craik paused to contemplate such an enquiry coming from a slave. "It sure doesn't seem so, Hercules. Not always. But I like to think that it is—I like to think that God will correct the inequities of the world in heaven, long after we're gone from this place—that someone like you will experience the glory of the Lord in ways that someone like me can never imagine."

"Glory of the Lawd," Hercules mumbled. "But not till I die."

It only took a few days for the news to hit New York, and it hit hard. A furious Alexander Hamilton railed against anyone who brought it up: "I ought to get on my horse right now, go down to Virginia, and hang Patrick Henry from the nearest tree!" He saw a lifetime's worth of effort go down in flames. The same news that brought about illness in James Madison unleashed a deep-seated anger in Hamilton that the young statesmen found difficult to control.

"We'll take a vote tomorrow, and then what? Allow Henry the power to mold America however he sees fit, and on his own terms? It's no joke, John. I really ought to hang him."

As usual, John Jay listened to Hamilton vent his frustrations at the Van Kleeck Tavern after the convention had adjourned its business. He struggled to remain the moderate voice of reason to a babbling maniac.

"Well, we must face the fact that tomorrow's vote will not be favorable. This delegation has been opposed to ratification from the start, and Virginia has now confirmed New York's greatest suspicions. It would be best for us to focus our attention on the future and what should happen after ratification is rejected." Jay's eyes bounced from side to side, following Hamilton's body rocking back and forth in his chair.

"I told you what will happen. I'm gonna hang the bastard," Hamilton mumbled.

"Alex, you can't just—"

"Did you know that the Pennsylvania militia is assembled right now to fend off Blue Jacket and the alliance of natives in the West? We could call out New York's militia—I'd be happy to lead it—combine forces and put a swift end to this ludicrous notion of a Southern confederacy before it is born. Listen to the rumblings in the streets. The people feel more fury in their guts than I do. And this is Poughkeepsie. Can you imagine the revulsion spreading down Wall Street right now? Can you imagine Philadelphia? Boston? I wouldn't be surprised if they've hung the bastard in effigy already."

Jay pushed Hamilton's rum a little closer to him. "Have you considered that this is not all bad news? Of course, it smacks of disunity, but what exactly are the ramifications of two counties instead of one? With the South abdicated, the Northern states could improve upon all the Constitution's shortcomings. The slave trade would die an instant death in a Northern republic; indeed, slavery itself would be abolished over time. Your dreams of a powerful financial sector would no doubt flourish in the absence of Southern obstruction. A strong bank, protective tariffs, direct taxes, internal improvements. If you despise these men of the South so much, why not set them free? You bang the drums of war too soon, and fail to see the opportunity in it all."

Hamilton tossed his empty shot glass back down to the table and leaned in as he swallowed, forcing his bloodshot eyes onto Jay, doing everything in his power to contain a visceral wrath. "You're going to vote no," he ventured. "You're going to vote no, aren't you?!" Astonished, Hamilton banged his fists on the table, knocking the empty glass to the floor, where it shattered to pieces. "You would throw away everything we've worked for—and after you've defended the Constitution with honor. You would really vote no?"

"Calm down, now. I didn't say that." Jay wiped the perspiration from his receding hairline, then began a sneezing fit, as he often did in moments of distress.

"Is it for political gain? Because John Jay can never be in the minority?" Hamilton's voice rose over the sneezing as Jay fumbled mucus between his fingers. "Everyone else will vote no, and you just can't bring yourself to stand up for something—to stand up for what is right! You are a weak little man!" Hamilton stood to exit and looked down on his friend one last time. "Vote your conscience, John. I, for one, will not bear witness to it. I refuse to sit through a vote of incompetent, phony statesmen, who design to bring ruin upon this exceptional nation. What an astounding embarrassment to associate with such a convention. I shall leave for home in the morning, and the convention will adjourn its business in my absence."

The sun crept away over the horizon. Hercules escorted James Madison to the coach house, explaining the liquid diet that Dr. Craik prescribed: mostly water, teas, and broths. Inside, they found Jonathan with Peter, washing Madison's carriage. It looked puny parked next to George Washington's immaculate barouche. Madison's gig was filthy from the miserable trip out of Richmond through swampy terrain created by the storm.

While Madison examined the carriage, Peter whispered to Hercules, "You meet Jonathan here? You see his clothes? They look even nicer than yours," Peter admired. "You see them buckles on his shoes?"

"We met last night, and yeah, I seen the shoes. Dirty as hell." He didn't need to be reminded—not by Peter—that he was no longer the best-dressed slave ever seen at Mount Vernon. "Why you so jolly 'bout some slave, anyhow?"

Peter could not stop showering adulations. "He been all over, to New York and Richmond, to Philadelphia, Baltimore, Annapolis, too. Imagine that. He been all round the world."

Jonathan noticed Hercules and gestured with a slight bow. "Good day, Mr. Hercules. A pleasure to see you again."

Hercules nodded, still wanting to throw a punch in Peter's side.

"It must have been you who prepared the delicious hoecakes and honey that Mr. Madison was gracious enough to allow me this morning."

"Yes, indeed. I hope you like 'em. Too bad you can't taste my lamb chops at dinner," he said. "They ain't for slaves."

"Too bad, indeed," he replied, impervious to the underhanded insult.

"Oh, yes, suh," Peter chimed in. "Uncle Herc here make real good food. You'd like it jus' fine, jus' like that food they got in New York. What kinda food they eat up there, suh?"

"Well, Peter, the cuisine—" He stopped.

A weak-looking James Madison stepped out of the carriage to address his slave. "We shall depart in the morning, Jonathan," said Madison. "But I must ask one question of you first," he announced in a monotonous voice. "Was it you who alerted General Washington to my illness and requested the presence of a doctor?"

Jonathan shuffled his feet in the dirt, thinking of an answer.

Before he could respond, Madison continued. "The doctor said I might not have lasted the evening."

"Yes, master. It was me." Jonathan exhaled.

He was one of the few men shorter than Madison. His master reached down and put his hand on the servant's shoulder. "Thank you, Jonathan."

Madison then paced out to the grounds of Mount Vernon to take in some fresh air.

Peter's eyes shone brighter than the North Star.

"You jus' hear that, Uncle Herc? A white man say thank you to a slave. Imagine that. Did ya hear it, Herc? He done saved that man's life."

"I'm standin' right next to ya. I hear what you hear, dummy," Hercules snapped. "Ain't none of my business who thanks who around here."

"Well, I hope you will both accept *my* thanks for the hospitality," Jonathan interrupted. "I must get some rest before we depart for Mr. Madison's home at Montpellier, and then back to New York in the Congress—if there is still a Congress. Good evening, gentlemen."

Peter tried to follow his idol out the door, but Hercules clutched his scrawny shoulder and pulled him back.

"What's the matter with you? Lookin' up to him like he's Mastuh Washton. That man a slave, no different than us. He goin' back home to slave, and then to New York to slave some more."

Peter seemed bewildered that his behavior might have chipped away at the big cook's ego. "Okay, Uncle Herc. I jus' think he look nice, that's all."

"Yeah, well, I look nice, too. But no matter how nice I look, I'm still a slave." His voice grew deeper. "I got no problem workin', but I ain't never gonna be happy 'bout bein' no slave, like you are. You so damn happy in chains, fool. No matter how good I cook, I'm still a slave. No matter how good you fit a horseshoe, you still a slave. That's all we ever gonna be."

Peter straightened his hunched back as best he could to address Hercules. "I ain't never been happy to be a slave. What I am, is happy to be standin' here on God's green earth. I'm happy the sun come up every day, and I'm happy to live under it—happy I got air to breathe. You best learn to be happy 'bout somethin, kid. Or else, you damn right. You ain't nothin' but a slave." Peter projected his usual, warm smile and departed, gazing up at the blue sky moon.

Imagine that.

Ona didn't sleep, woken again by the sting of a vicious whip in her dream. She threw on her clothes and stepped outside much earlier than usual. A sliver of the moon hung in the sky, like a whip, ready to crack her from above. Its light was all that guided her through the still, black evening. She took her time roaming in and out of the woods, then back to the yard, feeling an unusual sensation of tranquility. Darkness remained, but dawn would soon announce a new morning.

She galloped through the bowling green and into the lower garden, where her sleepwalk came to a sudden halt. Among a beautiful assortment of marigolds, Ona stood paralyzed, staring at what she thought was a leg. Her heart fluttered as she confirmed that a body lay in the garden. The size of the body suggested it belonged to one of two people: Hercules or George Washington. Fearful, she dashed toward it and found Hercules lying in the middle of the garden, flat on his back.

"Hercules? You okay?" She searched closer through the darkness to get a better look.

His body was stiff, and he stared straight up to the stars, his face void of expression, his eyes wide open, but he didn't acknowledge Ona.

"Hercules, say somethin'! You scarin' me!" she cried. "You sleep out here all night? Speak to me, Uncle Herc."

She tried to say more, anything to fill the empty silence. Finally, his body twitched, ruffling the flowers around him.

"You ever sleep outside, Li'l Miss?"

An adrenaline rush subdued her. She exhaled a deep, heavy sigh and took a moment to comprehend his question. "I sleep outside? Uh, yeah. I sleep outside once. Didn't mean to, though. Fell asleep out on the piazza, I was so tired. Lady Washton hollered somethin' fierce." Ona relaxed. "Hercules, why you out here in the middle of the night?"

"I like this spot right here. I like sleepin' here." He stroked a red rose resting against his thigh. "No one really knows—'cept you now . . . well, Mastuh Washton must know. He keep catchin' me out at night. I like this spot. I like lookin' up at the sky and can't see no end. I try to count all the stars, but you jus' can't do it. So many stars, you can't keep 'em straight. Apple tree right there if I get hungry. And all these flowers smell so pretty. I ain't never been no Godly man, but I think heaven smell like this place right here."

Hercules widened his nostrils and inhaled a massive whiff of a floral evening. Ona inhaled too, but then cringed in a coughing fit.

"That don't smell like heaven to me. Uggh," she said, choking. "Smells like—fish—like dead fish. You forget to clean up after supper?"

"You smell them weeds behind you," he said.

A patch of sharp, green wildflowers stood three feet high and were drooped over with yellow buds pointing to the ground. A curious mix of chemicals dripped from them.

"You stay away from them. Mastuh spray all the weeds with poison. Come over here. Find the right spot."

A true visionary in agriculture, George Washington had concocted an arsenic-based weed killer to fight off the ugly intruders in his gardens. So far, his experiment had showed promise, although not without consequences. On more than one occasion, the gardener employed at Mount Vernon had discovered dead rabbits around the weeds, no doubt killed from digesting the arsenic.

Ona pranced around the chemicals and sat down next to Hercules. She inhaled again and smelled the fresh roses and marigolds that surrounded her.

"Now listen real close to them songs comin' from the farm," Hercules said. "Every mornin', them songs wake me up."

She closed her eyes and heard the slaves, faint in the distance, walking to the fields, carrying their hoes and singing the most solemn melody she'd ever heard. She couldn't make out the words, but the song almost brought her to tears. She heard the call and response between a chorus of deep sounds and a high-pitched voice, probably a woman, squealing out in sorrow from the depths of her soul.

"So sad," Ona whispered. "So sad."

They listened together for a few minutes. Ona rested her head on his broad chest.

"So, that's why *I'm* here," Hercules said. "What in Lawd's name *you* be doin' out so early? Can't imagine you in a hurry to serve Lady Washton."

"Had a dream that woke me up. Had a dream you whipped me."

Hercules squinted. "*I* whipped you?"

"That's right. And not the first time. You whip me a lot at night. Bet you didn't know that. You whip me hard—harder than Mastuh Washton. It's okay, though. In the dream, I understand you gotta do it. It hurt real bad. But I'd rather it be you than mastuh. And Nelson was there, too. He was bleedin' from the side. The more you whipped me, the more he bled. I screamed, but Nelson did all the bleedin'. You ever dream out here?"

"Sometimes. But not about gettin' the whip. That's crazy. And I don't dream 'bout that damn horse neither."

"What do you dream about? I bet clothes. Clothes and food. All dressed up fancy, cookin' sirloin. Sirloin with potatoes, blackberries, and chocolate puddin'." She began to laugh. "And Lady Washton screamin' that it's too cold."

"No, not that either." Hercules paused.

"What, then?"

"I dream of my children. All three of 'em work the farm now. Might be them singin' songs that wake me up every mornin'. I dream 'bout them and their mama."

Ona knew very little about Hercules's family. She knew his wife was dead, but nothing else about her or the children.

"What are their names?" she asked.

"Son, Richmond, is the oldest. Two girls, Evey and Delia, the youngest. They don't know me as Papa. I see 'em sometimes, but now they jus' treat me like some other slave. Probably best that way."

"Do they call you Papa in your dreams?"

Hercules closed his eyes. "No. The dream's mostly 'bout their mama, Alice. Lame Alice, they called her around here. I hated that name. She come down with some sorta palsy. Lost control of her legs."

"Is that how she died?"

"That's how mastuh told me she died, but it ain't true. After Delia was born, Alice didn't get enough to eat on what they feed them field slaves. Bad harvest that year. Bad food. Cholera, or maybe dysentery, killed her. I know that's the truth, no matter what Mastuh Washton say. I dream of her sufferin'. I dream of her rollin' on the ground in pain 'cause I feel guilty 'bout it. She screams out like the devil, and I jus' stand there. I stand there and watch with food, so much food I can't even hold it all. Loaves of bread and fresh vegetables fall outta my hands. And then she dies. I think I dreamed it 'cause Mastuh Madison. I cook up all the food and medicine to save that man, but couldn't do it for my own wife. That ain't fair. And then stupid Peter say that Jonathan saved his life, when I did. That ain't fair neither."

Ona reached up to touch his neck. "Jus' a dream. I have 'em all the time, and they don't mean nothin'. I don't even mind havin 'em no more. Jus' a dream. Jus' part of life."

They told more stories, shared more dreams, and poked fun at Lady Washington, Nelson, and the high-and-mighty politicians who visited the mansion.

Still gazing straight up to the thin ray of light, he began to run his fingers across the top of Ona's head. "You think the sky in Philadelphia look like this one?" he asked. "I think it's the same—same big sky, same stars, same moon. We got the same things here."

"I thought Philadelphia was dangerous talk," she said.

"Very dangerous. Guess I'm a dangerous man tonight. You always been the dangerous one, but I ain't so shy. Ain't so safe sleepin' out here, ya know. I get a hell of a whippin' if mastuh find me here. Two whippin's. One for curfew, one for messin' up the garden."

Ona was excited to talk about Philadelphia. "I think in Philadelphia you sleep in any garden you want," she said, "and you don't get no whippin' and you don't worry 'bout no mastuh."

"I'd like that, Li'l Miss. You and me, and a garden in Philadelphia."

"You and me," she repeated.

Ona pulled him closer and rested her face against his. She closed her eyes, and her lips softened against his warm skin. Hercules nodded his head up and down her neck. Their faces caressed each other, and he kissed her. Just one slow kiss. Ona held her eyes shut and kissed him back. A light kiss. Their lips barely touched.

Still locked in his embrace, Ona opened her eyes. She cupped his face with both hands and pulled her lips away to speak. "We can't wait for mastuh. Mastuh ain't goin' to Philadelphia. We gotta leave from here. We go out to the river and follow it north—follow the stars."

Hercules listened, dangling his fingers over her cheek.

"Don't be causin' no fuss in the house," she said. "Someday soon, we leave this place. Mastuh and Lady Washton never know it comin'."

The sun prepared to rise, and they hurried together to the mansion.

Chapter 4

Everything happened so fast, even faster than James Madison had predicted. After New York's convention rejected the Constitution, the South did not bother waiting on the apathy of New Hampshire or Rhode Island. One by one, they seceded from the United States. Virginia and North Carolina led the way, followed by Georgia and Maryland. South Carolina held out the longest, but having very few options, the state legislature eventually succumbed.

George Mason, who would forever be known as the "Father of the Constitution," made a convincing appeal for a complete split from the North by abandoning the name "America" in favor of the Latin personification of freedom, lady liberty herself, *Columbia*. Other delegates insisted on a confederation rather than a consolidated government, and so christened the Confederation of Columbia.

The Southern Convention met in Charleston, South Carolina, as a courteous gesture to the most hesitant state. It played out more like a congenial social ball rather than a political convention, and the gentlemen in attendance unanimously approved the Columbian Constitution, written by

Mason. It began "We the States," rather than "We the people," followed by a Declaration of Rights, including twenty essential liberties. A large, unicameral legislature laid the cornerstone of the new government. The Columbian Congress, elected by propertied white men, would consist of one representative for every twenty thousand residents. They found no need for a Senate.

On November 25, 1789, a majority of the thirty-nine congressmen chose a president and vice president from among five candidates, one candidate from each state, nominated by his state's delegation. The newborn country chose its first executive leaders from an impressive ballot:

Maryland . . . . Charles Carroll
Virginia . . . . Patrick Henry
North Carolina . . . . Samuel Johnston
South Carolina . . . . Charles Cotesworth Pinckney
Georgia . . . . Abraham Baldwin

The citizens of Columbia expected the inevitable election of Patrick Henry, especially after the official retirement of a heartbroken George Washington. He sent a short message to Congress that read, "I shall not accept nomination to any public office, nor shall I serve if elected. I will forever pray for the reunification of our beloved nation."

In what would become a tradition, every representative voted for their own state's nominee on the first ballot, giving no candidate an absolute majority. To no one's surprise, Patrick Henry won the presidency on the second ballot, with twenty-nine votes. Choosing a vice president proved to be the more exciting contest. Carroll, Johnston, and Pinckney were deadlocked on the third and fourth ballots. None of them could boast strong anti-federal credentials, but all three were staples of American/Columbian democracy with unblemished honor. Charles Carroll had signed the Declaration of Independence, Samuel Johnston had served in the Continental Congress, and Charles Cotesworth Pinckney's military service had made him a genuine war hero with the implied endorsement of George Washington, who, in retirement, held his tongue on all political matters. Carroll's vote count began to wane on the fifth ballot, and his supporters threw their weight to Pinckney. With twenty votes on the sixth ballot, Charles Cotesworth Pinckney of South Carolina became the first vice president of the Confederation of Columbia, alongside President Patrick Henry.

The new government convened in Richmond and tackled its first order of business: choosing the country's flag. A small committee chose the crescent moon emblem over a blue sky from South Carolina's state flag and added a red canton to symbolize the courage and blood spilled in the struggle for independence. It passed unanimously as the Columbian Congress began its work amidst a strong aura of unity.

Their second decision was far more burdensome: Where to locate the nation's capital? Virginians insisted on a permanent capital in Richmond, but representatives from other states feared that rapid population growth in Virginia would result in an overwhelming proportion of the Congress. South Carolinians pushed for Charleston, but the Virginians pointed out an obvious hindrance: Charleston's coast had proved too susceptible to naval attack during the war with Britain, and building a powerful navy ranked low on the first administration's list of priorities. Congress also debated the possibility of Baltimore becoming the capital, but it shared the same coastal deficiency, in addition to its close vicinity to the Northern states that were likely to become adversaries.

After a week of debate, the Congress chose Richmond, Virginia, as the capital of the Confederation of Columbia. As a compromise, Virginia would cede more of its western land and put Kentucky on the fast track to becoming the sixth state. Congress intended to pass legislation to encourage settlement and an increased population there.

⟶

President Henry met with Pinckney as soon as the vice president arrived in Richmond. The two men shared very little in common and had much to discuss as they took an amicable stroll along the James River on a brisk Sunday morning. Opposites in almost every way, Pinckney wore his blue military coat with gold trim and a black, felt, cocked hat, compared to

Henry's typical, dirty, maroon jacket that hung over his slender body like an oversized bathrobe. The cold winter breeze could have knocked Henry into the river, while not raising a hair on Pinckney.

After a cordial exchange of pleasantries, Pinckney wasted no time in getting down to business. "Mr. President, it is no secret that we have had our differences on the subject of an army. But I beg you to consider that we may find necessity in calling up the state militias sooner than expected."

Pinckney was a strong advocate of a standing army, the one thing Henry feared most. Henry responded with caution. "As you know, this now requires a three-fourths vote in Congress. I doubt they are ready to make such a move, you would agree. And remember our Constitution: Ultimate sovereignty rests in the states. We are elected merely to carry out their will." He kept the conversation to politics, knowing that his knowledge of military matters could not match Pinckney's expertise.

"Of course, they are not ready now, but we must keep a watchful eye on our northern neighbors. Heaven knows what will come of their Second Constitutional Convention. Every day there is rumor of war."

"Rumor—exactly that. Rumors, all coming from a tyrannical madman that should have been run off this continent with the British." Henry had made a career of arguing with federalists like James Madison, and even Pinckney himself, but one man in particular incensed him like no other. Patrick Henry despised Alexander Hamilton.

"He is a dangerous man, Charles."

"Sir, I do not disagree. I find his unquenchable thirst for power repugnant. His vision of strong government stretches far beyond the imagination of most federalists. This is precisely why I urge you to take precautions. I served with Hamilton at the First Constitutional Convention, and I can assure you he is a knave, but he is a persuasive knave—wielding his power of persuasion right now in Philadelphia. He is an enemy that we dare not underestimate."

"We must tread lightly," Henry replied. "Any action we take will spark reaction—any tariffs we collect, any treaties we sign, any territory we claim. Peace between our two nations is fragile, like a leaf dangling in the wind, hanging on to a split branch. Now, if we go raising an army, haven't we invited the knave to attack?"

"I only ask that you introduce the discussion to Congress. They may not be ready now, but I fear when the time comes, it will be too late."

They walked on in silence. Pinckney added one last remark. "Mr. President, please do not think me a warmonger. Having served in battle, having seen it up close, I detest it more than anyone, and it would bring no pleasure to make war on my former compatriots."

The president smiled, pleased that his vice president sought his approval. "You are an honorable soldier, Mr. Pinckney. You are no warmonger."

The two leaders of a new nation continued their walk down the cold, hardened riverbank.

It was the performance of a lifetime. John Jay had seen his friend give long, eloquent speeches before, for lengths of up to five hours, but never with the controlled passion that emanated from Alexander Hamilton as he addressed the Second Constitutional Convention. Jay relied on Hamilton to convey their shared sentiments, never being one to give long speeches himself. At this moment, he looked proud to be sharing in the work of a great man, even though their friendship had grown a bit contentious in recent months.

A snowstorm descended from a gray sky, leaving the delegates with no choice but to take cover in the Pennsylvania State House, a captive audience for Hamilton. It was unusual for the work of government to continue into the winter months, but the grave political climate called for it, and Hamilton took advantage of the emergency situation. He was quite familiar with the venue, and with most of the delegates as well. Jay couldn't gauge how other men in the room received the speech because everyone had gone silent and expressionless, hypnotized by Hamilton's oratory.

This was no Patrick Henry speech. His arms didn't flail, and the earth didn't shake. Hamilton delivered more of sermon, mourning the loss of his countrymen in the South and transforming the emotion felt from that loss into a righteous call to action. Every word floated out of his mouth into the frigid air.

"I still hold firm to the belief that we are all Americans in our hearts. We all desire the blessings of liberty, and we all find nourishment in its fruit alike. But, like the different branches of a maple tree, both from the same root, our two countries must also set out in our own directions and find our own course. Our brothers to the south have paved their path, and so must we.

"I would say there is no need to alter the Constitution at all, if not for the abandonment of our brethren, which cultivates great opportunity to improve upon the Constitution's imperfections. The Southern faction has gone astray, and with it, Southern interests which are incongruent with our cause. We can, once and for all, dispense with the horrific slave trade. We can put the institution of slavery on a path to extinction as Pennsylvania and Massachusetts have done with great foresight. We can strengthen our government's financial system through a national bank, stable currency, internal revenues, and protective tariffs. Just five stubborn states impeded such progress, but have now jettisoned, and we shall all benefit from increased commerce, increased territories, and internal improvement projects.

"Yet, I warn every statesman present that the fracture of our beloved America will not move forward without encountering dangers. As we speak, our countrymen are fighting and dying against Chief Blue Jacket and his alliance of philistines to the West. It is intolerable. We now face foreigners to the South as well; brethren in our hearts, but foreigners in fact. Beyond our foes to the South and West lay countless, unclaimed acres, territory for the taking—the seeds of an empire. Now is the time to rid ourselves of the fear of a powerful military whose sole purpose would be to protect our lives and our liberties; a robust military to protect our borders and our shores and to aid in the expansion of the National States of America."

Voices in the hall began to buzz.

"Though I feel a fondness for our former countrymen, I cringe to think what will result when they are attacked without warning; when they depend on ragtag militia to scatter against the might of great empires. Let such a calamity never befall our glorious National States."

The New England delegates in the back corner of the hall buzzed the loudest—"conquest," "empire," "warmonger," "king." The accusations fluttered out in abundance.

Hamilton concluded his remarks after speaking for over two hours. With the exception of those in the back corner, most delegates reacted with exuberant applause. His views on the extent of federal power had always leaned a bit extreme, but drastic circumstances called for drastic measures.

Pennsylvania's Robert Morris rose to speak next on the subject of the presidency, which Hamilton had ignored, to avoid inadvertently campaigning for the office. Morris shared Hamilton's vision of a strong executive. He was the elder statesman of the Pennsylvania delegation, a newfound role for him since the retirement of Benjamin Franklin, who, like Washington, wanted nothing to do with the latest political developments in America.

Morris was a portly, miserable lump. Dressed in gray pantaloons, a gray shirt, and a gray jacket, he approached the podium, leaning on a cane, exhausted after the twenty-foot trek from his seat. What he lacked in physical luster, he made up for in the respect that he commanded from the other delegates. Morris's wealth bewildered most ordinary Americans, and he gave up much of it to fund the War of Independence. With Hamilton's help, he intended to build a powerful financial machine—a fiscal empire of the well-to-do.

"Gentlemen of the convention, I offer an amendment to the length of a president's term." He was quick and to the point. "I suggest that while the Confederation of Columbia, a wicked band of traitors, tear themselves apart every four years changing their chief of state, we, the National States of America, elect a supreme executive to a life term."

With this, the soft murmur from New England turned into a lion's roar.

"It would be"—he waited for the noise to abate—"it would be based on the exact reasoning for the life terms of judges. An independent executive is no less important than an independent judiciary, free from the passions of less refined men." He again stopped to wait out the caterwauling. "Of course, a system of checks and balances will remain, including an elected legislature's power to impeach. But why should we self-inflict the wound of instability by wrangling over vainglorious candidates for high office, over and over again?"

"Royalist!" someone shouted.

The noise died down to allow a response. Morris paused, waiting for his audience's full attention.

"You may call me what you wish, but every man here knows that Great Britain will do everything in her power to disrupt the general welfare of these states. France is in absolute chaos, and the duplicitous Columbian States sit idly by, waiting in our backyard to ally with either one of them. Escaped Negroes will soon spill across our borders while our people sit surrounded by an uncivilized, barbaric race of Indians prepared to scalp anyone in their path. Your weak executive may have applied six months ago, but it is a new world now, gentlemen!" Morris did his best to maintain his stamina. The tension-filled room could soon burst, and he stepped down from the podium for his own good.

Although Hamilton referred to "our southern brethren," out of respect for Washington and Madison, Robert Morris's views represented the overwhelming opinion in the Second Constitutional Convention, that the South had turned its back on America and should suffer the fate of treasonous traitors.

Next, William Findley made his way to the podium, shivering through the frozen hall. From western Pennsylvania, Findley looked nothing like a politician—because he wasn't one. He wore ordinary clothing, and his shaggy, unkempt hair offended some of the powdered-wigged statesmen in the room. Not just a representative of the common man, Findley *was* the common man. He often quarreled with Robert Morris and other politicians who sought profit out of a career in public service.

Findley addressed the convention in a thick Irish accent. "Gentlemen, in Pennsylvania's Ratifying Convention, I opposed the United States Constitution more than any man. I found the unprecedented power grab by moneyed men repulsive to good conscience. And today, I stand before you to announce"—he paused—"that I agree with my colleagues, Hamilton and Morris."

A collective gasp came from the floor. Robert Morris did a double take, scratching his temple. He must have misheard the Irishman.

"Mr. Morris is correct. It is a new world. And in such a world, I have no objection to an executive armed with power to protect the liberties for which I fought in the Continental Army. I have no objection to a standing army to defend those rights against all foreign enemies, Blue Jacket or anyone else who would terrorize my constituents."

The room vibrated with applause from a standing ovation by all of the delegates except for New England's.

"Yet I still caution my fellow delegates. Consenting to more government authority requires, more than ever, that this government be bound to protect our liberties in a bill of rights."

This finally generated applause from the New England representatives, who crowded around lanterns for heat.

"Our former ratifying conventions recommended such a bill of rights, and it now represents a reasonable compromise for a more powerful executive."

Alexander Hamilton and Robert Morris jeered at the suggestion, but they were outnumbered by a significant majority that approved the Findley Compromise. The convention created a committee to draft a bill of rights, which most delegates thought would pacify New England. They would be wrong.

—

The Second Constitutional Convention's committee to draft a bill of rights engaged in boisterous argument, similar to any other gathering of egotist politicians. They referred to George Mason's Declaration of Rights that began the Columbian Constitution, but found much of it repetitive or unnecessary. After days of deliberating, the committee presented its bill of rights to the convention:

> *Article I: In criminal prosecutions, every man has a right to be informed of the accusations against him, to be allowed council, to examine the witnesses for and against him, and to a speedy trial by an impartial jury. The right to trial by jury shall not be denied in cases of trespasses, torts, nor personal wrongs and injuries.*

Article II: Excessive bail shall not to be required, nor excessive fines imposed, nor cruel and unusual punishments inflicted.

Article III: No soldiers, in time of peace, shall be quartered upon private houses without the consent of the owners.

Article IV: The people have a right to freedom of speech and writing and publishing their sentiments, and therefore, the freedom of press ought not to be restrained.

Article V: There shall be no national religion established by law. All persons shall be equally entitled to protection in their religious liberty.

Despite its brevity, the bill of rights included an accurate sample of liberties that the committee found most imperative. This had no apparent impact on the New England delegates who screamed bloody murder after the committee presented its work. Oddly, a New Yorker, George Clinton, led New England's attack against the document.

A thick pool of saltwater perspiration dripped from his chin to the edge of Clinton's desk. The man smelled as if he defecated through his glands; swarms of odor exited his oily skin in waves, giving off a pungent tang of molded cheese and feces. Even the other members of New York's delegation kept their distance to avoid being exposed to the assault.

"A dwarf declaration!" Clinton began. "It is an insult to free men everywhere to leave absent any language that reserves powers to state governments!" Clinton's voice bellowed like a trumpet from his protruding potbelly.

Alexander Hamilton took the bait and blew right back. "The supremacy clause would render any such declaration useless. Our federal constitution will become the supreme law of the land. It will thus supersede your fantastical illusions of state sovereignty. We've been through this."

Hamilton had fought political battles with Clinton in New York for years; bad blood ran deep between the two. They stood behind the same table and spewed their breath in each other's faces.

"The *former* governor should sit down before he embarrasses himself further," Hamilton stated, hitting below the belt.

George Clinton served as New York's first governor and was quite popular. Voters reelected him several times before the recent fiasco that followed the First Constitutional Convention. Hamilton had accused the governor of working behind the scenes to stack New York's ratifying convention with anti-federalists, thereby assuring the US Constitution's failure. Out of raw retribution, Hamilton had campaigned to see an end to Clinton's administration. He endorsed Judge Robert Yates through scurrilous attacks on Clinton's character in the press and by befriending voters with methods that bordered on bribery. Hamilton had made enough powerful friends in New York to sway the outcome of an election, even for someone like Robert Yates, who shared Clinton's anti-federal beliefs. For Hamilton, Yates represented the lesser of two evils. Robert Yates became New York's second governor in a landslide.

Annoyed, Clinton ran both hands through his greasy, lightning-white hair. He would not allow Hamilton to humiliate him in public, in the presence of such prominent statesmen. "Nothing of due process, private property, nor the right to bear arms! Are we expected to accept a despot in return for this miniscule list that fails to even scratch the surface of the freedoms of man? It would amount to giving up a mile for an inch in return. Never! I say never!"

John Jay sat next to Hamilton and tried to pull him back down in his seat. After all, the screaming match was more about the two men's personal hatred of each other and less about the bill of rights.

Hamilton stood his ground, in firm opposition to the ugly glutton. "Perhaps the former governor should reexamine due process of law, for I'd say the first article defines it." He moved toward the center of the room in order to address the entire convention and to avoid coming to blows with his local nemesis. "Every man here knows that the obsession with 'property' in the South is a mere façade to protect the rights of slave owners. Lest we all become fleshmongers, Mr. Clinton's argument is nonsensical. Further, the South has guaranteed the right to bear arms for the purpose of putting down slave rebellions, and because they will rely on amateur militia for protection. The Columbians have been neglected by their federal government and are required to arm themselves. It is an admission by that government that they will provide no protection to their citizens, abandon them in a dangerous wilderness, and I assure you, they will come to regret it. Our military will safeguard this nation's freedom so that the people need not arm themselves out of fear."

"Armies and autocrats!" George Clinton walked away from his table. "Gentlemen, the Columbian Constitution includes a declaration of twenty inalienable rights, yet all we discuss in Philadelphia is oppressive armies and autocrats! I bid you adieu!"

And with that, Clinton stormed out the door, followed by every delegate from Massachusetts, New Hampshire, Connecticut, Rhode Island, and—to everyone's astonishment—half of New York's delegation.

The remaining delegates continued their work, and by the end of the convention, Pennsylvania, Delaware, New Jersey, and half of New York agreed to a federal government with more substantial power than was originally set forth by the United States Constitution, yet it did include the proposed bill of rights. The executive would indeed serve a life term, and the delegates found no use for the office of vice president. They abolished the slave trade, and the institution of slavery would be phased out. Each state reserved the power to determine how the phasing out would occur, but a deadline was set at twenty years. As of 1809, slavery would be outlawed in the National States of America. Over time, every state would adopt the model set by Pennsylvania. Children would no longer be born into slavery, escaped slaves from the South would earn their freedom after one year of residency, and after the duration of twenty years, any remaining enslaved people would acquire their freedom.

The National States army began recruitment to secure the undefined borders to the West, and Pennsylvania's southern border. They expected a mass exodus of escaped slaves, which would enflame civil discord in Columbia.

The ensuing kerfuffle in New York tore the state apart. Led by George Clinton, the eastern counties of New York formed the state of Saratoga with the intention of joining a New England Republic. The birth of Saratoga created a geographical gap of over one hundred miles that cut off New York City from the western county of Montgomery. Hundreds of land speculators from Albany and New York City relocated to their Montgomery property. In great need of a strong military to defend against native attacks, Montgomery crafted its own state constitution and became the fifth state to ratify the National States Constitution.

The failure of the United States Constitution gave birth to the Confederation of Columbia and the National States of America. The Republic of New England would form next, including Massachusetts, Connecticut, New Hampshire, Rhode Island, and three new states, Saratoga, Vermont, and Maine.

MONTGOMERY

SARATOGA

NEW YORK

Chapter 5

Blood. Everywhere, blood. Tiny speckles in the dirt, heavy clots flying through the air; each lash quickened the flow of red blood running down the helpless man's back in thin stripes. The volume of his screams dwindled with each blow as he lost the strength to cry out. He wandered in and out of consciousness, back and forth from a traumatic reality to a lethargic trance. George Washington ordered every house slave outside to witness the would-be escaped slave receive twenty lashes. The overseer's cowskin whip was stained with the man's blood after just one crack.

Hercules watched from the side yard with Ona. He felt no more shock or fear than he normally would at the sight of a man strung up and whipped by John Fairfax. He narrowed his eyes to confirm the victim's identity. The man looked older than most slaves at Mount Vernon because the flesh on his back was so soft; it ripped apart like the tender, bloody lamb that Hercules prepared for dinner. *Must be an old field hand*, he thought. *Why would an old man bother running?* His speculation stopped when the man turned his head and let out an awful howl, making eye contact with Hercules for the first time since the whipping began.

The light that always radiated from Peter's eyes—that carefree light that angered Hercules so much—had faded. Tears fell from his bloodshot bulbs. He accidentally bit his tongue, causing more blood to seep from his mouth and color his teeth. Blood and sweat doused his entire body. It all gushed together like a crimson cascade from his wet beard.

Hercules dropped his head in disbelief. Peter was the least likely man on the entire plantation to run away. Where would he go? What would he do?

As he stared down to the dirt, an unrelenting grip seized Hercules by the back of his neck.

"Watch, nigger! See what's coming to you, if you're making any plans."

Hercules hunched over. Fairfax pulled his head down to eye level and dragged him a few steps closer, making it impossible to ignore the slave driver's infernal work.

"Get a good look now," he said.

Hercules restrained his sudden urge to bite the man's face.

Fairfax was the perfect specimen of a white man. He was cruel and competent. He stood just shy of six feet, and his muscles bulged from his statuesque figure. His cotton shirt and suspenders wrapped his body tight. A full head of blond hair, brown eyes, and healthy skin gave the impression of a virile, thirty-two-year-old man in his prime.

Fairfax swung the whip gracefully and with ease, in perfect form as if practicing some sport. He was a perfectionist in every aspect of his life, and he managed Mount Vernon's house farm with an iron fist.

Each swing of the whip landed with more force than the last, and Hercules began to feel a deep remorse as he looked on in grief. No matter how much Peter had beleaguered him—in ways that no one else could—Hercules had never wished the man treated like this, beaten down like an animal. He began to regret any ill will he had ever felt toward Peter.

After the final lash, Fairfax addressed his audience. "Seems more niggers got a hankerin' to run these days. It seems you think there's a safe haven awaiting you up North. Well, hear it now—there is no safe haven. What awaits you is Columbian slave catchers, paid to repossess property. They will capture you or shoot you dead before allowing you to escape. And what awaits you upon your return is my whip. Let this one be the only example needed to spread the message. Your safest move is no move at all."

He untied Peter, and the pitiful bag of bones fell fast to the ground. No sooner than Fairfax began his stroll back to his horse, Hercules and several other slaves raced to Peter's aid. Ona sprinted to fill a bucket of water and then rushed it back to the scene.

"That ain't no man. He's a monster," Ona said as she poured water over Peter's head. She then poured it over his shredded back, forcing an ocean of bloody water into the dirt as Fairfax rode his horse off into the distance.

"Breathe in slow, now. You'll be all right," said Hercules. He wanted to say more. He wanted to ask what Peter had been thinking, but the wounded man got himself up and stumbled out of sight in embarrassment.

"Peter, wait!" Ona called out. "I hate him, Uncle Herc. I ain't never hated no one more than that monster," she said.

Hercules shook his head. "He used to be a decent man. I used to think if I's free, we'd be friends; we 'bout the same age. Then mastuh hired him, and he done changed."

Hercules remembered a time when John Fairfax was just an acquaintance, the son of a neighboring plantation owner. George Washington cherished his relationship with the Fairfax family and hosted them often. After Washington hired John to oversee the house farm, the kind, young neighbor transformed into a salacious demon.

"Didn't take long for him to change, neither," Hercules reminisced. "He whipped every slave out in that field—women, too; women most."

Ona whispered, "If I ever do get outta here, I'll kill a monster like that on my way out."

"What 'bout slave catchers, like mastuh say? Plus, folks in Alexandria say they got an army with guns turnin' runaways back at the border."

"You outrun the catchers and bribe the guns," Ona whispered. "Charlotte know a man in Alexandria. He saved money, made it to the border, and bribed the soldiers. Now, he in Pittsburgh."

"Ain't no way Peter woulda made it to Pittsburgh or anywhere else. Why you think he'd run?"

Ona seemed surprised at the question. "Same reason we gonna run. Same reason slaves all over be runnin' now. That monster can't catch us all."

The next morning, Hercules hurried through his kitchen preparations so he could check on Peter. He arrived at the stable just after a slow-rising sun eased up to illuminate the whole plantation. Hercules enjoyed the early spring at Mount Vernon, the lingering chill in the air, and the pockets of sunrays that beamed through the atmosphere and warmed his skin. A daylight moon rested in the clouds.

"Peter? You in there, Pete?" His heart sped up, worried that he couldn't find the man he usually preferred not to see.

"Back here." Peter's cracked voice came from the corner of the stable. He hunched over a rake, shirtless with his back in the air. "I'm back here, Uncle Herc. How you do today?" He welcomed his guest as if nothing out of the ordinary had occurred. "You see that big ol' moon still hangin' round in the sunshine?" Hercules nodded, closing his eyes as Peter continued. "Ya know, I think that moon be chasin' the sun, tryin' to catch up. When we see that moon in daytime, it's gettin' close. Close to catchin' the sun, imagine that. What you think'll happen if the moon catches the sun, Uncle Herc?"

Hercules shook his head. "I never really thought 'bout that, Peter." He peered over the old man's shoulder, trying to see the wounds on Peter's back. He didn't bother to ask about Peter's suffering. The excruciating pain was far too obvious. A few hummingbirds broke the pregnant silence, and Hercules spoke in a soft voice, "Peter, I jus' wanna say sorry If I's ever mean to you—impatient, or snap at you. I mean, I take work serious for mastuh and . . . and I admire you runnin'. I do. I never thought you to run, that's all."

Peter hunched over closer to the ground and gasped for air. He snickered, trying to resist a full-blown, painful laugh. "Well, imagine that. You admire me runnin'." He shuffled to the center of the stable and turned his back toward the sunlight. "You seen what that man done to me. You admire that? You admire the whip, boy?" He laughed harder, bearing the pain.

Flummoxed, Hercules explained, "I . . . I mean, I think you showed courage."

"Courage for takin' a whip? Ain't like I never felt a whip before. Fact, I felt Mastuh Fairfax's whip in the fields—many times, many years—before I's shipped off to the stable. This one ain't no different from the last."

Hercules knew Peter was lying—not about being whipped before, but about yesterday's beating feeling no different. Age had taken its toll on Peter, though he may sometimes have denied it. Regardless, Hercules had more questions about Peter's escape plot and how he planned to carry it out.

"Where was you runnin' to? How'd he find you? What happened?"

Again, Peter laughed, then said, "Boy, you jus' don't get it, do ya? I ain't got no courage; I ain't been runnin' nowhere. I ain't try no escape."

"But, why—"

"Mastuh Fairfax catch me outside, late, off the plantation, jus' beyond the house farm. I's jus' sittin' in the woods with food—potatoes, mush, apples, water. I ain't been runnin' nowhere, Uncle Herc."

"But I can bring you food from the kitchen. Why'd you go out the woods? Don't make no sense." Hercules thought Peter was lying again.

The battered man tried to straighten his back. He reached as high as he could to Hercules's shoulder and held on for balance. Peter spoke to Hercules's chest. "All kinda people be runnin' late at night, now. Imagine that. Slaves runnin' through the woods to freedom, chasin' stars, gettin' chased down like dogs. I jus' like helpin' out. Last two weeks I find five hungry people runnin' through these here woods. People from all over—Carolina, Georgia. I give 'em food and show 'em a path in the maples. Mastuh catch me feedin' three people—man, woman, child."

Peter lost his grip on Hercules and fell toward the ground. Hercules helped prop the man back up onto his rake. Peter continued to speak as a single tear crawled down his high, emaciated cheekbone. "I coulda run with 'em. I coulda followed that nice family to freedom. Mastuh was screamin' way off in the distance like Lucifer himself. I coulda made it out with 'em. But I jus' stay and watch 'em disappear in the woods. Imagine that, Uncle Herc. I coulda run free. Got whipped for it anyway. I coulda run free. But I ain't got no courage. None." Two more tears trickled from his eyes.

"But you the reason they got free," Hercules said, trying to lift Peter's spirits. "Mastuh Fairfax mighty quick on a horse. He'd catch that family if you didn't help. That's courage, Peter."

Peter ignored the compliment and continued his self-degradation. "Devil ride up on me and snatch me right up. He be screamin' on high, 'Who that out there? Who you with?' And I jus' say, 'I ain't with 'em.' Mastuh hit me over the head. 'You be runnin'!' And I jus' cry out, 'I am not! I am not!' Uncle Herc, I shoulda run."

"I don't know, Peter. I don't know." Hercules did his best to console the broken man. He patted him on the head, afraid to touch any of Peter's skin.

The roosters outside began to crow, and Peter regained his composure. As Hercules departed from the stable, Peter clutched his forearm to hold him back.

"Don't you ever make that mistake I did. You get a chance to run, you run on outta here, boy. I ain't got the courage, but you do. I'm old and weary, but you ain't. And these runners, Herc, they tell me stories. They gettin' rid of slavery up north. No more slaves. Causin' a big fuss round here. Use them big legs, Uncle Herc. You use 'em for me."

Hercules nodded his head and took two steps out of the stable, then stopped, surprised to see George Washington approaching. He hoped his master was coming to enquire about Peter's health, but Washington jogged toward them in an awful hurry.

"Boys, Vice President Pinckney will arrive this afternoon. We shall ride the grounds and go on a fox hunt. Peter, have the horses ready. And Hercules, you will prepare fresh cod for dinner. Soft courses. Soft dessert. My teeth have been aching. Now, back to the kitchen."

Washington paced back to his study, and his slaves labored away, just as any other day before this one.

___

Alexander Hamilton's performance at the Second Constitutional Convention almost guaranteed his election as supreme leader of the National States. The newspapers portrayed him as a savior. However, the political earthquake that fractured New York into three states altered the electoral math. Pennsylvania's population now significantly outnumbered the population of other states, as did Virginia's in the Confederation of Columbia.

Propertied white men of the National States chose an electoral college, and these electors selected Hamilton as supreme leader, but in a closer election than expected. Pennsylvania's ten electoral votes were split between Robert Morris and William Findley. One elector cast a vote for Benjamin Franklin, even though the sage refused to associate with the new government. Hamilton won all three of Montgomery's votes, New Jersey's six votes, and Delaware's three votes. In his home state, three of New York's four electors chose Hamilton, while, surprisingly, one held out for Findley. A candidate needed a fourteen-vote majority of the electoral votes to win the election. The final electoral count brought victory to Hamilton, but by a thread:

> Alexander Hamilton 15
> Robert Morris 6
> William Findley 4
> Benjamin Franklin 1

John Jay brought Hamilton the good news. "Congratulations, Supreme Leader Hamilton."

Jay loathed the title of "supreme leader," and he held moral objections to a life term, but he celebrated his friend's success nonetheless. If anyone possessed the genius to lead a nation, it was Alexander Hamilton.

"Please hold the applause, sir. We have much work to do," Hamilton snarled. "Forthwith, we must raise a military and secure our borders. I want escaped slaves turned back at our southern border, and I want Chief Blue Jacket's head waiting for me in Philadelphia when I arrive. Have you heard the latest? Six hundred of Arthur St. Clair's men—dead, scalped, and butchered in Ohio. Six hundred. It will not stand. Their deaths will be avenged."

"It should never stand. We are in full agreement," Jay concurred.

"I served with General St. Clair in the Continental Army. A fine man, but weak. Totally incompetent as governor of the Northwest Territory. The United States Government was foolish to appoint him. But make no mistake, the Northwest Territory—including the Ohio Country—belongs to the National States of America. It seems Chief Blue Jacket has yet to learn that. I want a military force invading Ohio as soon as possible. And not a motley militia. I want a national army. Secure the borders first. Second, we must be sure the press publicizes our victories."

John Jay raised his brow in suspicion but chose not to argue with the new supreme leader.

Hamilton had one other concern: "The election, John. There's one thing I must know. Which elector from New York betrayed me? I believe he voted for Findley?"

"Sir, I do believe it was Mr. Aaron Burr."

The Columbian vice president arrived at Mount Vernon without fanfare. Washington assumed Pinckney would try to convince him to serve in a military capacity, but the general had already made up his mind: the answer was no. Pinckney explained that his visit was first and foremost on the basis of friendship, but it didn't take long into their horse ride for the conversation to turn political.

"Loyalty is the most essential virtue of good citizenship," Pinckney said. "Loyalty to God, loyalty to one's family, and loyalty to country reign supreme over all other good qualities. I've learned this, in no small part, from you, General, which is why I choose to serve. I have been called to service by the people's representatives, and my loyalty shall not waiver."

"Ah, but have you forgotten about loyalty to your values, soldier?" Nelson snorted in agreement, carrying George along the path. Washington placed deep trust in his federalist allies like Pinckney, and it pained the patriarch to watch his disciple go astray. "If you remain loyal to your principles, then I have no qualms, and neither should you, if you remain true to the values that have carried you thus far through the noble course of your life. I, for one, find the new government inconsistent with my own values." He struck a cordial note, but never hesitated to make their differences known.

"I believe we still share similar values," Pinckney protested, "and I'm confident that President Henry will soon see the necessity of strong government as well. Of course, I do not ask for your immediate endorsement, but a visit to Richmond would do well to promote solidarity among the states. President Henry would be delighted to receive you at the capital, and a grand reception would engender positive press for all parties involved."

Washington didn't hesitate to reject the offer. "I'm afraid I must decline the president's invitation, out of no umbrage toward him personally, but due to the confederacy's general offense to my values." He ignored the obnoxious intimation that the great George Washington needed Patrick Henry to upgrade his reputation in the press.

Always a gracious guest, the vice president refrained from pushing the subject further. "Very well, sir. I do hope you change your mind soon."

"You should know that I've advised Mr. Madison to again take up politics," Washington added. "His values are most virtuous, and he has a career ahead of him, rather than behind. He does not afford the luxury of retirement as I do. He is younger and far more astute than I, and he would serve the people well—that is, if the weak structure of our government will allow him to do so. His health is improved, having slayed whatever demons reside in that man's solar plexus."

Pinckney shrugged his shoulders. "I had hoped to avoid the subject, but I cannot lie to you, General. President Henry plans to appoint Mr. Madison as an ambassador to France. Thomas Jefferson has been recalled from the post, and the reality is that the president would like nothing better than to ship his biggest adversary off to sea, thousands of miles away."

"And in the middle of a bloody revolution. He'll be lucky to get out alive." Washington shook his head. "I can't say I'm surprised."

"I assure you, it will not be a completely half-hearted appointment. The president wishes to maintain strong ties with a stable French government. Trade with the French West Indies is most essential."

"Yes, of course. The repulsive trading of African slaves." Washington attempted to advise and not chastise his protégé, but his words fell on the deaf ears of an ardent South Carolina flesh peddler. He knew that Pinckney felt no remorse for the enslavement of innocent people, but advanced his appeal anyway. "The country is already overwhelmed with runaways, and the same Southern gentry who protested against any internal taxation now calls for collecting taxes to fund government paid slave catchers."

"These slave catchers have become a national necessity." The vice president wagged his finger in the air as he spoke. "Word has spread that the National States will institute gradual emancipation. The number of runaway slaves has already increased tenfold. Hamilton has positioned some troops on Pennsylvania's southern border, but these men are bribed too easily. Our larger concern is Spanish Florida. The Spanish Crown recognizes the freedom of runaway slaves in Florida, so long as they convert to Catholicism."

Washington laughed at the irony. "What a peculiar dilemma for President Henry. He has been swept into office on the promise of limiting federal power and respecting states' sovereignty, yet border security will require major government intervention, a tax even, to protect Columbia."

"Indeed." Pinckney nodded. "The president requested state militiamen to patrol the borders, but only Georgia and Maryland responded. To most Columbians, Georgia's border dispute is Georgia's problem. No other state militia wants to pick a fight with Seminole Indians. They're ferocious. In addition, Alexander Hamilton has ignored our president's demands to return Columbian property. It is stolen property, and our citizens deserve compensation for their losses. Alas, Hamilton has done nothing."

"Oh, he's done plenty," George said. "Hamilton has published Henry's pleas in the National States press. The propaganda portrays President Henry as a weakling, crying to the supreme leader to return his slaves."

Pinckney grew irritated. "Regardless, the tax is a step in the right direction. A new Department of the Interior will be well-funded, and it will pay for agents to repossess property. These federal agents will play an essential role in the security of our country, and will prevent a senseless war with the National States. You see, the politicians in Richmond already find a greater need for strong government."

George Washington dismounted from Nelson as the cool breeze delivered a fresh scent. Early leaves of spring rustled in the trees above them.

"If the decision were up to me alone, I would rid our nation of the curse of slavery." He put a firm hand on Pinckney's shoulder, pulling him closer. "But it is not up to me. It is up to men like you and Henry, and you are both decent, moral men. Go back to Richmond, Charles. Go back to Richmond and understand your values before you understand anything else. Hold firm to your moral code, to the American ideals for which we fought, and you can effect positive change for us all."

The sweet aroma of fresh nectar spread across the whole plantation, as winter yielded to spring. Martha Washington's grandchildren played under the first April sun, much like the honeybees swarmed around George's poplar trees again. The bees whirled around in reckless patterns to Hercules's relief. He'd been unable to stock up on honey for months. He always gathered as much as possible in the spring and summer, and Washington usually imported enough to last the cold season, but a long winter threatened to create a serious honey shortage at Mount Vernon.

With Peter incapacitated, Hercules would have to pick a fight with the honeybees alone. He covered his skin with as much clothing as possible—three linen shirts, two pairs of trousers, and one of his fancy belts wrapped around his neck. He wobbled like one of the clumsy bison that wandered the woods of Washington's estate. The poplars grew in a yard downhill from the kitchen and stable, near a burial ground where Washington allowed his enslaved population to bury their own. The remains of his wife, Lame Alice, rested not far from the beehives. On every quest for honey, Hercules imagined Alice watching, laughing hysterically at his ridiculous-looking outfit and the gymnastics that he performed just to fetch a bit of honey.

"Mastuh loves his honey," he whispered toward Alice's grave. He tightened his gloves, lit a makeshift torch from his iron kitchen utensils, and marched off to battle the oppressive yellow runts.

The hunter spotted his prey, a small hive in a hollowed tree trunk.

"Can't jus' hide underneath a rock, huh? You gotta be difficult." He spoke to the bees. Hercules preferred harvesting honey from lower hives underneath rocks or logs. At least this hive was low enough that he wouldn't have to climb the tree.

Holding the torch high, he waited for a mass exodus of bees. Every muscle in his body tightened, and he ducked his head in fear of being attacked. He felt a rush of blood pushing through the veins in his arm, and his fingers began to tingle. In an instant, an army of black-and-gold vermin swarmed all around him. His shaky hand held the flame beneath a beating sun. His body simmered in sweat, wrapped in layers of clothing.

"Come on now, bees. Jus' leave me alone and let me do this." He heard Lame Alice's wild laughter.

After calming the bees with smoke for a few minutes, he reached out his free hand to snatch the honeycomb. A single, curious bee somehow managed to sneak under his work glove and release a stinger in the back of his right hand while he poked and prodded to loosen the honeycomb from the hive. As in past attempts, Hercules knocked the entire hive to the ground by accident. A swarm of bees zipped closer to his face, which was wrapped in linen, exposing only his eyes and mouth. His heartbeat quickened, and he began to wheeze. He lowered the torch, snatched the honeycomb, and fled from the bees, back up the hill. Two more stingers found their way into his shoulder, but just three stings in total—without the aid of Peter—was a clear success.

Back in the kitchen, Hercules struggled to extract the stubborn honey, locked inside its wax pockets like a thick tar. He cracked open the comb from different angles with a meat cleaver, but extracted just a few ounces. He did manage to steal an adequate amount of beeswax to make candles for the mansion. Still early in the spring, there would be much more honey to claim. For now, a few ounces would have to suffice.

Unlike most enslaved people, Ona knew the date of her birth. On the tenth of April, she celebrated her eighteenth birthday with Charlotte in the Family House. Not much different from any other night, they at least acknowledged the milestone.

"You a strong, young woman now," Charlotte said. "You startin' to remind me of myself," she boasted.

Ona couldn't focus on her age. Since watching John Fairfax do his worst on Peter, she obsessed over escape. She sat on the edge of a splintered bunk, trying to rock Eliza to sleep, imagining how difficult it would be to run away with an infant. Charlotte could never run away with Eliza. The baby cried more tears than any other infant in the slave quarters. Her screams would echo through the woods like coyotes and attract the slave catchers.

"You don't take to children easy," Charlotte observed, watching Ona's feeble attempt to put Eliza to sleep. "That's good. Don't go gettin' any ideas. Woman like you, eighteen now—mastuh like nothin' more than your belly full a slaves. You stay away from them overseers. I don't have to tell you that. And watch out for Uncle Herc. I see how he looks at you."

Ona's face turned red as an apple. "I ain't got no ideas, and neither do Hercules."

Charlotte stopped knitting and flashed Ona a stern look. The familiar, no-nonsense stare said, *Don't try to fool me.*

"I know where you go at night—out the garden with that man. You best be careful out there. I'd be stayin' in if I was you, now that Peter been caught. Ain't gonna be pretty when mastuh come out lookin'."

"We careful, Char. And we ain't got no ideas, neither."

"Mmmhmm," Charlotte mumbled as if she didn't believe one word of it.

"Honest, Char. I jus' like to cuddle with Herc—okay, sometimes we kiss, but that's all. I like talkin' 'bout—" She stopped short. She could never reveal their escape plans, not even to Charlotte. "I like talkin' to Hercules."

Charlotte's brawny, leather hands seized Eliza away from Ona. "Listen to me, girl. No man in the world be okay with jus' a kiss and some small talk. No man. Not Hercules. Not no one. So, you be careful. You old enough now—old enough for men to take advantage. You understand? You look out for yourself."

"I understand. But Herc ain't takin' advantage. He a decent man."

"He a confused man, is what he is. Lame Alice couldn't even walk and then starved to death, and Herc's emotions died with her. Man thinks he can escape that kinda pain by cookin' in his kitchen. That's why he so serious about work and servin' Mastuh Washton. He don't know what he wants. But I do. Hercules is a man, and a man wants jus' one thing from a woman. White or black, no different. A man is a man."

"Yes, ma'am." Ona felt like a child being scolded by her mother. "But I do feel safe when I'm with him. Does that mean I'm in love? Bein' safe?"

Charlotte sat down next to her. "No, child. Not bein' safe. Safe is how white people love—like Lady Washton be so safe—like all mastuh's house-guests come and be safe. Safe by havin' money, and land, and slaves, and jewels. That's how they love. But love is somethin' different for us. For us, bein' safe is the easiest thing in the world. Work, work, work. Shut ya mouth and work. That's safe. I loved a man once. Jus' once, and I wasn't safe one minute. Most dangerous thing I ever done, fallin' in love. Oh, you can have babies every year, and them babies be safe as mastuh's most prized possessions. But love? That's dangerous. Dangerous, 'cause mastuh can't own that. Mastuh can't take it from you. He can't sell it for a profit. Love's like you got somethin' you ain't supposed to. Somethin' you willin' to fight for. You know love when you scared like the devil."

In March of 1790, John Adams returned home from England to a quiet Boston Harbor full of roughneck sailors and poor fishermen, most of whom wouldn't recognize the famous founding father if they even cared to acknowledge him stumbling off the boat, waterlogged with sea legs. Though relieved to be home, an acute sadness overcame Adams as he gazed into the water. He could almost smell the British tea, as if it had just yesterday been thrown overboard and destroyed in protest. His eyes scanned for the blood spilled all over Boston in the early days of the American Revolution—and for what? A nation torn asunder, shattered in three. Events seemed to have spiraled out of his control since then, and all he could do now was hope and pray for the best.

Adams served as the United States ambassador to England, but after America's great rupture, he felt like a man without a country. Stuck in London, he grew impatient. The work of constructing the Republic of New England transpired in his absence, and for his own good, for he possessed the peculiar ability to aggravate most other statesmen and to earn their abhorrence through his biting arrogance. Had he been present in Hartford to contribute his talents to the New England Constitution, Adams would have lashed out at the compromises intended to limit the power of Massachusetts. George Clinton, the Saratoga delegate and nemesis of Alexander Hamilton, demanded assurance that Massachusetts would not dominate the political landscape of their country, as Virginia did in Columbia. He required affirmation that the New England states would not act as mere satellites of Massachusetts.

To appease Clinton, the convention agreed on the admittance of two new states, Saratoga and Vermont, to help mitigate the power of Boston men. Clinton further demanded that Massachusetts cede its northern territory to form a seventh state, Maine. Furthermore, the capital of the new republic must not reside in Boston. The convention chose Hartford, Connecticut, over the protests of Rhode Island's delegation, which favored Providence.

John Adams didn't consent to every word of the New England Constitution, though he did praise the unequivocal abolition of slavery. He published his vision for the new republic through the *Boston Gazette*: "We now find a Columbian government with no significant power other than that of kidnapping human beings escaped from the jaws of slavery. The South has chosen mob rule over sound authority. In stark contrast, the National States government overflows with power in the hands of one supreme leader who will trample the rights of free men. The task upon us in New England is to strike the proper balance between these two extremes. Our republic must be glorious in both its respect for human liberty and for the authority of good governance."

In his second essay, Adams pontificated on foreign policy: "There can be no doubt that in the constant turmoil between France and Great Britain, the Confederation of Columbia will side with France, and we New Englanders will feel more affinity toward Britain. Hamilton possesses a womanish infatuation for Great Britain, although he and his bank will most likely sell out to the highest bidder between the two."

His constant criticism of Hamilton and Henry indicated that Adams craved the opportunity to lead New England, even though his generation of revolutionary heroes had been pushed into retirement. Washington and

Franklin rejected outright the notion of three countries. Madison awaited his exile to France, and it was beneath Thomas Jefferson, the great Virginian and author of the Declaration of Independence, to serve in any capacity other than President of Columbia. But John Adams felt a greater sense of duty and of arrogance. He was best suited to lead the new nation, the unbreakable link between New England's revolutionary past and a steady course for the future.

After parliamentary elections though a sweltering summer, the new government chose John Adams as the first Prime Minister of the Republic of New England on July 4, 1790. He took an oath to uphold the New England Constitution, which included a bill of rights and clear instructions for his role in carrying out the legislation passed by a bicameral parliament, elected by the people. Prime Minister Adams began his five-year term with a speech to Parliament, in which he emphasized the priority of reestablishing trade and diplomatic relations with England. Under the leadership of Adams, New England seemed to have weathered the political storm.

The Republic of New England

Chapter 6

A typical July in Philadelphia reeked of steaming sewage that sizzled under the ferocious sun. The summer of 1790 proved to be no exception. Construction of two new buildings, the Federal Palace and the National States Bank, had already begun on Chestnut Street. Until their completion, Alexander Hamilton would have to work out of the Pennsylvania State House and its muggy, inadequate accommodations. An irritated supreme leader paced the floors of an upstairs office.

He held the newspaper close to his face and enunciated each syllable, as if the words taunted him from the page: "'This palace will become a sanctuary of despotism and the insidious bank, its financial lifeblood for King Alexander to corrupt the people's government!'" Hamilton threw the newspaper off the wall, unable to read any further. "The *New-York Journal* continues to sow the seeds on anarchy. To even consider publishing the unchecked rancor of an imbecile like Aaron Burr is walking the line of treason. And this dunce is running for governor of New York! We cannot allow that, John. We simply cannot."

John Jay sat hunched over, ill from the heat. Sweat poured from his brow and formed a small puddle on the floor beneath him.

"Your buildings will be erected, and you will run them as you see fit, regardless of Aaron Burr's opinion. I think your best move is to ignore the man. Why acknowledge someone whose talents are beneath yours?"

Hamilton grinned. "Mr. Jay, you know me too well to believe that I could pay no mind to a treasonous ignoramus like Burr." He gnawed at his fingernails and bent over to retrieve the paper again. "'The supreme leader has unveiled his true warmongering ways by waging senseless war in the West.'" Again, he threw the paper down. "Senseless war? Six hundred men are dead! And he would dare criticize me for defending our nation. He ought to move to Columbia and see how he likes living in a country with no army!"

"It is out of character for Mr. Burr to use such harsh language," Jay said. "Though, he is perhaps the best lawyer in New York. I've lost three court cases to him. He's almost put my private law practice out of business. And you've lost to Burr, too, correct?"

Hamilton bit the side of his tongue and growled. "Of course I've lost to Burr in court. Everyone loses to Burr in court. That little shit could convince a jury of anything, beyond a reasonable doubt. He poses a serious threat to my administration."

Jay gave Hamilton the raw truth. "Our bill of rights ensures a free press, and I'm afraid his election is all but certain. New England's annexation of Saratoga has taken with it many of New York's political thinkers. I agree, the man has inadequate experience to govern a state like New York. He is far too young. But Burr serves as New York's attorney general and is virtually unopposed for the governorship."

"No, no. *I* oppose him! And as you have pointed out—the man is beneath me. This is exactly why the supreme leader should be empowered to appoint state governors. It would prevent the uneducated masses from electing the likes of Burr."

"Our Congress would never allow it. Nor does our Constitution, for that matter."

"Perhaps the Congress needs a little pressure to amend the Constitution, and perhaps the *New-York Journal* needs a little pressure to abide by responsible journalism."

Jay squeaked out a few sneezes. He was just about to excuse himself when three knocks came from the door. He squinted as if the sound of each knock pierced his brain deeper.

"Ah ha! He has arrived!" Hamilton exclaimed. He threw down the newspaper one last time and motioned for Jay to open the door. The supreme leader straightened his wig and struck a gallant pose while Jay pulled on the doorknob and smiled at the two armed soldiers.

"Mr. James Madison, sir," one of the soldiers announced.

Jay gave permission to allow the guests inside. "Mr. Madison, how nice to see you," Jay said.

"Hello, old friend. We've not seen each other since the First Constitutional Convention."

The two men shook hands, and Jay nodded to acknowledge Madison's slave, Jonathan. It was quite unusual for a slave to accompany his master inside for a meeting of gentlemen, but Jay ignored the breach of custom.

Madison and Jonathan entered the humid office as if walking into a steam bath. Jonathan bowed in the presence of Alexander Hamilton. Madison opened his arms and smiled.

"Alex, how goes it?" he asked. An awkward silence followed.

John Jay positioned himself to the right of the supreme leader and lowered his head, raising his brow to Madison.

"Oh, of course," Madison said, before bowing down to his old friend, astonished that such a gesture would be required of him.

Hamilton addressed Madison. "James, how delightful it is to see you in good health."

"I thank you kindly, sir. Congratulations on your election. I trust the fine people of these states are in good hands. And congratulations to you, Mr. Chief Justice of the Supreme Court," he said, turning to acknowledge John Jay. "The supreme leader has made a fine choice."

"Thank you, James," Jay said with pride.

"A fine choice, indeed," Hamilton said. "In fact, we were just discussing how Chief Justice Jay might soon rule on cases of treason in the press."

The delegates at the Second Constitutional Convention altered the original Supreme Court set forth by the United States Constitution by expanding its jurisdiction and establishing a panel of three judges, appointed by the supreme leader. Hamilton chose John Jay as the chief justice, along with James Wilson of Pennsylvania and Delaware's John Dickinson to serve on the bench. Jay could not have been happier with the appointment.

"I find that the theatrics of politics and legislating are best left in the hands of you charismatic men," Jay said in his usual modest fashion. "I myself have no stomach for the ruckus of electoral politics, and prefer the quiet chambers of a judge."

"You are the wiser for it, sir," Madison said, turning his attention back to the supreme leader. "Mr. Hamilton, I hope you don't mind that I've taken the liberty of bringing my manservant, Jonathan, as he has business here as well."

Jonathan bowed a second time to Hamilton. At a mere five feet, three inches, he disappeared from the supreme leader's sight, like a ghost. Hamilton signaled for everyone to sit.

"No worries, Mr. Madison. All are welcome."

Madison positioned his small body in a chair that left his feet barely touching the floor. Jonathan's feet dangled in the air. Madison looked up and commenced with business. "As you both know, my wife and I are off to France on the morrow."

"Ah, yes, Mr. Ambassador. We've neglected to congratulate you, as well," Jay interjected.

Madison shrugged. "Well, I'm not sure I would congratulate a man on being deported by the president of his country, who is no doubt fearful of a little competition. Patrick Henry has every intention to pursue an isolationist foreign policy, with which I don't necessarily disagree, but he will need me in France to do little more than twiddle my thumbs—to avoid getting killed by the Jacobin mobs. In fact, that may be what he intends—for me to be killed by Jacobin mobs."

Hamilton leaned back and addressed his old chum. "Perhaps it is for the best, James. Please do not take offense, but I fear the turmoil that may be unleashed in your country in reaction to a powerless government. Your President Henry presides over an excess of democracy. He places too much faith in the ability of ordinary men to participate in government, and he will reap what he sows in Richmond. If I were you, I would enjoy a nice European vacation until the tidal wave subsides."

"Only time will tell the outcome of our political experiment in Columbia. I have come today for two other reasons. First, to visit old friends, and to see Philadelphia one last time before my journey across the sea. I have fond memories of this place, you know."

Hamilton nodded his head in agreement. Both men got lost in a pensive trance, reminiscing of the Constitutional Convention, the hardest work of their careers, even if the US Constitution had been a miserable failure. Jonathan nudged the arm of Madison's chair for him to continue.

"Ah, hmm. The second matter is more urgent, gentlemen. I have employed overseers to manage my farm and my accounts at Montpelier for the duration of my tenure as ambassador. Jonathan, here, is unfit for field labor. He accompanies me in my travels, but will be of little use in my dealings with the royal court in France. I also hesitate to make a poor first impression by representing the Confederation of Columbia abroad as just a nation of slaveholders. Left with very few options, and in the interest of doing what is right, I have chosen to emancipate Jonathan."

All eyes in the room converged onto the tiny freedman. He sat up straight and proud.

"He has in his possession manumission papers," Madison continued, "which I have signed. He is a hard worker, trustworthy, and loyal. He reads and writes, and I can attest to his untarnished character. Jonathan is quite familiar with Philadelphia and New York, as well."

"Hear, hear!" Jay shouted out. "Jonathan makes a fine example of what is possible when we eradicate slavery and embrace nature's liberty for all men."

"We are in agreement," Madison responded. "I have brought Jonathan along today in the hopes that he may find some gainful employment in your service."

Jonathan spoke for himself. "It would be an honor to serve at the pleasure of the supreme leader. I have devoted my life's work to assisting Mr. Madison and his principles. Naturally, it would bring great satisfaction to continue that work in your service, Your Excellency."

"Such a well-spoken slave—my apologies—such a well-spoken man," Jay corrected himself. "A wonderful plan, indeed, Mr. Supreme Leader. The employment of a Negro in government service—a decent gesture to humanity."

Still unconvinced, Hamilton addressed Jonathan. "And what of the multitudes of office seekers—white office seekers—who come from all across the National States every day, by the hundreds, in search of employment?

What am I to tell them? That I prefer a Negro? A foreigner?"

Jonathan didn't shy away from the challenge. "With respect, sir, you should inform them that they are unqualified, for none of those office seekers have been brought up and trained by the hand and wisdom of James Madison."

He had already made a terrific impression on John Jay, and the chief justice was prepared to offer Jonathan a job as an office clerk if Hamilton passed on the opportunity.

Madison chimed in again. "You understand I cannot take Jonathan to President Henry or anyone in his administration. They would shackle him and sentence him to a life in bondage before I even made it to France."

The supreme leader was curious. "You know New York, yes?"

Jonathan nodded.

"And you read and write?"

"Yes, sir." Jonathan didn't move a muscle, and he looked Hamilton in the eye.

Hamilton paused and glanced down to the floor at the torn newspaper containing Aaron Burr's libel.

"Jonathan, I think I have an important job for you. It is top secret. Mr. Madison, I can trust this man with sensitive information and classified, arcane work?"

"You have my assurance, dear friend."

Hamilton stood up from his chair and flashed Jonathan an austere smirk. "Very well, Jonathan. I will brief you in the morning, and, come Monday, you are off to New York City."

"Your servant, sir." Jonathan breathed for what seemed like the first time since he'd entered the room.

James Madison shook the supreme leader's hand. "And I thank you as well, Alex."

An uneasy silence hushed the slaves at Mount Vernon after Peter's whipping for his alleged escape plot. Not many workers ventured out of their cabins at night, expecting John Fairfax to be more vigilant since the incident. Charlotte even stopped going to the Sunday market in Alexandria, not wanting the hassle of being stopped and questioned by Fairfax or the government slave catchers.

After a three-week hiatus, Ona whispered to Hercules in the kitchen, "Meet me in the garden tonight?" She missed their private time in the evenings and looked forward to a reunion.

He grinned and put his head back down to focus on chopping vegetables.

Hercules usually found their spot in the garden first, but this time, Ona arrived early. She tiptoed through the horrendous smell of poison-laced weeds, startled after stepping over two dead rabbits staring up at her. She found their private patch of roses, tucked away in secrecy. Anxious, she hid under the trees like prey in the jungle, looking over her back for the overseers. Her first whipping could come at any moment. In her dreams, the whippings appeared more vivid and always punishment for disobeying Martha Washington. She imagined Martha standing by, delighted, and cheering for John Fairfax as he unleashed his fury.

Hercules interrupted her scattered thoughts. "Now, Li'l Miss shouldn't be out here all alone at night," he whispered as he entered the garden. He crawled down beside her and fed her a honey-dipped apple slice. Ona accepted the treat, smiling with thick honey dripping down the side of her mouth. Hercules kissed her before she was finished chewing, and he licked the honey from her lips.

The stubble on his chin tickled Ona's neck. She laughed out loud. Louder. Intentionally louder so he would stop. Ona replayed Charlotte's warning in her head: *A man wants just one thing from a woman.* She swallowed the apple and then held on to his cheeks to create some space. "Slow down, or Fairfax gonna hear us. Herc, it's time. We gotta run soon," she whispered.

Hercules gave in. He looked away from her, rejected.

"They jus' gonna keep sendin' more slave catchers. If we don't try now, we'll never make it. We get to Philadelphia, and then—maybe New England. Herc, no more slaves there, it's true. Mastuh Washton said it himself. It's in the newspapers that come from Boston. It's in letters that mastuh reads to Lady Washton. We get to New England, and we get freedom. That's how I wanna love you. I wanna feel safe."

"And how we supposed to do that? If Fairfax don't catch you, Mastuh Washton will. He's the fastest man alive on a horse."

Ona could now explain the escape plot that she had crafted in her mind. She had snooped in the mansion, hid out in chimneys, and gossiped in Alexandria for months, waiting for the chance to reveal her master plan. It was her own version of "Give me liberty or give me death," redemptive just to speak it out loud, but not too loud.

"Today's Monday. We leave Saturday."

Hercules rolled his eyes, doubtful.

"Mastuh Fairfax is easy. You put out coffee for the overseers every mornin'. Saturday mornin', you soak them weeds in the overseers' coffee pot." She motioned to the smelly weeds in the garden that Washington sprayed with arsenic. "Overseers drink that coffee in the mornin' and be too sick to go slave catchin' at night."

"Them chemicals? You can kill a man with that," he objected.

"Shhh. Then, three o'clock is dinner. No guests this weekend, so it's jus' mastuh and Lady Washton. We serve dinner like always, then after tea we run out to the woods. We follow the river north, run as far as we can, and find a spot to hide before dark. But we hide out at night. We can't be runnin' at night—slave catchers find us."

Hercules remained silent, shaking his head.

"You bring food for us," Ona explained. "Start makin' extra tomorrow mornin', but no meat. Them slave-catchin' dogs'll smell meat a mile away and eat us both alive. Save us some bread, potatoes, vegetables, cake. Don't be usin' no fancy spices. That gives us food to eat, and if anyone stop us with questions, we on our way to market to sell food, or we goin' to see family on another farm. That's why we wait 'til weekend. But we keep travelin' by day and hide out at night."

Hercules raised his finger to Ona's lips to stop her. He stood and began a nervous strut around the garden, almost tripping over his own feet. The whole proposal made him shudder, especially at the thought of brewing contaminated coffee, not just because it would jeopardize the health of those who drank it, but also because he took pride in brewing good coffee. Poisoning someone's food was against his entire work ethic; although, it wouldn't be so bad, giving John Fairfax a bout of diarrhea, after his treatment of Peter. But it would be too risky to escape in broad daylight. Even if they made it through the weekend, what hope would they have on Monday morning? They would never make it to Pennsylvania in just two days, and they would no longer have an excuse to be off the plantation.

Hercules tried not to offend Ona with criticism, so he held his tongue, with the exception of his biggest concern. "Suppose we do all that. We poison the coffee and leave after dinner. We hide out in the dark and run away under a blue sky. How do we get in Pennsylvania? We can't jus' walk into another country. They got soldiers. They lookin' for runaways, and we ain't got enough money to bribe them. I got some money saved, but that's Spanish coins and Continentals. Pennsylvania probably don't even want that. What we do then?"

"Shhh." Ona put her finger to her lips and scanned their surroundings to make sure they were alone. Her neck stretched upward into the open air, and her eyes searched again like a wild animal. She reached down to remove her shoe; a small leather sack fell out and landed in the palm of her hand. She lifted it upside down, and a necklace with a bright-red stone rolled on to her fingers. "Ruby," she said, with eyes wide open, captivated by the gem. "Lady Washton got so many, she can't keep 'em straight. I been holdin' this one for ten days. She still don't know."

Ona held out the precious stone away from her body and into the thin ray of moonlight. The ruby reflected a brilliant glow up to Hercules like the stars he gazed at in the night.

"She won't be dressin' up fancy with no company this weekend," Ona continued. "I'll take one or two more from the jewelry box this week, and then Saturday before dinner, I'll get a whole sack full. Ain't no white soldier up north gonna turn down these gems, Hercules."

"I wanna believe you," he said, still shaking his head.

"Then believe me." She touched his leg, waiting for him to agree to the plot so they could spend the rest of the evening in each other's arms, lying out under the light of the moon, dreaming of their future together.

"You playin' with fire now. We get caught, it ain't no whippin' comin' our way. Poison coffee, stealin' jewels, runnin' off—we'll be hangin' from that tree right there. You know that?"

She *did* know, and she thought about it often. "Then we'll be free from this place for sure."

Hercules said nothing again, and Ona grew impatient. "Herc, most slaves don't got what we got. Them runaways gettin' caught—they ain't got no rubies and pearls, they ain't got food, they ain't got a river to follow in the backyard. We got advantages, Herc. When you got advantage, you *take* advantage. That's what Charlotte says. I don't know 'bout you, but I'm gonna take advantage."

After a long pause, Hercules responded. "Saturday, after tea. But if I do this, you don't go backin' out. We leave Saturday after dinner, no matter what."

"No matter what," she said, surprised that she'd convinced him. She placed her hand on his chest and extended her neck upward to kiss his forehead. "Jus' hold me."

Together, their bodies fell to the dirt, where Hercules buried her in his brawny arms.

"We can make good money up north, you know." She smiled. "You can get paid for cookin', and not jus' for some mastuh. I can find work as a seamstress. We'd take care of our own selves. And you think you got nice clothes now? You'll be dressed like a king."

He pulled her petite figure in closer and ran his fingers through her hair, sliding his hand down to her breasts.

No man in the world be okay with jus' a kiss and some small talk, Charlotte's voice echoed in Ona's head again. Her body tingled. Hercules pet her arms and chest with more force than usual. *Old enough for men to take advantage.* He lowered his lips to her shoulders. *You look out for yourself.*

"Not like this," she said, jolting away. "Not like this, Herc. I want to. I really want to, but not like this. Up north, across the border," she whispered. "I wanna be free. I wanna be free with you, and the first thing I wanna do free is love you. But I ain't gonna love you scared."

Rejected for the second time, he shrugged his shoulders, wondering if

Ona was just using him to escape. He considered backing out of the whole plan; considered it—until images of Peter flashed in his mind. Old Peter, who had served his master for a lifetime, whipped to the bone, tossed aside like spoiled fruit. He imagined the bloodthirsty grin on John Fairfax's face. The man wouldn't hesitate a moment to rip up Hercules just the same. Toss him aside, just the same.

Hercules walked back to his quarters, carrying the weight of the world on his shoulders. Ona's plan depended on him taking gargantuan risks, and he needed to think them over to execute the plan just right.

Ona stayed in the garden alone that night. She inhaled the summer breeze and immersed herself in the smell of the rosebushes. She fell in and out of sleep, thinking about the National States of America and worrying about her escape plot. Just before sunrise, she awoke to the sounds of the plantation slaves marching out to work for another long day of labor, like they had the day before, and like they would the following morning, and every morning after.

Prime Minister Adams took no delight in having to relocate from Boston to Hartford, and he cursed George Clinton every step of the way. Clinton's political maneuvering and backroom deals had resulted in the new capital's Connecticut home, in addition to a significant decline in the influence of Adams's home state of Massachusetts.

If George Clinton was a thorn in Alexander Hamilton's side, he was already becoming a knife in the back of Prime Minister Adams. Clinton, the man most responsible for Saratoga's secession from the National States and admission to New England, was elected that state's first governor, and he got straight to work in his usual criticism of federal power.

"There can be no question that the prime minister's creation of a privy council serves the purpose of sidestepping our Parliament, the people's elected representatives. It is merely a council of elders, an oligarchy of old men past their prime."

Adams belted out a scornful laugh when he read the governor's statements. "Either Mr. Clinton forgets his own age, or he expects the public to be so unenlightened as to ignore his glaring hypocrisy."

"The man is at least fifty, lest he was born with that white hair," observed Elbridge Gerry, which brought a round of laughter to the room.

"You gentlemen do know that I have appointed you for your experience and good morals, and if some faux New Englander objects, then so be it."

The prime minister had chosen three advisors for his privy council, including Elbridge Gerry, Timothy Pickering, and Oliver Wolcott, the oldest at age sixty-two. Gerry and Pickering were both from Massachusetts and younger than George Clinton, as was Henry Knox, who would soon arrive to command New England's army.

As a Massachusetts delegate, Elbridge Gerry walked out of the Second Constitutional Convention with Clinton, and he knew the man's leadership abilities well.

"Clinton can be extremely persuasive. He is personable and likeable, and he is very good at making political friends where he needs them. He comes across as your jolly, old, gluttonous uncle, but his personal ambitions are great, and they will distract him from safeguarding the general welfare. Mr. Prime Minister, if you were to declare the sky blue, he would insist on it being crimson, and he would have a regiment of newspapermen backing him up within the hour. I have no doubt that he seeks your office for himself someday."

"Very well. On that day, I shall criticize *his* every move; that is, if I'm not too far past my prime." Laughter again filled the room. "But I'm afraid we have more pressing matters at hand than Uncle Clinton. By now, you are all aware of the bloody turn of events in France. From all of the intelligence I can gather, it appears that the same revolutionary spirit that swept through our three Americas has landed ashore in Europe. Violence began with the storming of the Bastille, much like our Boston Massacre. The people have since declared their independence through 'The Declaration of the Rights of Man,' no doubt inspired by Mr. Jefferson. The king is practically powerless; it is mob rule, gentlemen."

Adams cheered the news of a popular movement for liberty across the ocean, but the details of the revolt concerned him. He worried that a

French revolution would be led by ordinary men of no particular political skill. There was no French George Washington or Thomas Jefferson—or John Adams.

Adams leaned forward from behind his enormous desk to address his privy council of advisors. "King Louis has accepted an elected assembly, but there is no evidence to suggest that the assembly accepts him. They intend to write a constitution and establish a French republic. It appears that the French masses are well on their way to overthrowing their monarch."

Elbridge Gerry, always the playful jokester, interjected. "I wish them more luck than we had in our Constitutional Conventions."

"I wish them luck, as well, and I will champion the cause of liberty wherever it may exist," said Timothy Pickering. "But Mr. Adams, you must refrain from formally acknowledging any new government in France." His remark silenced the fading laughter. "We have pledged good relations with Great Britain, and the last thing we can afford is an alliance with the mother country's mortal enemy."

Pickering was one of the few Americans left to refer to England as the "mother country." At age fifty-four, Timothy Pickering looked about a hundred years older. Wrinkled skin of pastel-white hung from his face and from his stiff neck, which gave him the appearance of a turkey. His conservative attitudes completed the persona of a grumpy old man. Most observers, even those who knew Pickering, would have believed the man was as old as George Clinton claimed.

"I believe we should maintain our positive diplomatic relations with Great Britain and abstain from any engagement with the French, unless otherwise prompted by our ally," Pickering concluded.

Elbridge Gerry lowered his head and smirked. "Let's not rush too hastily to cozy up with King George. After all, it was French support that sustained our revolution against the tyrant. Do we not owe allegiance to our brethren who follow our lead in search of freedom?"

"We owe our allegiance to our prime minister, our countrymen, and God," Pickering threw back. "And that tyrant to whom you refer is responsible for providing the marketplace for our timber and shipping industries—indeed, for our entire economy."

Pickering grew more irritated, and Gerry chose not to argue with him any further. Instead, Gerry appealed to Adams. "John, I would just remind this council that New England is a sovereign nation now, and quite capable of handling foreign relations with more than one country. Establishing diplomatic ties with both England and France would allow you leverage in negotiations with the two. Each would compete for our support as they tear each other apart."

"Yes, but Timothy is correct," Adams interjected. "The British Navy is the most powerful in the world, and that is so because New England timber builds her ships. We must not jeopardize our economic relations with the king. We also have a lunatic calling himself 'supreme leader' and raising an army right across Saratoga's border. God forbid we should end up at war with the National States, but if so, we would depend on an alliance with Great Britain."

Adams rested his head in his left hand and scratched his balding forehead. "Mr. Wolcott, what say you?"

Oliver Wolcott, the elder statesmen from Connecticut, was the only advisor not from Massachusetts, and he provided a middle ground between the competing personalities of Gerry and Pickering. He hunched down in his chair and held on to his rounded belly.

"Neutrality, first and foremost, Mr. Prime Minister." He'd developed a habit of speaking in a soft voice to hush those around him. "We must publicly support the idea of popular sovereignty in France, but our young nation can afford neither financial nor military aid at this time. Neutrality also avoids alienating the British."

Adams slammed his fist down in agreement. "Military action is out of the question. Our shipping to both countries will continue uninterrupted, and we will delay sending an ambassador to France as of now. Poor James Madison has already landed in the inferno. God willing, he will return to Columbia unharmed."

Chapter 7

George Washington was a defeated man. He sat in the darkness of his library, listening to the flicker of a single candle and the wax teardrops that fell from it. His teeth ached in horrific pain, as did his back and his knees from riding all week across his eight thousand acres of farmland. General Washington would never take pity on himself, but he pitied the nation that he tried to lead out of ruin. The future seemed more uncertain now than during the most hopeless days of the Revolutionary War. As he came to grips with his failure to unite a nation, he leaned forward onto his small writing table and penned a letter to the supreme leader of the National States of America.

Mount Vernon,
Wednesday, September 16, 1790

Sir,

I have received your letters through the post that describe your recent assent to power. While I offer to you my most sincere congratulatory sentiment on your individual achievement, my feelings for our American nation have grown sullen. Without doubting your political talents, I remain fearful for the people's future security and welfare. It appears a reality that North and South cannot—and will not—continue intercourse in matters of government or economy. I have alerted you before to the dangers of political factions, and I now must confess the folly in my assessment that faction would lead to the downfall of a nation. In reality, our factions have prevented the birth of a nation at all, leaving the

United States of America stillborn. I trust you will strive to prevent the further fragmentation of our countrymen in your new role as chief executive.

I shall never relent in my hopes and prayers for a singular union of America, and I refuse on principle to acknowledge any more Americas than the one for which you and I, and so many courageous young men and boys, fought. Until our eventual reunification, my faith rests in your leadership, as well as the leadership of Mr. Henry and Mr. Adams. Americans have chosen their leaders well, and I am confident that such distinguished gentlemen will prevent bloodshed between these states. Henry and Adams are both decent men—distant from you in ideology, but they are decent men nonetheless—and decency must always prevail over ideological differences, lest we revert to a race of barbarians.

Of course, I support your efforts to put down the Indian rebellion in the West. The news of General St. Clair's defeat saddens me, and I wish you Godspeed in the defense of our countrymen.

Here in the South, Patrick Henry condemns the federal system that you and I prefer. The South has no common defense, no common currency, and no possibility for common enforcement of any federal law. Henry has been accused of presiding over an excess of democracy, and he will no doubt learn the advantages of federalism through trial and error.

Conversely, the rumblings in the South suggest that you, sir, wield an excess of power, true to any European monarch. If I may offer some insight: My belief is that whether an excess of democracy or an excess of power, the real danger lies not in democracy or power, but in excess itself—an excess of either of the two. I urge a path of moderation for all three new American chiefs. Even though empirical evidence suggests the clear advantage of strong government, and the British example serves us well, I caution you not to allow your admiration of England to blind you. English government serves Englishmen quite well, but you have been elected to serve Americans, and a transplanted British government will not suffice.

I refuse to believe that our revolution was fought in vain, and if it has proven anything, it is that Americans are not Englishmen. Americans are raw, unpolished, and coarse in demeanor. Americans represent a most irregular culture in the history of civilization, full of outlandish contradictions. They possess simultaneously the skepticism of Mr. Henry and your zeal for strong governance. They demand low taxes, and at the same time favor government-funded internal improvements. They desire recognition on the world stage while at the same time pleading isolationism. They want an army for protection, but offer it no quarter. Americans rejoice in freedom as the natural state of mankind, while enslaving an entire people who have committed no crime.

Yet if popular sovereignty is to become the norm in America, then the American people deserve all that they demand in all of its glaring inconsistency. In a way, you have been elected to accomplish the impossible. No one leader—no matter how honorable and righteous—no leader alone can fully satisfy this strange new nationality. For this reason, I request that you relinquish power after one specified term of service and abandon this aberration of a life term. The diversity of the American people demands representation by a diversity of citizens in rotating office; otherwise, power in the hands of one executive for too long will result in the very excess that America fought so courageously against. As I look out to my gardens, it is the diversity of species, the multitude of colors that impress the senses. So, too, are the American people—strange and beautiful with brilliance and imperfections alike.

I have no doubts in your ability to serve Americans with modesty and dignity. I am, dear sir,

Sincerely yours,
George Washington

The dining room table overflowed with an assortment of meats. Pork, roast beef, chicken, and veal. A wider variety of sauces and oils complemented the feast. Madeira wine and an imported sparkling white washed it all down, just before George Washington's favorite cherry pie for dessert. Hercules had outdone himself. He gave the impression of a most loyal slave, though he was preoccupied with thoughts of treachery, lawbreaking, and escape. He couldn't resist daydreaming about Ona's scheme, second-guessing at one moment, but elating in premonitions of freedom the next.

The dinner guest, George Wythe, showered the chef with compliments. "I've dined with governors and diplomats of all sorts, but no meal could compare to this. Mr. Washington, I must hire your cook, should I ever entertain guests of my own."

Wythe had spent the last year lamenting the fracture of the United States, like Washington and so many other framers of the failed United States Constitution. Since Wythe and James Madison's epic failure at the Virginia Ratifying Convention, the elder statesman remained out of sight. He and Washington both enjoyed immaculate reputations for being decent, moral, and fair citizens. Wythe's student, Thomas Jefferson, shared similar repute. Why should men of such standing waste their time with the political skirmishes that threatened to rip nations apart? Instead, they would observe from afar, wagging their fingers like disappointed fathers.

Over dinner, Washington and Wythe discussed family and farming, new technologies, and the weather. Over tea, the talks turned political, to the topic of Columbian slavery in particular.

"I just cannot imagine a future in which slavery continues to be profitable in the Confederation of Columbia," Wythe postulated.

A slaveholder for most of his life, Wythe's opinions had turned against slavery since the split of the United States. Washington's thoughts moved in the same direction, but not at the pace of Wythe's. For whatever moral dilemma confronted him, Washington's wealth depended on the three hundred enslaved people at Mount Vernon.

"The number of runaways from my farms has doubled in the last year," Washington bemoaned. "And why shouldn't it? The appeal of freedom in the National States is a curse, to both myself and my slaves. Nobody will convince me that those slaves lead a better life in hiding than here at Mount Vernon."

"Perhaps it is similar to our false hope in the US Constitution. The allure was powerful, like Homer's sea nymphs. And the allure for your slaves comes not just from Hamilton's National States, but from Spanish Florida as well. France, too, seems to be losing control of her slave economy in the islands. A widespread slave uprising in the Caribbean could be the death warrant of the institution. We may just be witnessing an international anti-slavery movement. My opinions have shifted, in part, because I wish to be on the right side of that movement. The pious side. I believe in your heart, you agree with me on the matter."

"Yes, in my heart, of course," Washington affirmed. "But my heart and my pocketbook are two very different places. How could my estate ever function after emancipation? It's unthinkable. Unthinkable in my lifetime. However, I've considered some amendments to my will, for arrangements after my time has passed."

"You would emancipate your slaves in your will?" Wythe's eyes beamed.

Washington shook his head in deep thought. "I have no control over Martha's dower slaves from her first marriage, but perhaps some of my own. Someone like Billy Lee or Hercules."

"A righteous gesture, indeed, and a fine example for others of the gentlemen class. A much-needed example. I'm afraid you and I reside in a small fraction of fair-minded slave owners, with Mr. Jefferson, too. New England and the National States have taken all the antislavery politicians away from us." They sat in silence for a moment, reflecting on all that had transpired in such a short amount of time. "I'm sure you will make the correct decision, General, whatever that is."

Washington laughed. "I'm glad *you* think so, Mr. Wythe."

As a regal-looking horse-drawn carriage drove George Wythe from Mount Vernon back to his home, Hercules began the most physically demanding part of his work: chopping wood. Every night, after laboring in the kitchen all day, Hercules sliced up a few tree trunks so that he could heat up the oven and the smokehouse first thing in the morning. Hercules called it "firing up the pits of hell." Martha's daily ham, and the feasts such as the one just served in honor of George Wythe, came straight from the fires of hell.

He raised the ax in a slow, scrupulous motion, high above his head, and accelerated downward in one forceful strike of the wood. Hercules handled the ax with the skill and precision that John Fairfax did with a whip. His right arm vibrated from the wrist up to his shoulder with each swing of the ax. After a while, it felt as if his arm was an extension of the ax, and it eventually went numb. If the grueling labor annoyed him, he didn't show it. Chopping wood was a good reminder of what kind of toil awaited him in the fields, should he ever be demoted from the kitchen. Field work was always a possibility for a young, enslaved man the size of Hercules.

A final glimmer of sunset faded, and the tired, hulking chef began to fixate his thoughts on escape again. How could Ona's plan ever work? If it did, what kind of life would they lead away from Mount Vernon? Should they trade a wealthy slave master for the uncertainty of freedom? He had already committed to Ona, but he questioned the decision more and more with each plunge of the iron ax.

"Hercules, doing fine work, as always." Washington's body appeared out of the darkness.

His voice startled Hercules, now rushing to complete his work before the pitch black could prevent it.

"A meal for the ages, I must say," Washington continued. "Nary an unsatisfied stomach in my dining room. You made quite the impression on Mr. Wythe tonight."

"Yes, suh. Thank you, suh." He continued his work, head down, stone-cold stare.

Washington placed his hand on his cook's shoulder, signaling for him to stop working for a moment. "I mean it with sincerity. You do exceptional work for me, and it shall not go unrewarded. Go ahead and take the left-overs to Alexandria. Make a few bucks for yourself. In fact, when you're done here, prepare some more lumber. You'd collect a good sum for it at the market, with the cold weather on its way. You could probably use a nice hat or a new belt to go with those fancy shoes of yours."

Hercules smiled and wiped the sweat from his brow. "Thank you, suh. Sure would like a nice hat," he said, gasping for oxygen.

Washington nodded. The tone of his voice changed: "Three more ran off from the farms this week. Your children are secure, but many of my slaves have misguided ideas about the world. It's not safe for you. Where will these people go? North? The National States is industrializing, like Europe. Your skills in agriculture would be useless. West? You'd be marching to your own death at the hands of Indians."

Sweat came pouring back over Hercules's forehead. He envisioned himself hanging from the ceiling of the smokehouse, roasting with the pigs in the pits of hell. Why would his master want to talk about escape? Had Washington already found out the cook's intentions? If so, Hercules would be sent to the field by morning, if not to the auction block.

"Hercules, you are one of my most trustworthy slaves. You would report any mischief or intrigue to me, yes?"

"Oh, no mischief here, mastuh." His voice trembled. "Them boys be runnin' from the farms, but not here at the mansion, suh. You a fair man, Mastuh Washton."

"Yes, of course. But you would report it to me, nonetheless?"

Hercules had no option but to lie. "Yes, suh."

"Information of the sort is valuable to me, and also, would not go unrewarded." The insinuation was not so subtle.

Hercules felt his heartbeat stagger. He was light-headed. He could rat out Ona right here and now. Rat her out and be rewarded handsomely. Never. He could never. However, the talk of reward piqued his curiosity. Was there a path to freedom other than Ona's scheme? A safer one that didn't require poisoned coffee? Hercules ignored the racing rhythm of his heart and found the courage to question his master.

"Mastuh, suppose—suppose I was to buy my own freedom, suh." Washington's eyes widened. "Got three hundred dollars saved, mastuh. And more comin' soon."

Washington's jaw dropped, speechless.

"Hercules, I'm stunned," he finally spoke. "*Buy* your freedom? Are you not treated well? As well any slave here or anywhere in Columbia, for that matter?" His tone grew angry. "Where on earth would you find a better situation? You have an entire workforce of slaves providing you every resource imaginable. Those vegetables don't grow themselves. The cattle and swine do not come from thin air."

"Yes, suh." Hercules took a step back. "I jus' thought of bein' rewarded with freedom, is all. Other cooks here do fine work, too. They'd work real hard, and you can buy someone new with my three hundred dollars, suh."

"Three hundred dollars!" Washington spit on the ground. "Hercules, I couldn't even get a decent coachman for three hundred dollars. For the sale of a lead cook, someone of your talent, I would need no less than one thousand dollars."

"Sorry, suh. You right, suh." Hercules raised the ax to continue chopping wood. He'd never made his master so upset before.

"Hercules, I'm disappointed in you. I've come here to commend you, and this is your response. If you're unhappy with your working conditions, then I can make alternate arrangements. My farms need plenty of muscle."

"No, suh." The slave's voice quivered again. "Happy right here, suh." He quickened the pace of his work, now in complete darkness. Washington walked toward the horse stable, baffled.

Ona and Hercules spent Friday night in the Family House, expecting it to be the last time they would see the enslaved workers who had become like family. They agreed to tell no one of their plot, and they both remained disciplined in keeping it secret. Feeling nostalgic, they made sure to say their unspoken goodbyes to everyone before lying down for their last sleep at Mount Vernon. Hercules made sure to leave Peter on good terms. They spoke about the last beehives of the season and Master Washington's horses and newborn mules. Peter pontificated that the moon remained in the morning sky because it had no reason to fade away. Why would the moon set, just to return at nightfall? The moon had an assigned place in the sky. Hercules indulged Peter and his simple pleasures. He even felt that he would miss the old man's ramblings.

Hercules shared stories with the other house servants, and he played games with the children. He would not get the opportunity to say goodbye to his own children on the outlying farm, but the sad truth was that he had a closer relationship with the children in the Family House.

Ona spent much of the evening with Charlotte. She tried not to act out of the ordinary because Charlotte was smart enough to figure everything out. Charlotte had always been a mother figure to Ona, teaching her how to sew, how to garden, how to deal with Lady Washington, how to be a young lady, and how to conduct herself in the presence of all sorts of people—white and black, men and women. She was a mentor in the art of resisting the horrors of slavery. The wise, old seamstress gave Ona confidence and a sense of purpose in a seemingly purposeless existence.

Neither Hercules nor Ona slept a wink that night. They crammed into their Family House bunks, never having felt so unsure of tomorrow, yet hopeful for freedom, and soothed by their thoughts of each other.

⌒

Hercules rose for work on Saturday a bit earlier than usual. The sun would stay hidden for a few more hours, and cool air filled the early darkness—a widespread, empty silence. He could hear the faintest noise made miles away. Even the birds still slept—or they knew to stay away from his mischief.

He carried a glass jar to gather the weeds on his way to the kitchen. The weeds still dripped with whatever chemical concoction the gardener had last applied. He bent over and pulled at them with all his might, his hands shaking, struggling to uproot them, as if the devil tugged on the other end from the depths of hell. After wrestling them out of the ground, he cut off the roots. Hercules would not tolerate dirt in his coffee.

The shakes and nervous twitches stopped once he arrived in the kitchen, where he felt at home, comfortable and confident in his expertise. It took a bit longer for his teeth to stop chattering. He grinded some coffee beans to brew a small test pot. There would be no way to taste the experimental poison, but Hercules wanted to sample the smell of arsenic-laced coffee. He knew the weeds gave off a peculiar odor long before Washington began to apply chemicals, so the arsenic was hopefully odorless and tasteless. He was over-prepared with a few additives to dilute any strange smell. Hercules poured a few sample cups with extra sugar, milk, spices, and even dandelions, but he still detected a slight fishy smell from the weeds. Always the perfectionist, he was not convinced that the wicked beverage would pass as fresh coffee.

He felt a slight panic and began looking out the window, then over his shoulders. The clock struck five o'clock, when George Washington began his day. Even though his master never bothered him in the kitchen, Hercules began to shake again in acknowledgement of how risky this business had become. What if Washington smelled something odd in the kitchen and came asking questions? What excuse would he give for having repugnant wildflowers in the kitchen? His heart pounded harder against the wall of his chest, pulsating through his uniform. Then, an epiphany. All at once, he stopped shaking and stood frozen, staring at a shelf on the wall that contained the answer. It was right in front of his face all morning: George Washington's treasured honey.

That's it, he thought with a cathartic sensation. He would just need honey and maybe a little milk. Hercules soaked a weed in honey, encasing the arsenic in golden syrup. He then dipped the sharp, green weed in a new cup of coffee, leaving the poison-laced honey to dissolve. He let the cup sit outside for a few minutes. *Success!* It smelled like coffee and honey. If only he could try it out on someone, or on something. He fantasized of poisoning Nelson, for all the times the famed horse had sneered and growled at him, but there was no time for revenge. He rushed to brew a fresh pot and soak some more weeds in a honey jar. John Fairfax would be expecting his morning coffee soon.

Ona rolled off her wooden planks at five o'clock to prepare for work. She hid a small knapsack full of her belongings under a blanket in the corner of the bunk. Charlotte had given her the knapsack as a Christmas gift almost a year ago. Until now, it had never been used. She packed it with a comb, some linen clothes, and a drinking gourd. The red-and-white livery uniforms worn at Mount Vernon would be too recognizable to slave catchers, so she planned to leave them all behind. Before walking to the mansion, Ona retrieved the stolen jewels hidden between two boards of her bunk. She placed seven rubies and six pearls in the bottom of the sack. This was the last day to pilfer any more from Lady Washington's bedroom.

Martha seemed her normal self when Ona arrived. She was old, tired, and demanding. Her general disposition had improved since events had made it clear that George would remain in retirement, but she still projected a miserable condescension when interacting with her human property. For the past week, Ona had begun to enjoy when Lady Washington became rude and demeaning. It motivated her to escape.

As Ona dressed her mistress's hair, Martha gave out her orders for the day. "After serving my breakfast, you will help in the spinning house. More shirts will be necessary for the coming winter, and I will expect you to produce more than Charlotte and the others. You are younger, you have more energy, and your fingers are more agile."

"Yes, ma'am," Ona said. Her cheeks rose in a quick, candid smile at the thought of being absent for the coming winter.

"Seamstresses have been whipped with sharp-edged sticks for not producing to their potential."

"Yes, ma'am." Ona continued curling Martha's hair.

"You will prepare the guest bedroom and Servants' Hall after spinning. A delegation of politicians will arrive tomorrow, no doubt in another desperate attempt to coax George into serving in the Columbian government. We will respectfully decline, but offer agreeable accommodations for their stay. And you, little girl, are not to commiserate with their slaves. Do you understand?"

"Yes, ma'am." Ona paid very little attention, not expecting to ever meet these people.

Martha continued. "Slaves have been sharing information like wildfire, and knowing more information will only do you harm. It is a dangerous world, and you would be best to avoid it. So, spinning, it shall be for you. Spinning and serving our guests."

Ona hadn't anticipated working in the spinning house on the day of the escape. Somehow, she would need to return to the bedroom alone to pocket more jewels.

As Hercules put the final touches on his honey-arsenic roast, he brewed a separate pot of straight coffee to prevent anyone else from drinking the toxic batch. Other kitchen help would arrive soon and maybe sneak a few sips for themselves. He turned his attention back to the "special" pot and soaked each honey-dipped weed in the coffee. He then disposed of the weeds down the necessary.

Just after six o'clock, like always, Hercules walked the coffeepot and a few cups to the overseer's doorstep. He felt positive that he'd eliminated the weedy aroma, but his hands still shook. He heard the chimes of rattling porcelain with each step. The plan left no margin for error. If the arsenic didn't work, then John Fairfax would catch the runaways later in the evening. If it worked too well, John Fairfax would be dead by evening. Even worse, if Fairfax grew suspicious after one sip of his morning coffee, there was a good chance Hercules would be the dead man, hanging from one of George Washington's beautiful poplar trees. He imagined himself hanging in between the beehives that brought him so much grief.

John Fairfax resided in the overseer's quarters, a small, brick building adjacent to the spinning house. Hercules arrived and arranged the coffeepot and four cups on the doorstep. Sometimes other farm managers came for coffee, so he always left extra cups. Hercules didn't breathe easy until he let go of the last cup. Heat rushed through his puffy fingers when he unclenched his grip. He trotted out of sight and then slowed his stride, taking backward baby steps, waiting to see Fairfax drink his morning coffee, anxious to witness the transaction.

Hercules stood about fifty yards away, in back of the mansion near the portico. Still, no Fairfax. He squinted to see a figure emerge in the distance, possibly a farm manager. As he took two baby steps forward, Hercules realized that this person had come from the Family House. Two more baby steps. It was definitely one of George Washington's slaves walking to the overseer's house. The sun had just begun to rise, and it shed a faint light on the mystery man. Hercules now jogged until he could identify the man walking toward the coffee.

Peter, no, he thought. Peter inched closer to the doorstep, and Hercules sped up even faster. He reached Fairfax's front door just in time to intercept Peter at the steps. He tried to speak but needed time to catch his breath.

"Mornin', Uncle Herc. Gonna be a fine day today, mmmhmm."

Hercules panted. His hands clutched his knees. "How come you ain't in the stable? You late?"

"No, no. I be workin' with Mastuh Fairfax's hoss today. Jus' need my orders." Peter reached out for a coffee cup, and Hercules slapped his arm away with a sweaty, open palm.

"Don't you be drinkin' that coffee, now," he commanded in a stern voice.

Peter was about to respond when John Fairfax opened the door and stepped outside with another overseer, William Garner, a bearded, burly-looking farmer. Fairfax looked at Hercules, having heard the slave's warning.

"Coffee no good?" he asked.

Hercules felt a burning in his chest again. "Oh no, coffee real good, suh. Strong today, with honey in it. But old Peter here got no stomach for honey. Ain't that right, Peter?"

Peter looked confused, but neither of the overseers cared to hear his answer. "Well, them honeybees don't bother me none. No, suh, not one sting. Imagine that." Peter chuckled.

Fairfax continued as if the old man didn't exist. "That's Hercules, always the perfectionist."

"He could make a fine overseer," Garner replied.

Hercules paid no attention as they poured the coffee. He stared deep into Peter's eyes, praying that his words would sink in to the old man's skull. "That's white man's coffee. Slaves don't be drinkin' a white man's coffee, Peter."

"A fine overseer, indeed." Fairfax laughed.

Garner and Fairfax continued their conversation and began sipping the coffee. Hercules grabbed Peter's shoulders with both hands and squeezed hard. "That coffee for Mastuh Fairfax, you understand?"

Peter's face formed a gullible smile, and he nodded his head in agreement, but Hercules was not convinced that he'd received the message. Peter was either too naïve to understand or he was the world's greatest actor. Hercules couldn't tell which. He wanted to wait around to make sure Peter wouldn't take even a sip, but that would seem suspicious. Meanwhile, Masters Fairfax and Garner both drank down their coffee with no complaints. Hercules watched out of the corner of his eye, relieved that they hadn't tasted anything funny.

"Well, go on now, nigger," Fairfax told Hercules. "You ain't no overseer yet."

"Yes, suh." Hercules looked at Peter one more time, then put his head down and walked back to the kitchen. *Lawd, don't let him drink that coffee,* he thought to himself. *Lawd, don't let it be.*

coffee. Hercules grabbed Peter's shoulders with both hands and squeezed

Ona reported to the spinning house after breakfast, still wondering how to sneak back into Lady Washington's jewelry box. Her head thumped from sleep deprivation combined with waves of adrenaline in anticipation of acquiring her freedom. She found Charlotte alone, already working. It calmed Ona's nerves to see her once again before leaving Mount Vernon.

Regardless of Martha's orders, Ona couldn't focus on her work. Instead, she envisioned John Fairfax catching her in the night, dragging her from the back of his horse, then tying her up and whipping her until no more blood was left to run from her broken body. Of course, a hanging was the more likely punishment, though she thought Fairfax would whip her anyway, for the pleasure, before killing her.

"What's the whip feel like, Char?"

The question caught Charlotte by surprise. "Why you askin'? You got one comin'? You get caught with mister man outside in the garden?" Her voice sounded irritated.

"No, nothin' like that. I jus' wonder 'bout it. Mistress say I get whipped with a stick if I ain't make more shirts. Why'd you get the whip?"

"Got caught sewin' extra shirts to sell at market once. Got the whip. Sewed too slow when I was sick. Got the whip. Next day, sewed too fast and didn't do a good job. Got the whip again."

Ona could sense Charlotte's discomfort in talking about it, but asked anyway in a timid voice, "It hurt real bad?"

"First couple cracks hurt real bad, yeah. They the ones that break skin. First couple cracks, you still alive; you still a woman. That's why they hurt. After that, them cracks whip your soul. Then the pain get so bad, you realize you got no soul. You start feelin' like a dog. Ever wonder if a dog got soul? Well, they ain't got none. The pain don't stop until you stop bein' a woman and believe you's a dog. You *is* the dog. That way, the whip make sense."

Ona listened and felt guilty that she had never been whipped. She'd spent the last year plotting an escape and growing far more defiant than Charlotte, at least in her thoughts. Why should she not have received a whipping? It didn't seem fair. Of course, Ona didn't want to get whipped, but she didn't want to seem so innocent either. She felt an urge to reveal every detail of the escape plot and to confess her love for Hercules. She wanted to prove her defiance and make Charlotte proud.

Her cheeks felt warm, and she was about to cry. She loved Charlotte more than anyone on the plantation. Ona was not just escaping the humiliation of slavery, she was also leaving home—a home that included fond memories and relationships.

Her rush of emotion was cut short by the reckless noise of two galloping horses coming to a screeching halt just outside the spinning house. George Washington and his body servant, Billy Lee, dismounted their horses and dragged John Fairfax's motionless body off of Washington's shoulder and up the few steps to his living space. Fairfax's eyes fluttered in and out of consciousness, and a thin stream of maroon blood dripped out the side of his mouth. Distressed at the sight, Ona imagined Fairfax whipping Peter to shreds. She imagined Charlotte's back torn open, telling herself, *He deserves it, the monster. He deserves it.*

They pulled his ragged body inside, and Washington pointed at Ona and Charlotte.

"Charlotte! Water! Plenty of water! Move!" Washington yelled.

Charlotte began a slow jog toward the well. Ona stepped back inside the spinning house, preferring not to contribute anything to Fairfax's recovery.

When Charlotte returned, George Washington assumed the role of general, which he played so well—taking quick action and inspiring confidence in those around him.

"Billy Lee, you will ride to Dr. Craik and bring him forthwith. Do not return without him. I will oversee the grounds today. Charlotte, stay with Mr. Fairfax until the doctor arrives. Keep him awake and alert. John, the doctor is coming, my good man!"

～

Charlotte stood next to the fireplace in the overseer's quarters. The room suffocated in silence, like John Fairfax suffocated in his tight, cotton shirt, soaked in sweat and a brown, liquid vomit, littered with random green chunks. His pitiful, famished figure was sprawled out across the bed. The big-boned, self-possessed seamstress stood over him, staring as he squirmed like a fish out of water. She studied the blood drying on his lips, with no intention of obeying the order to keep him conscious. She took a slow, satisfying breath in her nose, unfazed by the overseer's stench of agony. She felt content. She watched him writhe in pain on the bed, the beast who had whipped her on multiple occasions. His suffering brought her peace.

Before he slipped out of consciousness, Charlotte took a sip of the water herself, and then spoke in a calm, sadistic voice. "You can die right here in front of me, you son of a bitch. Go on and do it. That's fine with me," she said, her deep, raspy tone just loud enough to reach him, as his eyes began a series of spasms—up under his eyelid, then back down to reality.

"You can leave this place forever, go straight down to hell in the devil's arms, right where you belong. Leave me to take care of Eliza, and when you die, maybe, jus' maybe, I can look my baby in the eyes and not see your nasty face. I'm so sick of seein' you in my baby, seein' you hold me down, seein' you push that ugly pecker inside me. I still smell the whiskey on your breath. I still smell the grass stains on your hand that gagged me. Couldn't even wash up for the occasion? Oh, I thought of killin' you myself, plenty of times. But this'll be even better. I'll jus' watch you die in as much pain as you can feel, and I won't have to do a damn thing. But you'll take my pain with you, and your daughter'll have a better life once her daddy goes six feet under. Die. Right now, you son of a bitch. Go on and die."

She looked forward to witnessing Fairfax succumb to death, until interrupted by Martha Washington barging through the door.

"John!" Martha gasped as she darted to the bed, turning her head at the sight of him. "Well, don't just stand there. Help me get his shirt off."

Charlotte broke her stone posture and followed the orders of her mistress. Fairfax overheated as they struggled to remove his shirt, breeches, and stockings, leaving him in just his linen drawers. After a few minutes of dousing him with water, and his temperature refusing to budge, Martha sent Charlotte to the ice house. She returned with a large slab of ice and placed it over the grotesque man's body.

One hour later, Fairfax's temperature stabilized, and he fell asleep. Charlotte returned to work, and Martha Washington remained at the overseer's side, waiting for Dr. James Craik. The mansion was left empty for Ona to rob her mistress of all she desired.

Ona crept up to the bedroom, stood in the doorway for a moment, and stared at her mistress's bed. *Why not?* she thought. She had time. Ona fell backward on to the bed in joy. She spread out her arms and legs in every direction, trying to touch every thread and each corner of the blanket. She let her thin body sink deep in the mattress as she imagined herself descending into a sea of clear water, washing the freckles off her cheeks. Her heart fluttered and she let out a soft moan. The young slave turned and twisted her body in an improvised dance, a random assortment of movements, like a baby deer trying out her new legs. *This is what I will have in Philadelphia,* she thought. She closed her eyes and imagined Hercules lying next to her, his big arms wrapped around her. He kissed her neck, and they made love. She panted; she felt weightless. They ran through the dark woods together, holding hands, and again, they made love under a full moon. She imagined his chiseled body in the moonlight.

Ona had no idea how long she'd fantasized before standing up out of the bed. She pulled the sheets tight again and tiptoed into her mistress's closet for the loot. When she found Martha's jewelry box hidden under the bottom shelf of linens, a variety of gem stones, mostly rubies, stared up at her like flaming-red eyeballs, scolding her for her disobedience. Some were set in necklaces and rings. She threw her hands into the box, gripping as many as she could hold at once. While clutching the jewels in her palm, she felt a sharp edge stabbing the inside of her hand. On instinct, she released the stones, letting some fall to the hardwood floor. A large scratch ran from the middle of her palm to the base of her thumb, and she watched a thin, red line of blood creep out of the wound.

Most of the jewelry fell back in the box, but Ona would have to scavenge the floor for the remaining stones. She recovered a few pearls from under the shelf and then reached for the rubies and silver. When she turned back to the box, Ona noticed a prism of light beaming from across the room. She crawled across the floor on her hands and knees to get a closer look. Ona had seen diamonds on the guests who'd visited Mount Vernon, and occasionally around Martha's neck. She recognized the brilliant glow staring back at her. Ona reached out and lifted the diamond with two fingers. *Welcome to Philadelphia.*

She stole thirty pieces of jewelry, including a free-floating diamond, bundled up in a linen sheet, as if it were dirty laundry. It made an appropriate disguise since Martha had ordered her to prepare the guest bedrooms. After cleaning the rooms to perfection, Ona took the sheets to the wash house in a roundabout route so she could stop and unload the booty in her bunk.

Dinner would be served in a few hours. She headed toward the kitchen, wondering if John Fairfax was still alive. Butterflies raced in circles through her stomach. The escape was near.

Chapter 8

By September, the oppressive heat in New York had surrendered to the early chills of autumn. The corner of Wall Street and Water Street bustled like the old marketplaces of antiquity. People gathered from all over. A steady stream of merchants spilled out of the East River by the hour. They came straight from their boats to the Merchant's Coffee House, buying, selling, drinking coffee, drinking rum, gambling, and getting into any other trouble they could find. Politicians sat for hours in the coffee house, debating every idea under the sun. It was the center of New York politics.

Recently emancipated by James Madison, Jonathan could never have imagined walking into the Merchant's Coffee House in New York City as a free man with business of his own to conduct. His job was simple: Collect any information he could about Alexander Hamilton's political opponents—Aaron Burr in particular. The supreme leader wanted every last detail about the little swine: his beliefs, his plans, his financial investments, his family life, his personal life—nothing was off limits.

As Jonathan approached the front entrance, he circled around a small group of shaggy farmers who were in a heated argument about the health and price of a drove of cattle. He dodged their flailing arms, barely getting out of the way. The inside of the coffee house was just as crowded as the outside. He noticed a delicate-looking woman with light-brown, copper-colored skin sitting near the entrance as he stepped forward. She batted her eyes and slid toward him.

"Hello there, stranger," she said in a flirtatious voice.

Her tall, slender figure could be seen through a never-ending silky gown.

"Hello to you, miss," Jonathan responded. Her hair was a bit disheveled, which made her seem more approachable. "I'm looking for the man in charge here, a Mr. Bleecker, I believe."

"I think you should talk to *me*," she said with an alluring smile.

Jonathan blushed. He noticed her floral perfume, which smelled like James Madison's garden.

"Perhaps I could share stories from my travels in due time," he said. "But I do have important business here."

"But I'd like to hear stories now, kind sir. I'll bet you've been all around the world." The young woman exaggerated her pouting lips, waiting for him to submit.

He giggled and turned toward the bar, waving back at her with his fingers. "I will return soon, miss." *What a beautiful young lady*, he thought.

The man standing behind the bar looked far less amicable. His round stomach flopped over his belt in every direction, and his bald head sat atop some unusual side whiskers. Jonathan put his most buoyant smile forward.

"Mr. Bleecker, I presume?"

"Bleeker's off gettin' rich," was the monotone response. "What'll it be?"

"Well, I do have business with a Mr. Bleecker, sir. Do you know where I might find the gentleman?"

"Look, boy, Bleecker's got no business with a nigger. I can assure you that. Now, you're either gonna order a drink or go lookin' for some other banker. There's plenty of them up and down Wall Street." He turned to launch a dribble of tobacco juice into the spittoon behind him.

Jonathan refused to shudder at the brute's poor manners. He had been to New York plenty of times with James Madison, and he was well aware that attitudes toward black men were not much different here compared to the ones in Virginia. Gradual emancipation was a nice gesture, but banning the condescending treatment would take centuries.

Jonathan kept his cool. "I am to be given a room in the upstairs of this building, sir."

The fat man burst out in laughter. "That's a good one, kid!"

"Mr. Bleecker has been made aware of my arrival. He has agreed to make the proper accommodations."

Still laughing and shaking his head, the bartender got closer to Jonathan's face. "Says who?" His foul tobacco breath floated forward.

Jonathan stood tall and refused to yield an inch. "Says Alexander Hamilton, supreme leader of the National States of America. If my presence is some inconvenience, then I suggest you alert the supreme leader directly. But it *is* his wish that I reside here."

He finally got the man's proper attention. Even if Jonathan was bluffing, it would be too great a risk for the man to defy Alexander Hamilton's orders. The whiskered man stepped back and reached for a scroll from behind the counter. He showed it to Jonathan and spoke in a much less threatening tone. "Look here, man. The only expected guest is a 'Jonathan Taylor.' That's all. Doesn't say anything about puttin' up no nigger."

Jonathan smiled and reached in his back pocket for the manumission papers signed by his benefactor. He held on to the document with pride and an iron grip, presenting it to the bartender. "Jonathan Taylor. Pleased to make your acquaintance. I will see the room now."

The man stood speechless for a moment. "Arrogant prick," he grumbled under his breath.

He escorted Jonathan upstairs to a single room with a bed and nothing else.

"There you are, Mr. Taylor. I hope it'll do." Jonathan accepted with a nod, but the man continued. "Now there are just two rules downstairs in the coffee house. One, if you hang around, you buy somethin' to drink. It ain't no spectator's gallery. And two, whatever happens to you, I ain't responsible."

Jonathan narrowed his eyes in a puzzled expression. The man explained further.

"You get ripped off by some smooth-talkin' merchant—I ain't responsible. Lose all your money in bad land—I ain't responsible. You catch some fever from the whores—I ain't responsible. Got it?"

"Yes, sir," Jonathan replied, saddened to discover that the beautiful young woman at the door was a prostitute. "Oh, and one more thing," Jonathan interjected as his host walked down the stairs. "The supreme leader would not be happy if others were to discover my connection to him." He paused for the message to sink in. "Good day, sir."

Arrogant prick.

Jonathan hung around for a few days, and when Aaron Burr entered the coffee house, Jonathan knew it. Burr wore a slicked-back ponytail, black as tar, with large black eyebrows painted on to his vampire-like complexion. His wide, black pupils rested deep in the eggshell-whites of his eyes. Burr's chiseled features could turn the head of anyone, even though he was slim and unimposing in stature. Jonathan had only ever met one other man who could command attention by his mere physical presence. That man was miles away, talking to his horse at Mount Vernon.

The former slave, turned spy, carried a preliminary profile of Aaron Burr. Burr had practiced law in Albany and New York City before being appointed New York's attorney general. He'd settled in New York City after Saratoga's admission to New England. He seethed at the prospect of gobbling up political opportunities left in the tiny state of New York. Still in his mid-thirties, Burr set his sights on the governorship, and was expected to win it.

"Governor's here!" yelled a stockbroker seated at the bar. The crowd got a bit rowdier in acknowledging Burr. "Hey, gov!" a second voice greeted him.

"Ah, not just yet," replied Burr. "That depends on you good gentlemen voting. And you can count on me to remind you of that every day until Election Day."

In truth, these men held very little interest in who served as New York's governor. Their primary concern was making money, and as long as the state government allowed them the privilege, they had very few opinions on politics.

"Just keep your hands out of my pocketbook, gov!" shouted another stockbroker.

"Now *that*, you can count on," Burr said with confidence. "But King George—I mean King Alexander—over in Philadelphia, you'd better watch out for."

Laughter and a few hisses followed. Jonathan made a mental note of the comparison to a despot.

"Where ya been, gov?" asked the man seated at the bar. "Haven't heard you screamin' 'bout kings in a few days. Been kinda quiet around here."

Burr looked surprised at the question. "Haven't you heard the news, man? The office of the *New York Journal*—burned to the ground. Tragedy, I tell you. An utter tragedy. And foul play by the looks of it," he explained. "I've been helping with the recovery and raising donations. You gentlemen are welcome to contribute, of course."

The bartender listened and served Burr his coffee. "Foul play? Fat chance," he said. "These buildings go up in flames all over town. Hell, this here coffee house could go up any day now." More chatter came from the customers. "Who the hell'd wanna burn down a newspaper office, anyhow?"

"I'll tell you who," Burr shot back. "A political hack who just can't stand a free press. Someone who doesn't approve of the courageous dissent published in the *New York Journal*. Someone whose political ambitions are threatened by it. Believe me, gentlemen, politicians play dirty, just like the bankers on Wall Street."

"Well, then, gov," the bartender joked, "you ought to run for fire chief, don't ya think?"

The room swelled once more in laughter. Burr turned to Lydia, the prostitute who had propositioned Jonathan earlier. He placed a handful of coins in her palm. "Why don't you take the day off, my sweet? I don't like these men philandering with you all day."

She accepted the money and smiled, but remained seated just the same.

"Now hold on a minute, gov," a drunken, fat man objected. "I was thinkin' of givin' her a whirl myself," he said as he stroked his poorly trimmed handlebar mustache.

"Oh, Mr. Winthrop, please. There are many others who will gladly accept your magnificent whirl," Burr joked with a contemptuous grin. The fat man sat back down, too drunk to stand. "You have no daughters, I presume?" Burr continued.

The room exploded in laughter at the thought of a woman willing to bear the children of Benjamin Winthrop, a miserable glutton who had lost so much money in failed business dealings, it was a wonder he did not yet rot in debtors' prison. The government restricted suffrage to propertied white men to weed out degenerates like Winthrop—but he came from money.

"If you had a daughter as beautiful as mine, sir, you would understand my position on the matter." Aaron Burr took advantage of the opportunity for a good speech. "So when you elect me as your governor, you can rest assured that your daughters and mine will live in a New York that respects the delicacy of women."

Again, the room quieted in disinterest, so long as they could get rich.

Jonathan observed the banter and considered how to introduce himself. How could he get close to Burr and build a relationship on trust? Should he play humble and meek, and suck up to the future governor, or be bold and brash by challenging him? Jonathan had been in the Merchant's Coffee House long enough to know that humble and meek wouldn't play here.

"And what of the free black men and escaped slaves from Columbia? Will the governor respect their rights as well?" Jonathan's question sucked the air out of the room.

Before a stunned Burr could respond, Mr. Winthrop chimed in again. "Now hold on a minute, boy. The man said he's got a daughter, not a Negro." It broke the awkward silence.

The newcomer had put Aaron Burr on the spot, and he needed to give a tactful answer. The voters of New York would in no way tolerate social or political equality for men like Jonathan. Burr would need to construct an answer that satisfied Jonathan, but assured every white man in the room that former slaves would have no discernible impact on New York.

"The Negroes will play a vital role in settling the vast lands of Montgomery and of the Northwest Territory, once the Indian threat there has been removed. The National States will depend on more settlement to expand west and become an economic power." Burr paused and looked up from under his heavy eyelids, hoping that his cockamamie answer would suffice.

Jonathan approached Aaron Burr with confidence and an outreached hand. "Jonathan Taylor, sir," he said with a charming smile. "I trust you will allow me to buy you another coffee."

The gossip of Master Fairfax's illness flew through Mount Vernon. Some cheered the news and hoped for the worst, but Hercules wished for the overseer's survival, promising himself he was no murderer. He had other concerns, as well. What about Master Garner, who had also drunk the coffee? Two ailing overseers with the same symptoms on the same day would arouse suspicion. If Garner was indeed sick, the two culprits would have to make their getaway before news reached the mansion. And what about Peter? Hercules worried about Peter the most. If arsenic wrought so much havoc on a young, healthy man like John Fairfax, the old, broken stableman had no chance if he'd digested whatever evil festered in that brew.

The kitchen was a complete mess with food everywhere. Remnant feathers of a butchered pheasant flew through the air. Every bottle of oil and condiments sat on a stone countertop. Fire blistered in the brick oven, causing the room's temperature to soar above one hundred degrees. The heat didn't bother Hercules; in fact, it made him focus on his work. If this was the last meal he'd cook at Mount Vernon, then he was determined to make it a majestic one. In addition to the roasted pheasant and the smoked ham, Hercules prepared fresh greens with a champagne vinaigrette, baked oysters, and a chocolate paté for dessert, all to be washed down with Master Washington's favorite Madeira wine. Even on the night of his escape, Hercules wouldn't think of serving George Washington a half-assed meal.

As he moved back and forth from dish to dish, catching the sweat that melted off his forehead down to his apron, Ona slipped into the inferno through the back door.

"Fairfax out cold," she whispered, with her lips pursed beneath a smile.

Hercules twisted his neck in both directions to make sure they were alone. "Meet in the stable after tea," he whispered back.

Ona squinted in confusion. "We meet at the Family House. That's the plan."

"Plan changed. I gotta go to the stable first." Ona started to protest, but he cut her off. "Mastuh will be with Fairfax and Dr. Craik near Family House, anyway. We'll be safe leavin' from the stable."

In truth, he wanted to check on Peter before they ran. Hercules had asked every other house slave if they'd seen him, but on this day, Peter was a ghost. The cook would not leave Mount Vernon without knowing for certain that he had not harmed Peter in any way. Ona shrugged in disapproval, then went back to work setting the dining-room table.

Hercules usually castigated Ona for her spying on the dinner conversations, but tonight, it was he who listened a bit closer than he should. Doctor Craik joined George and Martha for a quiet dinner. No one said much of anything, other than expressing complete bafflement at Fairfax's illness. The doctor spoke in a blunt voice, without much confidence.

"In all my years, I've never seen anything like what I witnessed in your overseer. Severe gastritis for sure. Perhaps colic in the poor man. He will need plenty of liquids and rest."

Martha shook her head in disbelief. "What he needs, above all, is an impassioned plea to divine providence through our prayers. And he should be at home with his family."

"Yes, yes," the doctor concurred. "I must be on my way shortly. Perhaps your manservant, Billy Lee, could escort John home upon my departure."

Martha gave a disparaging look on hearing that the doctor would not stay longer.

"Other patients await, I'm afraid," he said before she could protest.

After dinner, Billy Lee tossed a weak John Fairfax over the back of his horse for the second time and escorted the raggedy overseer to his father's plantation. Doctor Craik set out as well, leaving behind an eerie silence at Mount Vernon.

⌀

While George and Martha sipped their tea, Hercules arranged for some of the house slaves to clean up the portico afterward, saying that he would be out scouting honeycombs as the sun descended and the bees took cover.

He had already prepared a large cotton sack full of belt buckles and shoes, vegetables, breads, and some cooking utensils for the escape. He wrapped his favorite butcher knife in an apron and placed it on top to avoid it slicing through the middle of the bag.

Before exiting, the master chef paused to take one final look at the kitchen. Memories swirled around in his head. He remembered his younger self making mistakes and learning the rhythms of the kitchen. He reflected on the man he had become in that boiling cauldron, the wisdom and talent acquired throughout his many years in the service of George Washington, whom he still believed was a decent and honorable man. But the time had come to dissolve the bands between master and slave. His service had run its course. Hercules departed the kitchen confident that he was indeed a man, and no matter what laws a government passed, no matter how hard a white man wielded a whip, no matter what amount of labor a master could throw on him, he was no slave. He ran upstairs to change into two pairs of pants and four shirts, one on top of the other, making an already muscular man look like a bulbous monster. The sweat began to drip from every pore on his skin, but each drop was worth it. He cherished his fancy wardrobe and would take as much with him as possible.

He walked at a normal, inconspicuous pace to the stable. No news about the health of Master Garner had arrived, which calmed his nerves for the moment. Hercules assumed the coffee had done Garner no harm. He smiled and looked up at the cloudless sky, gaining more optimism that enough daylight remained for a swift exodus.

The sound of Nelson kicking up dirt, snorting, and neighing rang loud and clear as Hercules approached the stable. *Yes*, he thought to himself, *I'm leaving, and I'm not coming back, you stupid beast*. He marched in long strides, closer to the stable entrance. His gigantic shadow fell diagonal to the ground from the sun preparing to set in the distance. Peeking in the stable, he saw Nelson, Blueskin, and Magnolia staring back at him. He saw nothing else until his eyes peered away from the horses, down to the ground. In utter disbelief, his blood boiled at the sight.

"Damn it, damn it! Goddamn, idiot! No!" Hercules shouted in a rage as he reached out for the closest object, a pitchfork leaning against the wall, and threw it to the ground, releasing a terrible metallic shriek that reverberated through the whole stable. Nelson remained calm but snorted a bit louder and stared down Hercules like he wanted to charge. Blueskin and Magnolia jumped and squawked in a blithering frenzy.

"Stop it, now!" Ona cried. "Stop that! You scarin' me, and you scarin' the horses. You want mastuh to hear you, fool?" She sat on the ground next to Peter, who lay flat on his back with his arms stretched out to both sides. Blood and vomit blanketed his bare chest, like it had John Fairfax's.

Hercules ignored Ona's cries and jumped on top of Peter's fragile body. He threw down his bag and gripped Peter by the neck.

"I told you five times! Don't drink that coffee. Don't go drinkin' white man's coffee. And what do ya do, you stupid ass? Goddamn it!"

He noticed Peter slipping in and out of consciousness, and then continued his rampage to keep the old man awake. "I can't help you now! Ain't goin' back to that kitchen, you stupid ass! Ain't no way I'm goin' back!"

Lethargic, Peter summoned enough strength to speak. "Ain't no stupid ass." His voice sounded slow and hoarse. "You think I drank that shit you give Mastuh Fairfax? Shit that damn near killed him? I ain't stupid, boy."

Hercules lowered his voice, and his shoulders drooped in a hopeless gesture. "You lie, old man. I told you don't drink that." Peter looked like death incarnate.

"Listen here," Peter said in a throaty whisper. "Ain't no coffee gonna kill me. I'm gonna die on my own accord. I'm gonna die right here in this stable, with these hosses, right here. I ain't drink no poison. Jus' my time, that's all. I'm a old man. Tired, weak."

As usual, Hercules didn't believe him.

"And don't think I don't know what you's up to," Peter continued, glancing at Ona, too. "Bags all packed. Imagine that. You two, run smart. Don't stop for no one. Don't trust no one." His body rested back down to the ground, and he closed his eyes with a deep sigh. Black shadows eclipsed Peter's entire body.

"We can't jus' leave him here," Ona said with tears rushing over her freckles, down to the corners of her lips. She stroked Peter's forehead with an open palm. His face was a wilted flower, and his eyes squinted, struggling to stay open, to stay in the world around him. Ona turned her head away from the old man's lifeless face. She spoke to the shadow on the ground. "Let's stay with Peter a little while. Fairfax is good and poisoned. We can still leave tonight, after mastuh asleep. We get to Philadelphia in a few days, and we still—"

Ona's voice came to an abrupt halt; she gasped for air, as did Hercules when he turned from looking out the back window. The imposing shadow had not come from the horses or from Hercules; it was the shadow of George Washington, who stood like a tower in the stable entrance, listening to every word.

Hercules froze. His heart skipped a beat and then raced like a chariot when it started up again. Peter remained on the ground, not yet entirely aware of the situation.

"Philadelphia," Washington said without expression. "Philadelphia is a long way—more than a few days—and your home is here," he said with authority.

Hercules bit his lip in frustration. His tongue rested in the gaping hole between his teeth. Washington had probably come for another nighttime talk with Nelson. If they'd run from the Family House, they'd be halfway up the Potomac by now. The plan had fallen apart.

Ona stood, uneasy, and in a kneejerk reaction, she charged George Washington. She made a helpless attempt to sneak past him. Washington took one step to his left, and her tiny body bounced back like she'd hit a brick wall, knocking her down next to Peter. As Hercules stepped forward, Ona reached for the two sacks of their belongings and rolled across the ground to the back wall of the stable.

"Don't you touch that woman," Hercules demanded, and for the first time in his life, he did not address George Washington as master or sir. It was also the first time he'd referred to Ona as a woman.

Hercules stepped over Peter, and the two men—master and slave—stood eyeball to eyeball in a standoff. Hercules possessed a clear physical advantage. His layers of clothing would even cushion a blow from General Washington—if indeed it came to blows, which Hercules did not wish, but was prepared for, nonetheless. The escape had to be tonight. After all of the day's events—after Fairfax, and now Peter dying in the dirt—it had to be tonight.

"We leave tonight. That's a fact," Hercules said as his eyes reddened. "You can stand out the way, or try to stop us. Either way, we leave tonight."

Washington showed no sign of backing down. "You would be wise to think this through. President Henry has employed hundreds of slave catchers to hunt you and return you to me, at which point you would be sold to the highest-bidding, Georgia trader. If you do as you say—leave tonight—then mark my word, slave, you have cooked your last meal. You will rot under the sun of a cotton plantation and take a daily whipping, after a few farewell lashes from me, of course. You and your sweetheart here will rue the day you deserted such a fine life in Virginia. Now, stand down."

Hercules stood inches away from George Washington. Ignoring his master's threat, he took one more step forward to close the small gap between them. Their noses nearly touched, and he knew Washington could feel the thick bursts of hot air exploding from his widened nostrils. The three horses breathed even louder from inside their stalls. Breathing, snorting; deep, heavy breaths hovered all around.

From the corner of his eye, Hercules saw Ona, crouched down against the back wall of the stable, shaking and hiding behind his oversized bag.

Washington spoke. "Hercules, you must understand the—"

"No more," was the response, as Hercules stepped forward again, this time pushing into Washington's broad frame, which Ona had failed to penetrate.

To Hercules's surprise, Washington didn't move very far. Instead, the great military leader lowered his head, and in an impressive demonstration of strength for a fifty-eight-year-old man, thrust his weight right back, budging Hercules off balance.

He tilted toward the dirt, but managed to grab onto Washington's shoulders. If he was going down, he would take his master with him. His knees buckled, and his feet reached behind him in a desperate search for flat ground. Ona screamed in the background, but neither man could afford to acknowledge her. Hercules took one final step back in the direction of Peter, who lay with his legs crossed at the calves and his bare feet pointed straight up in the air, like a tree stump rooted in the soil. Hercules tripped over Peter's feet and began to topple over. He thrashed his torso around to throw Washington violently through the air, overtop Peter and toward the ground, hoping he would land on top.

The two men plunged out of control, straight toward Ona, who belted out a piercing, high-pitched screech. Pushing her spine hard against the brick wall, she squeezed her eyelids together and braced for the moment of impact, still clutching Hercules's bag to soften the blow.

They plummeted to the ground, and Hercules found his face pressed up against Ona's, with George Washington's body pinned between them. He felt Ona's warm tears running down his cheek. Hercules rose to his feet quickly, confident, ready for a fight.

"Get up, George!" he seethed, but Washington's body lay stagnant, on top of Ona.

He pulled Washington up by the collar. Staring back at him was the pale white face of his master, eyes wide, with a stream of red blood spilling over his gums and the few teeth that he had remaining. Hercules saw his favorite butcher knife—the same knife he had packed in his bag—protruding from Washington's chest, where the blood gushed out fastest. The body crashed back to the ground, causing a storm of dust to rise up. Washington tumbled over onto the belt buckles and fine clothing that had spilled out of the bag when the knife had pierced his heart. Hercules reached down to his dying master's body and ripped the butcher knife out of his chest, then threw it to the ground. A sea of blood surged out, staining the dirt black. Washington gurgled out his last breath of air.

Ona remained smashed on the ground, with her head leaning up against the wall, her linen clothing doused in Washington's blood. Hercules seized her entire body and hid her eyes from the repulsive sight. She shook and panted, still unable to speak.

"Breathe, girl. Breathe," Hercules commanded. "My knife was in that bag. We gotta leave now, you understand. Right now. No time to waste." He looked down at Peter, who was also in tears, rolling over in anger and despair.

"No, mastuh! No!" Peter cried.

When Ona's convulsions stopped, Hercules let go and tried to salvage his belongings, throwing as many as he could back into the torn and blood-ied bag. He heard Nelson exhale a hurricane. The horse's body rocked from side to side; his eyes fixated on his master's corpse and the bloody weapon that had stolen the life away from it.

Hercules rushed to Magnolia's stall, but Peter intervened.

"Uncle Herc," he whispered. "Uncle Herc," he said, louder. He strained to nod his head toward the first stall. "Take Nelson."

Hercules paused. He despised that horse almost as much as slavery itself.

"Nelson's calm. That hoss got speed and calm. You need speed and calm. Go on, take 'em."

Hercules was always hesitant to believe Peter, but this was the man's expertise. He was a skilled horse breeder. He'd devoted much of his life to the care of George Washington's horses, some of the finest horses in all of Virginia—and Peter was dying. Hercules took the last advice the old man had to offer.

"Ona!" Hercules shouted, waking her from a daze. He opened the gate in front of Nelson and reached for Ona's waist.

Peter grunted from the ground: "Girl."

She leaned forward, but struggled to hear him. The volume of his voice descended, syllable by syllable.

"Girl. Put . . . Put . . . that knife . . ." Ona wept as she listened. " . . . in my hand."

She sobbed hysterically. Her body trembled as if she stood in the path of a tornado. Her knees bent to the ground and she turned her head, not wanting to see the weapon. Ona grasped the butcher knife and tossed it in Peter's direction. His palm became drenched in George Washington's blood, like the rest of the stable. He held on to the handle and rested his head back.

"Now . . . go . . . go. Run on outta here."

Ona kissed Peter's forehead and sprinted back to Hercules.

Hercules lifted her up, onto Nelson's hind, and then mounted the horse himself. He yanked a horse whip off of the wall as they exited in haste.

On their way out, Hercules caught one last glimpse of the stable. Blood everywhere. Two horses, a dying slave with a murder weapon in his hand, and the corpse of George Washington, father of a nation. The invincible George Washington, hero of the American Revolution, lay dead in a pool of his own blood, killed at the hands of a teenaged girl with a butcher knife.

Nelson galloped out of the stable, uphill toward the mansion, carrying Hercules—about the size of George Washington—and Ona, who added very little weight. The horse accelerated after a few hard whips from Hercules.

"Faster!" Hercules yelled. "Move! Move!"

They approached Martha Washington, running toward the stable in a terrible panic, having heard the commotion from the mansion. She waved her tired arms in the air to signal for her husband and Nelson.

Hercules shouted at Nelson in a red rage. "Move, damn it! Move!" He whipped again and again, harder and harder. They blew by Lady Washington, forward on toward the Potomac River. Hercules kept whipping the poor steed, his grip more unrelenting than the worst of the overseers. "Move, Goddamn it!" He whipped out of anger, he whipped out of fear, and he whipped for retribution; for Peter, for all of the heckling the horse had given him over the years. He whipped harder; for every beesting he'd suffered, for Lame Alice and his children, sentenced to a life of field work, for a life of enslavement, and for it all having come to a tragic end as it had. Harder and harder. His bulging biceps tired from throwing down the cowskin with so much force. Nelson whined, and blood began to seep from his back. Hercules didn't let up until Ona squeezed him tight from behind, wanting for him to stop. Nelson carried the two bloodstained, fugitive slaves into the woods and out of sight. Their journey north had just begun, though not as it had been planned.

Nothing could possibly have prepared Martha Washington for what she was about to discover in her husband's stable. A stubborn sun lay just above the horizon, refusing to sink, introducing the evening hues of purple, pink, and orange. She inched closer, expecting something unfortunate. With one look, Martha opened her mouth to unleash wails of misery at the ungodly sight, but nothing came, as if the sound had formed deep inside her belly but was blocked by her heart on the way up. She screamed silence. Cutting off the oxygen to her brain, Martha's body would not permit her to witness the grotesque scene. She passed out, falling next to her husband's dead body. Peter was unconscious. When Lady Washington awoke, he would be dead, too.

Martha Washington was widowed for the second time in her life. Over two hundred enslaved people lived on her plantation, yet she was abandoned, completely alone. At sunset, on September 19, 1790, the American Revolution died at Mount Vernon. Martha woke up in a new world.

Book Two

LIBERTY, JUSTICE, WAR

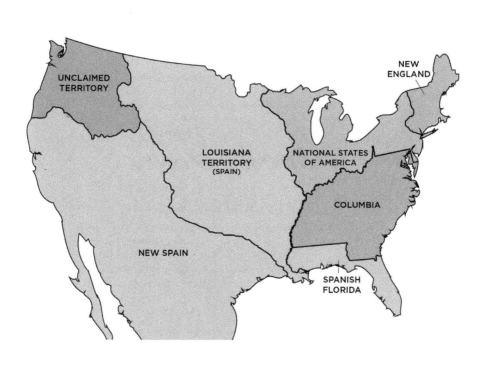

Chapter 9

ABSCONDED from the household of George and Martha Washington, ONA JUDGE, a light mulatto girl, much freckled, with very black eyes and bushy black hair. She is of middle stature, slender, and delicately formed, about eighteen years of age. She is a seamstress, with many changes of good clothes of all sorts—escaped on horseback on the night of September 19.

ABSCONDED from the household of George and Martha Washington, HER-CULES, a dark-skinned Negro, large in stature, six feet in height, over two hundred pounds in weight, missing one lower front tooth, about thirty-five years of age. Wears fine shoes and clothing and carries cooking utensils—escaped on horseback on the night of September 19.

Three nations mourned the tragic and seemingly cold-blooded murder of their patriarch. Like three religions spawned by Abraham, the National States of America, Columbia, and New England could all trace their roots back to George Washington's leadership in the Revolutionary War.

People crowded in churches across New England for days. Albany, the capital city of Saratoga, hosted an emotional midnight mass outside the North Dutch Church, where Governor George Clinton eulogized the fallen hero.

"We will carry on the work that he began so gloriously in our revolution. And so, as we carry on the work of a republic, we carry on the great battle of Saratoga. We build upon Washington's victories at Trenton, at Yorktown. We strive forward to prove that George Washington's battles were not waged in vain; forward to demonstrate that the people of New

England can keep a republic and nurture the liberties for which he fought."

Even Prime Minister Adams, Clinton's latest in a series of political enemies, sent a note congratulating Clinton on an "eloquent and unifying" speech.

In the National States, hordes of citizens congregated outside Philadelphia's Federal Palace, which still stood on bare bones, under construction by American slaves who awaited gradual emancipation. Church bells and gun smoke filled the brisk autumn air. Supreme Leader Hamilton spoke, still grieving the loss of his personal hero, his mentor, and his father figure. With heartfelt passion, he expressed his determination to apprehend the two alleged conspirators in Washington's murder.

"We will move heaven and earth in our obligation to see that justice is served. Neither I nor anyone in my administration will rest a day until these bloodthirsty savages hang for their crimes!"

The three justices of the Supreme Court, John Jay, James Wilson, and John Dickinson, delivered the most memorable speeches. Each man had personal experience working with the general. Dickinson reflected on the "American spirit" that Washington had instilled in him, even when the conservative Dickinson opposed independence from England. James Wilson agreed, revealing that he could never have found the courage to vote in favor of independence, if not for the passion and determination of the great revolutionary leader. John Jay, never known to have been a great orator, rose to remind the tearful audience that "Washington could have been king of North America after the war; indeed, he disappointed many in his rejection of a crown. Instead, George Washington allowed three countries to grow and flourish on their own. He raised his children well, and set them free to determine their own course in this world, like any loving father would."

In the Confederation of Columbia, Martha insisted on a private funeral at Mount Vernon for close friends and family. Religious leaders delivered the eulogies instead of rapacious politicians trying to take advantage of her husband's murder. Yet even at George's funeral, she would have to play the game of politics. Hamilton and Pinckney attended the service as close friends of the general. To avoid any political statement or favoritism, Martha also extended invitations to John Adams and Patrick Henry, even though the sight of Henry made her ill. In her mind, Patrick Henry was as responsible for her husband's death as the slave who had thrust the knife through Washington's heart. Still traumatized from having witnessed the murder scene, Martha spoke very little. President Henry did not even receive a greeting.

Washington would spend eternity in a desolate tomb on a hillside outside the mansion. After the funeral, the stable was destroyed, its contents burned, its bricks demolished to the ground. The body of Peter Hardiman, the assumed murderer, was burned, his remains spread out in the woods for the vultures. Martha spent most of her remaining days in deep depression, as John Fairfax and William Garner, both of whom survived the dreadful ordeal, managed the farms of Mount Vernon.

President Henry did hold a separate vigil in Richmond for Columbian citizens to attend. Martha, of course, stayed home while the South mourned the loss of their hero in similar fashion to the North. Private donors competed to give the most money for a statue in the capital. Famed Revolutionary War hero Henry "Light Horse Harry" Lee of Virginia eulogized Washington with his famous description, "First in war, first in peace, and first in the hearts of three great nations."

Ona awoke deep in the woods, shivering in the darkness. Muscular tree branches flexed high above in the heavy wind as if they would reach down, capture her, and send her back to Mount Vernon to face justice for the murder of a deity. No judge or jury would be necessary; her appearance pronounced the girl's guilt beyond doubt. Dried blood in crusted clots covered the freckles across her face; blood stained the entire front of her shirt and stiffened it like the cold leaves all around. In her half-conscious daze, she forgot everything that had transpired. For one brief moment, she rolled over in her straw-filled bunk with Charlotte and Eliza sleeping peacefully underneath. Someone must have left the Family House door open, letting in the strong winds.

The branches reached down closer, pulling her mind out of the trance.

She heard the echoes of attack dogs again, howling in pursuit of her scent; she was unsure if the noise was real or just haunting her imagination. Still in complete shock, she struggled to gauge how long it had been since that horrible night. Days? Weeks?

The moon had vanished. It hid behind those monstrous tree limbs, buried deep beneath the black clouds of an ominous night. The blackout aided in the fugitives' escape. Ona reached out her arms in search of Hercules. Her legs extended in all directions, feeling for his presence. She hurled her head back and forth until it collided with a sharp object that pierced the mud-caked skin of her forehead. A thin trickle of blood spilled from her temple as she pulled her head away. It was no use. The stone was a weapon, and it followed her with every turn, inching closer to her eyelid. Her heart pounded like a drummer marching off to war.

The blazing light of a torch fired up to the sky, sending a wave of heat over her body. A chorus of high-pitched whistles and war cries overpowered the wind while the shadows of four bodies came into view. Teardrops washed away the blood that had settled on Ona's cheeks.

"Machele ne tha-tha! Machele ne tha-tha! Sawanwa killa! Machele ne tha-tha!" Their voices bounced off the thick oak trees and echoed through the forest.

Ona widened her eyes while the screams assailed her. She shivered in cold fear.

"Squithetha mai-ah! Ps'qui miskaawi."

The tallest man among them hoisted his torch, and he howled into the night like a starving wolf. Light jumped off of their shaved heads and illuminated the red-and-black war paint that covered their bodies. Ona remembered Martha Washington's description of Satan when she talked about her religion, but Satan seemed tolerable compared to the four Shawnee Indians that confronted her.

A young man, no older than Ona, held the spear that rested against her eyebrow.

"Nooleewi-a," he said, looking just as nervous as Ona.

She shook her head, unable to comprehend a word. When Hercules and Nelson appeared from the forest, the Shawnees fell into another furious uproar.

"Mattah, neshwa! Negate hileni! Negate squithetha, m'seewa!"

Hercules's size was enough to threaten them. He dropped some fire-wood from his arms and lifted his hands above his head. One of the Shawnees threw up a British infantry rifle and shoved it toward his chest.

"Machele ne tha-tha!"

Nelson stood at attention, calm and cool as usual.

Ona had not seen many Native Americans other than the peaceful traders at Alexandria's market, most of whom had adopted European customs and language. She had never confronted a hostile war party. George Washington and his distinguished guests had nothing but chilling descriptions of uncivilized brutes, hell-bent on destroying innocent settlers. The newspaper reports were even less generous in their assessment. At the moment, the grim depictions seemed accurate.

"Okay now, fellas," Hercules said in a calm voice. He extended his neck, reaching out his face into the torch light that revealed his dark-brown skin.

How peculiar, Ona thought in a fleeting moment, that their skin color could actually save their lives in this odd encounter. These warriors would kill a white man on the spot if they had the chance.

"Don't want no trouble now, fellas," Hercules continued. "Jus' headin' north. Away from white man. Away."

The Shawnees held their weapons drawn steady until Ona reached inside her sack for a small handful of Martha's rubies. In a panicked reaction, the most aggressive member of the war party whipped his rifle around to Ona and aimed it at her throat. She screeched like an eagle. Holding out her shaky hands, her words fluttered as she spoke.

"Look, rubies. You take 'em. Lots of rubies we can trade." Ona searched for words that the Indians would understand, and their expressions told her that she had found one: *trade*.

"Trade," she repeated and handed a ruby to an unarmed Shawnee.

He glanced at it, but smirked and gave it back. The man picked up a rock from the ground and mocked her offering, drawing laughs from the other three. He threw the rock back to the ground and approached Nelson.

"Trade m'seewa," he said. "M'seewa," he repeated as he rubbed

Nelson's long neck.

"Horse," Hercules responded. "M'seewa is horse!" Ona looked on with skepticism. She knew Hercules would jump at the chance to get rid of Nelson.

"We want food. Food and shelter," Hercules continued. He made hand gestures to communicate, lifting his fingers to his mouth and drawing an imaginary box around his head. "We trade m'seewa for food and shelter."

The two runaways were dangerously low on bread since more than half of their supply had been ruined, stained in the blood of George Washington. Hercules kept a few of the soaked loaves, in case of the unthinkable—the worst possible scenario in which they had no choice but to eat the bloody dough. Flies swarmed in a frolic around their food supply. In desperate need of fresh food, they had to consider parting ways with Nelson. The aging horse growled a soft, low tone, and his eyes stayed fixed on the unarmed Indian.

"You'll be better off, old Nelson," whispered Hercules.

After another thirty minutes of tedious negotiations, the Shawnees agreed to escort Ona and Hercules back to their camp. Nelson would be the prize for some basic accommodations. The party traveled north to the Ohio Country, straight into a war zone. Gunshots and the screams of dying men in the distance—the sordid sounds of death—haunted the woods as they marched forward. The National States army plowed across Ohio with ease, paying little to no regard for the rules of warfare. Nelson looked the most comfortable with this setting compared to the rest of the party.

After stopping twice to provide a proper burial for the dead bodies they found cluttered in the forest, the Shawnees found a spot to rest that was a safe distance away from the bloodshed, a wooded area, again concealed from the moonlight. An aura of sadness surrounded them as they reflected on their loved ones who were being slaughtered by Alexander Hamilton's new army. Ona watched them pray to the Great Spirit. They prayed for their tribe, hoping that Chief Blue Jacket would still be alive when they returned.

For the first time since Mount Vernon, Ona felt a slight sense of security, knowing that she had made it out of Columbia and that her new acquaintances did not intend to kill her—at least not for now. Events had made it clear that she and Hercules had followed the Potomac River for too long, and too far west on their escape route. This was not Philadelphia—but it was no slave plantation either. Ohio felt strange, but beautiful. She had never seen such colors in the trees. Red, yellow, orange—like huge, fanning flames, cooled off by a biting breeze. The air tasted different to her, a pure chill that tasted like a calm wind at the gates of heaven compared to the flavor of blood that had plagued her insides since leaving Mount Vernon.

Ona lay down for a peaceful sleep on a bed of leaves; her body tingled. She wore one of Hercules's gigantic shirts, but blood still coated her hands and her face. It clumped in her hair. Despite her incriminating appearance, she stretched out her body and smiled. Ona closed her eyes, not knowing what tomorrow would bring. Tomorrow promised struggle and triumph. There would be fear and joy, and there would be freedom. She fell asleep in an instant, with Hercules lying by her side.

Ona's sleep lasted well into the morning. She remained in the leaves while Hercules and the four Shawnee Indians began their day. Basking in the brisk morning air, she awoke to the sensation of an acorn pelting her in the forehead. Hercules tossed the acorn to wake her in a playful gesture. A second acorn struck her thigh and commanded not just Ona's attention, but the attention of ten gray squirrels. The squirrels scattered, some running over Ona's body. Frightened, she jumped to her feet and bolted around in circles, trying to escape the little creatures.

"Hercules!" Her voice echoed throughout the forest.

Hercules shrieked in laughter, unable to stand straight. The Shawnees laughed even louder. Although at Ona's expense, the little joke began a communal bond with the Indians. They all laughed together.

"Go on, laugh it up," she said. "Jus' wait 'til you all go to sleep. You'll get yours. All of you."

"Haniwa Miskwaawi," one of the tribesmen said, laughing harder. "Haniwa Miskwaawi."

Ona couldn't comprehend a word of their language, but over the next few days she understood that "Haniwa Miskwaawi" was a nickname they had assigned her. They addressed her directly as "Haniwa Miskwaawi."

Their journey would last another week. One more week to Chief Blue Jacket and the Shawnee camp—assuming there was anything left of it.

In New York, the work of a spy came easily to Jonathan Taylor. He concocted a believable backstory and spoon-fed it to Aaron Burr, who now believed Jonathan was a freedman who'd inherited some money upon the death of his white uncle. Like everyone else in the city, he had come to get rich quick.

Jonathan's instructions were clear: Gather intelligence on Burr and report it to Alexander Hamilton, forthwith. Of particular interest were Burr's political beliefs and any possible plot to undermine Hamilton. Also, what information could be used against the aspiring statesman? What was most important to him? What information might embarrass him?

Jonathan struggled to pinpoint Burr's true political beliefs because Burr made a habit of pandering to whomever he was speaking to at the moment. At times, he seemed to hold genuine antislavery views and concern for the future of former slaves. However, when speaking to the rowdy, tavern crowd, Burr found it convenient to scorn free blacks and runaways. Jonathan did his best to provide an accurate report to the supreme leader. He had an important job and a responsibility to do it well, for his own sake and out of respect for James Madison, who had vouched for him.

Jonathan complied by sending two letters each week back to Philadelphia. They arrived at a modest, one-story building on Chestnut Street, built for the sole purpose of funneling clandestine communications. He was to address the letters to Mr. Samuel Lion, code for "supreme leader." Jonathan even took the liberty to disguise his own name with his initials, signing the name Joseph Teller. He had plenty to write about as New York's gubernatorial election approached.

New York City, NY
November 4, 1790

Dearest Mr. Lion,

Aaron Burr feels confident that a solid coalition of voters will sweep him to victory on Election Day. He refuses to openly campaign for office, other than the occasional speech at a coffee house or tavern. His charisma and oratorical skills increase by the day. Followers of Burr spread propaganda in the city newspapers as the election nears. In private, he confesses insecurities surrounding his age. Some have accused him of being too young for the governorship. He does not relent in criticizing what he calls an "overreach of power" on the federal level. The Federal Palace and the National States army have both been subject to his relentless attacks. He continues his pledge to strengthen the New York militia so that this state will not depend on the federal government for protection. He has eased criticism of the National States Bank because most men in New York approve of such an institution, in the hopes that a branch of the bank will be located in New York City. He now publicly advocates strong support for France during their tumultuous revolution. Enthusiasm for his candidacy continues to grow. Daughter Theodosia has turned seven years of age. Mr. Burr dotes on the girl. I will alert you of election results as soon as possible.

Your most humble servant,
Joseph Teller

No sooner than Jonathan had finished signing the coded name, a jolly Aaron Burr snuck up behind him and patted him on the back.

"Working on your memoirs, Mr. Taylor?"

Close call, Jonathan thought to himself. "Something like that," he responded in a nervous voice. He stuffed the letter into his satchel.

Other than Burr, very few white customers would socialize with a black man, so Jonathan sat alone most days. He would have to be more careful in the future and write from the privacy of his room above the Merchant's Coffee House.

"I say, Mr. Taylor, just between you and me, I imagine someday a Negro like you voting in New York elections. Now wouldn't that be something?"

"I imagine the same thing, sir."

"But Montgomery. Montgomery must be the testing ground. Ohio, too," Burr demanded. "More Negroes migrate to the West every day. Land is abundant. Many white farmers from Montgomery have moved to Saratoga in fear of the supreme leader. Montgomery is becoming the safe haven that I predicted, and once this bloody Indian war comes to an end, Ohio will follow suit. Negroes and Indians will be able to flourish side by side, without interfering with the progress of Anglo-America."

Jonathan sipped his tea to avoid smirking at the thought of blacks "interfering" with white progress. It also sounded odd for Burr to advocate for Indians. He had always referred to them as "Lucifer's children" until now.

Burr's eyes gleamed with merriment. "Did you know that just this past week, President Henry of Columbia criticized the National States for not securing the borders and for allowing his escaped slaves to find safety in Montgomery and Ohio? He even accuses Hamilton of assisting in the relocation. Hell, Hamilton may even be doing it. Even Patrick Henry recognizes the opportunities in the West!"

"Of course, they will need more than just land," said Jonathan. "Roads, canals, and how about a branch of that bank to lend money? Schools for the children. A university. Learning to read transformed my life for the better, and the citizens of Montgomery should have the same opportunity. But I doubt Philadelphia is interested in building up the young state with resources and capital. I've heard Montgomery's capital city—Buffalo, is it?—has but a few office buildings right now. It will take much more effort and commitment to realize this safe haven that you speak of."

An uninterested Burr looked over Jonathan's shoulder for some potential voters to solicit. "Well, the internal improvements in Buffalo are projects for their local and state governments to take on if Mr. Hamilton chooses to ignore them."

"So you would send people to an empty wilderness without assistance? It sounds like kicking them out of their home. People will say you have no principles," Jonathan fired back, regaining Burr's attention.

"What exactly do mean, man? I have done more for the advancement of your people than any other politician in New York."

"I mean just what I say. It is often necessary to read between the lines to determine your true principles. You are against a bank one day, and for it the next. The native tribes are monsters today and men tomorrow. You speak out against slavery with passion burning in your eyes, yet you continue to own a manservant. Talk straight with me, sir. I have no vote for you to lose, for I haven't got the right. Do you possess authentic concern for the welfare of these people in Montgomery, or are you just interested in getting them out of New York, out of the way? Is Montgomery a haven or a prison?"

For the first time since they'd known each other, Burr took offense. He paused to adjust the white collar underneath his dusty black jacket. "Mr. Taylor would like to know my principles, yes?" he said. "What I stand for?"

"Yes, sir."

"Well, here it is. I believe in representing the people. Representative democracy. If elected, I will do my best to represent the ideas of these ordinary New York citizens. It would be selfish of me to only represent my own passions. So, even though I personally despise the idea of a national bank, the people of New York welcome the idea, and I shall represent them. Now, Jonathan, in regards to the general welfare of others, men like you and I are more astute than the ordinary citizen. We understand the human experience and what it is to suffer, to sacrifice. Your ideas are good ones. And someday, Jonathan, the world will be ready for them. But the simple fact is that right now, at this very moment in our history, the world is not ready. Now, what is a politician to do until the world is ready? Sit here in a tavern? Get liquored up? Give up? No, sir. I will carry on until the world is ready."

"And if the people you represent want to strip former slaves of their rights? Suppose they condone a return to slavery. Will you represent them then?"

"Ah, but they do *not* condone such barbarity. A majority will not advocate for such extreme positions. A few oddballs here and there, yes. But never a majority of a truly representative democracy. That comes from the philosophy of a wise man, James Madison. If you wish to understand my principles, I would suggest you read the writings of James Madison. Are you familiar with Madison?"

"Indeed, I am, Mr. Burr. Indeed, I am."

The combination of sweat and oil on the body of an auction slave produced such a radiant glimmer that a prospective buyer could catch a glimpse of his own reflection by gazing into the torso.

"This one, strong as an ox!" the auctioneer exclaimed. "Age between twenty and twenty-two. You gentlemen can examine its teeth to confirm."

The slave market in Charleston, South Carolina, was hot as an oven—always hot. Even in the winter months when the temperature lingered around sixty degrees, the cramped, reeking slave chambers felt like it was ninety. Vice President Pinckney took the man up on his offer to examine the slave's teeth. He paid particular attention to their color and how worn down the molars looked. He was meticulous in purchasing slaves, even taking an opportunity to smell the slave's breath, to rule out any stomach ailments. Pinckney pried the young man's lips open with his mud-caked fingers and sniffed a healthy whiff of organic fish odor with a little metallic scent. No acid. Very good.

"Yep. This one'll do," he concluded.

Uncomfortable with the ritual, Patrick Henry stood by and wiped the sweat from his forehead. He'd owned plenty of slaves in his life, but why should the president of Columbia be responsible for buying the government's slaves himself? It did keep with his image of being a common man of the people. Still, he felt nauseated.

"That makes ten fine work slaves," Pinckney said, confident in his choices. "Trust me, Mr. President, this property is plenty capable of building up Richmond to your liking."

Henry and his vice president never agreed on much; buying slaves was no different. The president balked at the idea of separating slaves from their families, but Pinckney would have it no other way. Even as the children of his new merchandise wept in the corner of the room, pleading for their fathers to stay, Pinckney was insistent.

"I have managed a plantation for most of my life. I do not claim expertise in much, except military strategy and human property—especially the latter. We just spent two delightful days at my home, and the evidence speaks for itself. Did you notice any inefficiency whatsoever?"

"Of course not," Henry replied. "Your skill is beyond reproach."

"And in my expert opinion, sir, you do not want these niggers' wives and children anywhere around to distract them from their work. It is vital work of the state."

"Your experience is admirable, Charles, but after two wives and fifteen children of my own, my expertise happens to be on the subject of family. It pains me every day to leave Dorothea to raise our children alone. I would give anything for her to be with me in Richmond, and I would not wish the pain on my worst enemy, let alone some helpless slave."

"And that is exactly the point," Pinckney said. "You would do anything for your family! You would fight for your family! Do you really want these niggers fighting for theirs? Will you put up with that whining bitch over there every time her husband takes a whip? Will you fight off that greased animal when he defends his children's honor? I think not."

Henry shook his head, as if to say, "Goddamn it, you're right."

"Trust me. If you want roads in and out of Richmond—if you want the place to look like a functioning capital city—then separation is the only way."

And with that, the matter was settled. Henry turned to the slave auctioneer for some conversation with common folk. "Been busy here, have you?"

"Busy? Yessum, Mr. President," the man answered in a desultory Southern drawl. "But hawd, hawd work, slavin' is. Hawda than it eva been." He wore white pants, a white shirt stained in yellow perspiration, a beige jacket, tan suspenders, and a canary-yellow hat. It would be quite an undertaking to find someone blander than this scrawny merchant. "Hawd work," he said, even slower this time. They strolled outside together.

"But profitable, I trust." Henry maintained his politician's smile, especially since a crowd of onlookers had gathered after hearing the man address him as "Mr. President."

"Profitable eee-nough, I s'pose. But more and more niggas come through here every day. We get overrun. Yankees up north done banned slavery—demand go down. Price of a slave gone down, down, down. You get a fine house nigga for half of what you'd have paid five years ago."

Henry tried to interject, but the slaver was not finished.

"Slaves nowadays run like the wind, too. Runnin' north to Montgomery and runnin' south into Flawda. Every day, escape to Flawda. I can't no more guarantee property's a long-term investment. Price goes down, down, down."

"Now, that needs corrected," Henry said to the vice president. "We have a distinct economic advantage over the National States, and we must maintain it. We have an economy that actually produces things: sugar, rice, tobacco, wheat. What does the NSA produce? Nothing. An economy based on worthless greenbacks and placing bets on how much someone might pay for a piece of land. Sooner or later, they'll come begging us for food. And what will they have to trade us? Dirt. Dirt and worthless paper currency."

Pinckney nodded in agreement. "And the crops they do produce are harvested by *our* escaped slaves in Pennsylvania and that wretched state of Montgomery. Hamilton speaks of industrializing. New industries, manufacturing in New York, Philadelphia, Pittsburgh, Buffalo. But who will do the work of this industry? Inferior runaway slaves? That's laughable."

The beige man returned to the auction block and attracted most of the small crowd with him. Pinckney decided to address the elephant in the room. "Florida, Mr. President."

Henry listened, but this time would not shake his head to say, "Goddamn it, you're right."

"There has been violence on the border for over a month. Blood has been spilled. The blood of innocent Georgia planters merely trying to recover their property."

"And the Georgia militia will be called upon to handle the matter. That is in addition to our federal agents to repossess property." The president's tone grew a bit feisty. He had become the least popular man in Georgia as more escaped slaves found freedom in Florida and more slave catchers died on the hunt.

"Mr. President, I beseech you! Spanish Florida has become a powerful threat. Its population has doubled with our escaped slaves, Indian tribes, and refugees from the French colony of Saint-Domingue. Slaves have rebelled against the French and taken control of the island they now call Haiti. Call on Congress to raise an army. The Georgia militia will not suffice. I assure you, this is much different than Alexander Hamilton's silly quarrel with a feeble band of Shawnee. The Georgians are fighting Seminole Indians. Creek and Chickasaw, as well. These are vicious warriors, much more skilled, and with the backing of Spain. For all intents and purposes, the state of Georgia is at war with Spain—not to mention with wild runaways, thirsty for revenge."

"Then South Carolina's militia should be more than willing to help," he said, putting the South Carolinian on the spot. "North Carolina, too. I did not risk my life and honor waging war against a tyrannical English army only to construct a new army that would abuse the rights of my countrymen just the same. I will not abandon my values, and my values dictate that I stand against tyranny in all its forms, including the form of a national army."

"But sir, the real tyranny is Spanish Florida, thieving property from decent Georgians! Are you aware that the Spanish lure them in? They promise freedom to escaped slaves if they convert to Catholicism. Just like the promise of freedom in Montgomery. Calling out the militia further compounds the problem. When militiamen leave their plantations to take up arms, they leave more unsupervised slaves and increase the likelihood of escape."

"Mr. Pinckney, I know my intransigence incenses you, but my values are impenetrable. I will not raise an army. This will be the confederation to prove, once and for all, that self-government must survive by self-defense. Our citizens have a constitutional right to bear arms, and are duty bound to defend our nation with militia."

"Mr. President!" a voice called out in the distance, interrupting the debate. It echoed from no particular direction. Henry and Pinckney both turned to look. "Mr. President!" the voice called, coming closer. Henry squinted to see a figure approaching. In a flash, Pinckney's massive body projected through the air and sacked the man. A shot rang out, and gun smoke blurred the scene.

The vice president overpowered the man like a predator hunting vermin. With one arm lassoed around the assailant's neck, he ripped him up from the ground, holding the confiscated dueling pistol in his other hand.

"For the patriots of Georgia!" the man screamed out before getting pistol-whipped in the face. Blood dripped between his teeth.

An angered Pinckney shouted out, "Rope! Someone get a rope!" He turned to the president. "We'll hang 'em right there from that elm," he said, pistol-whipping the man again, just for the satisfaction.

Henry brushed off the dust and smoke from his jacket and regained his composure. The bullet had missed and gone straight up to the sky.

"We will do no such thing," he said, taking the gun from Pinckney's hand. "Belay that order! Someone get this man a lawyer!"

A shocked Pinckney loosened his grip on the man.

"A lawyer," Henry repeated. "I will never compromise my values. Never. This man has a right to legal counsel, and Columbia has no standing army. These are non-negotiable." With fire burning in his eyes, Henry stared down the would-be assassin. "May God have mercy on your soul."

Chapter 10

Alexander Hamilton preferred running the National States Government by himself, but he discovered the need for a cabinet, similar to Prime Minster Adams's Privy Council in New England. Adams had assembled a brilliant council in Oliver Wolcott, Timothy Pickering, Elbridge Gerry, and Henry Knox. Hamilton regretted losing such honorable statesmen with New England's secession. After deep consideration, the supreme leader had decided on three trustworthy patriots for his cabinet: Robert Morris, Jonathan Dayton, and Rufus King.

No one in the National States could possibly be more qualified for the post of treasury secretary than Pennsylvania's Robert Morris. He demonstrated unwavering loyalty to Hamilton at the Second Constitutional Convention, and he understood finance almost as well as the supreme leader himself. Morris would oversee all operations of the National States Bank, including printing paper money, collecting tariffs, and issuing government bonds.

Hamilton chose Secretary of State Rufus King of New York and Attorney General Jonathan Dayton of New Jersey for their youth and their eagerness to please the supreme leader, although this was about all they shared in common. Jonathan Dayton's handsome features and elegant style projected an air of entitlement. His chiseled bone structure made his face resemble the Great Sphinx of Giza. Rufus King, on the other hand, was more introverted, rough around the edges, extraordinarily ugly with pockets of baby fat and scabs staining the blotchy, red skin of his face. Dayton wore a powdered wig groomed to perfection, while vines of thinning hair crawled down the sides of Rufus King's scalp, hanging on in a desperate attempt to conceal the baldness of such a young man.

In addition to the cabinet, Anthony Wayne would serve as commander general of the National States army. Wayne continued to spend his days hunting down Chief Blue Jacket and the Shawnee Indians in the Ohio Territory with spectacular success.

For his first cabinet meeting in the new Federal Palace, the supreme leader sat behind his gold-trimmed desk, gazing out at his new group of advisors. A large, awkward-looking box sat in the corner of his office, overflowing with a long rope, sharp pieces of metal, and wooden parts.

"Are you building a playground?" Morris joked.

"Oh, that? I call it the 'French contraption.' It's a gift; arrived yesterday from the revolutionaries in France. I haven't a clue as to what it is, or its purpose."

"The French contraption," Morris repeated. "Curious."

Hamilton shook his head. "They can send all the gifts they want; I will never throw my support behind bloody mobs against the rule of law." His three cabinet members all nodded their heads in agreement. "But first thing is first. How soon until we capture the conspirators in Washington's death? I want them hanging on display in the capital for all to see."

An awkward silence told Hamilton that very little progress had been made.

Rufus King broke the silence. "As long as they are not arrested in Columbia, I think it's safe to say that the two slaves have made it across the border into our country. Pennsylvania or Montgomery would be their best bet."

"We must arrest them before Henry gets his hands on them. And we will not extradite them to Columbia. Never. Their crime is treason here, as much as there. Rufus, you will continue to put pressure on the local authorities in Pennsylvania and Montgomery. And General Wayne will find them if they go anywhere near Ohio."

"Yes, Your Majesty."

"Now, speaking of Ohio, gentlemen, expansion of the National States is a top priority. America first. We must think bigger. Much bigger," Hamilton challenged them.

As usual, Jonathan Dayton rushed to respond. "Your Majesty, there are big plans to attract settlement in Ohio. We will sell off tracts of land and provide Mr. Morris with an impressive stream of revenue—just as soon as Blue Jacket and his followers are removed."

"Which is any day now," King interjected. "The Indian alliance is falling to pieces. Some tribes are abandoning the fight, and we've enlisted support of the Seneca Indians. Anthony Wayne is the most skilled general in the National States, aside from you, Your Majesty. Wayne will deliver complete and total victory. Not just defeating the Shawnee in some battles, but completely eliminating them from our midst."

"Yes, but even bigger! Bigger than Ohio," Hamilton insisted. "The entire Northwest Territory is ours for the taking. I have decreed this to the public. Columbia and New England chose to secede from us. Therefore, all lands and treaties of the former United States belong to us. That includes the Northwest."

"We've already begun to survey those lands, Your Majesty," Dayton said, desperate for approval, pushing back the flowing, white locks of his wig.

"Very good, Jonathan," Hamilton lauded, as a knock on the door interrupted him. "Yes?"

One of the six armed guards poked his head in. Security had doubled since the attempt on Patrick Henry's life.

"The Spanish ambassador has arrived, Your Majesty. Will you receive him now?"

"Of course. Send him in at once." Hamilton struck a gallant pose behind his desk.

Don Diego de Gardoqui entered the office and bowed down before the supreme leader. His perfect posture; flowing, gray hair; and pristine, red jacket, decorated in gold, made him look like a much older version of Jonathan Dayton. Robert Morris noticed the resemblance and snickered. After a short exchange of pleasantries, they got straight to business.

"Our business here today is Florida, yes?" Hamilton enquired.

"It is, indeed, Your Majesty. Spanish Florida is under siege. Columbian robbers enter the colony at will to recover slaves, and they partake in illegal filibustering. They often become violent in their quest and have even gone so far as to kidnap innocent Africans, enslaving Spanish citizens. We've also had a young Spanish government official murdered. His Majesty, King Charles IV, offers his utmost gratitude for your assistance."

"And what assistance could I possibly provide to Florida that the king of Spain cannot?"

"Supplies, weapons, soldiers. These can be transported much faster from your country than from Spain. The king is interested in securing a permanent settlement in West Florida. And we know you would have no qualms with a Columbian defeat. We would appreciate any assistance you may be able to offer."

"No qualms whatsoever," Hamilton said. "Supplies and weapons can certainly be negotiated. Mr. King here would be happy to make accommodations. Mr. Morris can also arrange any financial assistance you may need. But National States soldiers are fighting in Ohio to protect our borders. I'm afraid it will be hard to provide boots on the ground."

The ambassador tilted his head with a half-smile, hoping for more aid.

"But may I suggest an alternative route?" Hamilton continued. "Why be satisfied with just West Florida? The Confederation of Columbia has no army. None, whatsoever. The Spanish military could overrun the Georgia militia and conquer the entire state. Georgia barely has a population, and half of it is enslaved. Those slaves will rebel and join your fight."

"These military decisions will be made at higher levels of government—by King Charles," Diego replied.

"And if he were to make this decision, sir, then the National States would be prepared to offer as much assistance as necessary. Even soldiers, though I doubt they will be required." Hamilton seethed with ambition. "Take Georgia. But only Georgia," he cautioned. "Any more would entice President Henry to raise a national army. So long as each state depends on untrained militia, we could pick off one state at a time from this quasi country. Georgia could be taken so fast that Patrick Henry would not even know until it's gone. And if Spain hesitates to conquer Columbia, I can assure you France will not. Napoleon will be here personally to reestablish a French presence in North America. That benefits neither of us."

Diego eyed the supreme leader with suspicion. "Why do you encourage such full-scale war? How do you benefit from Columbia's loss of Georgia? I must assume you would want something in return for such support."

"Yes, of course," Hamilton smiled. Now they were negotiating.

The ambassador continued. "Spain would be willing to open up more navigation along the Mississippi River, or perhaps land ownership in this Georgia territory?"

"Louisiana!" The room went silent. "Louisiana," Jonathan Dayton burst out the word again.

Hamilton had a shocked look on his face. Rufus King fumed in anger, about to explode like the pus from one of his warts.

"We help you take Georgia, and you cede the Louisiana Territory to the NSA." Dayton's body shivered as he made such an audacious proposal. "We must think bigger."

Having overcome his bewilderment, the supreme leader chimed in. "Now that sounds fair! Georgia for Louisiana."

Don Diego shook his head with derision. "Surely you jest, young man. Spanish Louisiana is ten times the size of Georgia."

"But Georgia is ten times more productive and profitable." Dayton didn't back down. He was too skilled a lawyer. "Savannah? Augusta? Have you been to these places? We're talking about some of the most fertile soil and the greenest grass in the world. That is no exaggeration. In the *world*. Now what does Louisiana have to offer? Frozen tundra and savage Indians."

Hamilton jumped back in the discussion before Dayton offended the ambassador. "We both know that Spain has overextended itself in North America. There are not enough Spaniards in Spain to come settle this vast land. It sits vacant, undeveloped and unmanaged to our west. We, on the other hand, have a growing population. Europeans continue to flee the chaos in France and England. We are industrializing. We could settle the land and, in the long run, benefit Spain through trade."

Ambassador Diego rocked his head back and forth. "Again, this is all above my authority. However, I can guarantee one thing: The Crown could never part with New Orleans. It is far too valuable in terms of commerce.

Any negotiation of this sort must be for Upper Louisiana only. Lower Louisiana is off the table. Not to mention that a large price tag would need to be negotiated as well."

"Of course, my friend," Hamilton agreed. "You take this proposal back to King Charles—the sale of Upper Louisiana in exchange for military assistance in the acquisition of Georgia."

"And the sale would not transpire until after such acquisition of Georgia is accomplished," Diego asserted.

"A reasonable arrangement, indeed," Hamilton affirmed.

The conquest of Georgia could not possibly fail. The supreme leader and Spanish ambassador shook hands. Jonathan Dayton had never felt so alive.

"Goddamn it! Damn that man to hell!" Shards of broken glass formed a puzzle on the coffee house floor. "Schuyler? Philip Schuyler? Is this some sick prank? Schuyler!" Aaron Burr grunted like a beast, lifted another table with all his might, and tossed it on its side, shattering three more bottles in the commotion. Lydia and two other prostitutes hurried out the front door to safety as Burr continued his rage.

"Philip Schuyler, the father-in-law of the supreme leader! His goddamn father-in-law! Governor Schuyler? The man is older than the original dirt brought here from Amsterdam! I thought they put his corpse underground years ago. Is he even a National States citizen? The man is from Albany, Saratoga! A New England state! He will be the governor of New York?! And you people just sit here, sipping your whiskey as if no usurpation has taken place!"

Burr intended to spend the day making arrangements for his move into the governor's mansion, but the election results had interfered with his plan. He reached underneath the closest tabletop for another show of strength, but this time the side-whiskered bartender seized his arms from behind. He tossed Burr's body like a sack of trash into a broken chair that remained standing on the glass shards.

"Now you're gonna sit your ass down and shut the hell up! You hear me?"

Burr turned his head in disdain, but the bartender continued to lecture him.

"After you done cooled off, you're gonna clean up this mess, and then you and me are gonna have a nice chat about how you'll be paying for the damage you done here."

Burr tried to compose himself, but still ignored the man.

"I gotta mind to kick you outta here for good," the barkeep said, raising his voice, chiding the petulant statesman.

"Settle down, Burr," a voice came from the bar. "You lost. We all lose sometimes, so deal with it. Pull yourself up like a man and move on."

Burr was about to stand again until the overweight bartender stomped on his foot. The low, squeaky chair would have to do.

"You cannot seriously believe that I lost the election. You cannot, in all good conscience, submit to the idea that Alexander Hamilton's father-in-law, never even nominated for the office, secured more votes than I did."

"Well, it seems he did," the man at the bar responded. "Now, who do you suppose would have the gall to cook up an election like that?"

"Good God! Do I have to spell it out for you? He's the man's father-in-law. And surprise, surprise, another printing press went up in flames two nights ago. The one newspaper that would dare investigate such impropriety—ashes—burned to the ground. You think that's coincidence, do you?"

A little less drunk than usual, but drenched in sweat just the same, fat Benjamin Winthrop came to Burr's defense. "There were quite a few suits from Philadelphia here on Election Day, I can tell you that. And they didn't spend much money. Had a few drinks, saw the sights, laid a few whores, and off they went. Didn't make one trade." Winthrop usually just doused his liver with whiskey and flirted with the prostitutes, but the girls had all run off, and he was always up for a good conspiracy theory.

"Plus, an inflated number of votes cast on Staten Island," Burr added.

Jonathan Taylor watched on, just as puzzled as Burr. "Be careful, Mr. Burr," he said. "If I understand you correctly, you accuse the supreme leader of fraud and arson."

"I accuse him of total usurpation of liberty!"

But the more he shouted, the less anyone in the Merchant's Coffee House bothered to care. They'd done their civic duty. Every last one of them had voted for Burr, but it wasn't Burr's day. Would a Governor Schuyler affect the lives of these men any differently than would a Governor Burr? They thought not. So long as they were free to get rich, politics was just a sideshow.

"What this nation needs is a genuine Whig Party. A party true to Whig principles, not under the influence of aristocratic families, nor the moneyed interests alone," Burr rambled as he began picking up the shiny pieces of glass from the floor. "A Whig Party to represent the middling classes of New York. And not just New York, but all of the National States. Ouch!" he cried, cut by a piece of glass. "We'll hit Hamilton where it hurts—in his prized federal government. Elect a few Whigs to Congress to shake things up."

By now, Jonathan was bent over, picking at the broken glass as well. "But Mr. Burr, you speak of faction. You yourself have warned against the dangers of faction."

"You are correct, sir. I abhor it. But it is a small price to pay for checking the power of the supreme leader. Now, a newspaper will be essential. And of course, security for such an operation, given the suspicious bad luck our press has had with spontaneous combustion."

Burr lectured Jonathan for another hour, speaking with great fury and passion, and he ended up recruiting the first member of his Whig Party—the very spy who was sent to destroy him.

Jonathan lay awake in mental turmoil, struggling to word his latest report to Alexander Hamilton. He made countless late-night edits, changed a word here, a phrase there, and then lay back down to bed for ten minutes before rising again to edit the edits. "Burr aspires to political faction," or "Burr excites more citizens to participate in government." *The man poses no dire threat whatsoever*, he thought. Was it a "victimized press," or "the unlucky casualty of happenstance"? He finally resigned to the fact that honesty would be the best strategy for him to pursue if he ever wanted a good night's sleep again.

"Burr continues to sow the seeds of faction, though with no malice of heart. He has begun the work of politicking for a new Whig Party, a party to represent the interests of common New Yorkers, laborers, freed slaves, the unconnected, even the interests of women. His wife, Theodosia, no doubt influences his thoughts on the latter. She comes from a proper upbringing and the finest quality of education. Plans have already begun for a Whig newspaper to spread propaganda. The location of this press is still undecided and will be kept secret due to the suspicions of political rivals engaging in extralegal means to abolish dissent. I will, of course, alert you to the location of this press as soon as possible.

"He has taken this route in the stead of challenging the election results in court. Burr maintains that any legal challenge would be futile in the face of federalist judges who dominate the courts. In public, he maintains that the recent election was riddled with fraud, in a conspiracy that reaches the highest levels of government, including the supreme leader of the National States of America."

Hercules stared, dumbfounded in the presence of Chief Blue Jacket. The great Shawnee warrior, the feared villain of so many Americans, the evil renegade who had killed so many settlers, looked so timid and fragile that the slightest breeze would blow him away with the wind. His skin appeared white, no darker than George Washington's, and he wore a red jacket, a British redcoat, despite his moniker that struck fear in the hearts of so many. Frail, bald, and almost as thin as young Ona, he faked a pitiful smile for his two guests, revealing the extreme melancholy that had overtaken his tribe and his soul.

They sat together to share a peace pipe in a wigwam buried deep in the Ohio Territory. Hercules held his arm around Ona as she trembled like the last leaves of autumn, never having experienced cold quite like winter in Ohio. She curled up tight in a blanket of buffalo fur, offered by their host.

Hercules was unimpressed with the peace offering, having tasted the finest tobacco of Virginia at Mount Vernon. Blue Jacket's tobacco had a bitter, grassy flavor and no particular odor—other than pure smoke combined with the rotting smell that flew throughout the camp since they'd arrived. The stale stench of death stung in his nostrils.

"I apologize for such a meager offering to guests who have traveled such a long way." Blue Jacket spoke perfect English, also not what the two fugitives had expected. "You are Chasing Honey, of whom my tribesmen have spoken," he said, passing the pipe to Hercules. "And your companion, Red Squirrel."

They both stayed silent, confused. "Red Squirrel," the chief repeated. "Haniwa Miskwaawi."

"Ah ha," Ona said, recognizing her new name. "Red Squirrel and Chasing Honey."

She glared up at Hercules. Her bloodstained clothing and her dalliance with the squirrels had earned her the nickname. The new Indian name for Hercules also made sense. Early in their journey, when the honeybees still gathered, Hercules had tried to extract some honey from a beehive as a token of good faith to his Shawnee escorts. To everyone's amusement, he'd failed in the attempt, forced to flee from an angry swarm of fierce, yellow warriors. The name "Chasing Honey" sounded appropriate. Neither escapee objected to the new names. They needed a new identity, now that most people on the continent yearned to see them hang for aiding in the murder of George Washington.

"We thank you for shelter and what food is available, great chief." Addressing royalty was nothing new to Hercules. "Our horse is strong and speedy and will serve you well." As he spoke, Hercules looked outside at Nelson searching for hay in Blue Jacket's ransacked camp. He wondered if they wouldn't be eating old Nelson for dinner any time soon.

"You are welcome to share in whatever the Great Spirit has left to deliver," the chief said. "But I am afraid the white man takes faster than the Great Spirit can replenish. The National States army massacres our people, but also wages war on the Great Spirit itself. They have burned our homes, destroyed our crops, assaulted our women, children; they spare no bird of the air nor fish of the sea."

Hercules sighed. "Americans crazy 'bout their property, and they fight like hell to defend it."

Blue Jacket choked as black smoke rushed out of his nostrils. "*Their* property, you say? *Defend*, you say?"

Hercules dropped his head low and spoke the first words that rushed to his mind. "Sorry, mastuh"—even though he'd promised himself never to speak those words again.

"Chief Hamilton is a new breed, Chasing Honey. He will stop at nothing but total destruction of our people. He aims much further than taking our land. He would rid this place of Shawnee and every other tribe if he could, and my greatest fear is that he is succeeding. This place was once full of our people, our culture. Families, happiness, abundance of nourishment for the body and mind. Now I am left with this putrefied tobacco, some corn, and one hundred warriors. One hundred are all that remain."

"Have your people resettled? West?" Hercules enquired, desperate for a safe hideout.

Blue Jacket paused, acknowledging the dead souls of whom he spoke. "Very few have fled. Some to the west, some south—Florida, if they are lucky. Most were fearless warriors. Thousands defeated Chief St. Clair's army. We stood our ground. Then Hamilton sent enough white men to conquer the world over. Those thousands of souls are what you smell across this wasted wilderness. Our lands have become nothing more than one big burial ground. You should be quite familiar with the white man's ways," he continued. "I understand they have enslaved you both before your arrival here, yes?"

Ona and Hercules both nodded, hoping Blue Jacket was ignorant to the fact that the two most-wanted fugitives in North America sat in his wigwam. The chief could give them up in exchange for Shawnee land undisturbed for generations. Stories would be written about the great Chief Blue Jacket and his courageous capture of the most vicious slaves in America. Blue Jacket could have such fame and fortune.

"Slaves from birth," Red Squirrel acknowledged. "And we'll never go back."

"Why do you suppose the white man enslaves your people, but slaughters mine? Why not enslave or slaughter us all? What difference would it make?"

Chasing Honey exhaled a thick cloud of soot as he spoke. "I guess your people don't make good slaves. And mine don't make good corpses."

"And what of the white man? Their day will come, too, my friends. My people have shared this land and kept peace for generations, since the Great Spirit brought forth life and the earth. It seems that now our time has run its course. But someday, it will be the white man's turn to be slaves, and the white man's turn to be corpses. Someone else will conquer them as they have conquered us. Then they will know."

Hercules recalled the tales of General Washington, disadvantaged and outnumbered, leading his men to victory. "Is there any fight left in your men? Are they conquered?"

Blue Jacket hung his head in despair. "The enemy is not far off. When they arrive, we will surrender."

In New England, Timothy Pickering rose to become Prime Minister Adams's most trusted advisor. They often dined at the Oliver White Tavern, just outside of Hartford, while construction of the prime minister's official residence was delayed. New England lacked the benefit of slave labor to build its capitol.

The Oliver White Tavern hid in seclusion, far away from distractions. In complete privacy, Adams and Pickering could discuss public policy matters and feast on some of New England's finest cuisine. Adams enjoyed salmon in prawn sauce, a dish to which he had first been introduced by a young Hercules at Mount Vernon many years ago. Tonight, they sat down to oysters in beef sauce with pease porridge, washed down with a thick, dark New England porter.

The prime minister hunched over to devour his meal. He spoke with his mouth full. "These developments in Canada are quite interesting. I am one to believe that the Constitutional Act passed by the British Parliament presents a certain advantage to us."

"And I am one to agree, sir," Pickering said in his usual, cool demeanor.

"The creation of Upper Canada and Lower Canada will allow our government to negotiate and trade with each colony on separate terms. A stronger alliance with both should be the natural outcome. It will build on our cordial relationship with New Brunswick and Nova Scotia." Adams chugged the last of his beer and signaled for another.

"Of course, our pro-French faction will disagree. They will say that you violate the neutrality pledge—favoring Britain over France—same old arguments," Pickering responded, rolling his eyes.

"Well, they'll just have to disagree. It wouldn't be the first time. I have looked at this from every angle, and it makes no sense to sacrifice our good standing with Britain just to appease the French. President Henry may need James Madison to kiss France's ass because Columbia's economy is a slave to agricultural exports, but we don't need to kiss anyone's ass. Regarding our military, I intend to remain neutral. But our fishing, whaling, timber, shipping, and textile industries will flourish through trade with Canada, so long as Hamilton insists upon higher tariffs in the National States."

Pickering nodded in agreement. "It seems King Louis will be gone any day now. Perhaps we renegotiate when a more stable government consolidates power in France. But in the meantime, George Clinton has already begun to organize the pro-French, Anti-Federalist Party. I dare say, Elbridge Gerry may very well resign from the Privy Council and join the old stooge to protest against a stronger alliance with British Canada."

"That is his privilege. And quite frankly, I've grown tired of Gerry's constant dissent. He's a perfect match for George Clinton and his new political party. I shall require more prudence in my council."

"Of course. However, Gerry is quite the orator, quite persuasive. Someone you may want inside your tent instead of out. He will pounce on us in the press. He'll say you would have New England be more Canadian than American. He'll rouse up nationalist sentiments among the masses."

"Well, now, that is interesting." Adams sat up to wipe his mouth. "Our interests do, in fact, align with Canada more than the National States, which envisions military empire, or Columbia, which envisions a slave empire. A British colony, we are not. But to accuse us of having strong cultural ties to Canada is no insult."

Pickering laughed. "I would not say that in too loud a voice," he said, watching the bartender approach with Adams's second glass of porter. "Upper Canada is essentially a colony of loyalist deserters from our revolution. A land of traitors to our cause, according to many."

"I suppose you are correct." Adams replied.

"But you have my full support for trade agreements with Upper and Lower Canada. You would even have my support for a strong military alliance with Great Britain, though I know you remain hesitant."

Adams leaned back to relax, rubbing his satisfied tummy. "You know, Timothy, Dr. Franklin was wrong in his assessment that nothing can be certain except for death and taxes. He was wrong. Even more certain is that Britain and France will be at war with each other more often than not. Should we form this military alliance with King George, it would only drag us into war with France when the hostilities boil up again, which, in turn, means that Columbia would be dragged in to support France. The result? An unnecessary war between New England and Columbia, each doing the bloody bidding of European powers. We may as well be colonies again."

"But, sir—"

"I remain committed to neutrality."

"Of course, Mr. Prime Minister. However, we would indeed win a military contest with Columbia."

"Win? And what do we stand to win? Bragging rights? Pound our chests like a pack of gorillas? I have zero ambition for territorial conquest. All we could ever win is the title of strongest pawn of the British. No, no, no. New England may not be a shark in the sea of world powers, but we shall not be a minnow either."

Pickering swallowed his last oyster. "I cannot argue with that, Mr. Prime Minister. New England is the fortunate beneficiary of your wisdom."

"And yours, as well, Mr. Pickering. Yours, as well."

The two men shared stories of their families for another half hour before mounting their horses for a quaint trip back to Hartford.

Chapter 11

1791

The surrender was not so simple. Commander general of the National States army, Anthony Wayne, arrived with five hundred soldiers dressed in matching blue, and well armed. What was left of the Shawnee war party and their allies fled across the Maumee River, abandoning their muddy settlement. Red Squirrel and Chasing Honey followed, fearful that some ambitious young troop would recognize them as the most-wanted fugitives in the land. Chief Blue Jacket and his brother, Red Pole, stayed back to surrender.

The first line of soldiers advanced on the camp and were greeted by the two brothers, knelt down in prayer to the Great Spirit. At gunpoint, Blue Jacket looked up into the baby-blue eyes of a young, pale-skinned, blond-haired private. The unsteady musket danced back and forth from Blue Jacket's temple to his ear, trembling with the boy's body, quaking in terror. The great Shawnee warrior sensed the boy's trepidation and could easily have overpowered him to confiscate the weapon and scalp him in the process—but there was no use.

Saddened, the chief spoke in a guttural voice. "I am Blue Jacket, chief of the Shawnee. Under protection of the Great Spirit, my people will fight no longer. We put down our guns and tomahawks to rest. We surrender."

The meek, young soldier took a step back, signaling for General Wayne. Hundreds of soldiers emerged from the woods like locusts as Wayne followed on horseback.

"General Wayne, Chief Blue Jacket surrenders," the boy said with a deep sigh, expressing his relief that someone else would take charge from here.

Wayne dismounted his horse, sword in hand. His oversized tri-cornered hat concealed the plumpness of his red face. Known as "Mad Anthony," the nickname suited his short temper.

Still on his knees, Blue Jacket remained calm as ever.

"This one is Blue Jacket?" Wayne nodded toward the chief. "In a British redcoat?"

The men behind him laughed.

"Silence!" His scream echoed through the forest.

Mad Anthony leaned forward and grunted up a thick wad of mucus before letting loose, firing it from his mouth like a cannonball onto Blue Jacket's nose. Before the chief could respond, Wayne's sword rested under his chin, much steadier than the young boy's firearm. The yellow loogy dangled from Blue Jacket's nostril.

"You're damn right you surrender. To the supreme leader of the National States of America, Alexander Hamilton!"

"Hoorah!" The army shouted in unison, again echoing through the woods.

Red Pole spoke, trembling in despair. "We are willing to negotiate prisoner exchange and free passage to new lands." Red feathers waved in the wind above his long, black ponytail. They taunted Mad Anthony, coming closer and closer to touching his thigh.

Wayne grabbed Red Pole by the feathers, almost snapping his neck. "When I want you to speak, I'll tell you to speak, savage!" he shouted, splattering phlegm over Red Pole as well. "And you ain't negotiating a damn thing. You will accept our terms of surrender, whether you like 'em or not." He threw Red Pole back into the mud, overturning him with his moccasins up in the air.

"Nice little place you got here," Wayne addressed Blue Jacket with a sardonic grin. "Where'd all your buddies go? Too scared to come out?" His eyes scanned the abandoned settlement. Not much remained but a few rows of wigwams and a food supply that wouldn't last two weeks. "Burn it," he said.

Red Pole stood in protest. "We surrendered!" Three uniformed soldiers seized him and began to shackle his legs. The prisoner kicked and hissed until a whack over the head with the butt of a rifle knocked him out cold.

"Burn it all down," Wayne repeated the order.

Chief Blue Jacket remained on the ground as a stone. He did not look behind him to witness the barbaric act of torching the homes of the helpless. He did not watch the soldiers abuse his brother. He sat in silence, somber, accepting whatever fate may bring.

The soldiers laughed as they torched each individual dwelling. The tree-bark roofs caught fire much easier than expected, sending enormous smoke plumes into the air. They looted whatever they could get their hands on, which wasn't much. A few blankets, arrows, and Blue Jacket's last bottle of rum. All the food worth taking was a very short supply of corn, beans, and a little squirrel meat.

Blue Jacket smelled the charred remains of his encampment, choking on the smoke. He stood and walked toward the inferno. Standing dangerously close to the heat, his eyes began to water. The skin on his forehead blistered in pain.

Anthony Wayne held his men back as they observed the great Shawnee war chief. "You think he's gonna jump in there? Save us a lot of trouble?" Wayne squinted his eyes.

The lieutenant general by his side interjected. "Sir, the supreme leader's orders are to take him alive."

Mad Anthony nodded his head. "All the same, I'd like to see the son of a bitch do it. Go on in there, buddy."

Another tense minute passed. Blue Jacket began to remove his clothing. First the redcoat, and then the deerskin shirt underneath.

"This is absurd," said the lieutenant, who rushed toward the fire.

By the time he reached Blue Jacket, the chief had tossed his coat and shirt into the raging fire. "If my people must sacrifice their possessions, then so shall I." His clothing lit up and vanished into the blaze. "They return to the Great Spirit. Return to where they came from, as we all must do. Even the white man."

The lieutenant apprehended a shirtless Blue Jacket, covered in sweat from head to toe. He escorted him back to Anthony Wayne. The commander clasped Blue Jacket by the neck and spoke.

"You and your pal there are gonna take a trip with us to Fort Pitt. You'll surrender to the supreme leader himself. But if it were up to me, I'd toss you right in there with your redcoat."

From the other side of the Maumee River, the surviving Shawnee Indians watched their village evaporate to the sky. They mourned together. Chasing Honey held Red Squirrel in his arms. They were running out of advantages.

～

Alexander Hamilton loved a brisk Pennsylvania winter. It brought back memories of assisting General Washington at Valley Forge, the worst winter that he or anyone else who endured the horror could remember. Though two thousand soldiers had succumbed to the cold at Valley Forge, it was there that Hamilton had earned Washington's respect as a military strategist. He looked back with fond memories on Mother Nature's massacre of the Continental Army. Surviving the tragedy proved his superiority in his own mind. Fond memories.

Pittsburgh's winter didn't feel much different. The landscape froze in the color gray, still as a painting. The sound of horse hooves crunching into the frosted grass and the sound of his own breathing echoed in his ears. He enjoyed the powerful gusts of wind, which carried a clean, pure air that he could never breathe in Philadelphia. Hamilton relished the slight flavor of blood that ascended from his lungs as the temperature dropped. Just like Valley Forge.

From the ashes of the Shawnee settlement, General Wayne's army and their captives, Blue Jacket and Red Pole, followed the frozen Ohio River on horseback to Fort Pitt. Delayed by the elements, Hamilton arrived a few days late, eager to end the Indian war. It was time to move on with the work of expanding the National States.

The supreme leader and his entourage arrived on a Sunday, just after dinner. His bodyguards unhitched the carriages upon entering the fortress.

"You gentlemen proceed," Hamilton ordered. "I will show the horses to the stockade."

Always a student of animal behavior, he looked forward to seeing the horses at Fort Pitt.

Barney, the enslaved stableman, welcomed Hamilton at the gates of the stockade with a bow. "It's a honor, supreme leaduh." Though the National States Constitution provided for a gradual abolition of slavery, Barney was one of the many slaves who'd fallen through the cracks and would not see freedom in his lifetime. "Overflowin' with steeds right 'bout now, suh, but we'll make room. Bring them hosses right in here. Let's get them out da cold."

Hamilton removed his hat and wiped the sweat that dripped from his wig. "We used to eat horses just like this at Valley Forge. It was all we had to survive." Hamilton smiled. "But I won't bore you with stories. You've got work to do."

Barney got to work feeding and currying the supreme leader's horses. Before heading back to conduct business of his own, Hamilton took a stroll through the stockade, petting each horse on the face as he passed. It stunk just like a barn should stink. Horse feed, manure, and Barney's pungent body odor. Thirty horses rested just on this side of the fort alone.

The horses acknowledged his presence as he passed, just as citizens would to a king. They nodded their heads and neighed in his direction. Hamilton awed at the beautiful creatures.

"A fine-looking mustang," he complimented. "And an Arabian. How I love the Arabians," he said as he massaged the muscles of a tall, brown, Arabian horse. "But sorry, young fella. The thoroughbreds are my favorites. Nothing quite like it. You understand, little filly." He gave himself a laugh. As he continued to scan for thoroughbreds, a particular horse caught his eye, hidden in the back corner of the pen. "Like that guy right back there. Indeed, nothing like a thoroughbred." Hamilton approached the horse in wonder. "Like it's sent from the heavens. A model of anatomical supremacy."

The horse reached out and rubbed its long, white forehead over Hamilton's cheek, warming his face so it was no longer numb from the cold. The supreme leader held the steed's head with both hands to get a good look.

Chestnut coating with a white face and white legs. Powerful legs. Probably a skilled charger.

"I once knew a horse just like you," he whispered. "*Just* like you. Most graceful horse I've ever seen. And the most graceful master."

Hamilton leaned against the wall and closed his eyes, envisioning George Washington on a horse. He imagined General Washington riding at Mount Vernon, so splendid a sight, so natural on a horse. He thought of the unimaginable speeds he could reach. Washington in command at Valley Forge, in action on the battlefield. The man was born to be on horse-back. But alas, he would ride no more. The supreme leader held back a tear. He remembered the general insisting that horses felt emotion, as much emotion as the most sensitive of the poets and playwrights.

One tiny tear managed to escape his eye as he reminisced. He twitched and opened his eyelids again upon feeling the horse, rubbing against him a second time, wiping away the tear. A short flutter sound escaped from the horse's neck. Again, a quick pulsation. Hamilton opened his eyes wide and wiped hard. The trembling from the horse's neck became a consistent quiver that mesmerized the supreme leader.

"A purring horse," he whispered. "It can't be. This can't be Nelson. Nelson?"

Hamilton reached for the horse's mouth. He examined the teeth like the most astute slave owner would examine the teeth of an African slave up for sale. Nelson would have to be over twenty years of age by now, and his teeth would reveal it. Hamilton's observations confirmed that this was indeed Nelson. His teeth were stained brown at a sharp angle, as would be expected in a horse past twenty years. The corrosion, the cavities, all pointed to a horse about the age of Nelson; although, Hamilton needed no further confirmation. No other horse purred like a kitten. Only Nelson.

"To whom does this mount belong?!" Hamilton shouted to no response. "Whose horse is this?"

Barney rushed back inside the stockade. "So sorry, mastuh. You callin'?"

"How did this horse come to Fort Pitt, man?"

"Thas ah . . . thas ah . . . Oh, that hoss come wit da Injun inside. That Injun chief rode that hoss in, suh. He mighty strong, too, that hoss. But cut up by da neck, you see. Got scars on his back. Fine hoss, tho, mastuh."

Hamilton was astonished. "You're telling me that Chief Blue Jacket arrived here on this horse? This very horse, right here?"

"Yes, suh. He surely did."

"Inconceivable." The supreme leader marched back outside through the freezing temperature and toward the main fort. His security team awaited him at the entrance. Hamilton's breath still fogged up as he spoke. "Where is this piece of shit? Take me to him, without delay."

An armed escort of five military men led Hamilton with a torch through the dark, stone halls of Fort Pitt. Their voices echoed throughout the dungeon. Hamilton removed his hat again and hunched over to avoid hitting his head off the low ceiling. They arrived at a tiny, cold cell for interrogations, containing nothing but a few chairs and a candle on the floor. A patient Blue Jacket sat on his knees while Red Pole bit his nails and paced the room from wall to wall.

When the supreme leader entered, Blue Jacket stood at attention next to his brother. The flickering candle provided quick flashes of light across the prisoners' faces. Hamilton's deep-navy eyes focused on Blue Jacket through a squint.

"What in God's name is this brute wearing?" Hamilton asked.

Blue Jacket fixed the collar around his neck and looked down at the uniform, a long, blue coat with tails and red cuffs, issued by the National States army.

"Is this a sick joke?" Hamilton continued.

A lanky brigadier general addressed the supreme leader. "Your Majesty, he arrived shirtless. The temperature has been frigid, even inside. We just thought—"

"You just thought? You just thought what? That this worthless beast in any way resembles the men of good morals and character, deserving of being robed in our sacred uniform? Is that what you thought?"

"My deepest apologies, Your Majesty."

"That will be all, General. Remove yourself. Now!" Hamilton turned back to Blue Jacket. "And you will hand over that cloak!" He pulled from the sleeve before the Shawnee could remove it himself. Blue Jacket sat back down in the chair, shirtless again.

"And which one of you would be the mighty Blue Jacket?" Hamilton asked, indignant.

The chief leaned his head forward in acknowledgment.

"Half naked and starved, from the looks of it."

Blue Jacket remained silent.

"Your Majesty," Red Pole interrupted, his forehead black and blue from the beating he'd received from General Wayne. "The Shawnee people have laid down their arms. We have surrendered. We ask for your mercy, and to be left undisturbed on the Maumee River. We can do you no harm there."

"You have killed hundreds of National States citizens, and you will receive no such mercy," was the callous response. "You will make your mark on a treaty that establishes a cease-fire, but nothing else. We are not haggling over your whereabouts."

Red Pole sighed in disparagement.

"Now, let's not waste time," Hamilton continued. "We all know that a land treaty with your people has about as much worth as the shit-stained leaves in the forest. Settlers don't care about your treaties. Governors won't abide by them."

Red Pole did not let up. "The British still occupy Fort Detroit. They should leave, as they promised after your great war. The few Shawnee survivors could dwell in Detroit. Or elsewhere in Ohio or Montgomery, where the Seneca live in peace."

"The Seneca Indians have been our ally in this war. They have earned the privilege. Neither your people nor the tribes that assisted you will ever again step foot in that state or any other state. Now, maybe you didn't understand me just now. You will leave this country. As of my return to Philadelphia, the Shawnee, Delaware, and Miami Indian tribes are banished from the National States of America, by decree of the supreme leader. Blue Jacket will hang, on display for the public—or maybe we'll use the French contraption." The other soldiers laughed in an uproar. "And you will take your people out of the National States. It is the destiny of this nation to expand further west; therefore, I suggest your people go north to British Canada or south to Columbia. Then you can be Patrick Henry's problem. Kentucky is in the process of gaining statehood. Perhaps you will settle there. And good riddance. After six months have elapsed, any of your people who remain in my country will rot in a prison cell like this one."

The two Shawnee leaders sat, despondent and defeated.

Hamilton hovered over them in his usual intimidating stance. "Now, Mr. Blue Jacket and I have other business." He signaled for the guards to take Red Pole away.

Left in privacy, Hamilton cooled his temper and sat down next to Blue Jacket. "I got a chance to see the horse you rode in on," he said. "A unique horse, indeed. A beautiful creature."

Chief Blue Jacket had learned to say nothing to a white man unless asked a direct question.

"This will be much easier if you speak."

Still, Blue Jacket said nothing.

"You do speak English."

Silence.

Hamilton laughed. "Perhaps we need some alcohol to break the ice. How about some rum?"

Finally, a question.

"I accept your offer," Blue Jacket spoke.

"Ah ha! You have vocal cords, after all. It just takes a little of the white man's poison." Hamilton reached for a flask, half full of rum, from his coat pocket and tossed it on Blue Jacket's lap. "You know, I grew up in the Caribbean," Hamilton explained. "St. Croix. They produce the best rum in the world there." The supreme leader did not often share information about his foreign upbringing, but Blue Jacket would be executed soon enough. Hamilton felt a sense of freedom talking to a dead man who had no choice but to keep secrets to the grave.

Blue Jacket tossed back a gulp of rum and exhaled the loudest noise he'd made since arriving at Fort Pitt. He reached out to return the flask, but Hamilton refused.

"Now let's get back to this horse," he said. "Pray, how did you come to possess such a fine horse? I'm certain you don't breed thoroughbreds like that in the wilderness."

"I do not *possess* a horse. The Great Spirit has brought horse and man together to share the land."

"Pure folly," Hamilton said. "Now tell me the exact circumstances of when and where your spirit brought you that particular horse out in the stockade."

"The Great Spirit is named Kokumthena. She created my ancestors on the back of a turtle—"

"Stop!" Hamilton commanded. "Enough of this bullshit. Two escaped slaves. A well-built man, very dark, and a teenaged girl. Mulatto. You got the horse from them."

Blue Jacket remained silent and took another sip of rum.

"Fort Detroit, then. I am the most powerful man in North America. I can give you Detroit. Hell, I could give you a Goddamn palace, with all the rum you like, too. Just take me to the two Africans who brought you that horse. In exchange, I will refrain from making my order to ban your people. They may live in Detroit. Of course, you will still hang for your crimes; but your people may have peace." Hamilton grew frustrated by the silent treatment. "Do you have any idea who these two slaves are? Do you have any idea of their importance?"

"I know exactly who they are. They killed your great spirit. Your creator, Washington. I will not give them up." Hamilton's eyes burned as Blue Jacket continued. "I have spent a lifetime battling your Chief Washington. I fought against him in the Seven Years' War. I fought against him in your Revolutionary War. He was responsible for the destruction of my people before you replaced him. Perhaps your Great Spirit killed my Great Spirit; but these two runaways killed your Great Spirit. They have taken vengeance for the Shawnee. They are heroes, and I will not give them up. I would have killed Washington myself if given the chance. His death was justice."

In an angry rage, Hamilton swung his fist at the Shawnee Chief, splitting his lip in an instant. Blood dripped like a fountain. Hamilton seized his flask out of Blue Jacket's hand and chugged every last drop of alcohol that remained in it, then whipped Blue Jacket's face with it, slicing his forehead, causing more blood to run. He kicked Blue Jacket hard, out of his chair, and then kicked the chair on top of him.

"Your spirit is a fraud! You are a fraud! You will die in Philadelphia, and that horse is now mine!" Hamilton kicked the second chair to the floor. Hearing the ruckus, three guards rushed into the room to protect the supreme leader. Hamilton barked out his orders. "The fugitives are in Ohio. I want every black man, woman, and child in Ohio arrested and held here at Fort Pitt! Mulattos, too! Any drop of African blood. Round up every last one of them. I will send military reinforcement to assist you."

"But, Your Majesty," a young officer pleaded. "There are so many. They still escape Columbia every day."

"Every single one in Ohio! That is an order! And this son of a bitch will get the French contraption!" he screamed, kicking Blue Jacket in the gut one last time.

Hamilton and his men prepared for their return to Philadelphia. The supreme leader rode Nelson, escorting Chief Blue Jacket to his execution. With the chief's surrender, Congress could now finalize statehood for Ohio, and Hamilton could focus his military's attention on the conflict between Spain and Columbia. He had pledged his support to Spain, and as tensions grew on the border, war was no longer a matter of *if*, but a matter of *when*.

It usually takes just one trivial episode to trigger full-scale war. A mere accident sets off a chain of events that lead to uncontrollable violence, or some unfortunate soul ends up in the wrong place at the wrong time, and war is the inevitable consequence. In the spring of 1791, John McIntosh was that poor soul.

The twenty-year-old McIntosh, tall, proud, with a soft baby face, took his teenaged bride Elizabeth to Southern Georgia, where he inherited five hundred acres of land on the Satilla River. A picture of youth and beauty, the smitten couple journeyed south to their new life with optimism. Elizabeth's radiant, auburn hair flowed on forever, like her husband's ambition. She was the most sought-after maiden in Georgia, a stunning symbol of grandeur, and from the distinguished Bayard family in New York. She resembled a young Martha Dandridge before becoming Martha Washington.

Indeed, the Bayards preferred a more eminent and suitable match than John McIntosh, but Elizabeth could not deny her feelings. She fell passionately in love with John's charm and aspirations, and John loved her even more in return. Nothing could stop him from marrying his bride; he claimed her.

When they arrived at their home in Camden County, Georgia, the newlyweds discovered an old, two-story, white house covered in fern-green moss. It needed much work, but nothing John couldn't handle. The surrounding plantation was ideal for growing rice. Beyond that, John McIntosh owned hundreds of acres of swamp—wet, muggy swamp. He had also inherited twenty slaves with the property, yet only eleven remained. The other nine, and thousands of other slaves from Georgia and the Carolinas, had taken advantage of the swampland for their escape to Florida. Though not the most comfortable hiding spot, the swamps offered perfect cover and difficult terrain for a slave catcher's pursuit. The swamps of southern Georgia were ground zero for fugitive slaves making their way to freedom in Florida, and John McIntosh's plantation sat in the eye of the storm.

Once settled in his new home, John decided to travel south to the border town of Saint Marys, where he would enquire about his nine escaped slaves. The town served as an outpost for Columbian agents to repossess property, or ARPs. These government agents captured fugitive slaves and returned them to their owners. Sometimes, the agents kept the confiscated property for themselves or sold them for a profit. If McIntosh couldn't regain his runaway slaves, then perhaps he could purchase unclaimed fugitives for a decent price.

Spanish Florida sat on the opposite side of the Saint Marys River. Since negotiating with the National States government, Spain had already stationed a few hundred soldiers in the capital city of Saint Augustine. The stage was set for war. A tiny spark to ignite the flames was all that was needed.

John kissed his wife goodbye on a quiet Saturday morning, admiring the sparkle in her aqua-blue eyes. "I love you more than life itself, my sweet."

They would never see each other again.

At Saint Marys, John learned that tracking down his escaped property would be almost impossible. He had an inventory that listed names and ages, but he'd never even seen these slaves to be able to give a proper description. In addition, the eleven slaves that remained on his planation were never branded, which meant the nine fugitives also did not bear a mark to prove his ownership. The very first advice given to John by the ARPs was to tattoo his remaining slaves with a stamp of ownership, just like cattle.

"Brand 'em good with a hot iron. Use your initials or some symbol or mark. And make sure you brand the head. I'd stamp the neck or the cheeks."

"Brand their faces? But that's torturous," the young slave owner replied, inexperienced in the brutality of the slave system.

"Torturous, but efficient. Lot a these fugitives been mutilating themselves to get rid of evidence. I seen one who chopped off his own hand, 'cause he was branded on the palm. Now, you brand 'em on the neck, they'll have a harder time choppin' off their head."

John smirked and nodded in agreement, but found the practice barbaric. He was not impressed by the ARPs. Instead of government agents working and sacrificing to serve the public, these men seemed like bloodthirsty monsters who took pleasure in hunting human flesh for sport. They tracked down slaves for the thrill of the hunt. It gave them a reason to chew more tobacco and drink more whiskey. As members of the militia, the Columbian Constitution guaranteed their right to bear arms, and they now had the opportunity to take some additional target practice on fleeing property. John concluded that the ARPs had no actual interest in helping to solve his dilemma.

He left the ARP garrison and went to the Saint Marys River to see the situation up close. McIntosh did not expect to capture his escaped slaves, but he could survey the border and maybe catch dinner out of the river. He rented a small fishing boat from an old, worn-out Georgian who thought the young man was crazy.

"Kid, you sure you wanna be doin' this? These are dangerous waters, these days," the old man asked.

"Yes, sir. I'll be just fine. I'm taking a peaceful boat ride, and that is all. I mean no harm to anyone—free or slave, Georgian or Floridian."

The old man raised his brow at John's naivety. "Seminole Indians don't care much for your leisure, you know? Neither does an alligator. You got protection? Somethin' to defend yourself with?"

John had never considered having to arm himself for the expedition, but the old man convinced him. In addition to the dinghy, McIntosh rented a six-inch, flintlock pistol, loaded with four lead balls. The gun was old and rusted with a high probability of malfunctioning. Even newer models misfired often.

"Listen good, now," the old man gave one last warning. "You don't hesitate to fire that thing. Seminole Indians is the most vicious people around. You run into any trouble at all, you fire. Understand?"

"Yes, sir. I understand." John smiled.

He set off upstream, assisted by a steady breeze; yet even the wind couldn't kill the miserable humidity. The Saint Marys River weaved in and out of the swampland like a snake slithering between two countries. He scanned his surroundings in awe. To his right, Columbia; to his left, Spanish Florida. John traveled through a sea of thick, green marsh. Odd sounds came from all over; from the frogs and the occasional otter. No doubt, noises in the woods came from fugitive slaves, hiding in fear, but hopeful for a new life of freedom in Florida.

A few miles into his trip, John came across a boat of ARPs hunting their prey. Like the old man at the dock, they stared at McIntosh as if he were a complete lunatic. Further upstream, he rowed past a group of Seminole Indians on the Florida side of the river. In a tense moment, John made sure his pistol was concealed and the natives could see his fishing gear. He smiled and nodded his head in acknowledgement. The Seminoles looked on with suspicion but took no action. *Ah ha*, he thought to himself. The elderly man was just a sour, old worrywart.

As the sun began to fall, John knew he would have to make his way back to Saint Marys before dark. The water swerved into a thick patch of forest that blocked out the sunlight. A peculiar silence took its place. Not a sound from the frogs. The wind slowed down, muting the leaves that danced in the trees. John sat motionless. He felt as if he were being watched. Could it be an alligator? The dinghy inched along, stuck in time.

A few bubbles rose to the surface of the swamp and broke the silence. Before John could turn around to see, a whooping splash erupted from the water and onto the boat. He was sure it was a gator, but when the wave subsided, John found himself in the grasp of two Seminole Indians, pirating his boat.

Shaking in fear, the young McIntosh needed to think quickly. He still had a loaded pistol concealed in his jacket, but both his arms were held behind his back, one by each intruder.

"You are in Florida territory!" shouted one of his captors.

"I am on a fishing expedition. I have no quarrel with you gentlemen." Panic rose from the boy's voice. It cracked in a high-pitched cry.

"You have no right to fish in Florida water," the Seminole responded, "and you have no right to kidnap." He was dark-skinned with red war paint on his face, an escaped slave accepted into the Seminole Tribe. As he grasped both of John's hands, his partner took control of the boat and rowed toward land.

They docked on Florida soil, and John saw a larger group of Seminoles approaching. He was more muscular than his two captors, but he would have no chance of escape once the war party arrived. He flexed every muscle in his body and bent down into a squat. With the dark-skinned Seminole still behind him, John's body exploded upward, tossing the man over his back and down hard on to the edge of the boat. Without thinking, he threw a fist at the second hijacker's face, knocking him out cold. While making his way off the dinghy toward the woods, John reached for the pistol. Without hesitation, he turned and fired a single shot into the crowd of Seminoles, now racing to catch him.

McIntosh did not know if his shot hit anyone. He hadn't aimed at anyone in particular. He'd fired his weapon just to create a distraction and buy more time to escape into the woods. If he happened to have injured or even killed a Seminole Indian who would have held him against his will, then so be it. He did, in fact, have every right to be on the Saint Marys River.

When the smoke cleared from the chaotic scene, it revealed the worst-case scenario for John McIntosh and for the state of Georgia. The bullet had not only hit someone; it had killed a man—and the man was no

Seminole Indian. John had fired into a group of twelve Seminole Indians and one Spanish general, sent to train them and prepare for a possible war with Columbia. Of all thirteen people, John's bullet had managed to strike Captain General Juan de Courten between the eyes. One of the most famous and most skilled Spanish generals lay dead in a swamp on the Florida-Georgia border.

The Seminoles continued to chase McIntosh, who had no knowledge of his surroundings. They captured him within an hour. As soon as word reached King Charles, Spain declared war on Columbia. John McIntosh was taken to Saint Augustine, where the government of Spanish Florida hanged him for the assassination.

With tears in his eyes, his last words were, "Elizabeth. Elizabeth."

Aaron Burr celebrated the opening of the *American Whig Journal* with a modest gathering of employees, financiers, and friends at the newspaper's headquarters on Broad Street, next door to New York City's volunteer fire department. Burr chose not to erect a sign on the front of the building, and he hired overnight security guards to protect his press from arsonists. The *American Whig Journal* promoted Burr's new political party, founded in opposition to the supreme leader's alleged abuse of federal power. He funded operations with money from his private law practice, Wall Street speculators, and ironically, a generous loan from the New York branch of Hamilton's National Bank.

Burr wanted the paper to promote Whig ideas and policies. It would support Whig candidates for office and wage total war on the usurpations of the Hamilton administration. If he intended to shock the political status quo, then the headline of the debut issue did not disappoint: "IMPEACHMENT NOW!" The scathing cover story, written by Burr under the pen name H.E. Edwards, unleashed a series of accusations against Hamilton in the style of Thomas Jefferson's grievances to King George in the Declaration of Independence:

He has interfered with state elections and denied office to the people's chosen representatives.

He has denied due process to settlers in Ohio by arresting and detaining Africans who have committed no crime, in violation of the first article in the National States Bill of Rights.

He has used extralegal means to shut down the free press in the National States, in violation of the fourth article in the National States Bill of Rights.

He has banished an entire population of peaceful residents from the National States of America.

He has handpicked the beneficiaries of the national government's fiscal policies . . . .

Burr lambasted the supreme leader, citing the National States Constitution several times in the article. He closed with a strong appeal for citizens to call on Congress to impeach Hamilton, using the impeachment process outlined in the Constitution.

Other articles in the debut journal covered topics such as lower tariffs; transitioning the military to peacetime; putting former slaves to work in the state of Montgomery; statehood for Ohio; and endorsements of political candidates, including Albert Gallatin and William Findley in Pennsylvania, William Floyd in Montgomery, and of course, Aaron Burr in New York.

Although still serving the supreme leader, Jonathan Taylor attended the celebration on Broad Street. The Whig Party energized Taylor more than most people in the room. He cheered for the improvised speeches given by partygoers, and he paid close attention to criticisms of Hamilton's mistreatment of black settlers in Ohio. The supreme leader had ordered the military to round up every black person in Ohio. According to Hamilton, escaped slaves in Ohio gave aid and comfort to Shawnee enemies, and the decision was made in the best interest of national security.

By the time Jonathan could chat with the man of the hour, Burr had already consumed a bit too much wine.

"Congratulations, sir!" Taylor shouted over the noise.

"It will be a marvelous success, Jonathan! I just know it. The Whig Party, the journal, all of it. We will take back our country from this monster. And you will be a part of it, Mr. Taylor. I hope I can depend on your services."

"It would be an honor, Mr. Burr. But do you not worry about the supreme leader? Might he seek retribution for such dissent? Will he not call it sedition?"

"Let him do his worst, man. If he does cry foul and accuses us of sedition, then we will have righteousness on our side. And if our court system has any independence at all, it will side with us, as will the court of public opinion. It will side with us—with liberty, with righteousness."

Jonathan had his doubts, but remained happy for Burr. "I will serve in whatever capacity you see fit."

Burr tossed back another swig of Bordeaux, straight from the bottle. "That is good, Jonathan. Very good. I'm thinking Montgomery."

"Montgomery, sir?" Surprised, Jonathan assumed it was the wine talking.

"Of course, Montgomery. An educated Negro like you could make a fine leader of freedmen as slavery is phased out. You could help organize the Whig Party in Buffalo. Help convince the state government to be the first to allow Negro suffrage, and then get us the black vote! Maybe even run for office there. State House? Or how about the National States House of Representatives? A Negro Whig in the House. Now wouldn't that make Hamilton just shit in his britches? Ha!"

"More than you know, sir." Jonathan didn't worry about blowing his cover. Burr was too drunk. "More than you know."

Jonathan found the prospect of moving to Montgomery attractive, but he would no longer be able to spy for the supreme leader if he moved away from Burr. He could be arrested for turning his back on Hamilton, working toward his demise with the Whig faction. Yet, something about the Whigs gave the ex-slave a sense of empowerment. It stirred up his soul. For as unprincipled as Aaron Burr seemed, Jonathan had grown to admire the man. He understood Burr's method of doing whatever it took—whatever it took to raise money, to spread the message, to get elected. Say whatever needs said. The style wasn't always pretty, and it created plenty of enemies. However, Jonathan once knew a brilliant man who played by the rules, stood by his convictions and never wavered; a man who would not bend. James Madison lost his fight for the United States Constitution, watched his country divide in three, and now served his political enemy as ambassador to France, a country without any semblance of a stable government.

Jonathan would give serious consideration to the thought of moving to Buffalo, Montgomery, but for now, continued to perform his duties as a spy. He pocketed an extra copy of the first *American Whig Journal* and mailed it to Alexander Hamilton in Philadelphia, without hesitation.

~

After mourning the loss of Chief Blue Jacket and the barren, scorched-earth village they'd once called home, the few surviving Shawnee decided to migrate south, across the Columbian border. They traveled to Kentucky, a growing slave state in which Red Squirrel and Chasing Honey could never step foot. Instead, the fugitive slaves followed a band of Seneca Indians toward their central Ohio settlement on the Scioto River.

Having aided the National States army, the Seneca Nation traveled with confidence and a joyful exuberance that was absent from the defeated Shawnee. They were better equipped with more supplies, and healthier in general. Red Squirrel and Chasing Honey ate the most delicious venison and freshest vegetables since their escape from Columbia. They hoped it would be safer to travel with the NSA's allies, rather than be chased by them.

The war party stopped to rest at a desolate lake in the middle of the Ohio country. Even in Ohio, so many miles away from Mount Vernon, Hercules still woke every morning just before four o'clock, ready to prepare the kitchen. Although his body had fled the horrors of bondage, a lifetime of mental enslavement would take longer to escape. As he threw another log on top of the fire, his thoughts returned to Virginia. He would need to chop more wood for the kitchen and the smokehouse. Lady Washington expected her daily ham cooked to perfection. The crackling wood sounded like Fairfax's whip. He flinched at each pop in the flames, and so did Ona. She woke up, startled.

"Honey, is that you? Come lay with me." She yawned.

"You can call me 'Herc,' ya know. We ain't real Indians here." Hercules scowled at the name he'd earned by humiliating himself in the beehives. He swatted at the mosquitos that circled near the lake.

"We ain't real slaves no more either," she explained, pulling him back down to the dirt. "I'm Red, and you Honey. We gotta take new names, 'cause them soldiers lookin' for Hercules and Ona Judge. They lookin' for slaves, and they ain't gonna find none here."

Chasing Honey closed his eyes and rested his head on her chest. They lay under the stars, just like they had in George Washington's garden.

"I can still hear them songs," he whispered. "I still hear them slaves marchin' off to work, singin' them songs, like they right here, followin' me. And I still dream. I dream 'bout honey. Mastuh need more honey. I dream 'bout waffles and coffee. Gotta brew more coffee. I jus' can't leave that place." He pointed to his temple. "Up here, I can't leave," he said, straining his cheeks to push back a tear.

Red Squirrel held his head in the palm of her hands. "We still on our way out," she said with a smile. "We still on our way. Don't know where we goin', but we still on our way."

Just as Chasing Honey began to slip back to sleep, the sounds of National States horses stomping their hooves echoed through the forest, coming closer and closer, searching for any escaped slaves. The soldiers even used dogs for the hunt, just like the slave catchers of Columbia. By the time the hounds arrived, the whole Seneca party awoke.

Two soldiers on horseback interrogated the tribe, caught off guard at the moonlit lake.

The lead officer shouted, "Halt where you are! We must inspect your party, by order of the supreme leader of the National States of America, Alexander Hamilton!"

The Seneca Chief Blacksnake spoke for the group: "We are Seneca. Your allies. Allies of supreme leader. We have nothing of yours, I am sure."

"Then this should be easy," the officer said. "We will inspect your party, and you can be on your way."

The two men dismounted their horses and approached, guns drawn. Red Squirrel may have had a faint chance of blending in, but Chasing Honey could not conceal his complexion. The lead officer lifted his rifle to Chasing Honey's head.

"Nothing of ours, huh? This nigger is under arrest."

"Major!" the other soldier shouted. "I think there's another!" He examined Red Squirrel's light-brown skin. He touched her face and ran his fingers through her hair.

Red Squirrel pushed him away in anger. "Get ya dirty fingers off of me, you dog." She squirmed.

"Yeah, we got another, all right!" He held Red Squirrel at gunpoint as well.

The major now addressed Blacksnake: "All Negroes in Ohio are to be placed under arrest, by order of the supreme leader! These two will come with us. And I oughta arrest you, too, for hiding them."

"Sir, we travel in peace, to land promised us for fighting against the Shawnee. We have done our duty. We have fought with bravery. Our two companions will be important in building our settlement. They have nothing you are looking for. Please, sir. We will go in peace."

Red Squirrel reached down to her shoe, sending her captor into a rage.

"Don't move! I'll shoot—you just try me. I'll shoot you dead, girl!"

Red Squirrel opened her palm slowly to reveal Martha Washington's diamond and a handful of rubies that she'd not needed until now.

"Is this all necessary, suh? We friends, as our chief explained. We helped you in battle, and we close to our destination."

"Major, you better take a look at this," the young private responded, uneasy.

The major inched closer, still aiming his weapon at Chasing Honey's head.

"So you think you can bribe us that easy?" he asked.

"Can you really arrest every single one?" Blacksnake wondered. "There are hundreds of Negroes here. Plenty more await their arrest all through this territory. Will your masters ever notice if these two do not arrive at prison?"

"Take 'em," Red Squirrel continued her appeal. "A thousand dollars, easy. We go on our way, and you go on yours. Nobody knows a thing about this. We'll be gone and outta your way."

The major stepped closer. His arm shot out to snatch the jewels from Red Squirrel's hand, but she pulled back faster than a rattlesnake. Her heart skipped a beat in fear that he would take the gems and arrest her anyway. She tilted her head back and held a single ruby above her mouth, wide open.

"I'll swallow every last one of these. Promise. If you want this treasure, we walk. That's how it works."

The soldier laughed and shook his head before giving in. "You all be careful in your travels, now," he said. "Go on, now. And leave what you got on the ground in front of you."

She did as he instructed. The whole group continued around the lake, with Red Squirrel keeping a watchful eye behind them.

The two men mounted their horses and rode off into the woods, a handful of precious jewels richer. Chasing Honey fell to his knees and began to hyperventilate. He could taste the bitter vomit pushing up his esophagus, threatening to spill out.

"I thought that was it," he whispered. "I thought that was the end."

Red Squirrel bent over and kissed his forehead. "Not now, Honey. We still on our way."

The tide swelled up and washed the rocks on the shore clean. Red Squirrel watched the water sparkle like the diamond that saved her life, like thousands of glowing diamonds, unable to hide beneath the exposure of a rising sun. The glow on the water lit up her path to freedom. It pushed the sun above to the horizon, sending it off to the world in a dazzling array of color and light across the sky. Pink, then purple and orange, each color chasing the other, capturing the clouds. Red Squirrel had seen countless sunsets over the Potomac River, but couldn't remember a single sunrise.

She remembered Martha Washington quoting the Bible and how those quotes had lacked meaning for her, but she remembered them nonetheless. So many quotes about light. She gazed at the sky with Chasing Honey and, for the first time in her life, quoted the Bible.

"The Lord is my light and my salvation." Chasing Honey squinted his eyes, confused. "God is light. In Him, there is no darkness at all." She laughed at herself as the words came out.

In the evening, they built a private fire underneath a soaring hickory tree, its limbs penetrating the nightfall. Flickering embers cracked in the air and heated their naked bodies. Her coffee-brown skin and freckled chest pressed up against his deep-black sternum. She felt his pulse throbbing against her. Red Squirrel held on to Chasing Honey, stretching her arms around his muscular frame and gazing into his eyes. She growled out her desire in deep tones, a timbre from within that she'd never heard before. Chasing Honey cried out, too. He could taste the drops of sweat from her neck. Completely vulnerable, his façade of raw masculinity melted away by the fire, his compassion secure under moonshine and hickory.

After two years of intimacy, it was the first time they'd made love. Red Squirrel cleared her mind of Charlotte's warnings—warnings about wicked men and all that they craved. She craved it, too. Red Squirrel loved Chasing Honey on her own terms.

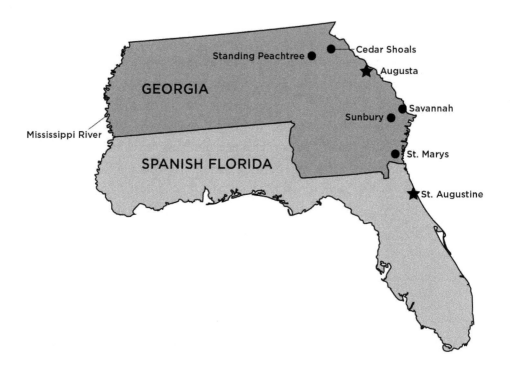

Standing Peachtree ●

Cedar Shoals ●

★ Augusta

GEORGIA

Savannah ●

Sunbury ●

Mississippi River

SPANISH FLORIDA

St. Marys ●

★ St. Augustine

Chapter 12

When five thousand Spanish soldiers marched from St. Augustine, Florida, to the Georgia border under the command of General Antonio Ricardos, it seemed that the Georgia War would play out just as Alexander Hamilton had pitched it to the Spanish ambassador. Instead of a war, it felt like a joyous parade to Ricardos, who marched his army straight into Columbia without the slightest resistance, the wind at their backs and the sun at their faces.

But if the Georgia militia did a poor job of defending the southern border, Mother Nature did her best to compensate. The Spanish general's delight soon turned to frustration with the wet terrain.

"Endless swamp," he complained to his lieutenant general. "Could we have possibly chosen a rainier place on earth to invade? At this pace, we won't see combat for months."

"We'd have been better to bring swimming trunks and fishing gear," the lieutenant joked, although Ricardos found no humor in it.

"It's much more serious than that, General. These wetlands don't just slow our pace to a crawl. We are burning through food and supplies at an untenable rate. We'll need Supreme Leader Hamilton to resupply us in a hurry; and if he is not true to his word, we could be in grave danger. Starved to the bone. Food for the gators. Hamilton has promised powder, muskets, and artillery, but I pray he sends food, and socks and boots, as well."

His second in command agreed, but remained optimistic. "We at least have the advantage of keen navigation. These Africans and Indians know the swamp like it was their home, like they lived on the lily pads."

Escaped slaves from Georgia plantations pointed the way north to their former homes. Seminole, Creek, and Chickasaw Indians also provided distinct knowledge of their ancestral lands, stolen from them by Georgia landowners. These exiles returned to their old masters with an army, and with determination. They returned bloodthirsty, tasting revenge on the tips of their tongues.

Once out of the swamps, tales of absolute horror and vengeance played out at each plantation Ricardos and his army plundered. Nathaniel Ashley, a wealthy landowner from a distinguished Georgia family of planters, was paid a visit by his former property. Now free men, these proud soldiers stripped Ashley nude, tied him to the whipping post and took turns whipping their old master, just as he had whipped them in the past. Each threw down at least twenty-five lashes before passing the cowskin around like it was a peace pipe. They forced his wife to watch, shrieking in terror, just as their wives, their brothers and sisters, their sons and their daughters, had shrieked when they'd witnessed the same abuse. Jane Ashley sobbed uncontrollably. Her husband passed out after one hundred lashes, yet the torture continued after he lost consciousness. They whipped him until his spine and vertebrae were exposed to the elements.

When the whipping stopped, Jane thought she had endured it all, but she could not escape the same suffering. Her former field hands ripped off her genteel clothing, starting with the fluffy white cap. They slashed her silk gown and tossed it aside into a pool of her husband's blood. Off came the petticoat, then the stay, sliced open with a knife that pierced the soft flesh of her breast. A thin stream of blood trickled over her stomach. Undressed sufficiently, Jane was strung up to the same post as Nathaniel. She didn't last long. She dangled, unconscious, lifeless after the first few cracks of the whip.

Before marching onward, the black soldiers forced Nathaniel and Jane Ashley awake again. They hanged the couple from an enormous sugar maple that welcomed visitors to the plantation. Its orange and red leaves hovered over the main house like it set fire to the sky. Thirty-five slaves watched in silence as their masters' dead bodies swung into each other in a morbid tango. These men and women were now free from their masters. If they chose to convert to Catholicism and give service to the military, then

King Charles IV would acknowledge their permanent freedom in Spanish Florida.

Ashley's sons, William and Ludowick, owned the neighboring plantations, and they met similar fates. William Ashley was tortured before being shot in the heart. A band of Seminoles got hold of Ludowick and drowned him in a nearby creek—slowly. Next, they scalped him—slowly. These incidents became commonplace for the landed gentry as the Georgia War began.

"General, these atrocities must cease," the lieutenant general pleaded with Ricardos.

"And they most certainly will, after the Georgians cease their atrocities toward our colonists in Florida. Were you aware that Nathaniel Ashley crossed the Florida border in search of his slaves and shot and killed a Spanish official in the process?"

"But, General—"

"But nothing. I encourage the passion that my army has demonstrated. And if you ever question my authority again, I will have you court martialed."

⌁

Ricardos's men plowed over Camden Country, taking control of Saint Marys without a fight. While they inched north, still at a snail's pace, the Georgia militia found time to organize and rebuild at least one strategic fort lost in the Revolutionary War. They reconstructed Fort Morris outside the town of Sunbury. Seven hundred militiamen, young boys and privileged farmers, converged on the small community just southwest of Savannah, setting the stage for the first major battle of the war.

The lieutenant general jogged to catch up with General Ricardos. "General, two more have fallen ill to this nightmarish heat wave. Dehydrated and useless." Mother Nature had continued her resistance during the hottest days of summer. "I'm afraid the added weight of our uniforms has complicated matters." The Spanish soldiers baked inside their heavy blue jackets and red shirts festooned in gold and silver.

Irritated, Ricardos swiped his sword at the nearest tree. "If King Charles knew what an absolute hellhole this place is, I doubt he'd be interested in acquiring it. I've lost valuable weaponry to the swamps and now trained men to the heat. We need an entire regiment just to fight off the mosquitos." He lit a tobacco pipe to calm his nerves. "So, let the Georgians win the battle of comfort and style. I'm much more interested in victory on the battlefield. Fort Morris cannot hold enough men to defeat us. How much artillery has lasted the journey?"

"Sir, about one hundred small field cannons and just a few mortars. The larger siege cannons and howitzers couldn't make it through the swamps. We'll have to smoke the Georgians out of their fort with no artillery to penetrate the walls."

Ricardos ordered his men in formation, two hundred and fifty yards away from the fort. He initiated the battle with small cannon fire—six pounders, not really intended to inflict major damage. Just a "Hello, how do you do?"

The Georgia militia responded with musket fire, preserving their heavier artillery until the Spanish came closer.

"That a boy," Ricardos spoke out to nobody. "Now let's give this militia some pride." He ordered his first line forward—every one of them black or Indian. They marched straight into gunfire. As they gained ground, the enemy resorted to cannons, cutting down the entire line with grapeshot.

Ricardos watched and laughed at the sight of losing several of his men. The lieutenant general gave a puzzled look.

"Not to worry, General. How much ammunition do you think they have back there? We'll take our time and watch them deplete their resources. It may take a day, and it may cost some men. That's fine. They're not equipped well enough to outlast us."

The game of cat and mouse pursued all day. By nightfall, the Spanish had advanced very little, but succeeded in getting the enemy to waste artillery fire. The real fighting came with the rising sun.

Just after dawn, a smug Ricardos sat atop his horse and watched from a distance as his men marched forward to capture Fort Morris. His orders were clear.

"We'll finish this business before noon and avoid the worst of the heat. Coax them out with gunfire and cannon fire over the walls of the fort."

It took little more than an hour for Fort Morris to go up in flames. The militiamen who remained inside were forced out, into the open field, where they discovered the Spanish lines already closing in. Each army charged the other, leading to most of the battle's bloodshed. Outnumbered, the Georgians fought in desperation against the most professional army in North America.

"Like I said, a joyous parade," Ricardos gloated. With victory in sight, he ordered the finishing touch. "Send in the dragoons! It took the horses long enough to get through the swamps. I'll be damned if we don't get some use out of them."

Doomed to defeat, the commander of Georgia's militia, Jared Irwin, ordered his men to retreat, leaving behind the ashes of Fort Morris and over three hundred dead Georgians. The Spanish suffered one hundred and twenty casualties in battle, but over one hundred more to malaria and dysentery. Overall, General Ricardos was quite pleased as the first battle of the Georgia War ended in a victory for the Spanish. He would be reinforced with another thousand men before marching farther north into more suitable terrain for warfare.

~

For two years, Columbian Vice President Charles Cotesworth Pinckney had pleaded with President Henry, urging him to call on Congress to raise an army, even though the president loathed the idea. Once the Georgia War began, it became clear that militia would not stand a chance in a fight with Spain. Congress no longer needed Henry to persuade them. They mustered up the required three-fourths vote to raise an army. The Columbian Constitution specified that this was a provisional military, to be disbanded during peacetime. The founding document placed a strict prohibition on standing armies.

"You won't go through with it. Please tell me you won't veto this bill, Mr. President." Pinckney sounded like a madman. Hazy, bloodshot eyes pulsated through his red face, dissected by a bulging vein from the top of his forehead. Would the president use his veto power to reject an army while the country was under attack? His silence seemed to suggest that he would.

Henry slouched in his chair with his head down. "I'd be pilloried. And how much difference would it really make, Charles? Congress would override my veto anyway, with the same overwhelming majority they used to pass the bill in the first place. No, I'm afraid I've lost this battle. We will recruit your coveted army."

"It is the right move, sir. We owe it to the people of Columbia to provide for the common defense. In Georgia and South Carolina, they've seen this act before. The British romped through our homes and our farms before we won independence. We must be strong in our resolve to defend Columbia."

"Yes, of course. But for me, defending them won't convince anyone otherwise. I am about as popular as the plague. I've devoted my life to the principles of democracy, of a people's republic, and as a result, the people would like nothing more than my demise. And not just voters. My own administration. Did you know James Madison resigned?"

Pinckney shook his head in surprise.

"He'll be coming home from France," Henry explained. "To escape the violence there and be welcomed by violence here. He wants to protect his family. And if you were wondering, he was unable to secure French support for our war effort."

"Well, of course he was unable. Why would the French support us when we haven't supported ourselves? A strong army will change everything. But never mind the French. They're still caught up in their own revolution."

Henry wallowed deep in depression at a time when the country needed his leadership most. The color and emotion had vanished from his face, and every muscle in his body seemed to slouch in paralysis. The vice president attempted to piece the broken man back together. They had a war to conduct.

"Mr. President, I would like to discuss with you the proposed constitutional amendments."

"Ha! The amendments! And what of them?" The president laughed in sarcastic derision, pouring himself a second shot of whiskey.

"Well, sir, if the commander in chief amendment passes, I would like you to know that I will accept the commission. It would be a tremendous honor. I hope you will support the measure, as I think it could do a great deal of good."

Congress went far beyond just raising an army. They compiled a series of constitutional amendments to ensure that war could be waged effectively and that Columbia would never again face such a calamity. With Pinckney in mind, one of the proposed amendments established that the vice president would serve as commander in chief of the armed forces. It was an acknowledgement of Pinckney's military experience, but no doubt a vote of no confidence in Henry. If passed, every future vice president would follow the precedent. It provided a unique division of power in the Executive Branch and an additional check on presidential power.

"Have no worries," Henry mumbled. "I will not stand in the way of anything congress wants—short of my execution," he joked. "I'm just a figurehead at this point. I couldn't get reelected if Jesus Christ himself came back to endorse me. In fact, they're considering an amendment on a term limit to make sure I can't even run for reelection. Well, let them have their fun. No, sir, you won't find opposition from my office."

"That is splendid, sir. With your permission, I would very much like to proceed in anticipation that the commander in chief amendment will pass. An army needs training, weapons, uniforms, supplies."

"You go right ahead, Mr. Pinckney. You are the commander in chief now."

"Thank you, Mr. President." Pinckney turned to exit the office with gusto, determined to serve his country with honor. He was a fish put back into water. As he approached the door, the vice president stopped and turned back to Henry with some words of encouragement. "Patrick, you are a national hero. If not for your leadership, this nation would still call itself British and the Confederation of Columbia would remain mere fiction in the minds of true patriots. Pull yourself together, man. Columbia needs your strength. She needs your passion."

With Patrick Henry's begrudging approval, Congress assembled the Columbian army and deployed it with great haste throughout the summer of 1791. On August 5, Congress, and the state legislatures of Virginia, Maryland, North Carolina, South Carolina, and Georgia, ratified the first three amendments to the Columbian Constitution:

> *Amendment I: The Congress shall have power to raise and support a standing army in order to provide for the common defense.*

> *Amendment II: The Congress shall have power to provide and maintain a standing navy in order to provide for the common defense.*

> *Amendment III: The vice president shall be commander in chief of the army and navy of the Confederation of Columbia, and of the militia of the several states when called into the actual service of the Confederation of Columbia.*

The proposed fourth amendment fell short of the votes required for passage. Limiting the president to one term of four years would guarantee an end to Patrick Henry's administration; however, most congressmen and state legislators found the amendment unnecessary since Henry had such little chance of reelection.

"Enemies of the state, Goddamn it! We are surrounded by enemies of the state, and my administration cannot and will not tolerate it. I'm sure you've all heard of this violent rebellion of farmers in western Pennsylvania against the whiskey tax. Rest assured, they've been apprehended. Blue Jacket sits in prison, and thank God for that. But the two conspirators in Washington's murder remain on the loose, here within our borders, and now we have a dangerous Whig faction to deal with. And deal with it, we will."

Hamilton's cabinet applauded his commitment. Every cabinet member attended the meeting: Secretary of the Treasury Robert Morris; Secretary of State Rufus King; Attorney General Jonathan Dayton; and the newest cabinet member, Secretary of War Anthony Wayne. Wayne had acquired celebrity status after the capture of Chief Blue Jacket. A thankful nation cheered his appointment to lead the new Department of War.

"Gentlemen, please welcome Mr. Harison again to the meeting," Hamilton said, lifting his wine glass.

Richard Harison was a master of propaganda. He had published several newspaper articles in defense of the supreme leader's policies, and his bombast produced the intended effect. Admiration of the supreme leader soared to new heights across the country. Hamilton defeated the Indian menace and was expanding the country west while Columbia suffered more casualties every day in their war with Spain. "He keeps us safe," was Harison's mantra in the press. "He keeps us safe."

Hamilton sat down to begin the meeting. "Our first order of business is the roundup of Africans in Ohio."

"Your Majesty, we've detained 585 Negroes, with more arrests being made every day," Secretary Wayne explained. "Our biggest dilemma now is space. The prison at Fort Pitt overflows with Pennsylvania farmers from this whiskey rebellion. We've begun construction of new holding cells, which should accommodate the influx of detainees."

"Very good, Wayne. The farmers will be hanged, every last one of them, so that will free up some space for you. As for the Africans, not one of them goes free until this infamous cook and housemaid are apprehended. Is that understood?"

"Of course, Your Majesty."

"I'd recognize Washington's cook anywhere. Big guy. Jet black. The girl, I don't recall as much, but I'm confident we'll get them both. They'll be executed as well. And if any son-of-a-bitch Whig has a complaint, you tell them these are prisoners of war, just as Mr. Harison has explained in the press. They have given aid and comfort to Blue Jacket and the Shawnee. I'd also remind everyone that our constitution grants the supreme leader power to suspend habeas corpus during wartime. These arrests are necessary and proper for the security of the National States."

"Hear, hear!" The cabinet applauded in unison.

They discussed new roads connecting Ohio to Fort Pitt and the inevitable statehood for Ohio.

"The bank has been quite busy these days," Robert Morris said with pride. "Men of good standing, good reputation, and fine families have taken out loans to purchase property in Ohio. The population should soon exceed fifty thousand."

"Just make sure we get a loyal state government out there." Hamilton scratched his head. "I sure as hell don't want Arthur St. Clair as governor. The man couldn't even lead an army to defeat a tribe of savages. Good thing Wayne, here, bailed him out. St. Clair is an embarrassment to our nation. Whigs, too. Keep 'em out. A Whig should have as much chance of buying land in Ohio as a Columbian slave driver."

"As you wish, Your Majesty. We should see a new state, chock-full of loyal subjects by the next round of congressional elections."

Next, the secretary of state updated Hamilton on the Georgia War. "They're getting stomped on, just as we anticipated. They rebuilt Fort Morris, then lost it a few days later." Laughter filled the room. "The Spanish should be in Savannah soon. After that, nothing stands in the way of them taking the capital in Augusta. However, Henry did give in and raise a national army. Pinckney will lead it."

"Yes, I've heard. But I still have no intention of using our soldiers." Hamilton pointed to Rufus King and Anthony Wayne. "Just money and supplies should be plenty for the Spanish to conquer Georgia. If King Charles cannot defeat an imbecile like Patrick Henry in battle, then he has no business wearing a crown. He'll end up sharing sob stories with Arthur St. Clair in the local saloon. Mr. King, I want you to hire some men to survey Upper Louisiana. You and Morris start working on land plots to sell to settlers, just like in Ohio. These new territories will be a cash cow for the government!"

Secretary King dared to ask, "Your Majesty, have you considered the constitutionality of adding territory? Our Constitution is quite vague on the matter, but should we not seek congressional approval to acquire Louisiana?"

The room went quiet. Cabinet meetings always included a smidge of debate, but nobody had ever questioned the constitutionality of Hamilton's decisions. If the supreme leader made a decision, then the decision was constitutional. End of debate.

King tried to amend his question. "I only ask because Congress would no doubt consent to the annexation. I mean, why give the Whigs something else to cry about?"

The silence was deafening before Hamilton responded. "Does the supreme leader have exclusive authority to make treaties with other nations?"

"Yes, Your Majesty, he does," Jonathan Dayton said with smug confidence.

"Good. Then the matter is settled. At the conclusion of this war, I shall sign a treaty with Spain, ceding Upper Louisiana to me. Is that more to your liking, Mr. King?"

"As you wish, Your Majesty."

"Very well. Now since you mentioned the Whig faction, what are we to do about it? How do we dismantle it?"

An eager Jonathan Dayton chimed in again. "I've had some thoughts on the matter, Your Majesty."

The other cabinet members rolled their eyes when the goody two-shoes spoke.

"And they are?"

"Suppose a new executive department was formed. The Department of Press. Its function would be to review any new publications and prevent seditious ones from going into business. Mr. Harison here could head it up. The secretary of press. He's a skilled journalist, and he attends the cabinet meetings now anyway."

Richard Harison smiled, delighted at the proposal. "His Majesty and I have discussed similar ideas. I've already been working on the publication of a newspaper. *The Federal Gazette*. It will be the government's newspaper, circulated in every state, with essential stories about the progress and prosperity the supreme leader has brought to us, and we will not hold back from scathing reviews of the Whig faction. This new Department of Press could issue the paper weekly."

Rufus King grew more agitated by the minute. "Gentlemen, it pains me to sound like such a lawyer today, but article four of our Bill of Rights establishes freedom of the press." He was more comfortable arguing with Dayton and Harison instead of the supreme leader. "You can't just stop publication of a paper because you don't like what it says, Mr. Dayton."

"Oh, but we can, Mr. King. We most certainly can. The function of press is to inform citizens with accurate information, so they make good, sound judgements. The press needs to be held accountable for achieving those aims. What Aaron Burr is doing with the *American Whig Journal* does not meet the criteria of press. Not even close. The paper does not inform. It publishes libelous trash. It makes it more difficult for voters to make sound judgements. Press? I think not. It is disgusting filth. However, it does meet the criteria of sedition and, during wartime, I would argue treason. Now, if you'd like to discuss the Constitution, it includes just as much language about prosecuting sedition and treason as it does a free press." Dayton may have annoyed the other cabinet members with his youthful enthusiasm, but he was perhaps the most skilled lawyer in the country. Hamilton had appointed him to the post of attorney general for good reason.

Thrilled, Richard Harison jumped from his seat. "Indeed, you are correct! The Department of Press will prevent the publication of libelous content and promote the *Federal Gazette*. We can even make sure that our gazette is the cheapest publication available."

"Free," Hamilton added. "The paper will be free, paid for with government coffers, and delivered to every household. The idea is brilliant in its simplicity!" The supreme leader's concurrence was enough to silence Rufus King.

The discussion turned to women and booze for another thirty minutes, and Hamilton bragged about the Roman architecture of the Federal Palace that was sprouting up around them.

After dismissing his cabinet members through the gargantuan columns that guarded the front entrance to the palace, Hamilton held Jonathan Dayton back for a private talk.

"You've been quite a busy man, Mr. Dayton. It has not gone unnoticed."

"Thank you, Your Majesty. It is an honor to be so busy in the service of your reign."

"Yes, well, I have some more business for you to conduct. Send your men to New York as soon as possible. Have them arrest Aaron Burr on the charge of sedition and bring him to Philadelphia."

"Of course, Your Majesty. It would be my pleasure to lead the operation and to see the look on that bastard's face when we detain him. I can personally escort my men on the morrow."

"No. That won't be necessary. You have a different, more urgent assignment, more classified. These slaves from Mount Vernon, the fugitives. They have become a nuisance, a thorn in my side. And this roundup of Negroes in Ohio is wasting valuable resources. Should Mr. Pinckney's Columbian army prove to be a formidable opponent, we will need those resources to fight in Georgia. If it were anyone other than Charles Cotesworth Pinckney, I would not devote a second thought to it. However, as a military general, Pinckney is not to be taken lightly. So, we need solid closure to the matter of chasing the fugitive slaves from Mount Vernon. The American people deserve closure, and God knows I do. I want you to ride to Fort Pitt in the morning. Do not return without two suspects. You should have almost a thousand imprisoned slaves from which to choose. A large, dark, toothless male and a skinny, teenaged, freckled girl. You've seen the descriptions. Again, Mr. Dayton, your instructions are to not return without them. It is essential to put this episode behind us."

Chapter 13

1792

To any of the Columbian soldiers who served in the Revolutionary War, Vice President and Commander in Chief Pinckney resembled the late George Washington in more than a few ways—his slow movements and erect posture atop his horse, the way his uniform hugged his body like a knight's armor, his razor-sharp focus and controlled, emotionless demeanor. Alexander Hamilton may have admired Washington, but Pinckney mimicked him. If Washington could defeat the British with an inexperienced, outnumbered army, then Pinckney could do the same against the Spanish.

In his first and most popular decision of the war, the commander in chief called upon Revolutionary War hero Henry "Light Horse Harry" Lee to take up arms once again and lead a platoon. The storied leader of the Siege of Augusta had ripped Georgia's capital city from British control during the Revolution. He would not hesitate to defend it a second time. Lee resigned the governorship of Virginia and headed off to Savannah.

"Give it to me straight, Mr. Vice President. The good, the bad, and the ugly. What kind of behemoth are we up against here?" Lee asked with great enthusiasm.

"The good news is that we have an advantage in morale, just like our fight with the British. Our soldiers will fight for a cause. A loss for Georgia could spell the death of our infant republic before having the opportunity to flourish—and flourish it will, Mr. Lee."

Lee punched his chest like a gladiator. A seismic ball of energy, he hadn't stopped moving since he'd arrived at Pinckney's headquarters. The vice president hoped that Lee would instill the same passion and fury in his men.

Pinckney continued his assessment. "On the other hand, a loss for the Spanish? What would it mean? Absolutely nothing. Just another mark in the loss tally from her wars of conquest across Europe and North America. Georgia is nothing to them. A speckle of salt in the sea of their empire. I doubt the Spanish soldiers possess the slightest understanding of what they're fighting for. Hell, *I'm* not even sure of that. The invasion is utter madness."

"Madness, indeed. It reeks of Hamilton!" Lee clenched his fists and his teeth at the same time.

"Ricardos has had an unhealthy dose of confidence, prowling out of the swamps and through the countryside without opposition. He feels invincible. We must take advantage."

"General, I'm just the man you need to crush the son of a bitch," Lee growled.

Experienced well beyond his years, Light Horse Harry Lee had begun his career in the Virginia dragoons, worked his way up to the rank of major, and then to lieutenant colonel—all before the age of twenty-five. Now in his thirties, he felt about eighteen.

"But of course, there are disadvantages," Pinckney cautioned.

Lee guzzled his third cup of coffee. "The slaves."

"There you have it. The slaves, our biggest conundrum that has dogged us since 1789, since our 'enlightened' neighbors decided on gradual emancipation. Our slaves run away in stampedes, even more now that war's begun. Before, they had to trek all the way to the National States or Spanish Florida. Now, they just need to find enemy lines, and when they do, many of them enlist on the spot."

"No need to tell me, General. I've lost more property this year than I have in the last ten years combined. That is why my first move as governor was to order the Virginia militia to serve as slave catchers and help out the ARPs. Although this complicates matters further. With slaves running and masters chasing, nobody remains on the farms to grow food. Food that could be very useful for an army."

"Just thank the Lord we *have* an army, Mr. Lee." Pinckney shook his head. "Recruitment has been quite successful, though. About ten thousand volunteers and conscripts; plus all five state governors have called up their militias. A nationalist spirit has intoxicated our people, and we must take advantage of it. I've ordered most militia to the western front. Rumor has it that the National States have already begun arming the Chickasaw and Creek Indians to fight against us."

"And to the east as well!" Lee shouted. He punched the air in excitement. "My advice is to shield South Carolina's coastline from the Spanish Navy just in case they're making any plans."

Pinckney wouldn't admit it out loud, but he hadn't considered the possibility of a naval attack. The Spanish sent a constant flow of soldiers and supplies to Florida, but an attack from the Carolina coast did not escape the realm of possibility.

"Very well, Mr. Lee. I shall order the South Carolina militia to the beaches."

"And fortify Savanna forthwith!" Lee drooled with confidence. "We'll push the thornbacks all the way back to the Atlantic!"

Pinckney raised a finger. "Here, we must be more tempered, sir."

Lee's mouth gaped in disbelief. "Tempered warfare, General? Seems quite paradoxical." His coffee breath hung in the air.

"To the contrary. We'll be pulling out of Savannah. It is in our best interest."

"Mr. Vice President, you've got me all worked up for nothing? Lure me to the bedroom and leave me unsatisfied? I'll take on the Spanish single-handedly if need be." The light humor couldn't conceal Lee's irritation.

"No, no, sir. You'll see plenty of action. That, I can guarantee. But Savannah is the wrong battle at the wrong time. I fought in the Continental Army, just as you did, and if General Washington taught me one thing, it was the art of retreat. Washington chose his battles wisely, and so must we. As we speak, General Ricardos is marching toward us with an army of thousands. I've already ordered the evacuation of Savannah."

"You would hand it over without a fight?" Lee stomped his foot like a toddler. "It won't go over well with the townspeople, you must know that."

"I'm well aware, General." Pinckney's slow drawl made it clear that he would not be negotiating, but Lee wouldn't let up.

"You want them to gather their possessions, their livestock, their slaves, abandon their farms and shops? This is no small undertaking."

"Sometimes the best decisions are not. Sometimes they're unpopular. How many times was Washington threatened with demotion? Now our best move is retreat. When we leave this place a ghost town, the Spanish will have no reason to torch it. We'll regroup with more volunteers in Augusta, organize an unstoppable resistance, and then push Ricardos back on his heels from there. We'll begin our assault from a position of strength, and when we return to Savannah, the townspeople will find it just as they left it. At this moment, all of our resources must be devoted to defending the capital city."

The vice president watched Lee turn to the wall and pout, in desperate need of some ego-stroking. "Augusta is the right battle, and you are the right leader for it. The British capture of Augusta and your siege to retake it are still fresh in the people's memory. They'll be happy to see you again, Mr. Lee."

Still unsatisfied, Lee mumbled, "So we fight in Augusta."

"We fight in Augusta," the commander in chief confirmed.

In truth, the Battle of Augusta was over before it began due to Pinckney's skill as a military tactician. After fortifying the town, Pinckney and Lee split their men into two divisions. Pinckney marched four thousand men to the fields, south of Augusta. Lee stayed back and surrounded the capital with more Columbian regulars ready to advance and protect Pinckney's flanks. Hundreds of ordinary citizens—men, women, and children—remained in Augusta to defend their homes if the Spanish broke the lines.

When the two armies squared off in open field, Pinckney shocked Ricardos with bold aggression and a willingness to immediately go on the offense. They showered the Spanish intruders with a barrage of iron, howitzers, and mortars before the enemy could even complete their formations. From the start of the battle, Pinckney's men advanced forward, pushing the

Spanish soldiers back toward Savannah. Had General Ricardos learned George Washington's lessons on retreat, he would have aborted the futile mission earlier than he did. The Spanish reformed their lines on unfamiliar grounds and wasted a second afternoon on needless bloodshed.

By the time Light Horse Harry Lee's division had arrived for some action, the Spanish were sitting ducks. Lee's men flanked Ricardos from the west and forced them to retreat. In an otherwise flawless battle, Lee sent the Spanish on a clear path straight back toward Savannah. Had they attacked from the east, Ricardos would have been left to wander in an unforgiving wilderness in the middle of Georgia.

Charles Cotesworth Pinckney had been correct in his insistence that a national army could stand toe to toe with the Spanish military. As news spread, the people's reverence for their vice president approached a level only enjoyed by George Washington before him. But he had not won the war yet. The Spanish still controlled Savannah; fresh regiments of soldiers, ex-slaves, and Seminole Indians came from Florida; and their defeat at Augusta provided a more convincing argument that the Spanish required assistance from the National States army.

***

Benjamin Winthrop stunned them all. Even in his brand-new overcoat and top hat, he still looked like a greasy beast with a floppy, egg-shaped belly protruding through his sweat-stained shirt. Yet he did, indeed, stun them all. He never lost faith in the supreme leader's ability to conquer Ohio, and had been investing in cheap Ohio land for years. The Ohio Land Company, previously owned by New Englanders, all but gave the land away after New England's secession from the National States. The Treasury Department also sold Ohio land at a bargain. Others in the Merchant's Coffee House declared Winthrop crazy to buy up land in the middle of a war zone; but after Blue Jacket's surrender, investors and settlers flocked to buy up the Ohio frontier, making Winthrop the lucky beneficiary. A few thousand acres here, a few thousand acres there; the value skyrocketed, and he sold faster than he could count up all the profits. He remained the plump, chauvinist drunk at the bar, about a million bucks richer.

Mr. Winthrop stumbled down the creaking stairs of the coffee house, a bit weak in the legs, followed by Lydia, Aaron Burr's favorite prostitute, still coming to grips with her new role as the opulent Winthrop's regular concubine. Though he paid well, Lydia shed a little more dignity with each sexual escapade, with each drop of sweat that drizzled from the boar's matted chest hair to poison her beautiful caramel skin. Burr and the rest of the politicians sweet-talked her and promised a glorious future for such a stunning young lady, but they were all talk. They were politicians. Lydia found herself trapped underneath three hundred pounds of Winthrop's penetrating blubber almost every day. No matter how hard she scrubbed, Lydia could not rid herself of his rotten-egg stench.

"You better pace yourself, Winthrop," a voice from the bar suggested. "It's not even noon, and you're well on your way to contracting the French disease!"

"No, sir, my gal is as clean as they come! No disease here—except Ohio fever. Sweet, sweet, Ohio fever! I've sure got that!" Winthrop's voice soared through the room.

The whole building vibrated as the clumsy man wobbled off the last step as if he struggled to keep his balance in an earthquake. He removed his new hat to wipe the swamp of perspiration from his forehead.

"Of course, if you're interested, I could spread that fever to you, good sir. A nice tract of land near Cincinnati, perhaps? Better buy now. The price goes up every day."

"If I had any interest in Ohio, Benji, I would take you up on it. But I've got some prospects in Pittsburgh right now. A bustling town is sprouting up around the supreme leader's new prison out there. Lots of jobs to be had, attracting thousands of settlers. I think if I strike now, I'll come out on top."

"Suit yourself. But don't come crying to me when the first jailbreak renders your land worthless."

The man shook his head and sighed at the thought of Benjamin Winthrop, New York's village idiot, lecturing him on value and worth. Hamilton's financial plans must have been a genuine success if a buffoon like that could become so rich so fast.

When Lydia made her way downstairs, Jonathan Taylor helped her to the bar and ordered her a coffee.

"And what about you, Mr. Taylor?" A jealous Winthrop interrupted. "A fine, respectable Negro like you could do very well for himself in Ohio. I'd give you a fair price—the word of a gentleman." More laughter emerged from the bar at the notion of Winthrop, the gentleman. "Never mind them, Taylor. How about it? Even if you don't want to live there. Buy now, hold on to the property, and then sell for a healthy profit."

Before committing to the conversation, Jonathan stirred the milk in Lydia's coffee and reached his finger to her forehead to rearrange a few sopping hairs that fell in front of her face.

"Believe it or not, I've actually considered it, Mr. Winthrop. My work here in New York has become, well, a bit unsatisfactory."

Winthrop cozied up next to his potential buyer at the bar, prompting Lydia to walk away. "Of course it's unsatisfactory. New York is no place for a Negro to succeed. And I say that as a friend to your people, Jonathan. I'm no slave driver like some of these men. Montgomery and Ohio. That's where you'll find opportunities for Negroes."

"That may be true, but I'm afraid none of these bankers will extend financial credit to a black man. So, I wouldn't be able to afford it, despite my interest."

"None of these bankers in New York, of course not. But in Ohio? I'd personally vouch for you. Trust me, I sold all the bankers their land in Ohio. I can call in a favor, and you'd afford a small plot of land before suppertime."

Jonathan turned to look at Aaron Burr chatting up another politician in the coffee house. The ex-slave considered his devotion to Whig principles and the irony of spying on Whigs in the service of Supreme Leader Hamilton. Winthrop interrupted his thoughts.

"You know what your problem is, Taylor? You get too involved in politics around here, too smitten by the likes of Aaron Burr. Trust me, I've seen a hundred Aaron Burrs come through here. Today it's him, tomorrow it will be someone else. They're all the same. They all talk out both sides of their mouth, and ain't a one of 'em gonna do anything for you. Look at me. I have no political principles one way or the other. I don't give a damn about any of it, and look how well I've turned out. I pledge my loyalty to Hamilton—genuine loyalty, everlasting trust in our leader. But that's the extent of it. You'd be wise to do the same, and stay away from all that Whig business."

Jonathan pondered the salesman's pitch, unable to reveal the true political nature of his work. "And what would I do in Ohio, this land that's free of politics? I suppose working for a Whig newspaper is out of the question."

"You can do whatever the hell you'd like. Go ahead and start a newspaper. Start a little coffee house for the merchants like this one. You good with numbers? I'll be moving out there myself and could use someone to handle my accounting."

"Indeed, I am good with numbers, sir. I may take you up on that. However, I still have pressing business to attend to here. I will keep your offer in mind, though."

After a firm handshake, Jonathan wiped his palm clean of Winthrop's sweat. He rejoined Lydia at the other end of the bar.

Across the room, Aaron Burr concocted political strategies, as usual.

"We're already seeing progress," he explained, wide-eyed. "In Pennsylvania, Albert Gallatin is sure to win a Senate seat, and we'll put William Findley in the House. We just need to prevent any mischief or intrigue like we saw in the governor's race. I've arranged for some lawyers to observe the polls on Election Day. And we'll do the same for you in New York," he said in excitement, pointing at his guest. "By God, we'll get you elected. Senator Edward Livingston of New York. Now how does that sound?"

Edward Livingston had inherited political opportunities from his esteemed family, as had many politicians in New York. He was the handsomest statesman available, and the second-best lawyer in the state, next to Burr. Livingston's vibrant good looks concealed a very serious side to the man, but it was vibrant good looks that won elections. Burr intended to prance the charismatic young jurist around the state so he may shake the hand of each voter in person.

"But our ideas, too," Livingston protested. "I'm eager to share our progressive policies with the American people."

Burr's torso pushed forward as he spoke. "Sure, Livingston. But if there is one reliable maxim of American politics, it is this: The American people don't want policies. They want to be entertained."

"Yes, well, perhaps I can entertain them with roads, canals, and universities."

"You and Gallatin will stir things up in Philadelphia, for sure. Keep this obnoxious tyrant on a short leash. Lest our constitution is meaningless, just for show. I still believe our legislature can check the power of the supreme leader."

"I share your optimism, sir. Yet the supreme leader's popularity expands every day, along with his power. This new *Federal Gazette* and the Department of Press has elevated Hamilton's reputation to that of a deity. He somehow becomes more beloved as he abuses more power. A frustrating situation, I must confess."

"Department of Press? More like the Department of Lies and Propaganda," Burr said, shaking his head. "And they criticize me for petty campaigning. Ha! That little paper is practically an organized campaign to perpetuate the big lie that Alexander Hamilton is our savior. And just take a look around. Every man in this place has a copy, like it's the damn napkin served with your cocktail." Burr noticed Livingston drop his head. "But do not despair, young friend." He wrapped his arm around Livingston's shoulders. "*The American Whig Journal* is fighting the good fight. Our circulation continues to increase, and we shall continue to wage this battle of ideas! As you say, we will entertain them with our ideas because our ideas are better. We'll put on one hell of a show, and on Election Day, we'll win."

"Better tell that to Benjamin Winthrop." Livingston laughed. "To that fat ass, Hamilton is the Second Coming of Christ."

Burr joined in the laughter. "Well, we can't save them all, sir. We can't save them from themselves."

When Livingston headed to the bar for a second round of whiskey, Burr glanced down at the latest edition of the *Federal Gazette*, left on the table next to him by the last patron. The headlines jumped off the pages and targeted Burr like the bullets he'd dodged in the Battle of Quebec during the Revolutionary War. An article titled "Negro Town in Montgomery Thrives" described a vibrant community of free blacks working hard to build a city of their own, Liberty City, separate from white Americans. Another article, "The New Fort Pitt," praised the expansion of the fort and its conversion to an effective jail that held hostile natives and prisoners of all sorts, including political prisoners. It lauded the city of Pittsburgh and, of course, credited Alexander Hamilton. "He keeps us safe," the article refrained. "He keeps us safe."

Burr paid particular attention to an article titled "Spanish Take Savannah." It described the heroism of the Spanish army and Spanish Floridians in their war against Georgia. He did not know whether to believe the claim that Savannah had fallen and that Augusta would fall next. It was no stretch of the imagination to believe that a world power like Spain could overrun the entirety of Columbia.

As Edward Livingston returned with two brandy snifters, Burr forced another smile and crumpled up the gazette, using it to wipe off the tabletop.

"Compliments of Benjamin Winthrop," Livingston said. "I tried to refuse. I really did, but he would not hear of it." Livingston plopped back down in his chair, almost falling off the edge.

"Very well, then. Now, what of this business with Spain? Following your imminent election to the Senate, the Whig Party will have to take a stance on this fighting in Columbia. What say you?"

"Quite honestly, I don't know what to make of it. I fail to see how the National States could benefit from being surrounded by Spanish territory. Would it not swallow us up? It seems that Hamilton's personal hatred of Patrick Henry runs so deep that he'd rather share this continent with a hostile European power than an independent American republic. Unbelievable."

Burr scratched his chin in deep thought. "I tend to agree with you. However, he's done quite a job of stirring up patriotism that we haven't seen since the days of Revolution. I think we can ill afford to throw support behind Columbia at this juncture."

Livingston could not respond, interrupted by a booming noise at the front door of the coffee house, as if a team of horses had barged inside. Five men dressed in ominous, black uniforms stood at the entrance with guns drawn. The room went silent.

"Are we being held up?" Burr asked.

"Aaron Burr!" the lead officer shouted with authority.

Burr remained silent and puzzled, as did everyone else in the room.

Jonathan stayed at the bar and placed his hand on Lydia's knee when she began to shiver out of fear. "Probably just some police officers looking for a scam artist," he whispered.

"Which one is Aaron Burr?" The man had addressed his question to the side-whiskered bartender this time.

About to soil his trousers, the bartender gestured with a subtle nod in the direction of Burr, in the back of the room.

All five Blackshirts marched toward Burr, knocking over the chairs that stood in their way.

"Are you Aaron Burr?" asked the foul-breathed leader.

Burr decided to stand and confront the man. "Now just who is it that searches for Burr?"

"Agents of the Department of Justice: National States of America! You are Aaron Burr? Publisher of *The American Whig Journal?*"

"The name Burr appears nowhere on the Whig journal you speak of." Burr and the other journalists used pennames in the publication for their own safety in situations such as this.

"Of course it's Burr! And he peddles that Whig paper you fellas are talkin' about." Benjamin Winthrop turned on Burr as fast as he'd bought him his last drink. He wouldn't pass up an opportunity to kiss up to the National States government. "He is Aaron Burr."

Winthrop received a few sneers of derision.

"Now just wait one minute," Edward Livingston interjected. "Supposing this is the publisher, what business is it of yours? He has a constitutional right to speak his mind through a free press."

"He does not have a constitutional right to commit sedition or treason," was the response. "Now that'll be enough bickering. Mr. Burr, you're under arrest!"

Three men began to apprehend the suspect, who was powerless to resist their strength. Fearing for his own safety, Livingston reached in his coat pocket for the revolver that he carried. The lead Blackshirt caught the gun out of the corner of his eye. He turned and fired without hesitation, sending a black cloud of gun smoke into the air and a lethal dose of lead into the chest of Edward Livingston, ending his life in an instant and killing his political career before it could begin.

Burr surged out of his captors' grasp and fell to his dying friend. Slipping on Livingston's blood, the officers tackled Burr and hogtied him.

Most of the customers had bolted out of the Merchant's Coffee House at the sound of gunfire, but Jonathan moved closer toward the chaos. As the four Blackshirts escorted Burr outside, Jonathan tried to locate a pulse in the lifeless body.

"Jonathan!" Burr shouted in desperation. "A lawyer, Jonathan! Secure a lawyer!"

Stunned, Jonathan fought back tears as he sat motionless next to Edward Livingston's dead body. His spying for the supreme leader had led to the arrest of Aaron Burr and the murder of Edward Livingston. The man was dead.

One tall, slender Blackshirt remained standing over the bloody scene. He leaned over and nudged Jonathan's shoulder to get his attention. "Mr. Taylor? Jonathan Taylor?" the man enquired. Jonathan stared at the ground, still in complete shock. "Mr. Jonathan Taylor?!" the man shouted now.

Jonathan's eyes bulged as he looked up at the stranger.

"Please come with me, Mr. Taylor."

"Now wait just a minute. Who are you? And how do you know my name? I have nothing to do with Mr. Burr or his political fantasies."

"Mr. Taylor, it is not necessary to create a spectacle. If you would please follow me outside, you will see that I mean you no harm."

"Not on your life, pal." Jonathan stood and backed up in a defensive stance. "Whatever you have to say, you can say right here."

The armed officer rolled his eyes. He came closer to Jonathan and lowered his voice to a whisper. "If you are indeed the Jonathan Taylor that I'm looking for, then you will be interested in reading a correspondence from Philadelphia. From a distinguished Mr. Samuel Lion."

"Samuel Lion," Jonathan repeated. He'd recognized the supreme leader's code name before uttering the words.

"Follow me, Mr. Taylor."

Jonathan complied and followed the Blackshirt outside to a bustling Wall Street, where the officers' five horses observed the gathering crowd. The man scanned their surroundings before handing Jonathan a note.

Jonathan turned away from the Blackshirts and opened the correspondence, which was indeed from Alexander Hamilton.

Mr. Taylor,

Congratulations on the completion of your assignment. This police escort will take you to Philadelphia, where we will meet to discuss instructions for your next mission.

Samuel Lion

Benjamin Winthrop owned such an imposing landmass in central Ohio that its emerging town became known as Winthrop. He sold small plots of land up and down the Scioto River to enterprising young pioneers, predominantly German immigrants, who came in flocks to join the French and Indian settlers who had lived there for decades. By the fall of 1792, the small but diverse population of Winthrop entertained itself in a few taverns and a flashy brothel. A town named after Benjamin Winthrop would have to contain the finest of whorehouses. The First Bank of Winthrop towered over the Winthrop Lutheran Church and the volunteer fire department.

Benjamin had a private, two-story mansion built of stone and clapboard on Main Street, overlooking the river. Here, he would spend his days in retirement, enjoying the breeze, drinking himself to a stupor on the extended

Colonial porch, and stuffing his stomach full of unimaginable quantities of comfort food in a dining room designed for a royal family. He shared the mansion with his pet hound dog, Smokey. By night, Winthrop frequented the town's women of ill repute as much as possible. Old habits die hard.

He had the outer walls of the mansion painted in a revolting combination of purple and bright yellow—because he could, because Benjamin Winthrop had been kicked around and ridiculed his entire life, taken advantage of, and held down, until now. Now it was his turn to call the shots, to live like a king, and if he wanted a purple-and-yellow castle, then so let it be done. He called the colorful estate "Whetstone Manor."

Winthrop had moved from New York with boatloads of money, but very few possessions and no furnishings for the mansion, except for an armchair, a dining-room table, and two portraits: one of Supreme Leader Hamilton, a common decoration in wealthy NSA households, and a portrait of his other hero, George Washington.

Fulfilling his insatiable appetite for a lavish lifestyle would require some help. Winthrop needed a housekeeper to tidy up the pigsty at Whetstone Manor. However, most ladies in town had learned to keep a safe distance from the drunken village buffoon, a known womanizer already. If Winthrop thought he could start anew with a fresh reputation in Ohio, he was mistaken. He needed a desperate woman, indeed, to take on the challenge of scrubbing the muck and grime at Whetstone Manor.

"My name is Red Squirrel, of the Seneca Tribe, but people call me Red. I spent years as a housemaid for my old mistress before makin' it to Ohio."

Winthrop reclined in his chair, blowing smoke rings from his tobacco pipe. He was uncharacteristically sober. "I suppose you use the surname Johnson."

"Johnson, suh?" Red Squirrel had never considered a last name.

"The fugitive slaves in New York all go by Johnson. Makes it mighty difficult for some slave catcher to find you when everyone goes by the same name." Smokey jumped on Winthrop's lap and licked his face clean of dried spaghetti sauce from lunch.

"Yes, suh. Red Johnson, as you wish."

"I have no quarrel with your kind, the Negro race," Winthrop explained, revealing a soft side. "If fact, I damn near fell in love with one in New York. I would've brought Lydia here as my wife, but she wouldn't have me. You see, most people find me repulsive. I know this; it's no secret. But a man's got certain needs, and I'll be damned if a brown-skinned beauty can't satisfy my needs."

Red Squirrel ignored his philandering. "I've worked as a body servant and a seamstress. I know how to garden, and I'm a decent cook." She stretched the truth on the cooking.

"Ya know, you sure could satisfy my needs, speaking of brown-skinned beauties." Winthrop was more interested in other qualifications.

"Mr. Winthrop, this house is a mess, and there ain't no one waitin' in line behind me who is willin' to clean it. I'm a free woman, and I'll walk out that door if your sexual advances continue. Now would you like a housemaid or not?" Red Squirrel shivered. She'd never spoken to a white man with the confidence or attitude that she'd just forced upon Benjamin Winthrop. A heat wave rushed through her chest, and she imagined Charlotte smiling in approval.

"Well, as I said. People find me repulsive. I suppose my maid ought to be no different. Pay is one dollar a day; that ain't negotiable. You can start in the dining room right behind you. Also, just down the road, on the corner of Main and High Streets, is a Negro boarding house. I own the property. Nothing extravagant, but it should suit your needs for three dollars a week. It'd be much more comfortable than a cramped longhouse of Seneca Indians."

"Thank you, Mr. Winthrop." She paused before exiting. "I don't find you repulsive, suh. I think you got a big heart, and I'm grateful for the job. But I got a man, and I've been taught to stand up for myself. I'll work hard. You won't regret it."

She walked to the dining room and fell to her knees in panic, wincing at the sight of Winthrop's painting of her former master, the man she'd killed. She reached for the edge of the dining-room table, rattling the dirty dishes, almost knocking them to the floor. Smokey barked to alert his master. She pulled herself up before Winthrop entered the room.

"What is it now, girl? Can't handle the stink already? I told you I'm a repulsive man." He laughed. Smokey barked even louder.

"No, suh. It's the paintin', suh. Scared me, is all. It's so lifelike. It look jus' like Mas—General Washton." She kept her head low to the ground, unable to look Washington in the eyes. In her mind, she imagined the last facial expression he'd ever made, utter shock, bleeding from his mouth onto Ona's freckled cheeks. Her face was the last thing he'd seen before succumbing to death. Frightened, she looked back up to the artwork. Better to see the lionized portrait of a courageous leader than the horrifying image that she could never erase from her memory. Inside the picture frame, Washington posed with a white horse standing in a snowstorm at Valley Forge. His eyes admonished her. She heard him scream out for vengeance in the exact tone of voice he used when angered by bad crops, incompetent politicians, or lazy slaves. "Justice!" she heard his voice repeat again and again in her ears.

"It's my favorite piece," Winthrop interrupted the turmoil in her head. He adjusted the crooked frame on the wall, still leaving it a bit off-center.

She glanced back up at the horse, avoiding eye contact with Washington. *What a terribly inaccurate portrayal of Nelson's coloring*, she thought.

"And we should be celebrating this portrait today, of all days," Winthrop announced. "They finally captured the two slaves who conspired to murder the man. Go on, pour me a glass of whiskey, Red!"

Her eyes tremored. "What'd you say? They capture who?"

"In today's paper!" He reached for the *Federal Gazette* to show her. Red ignored it, unable to read its contents. "They found the two slaves, Hercules and Ona Judge, detained at Fort Pitt and being transferred to the capital for justice to be severed. Goddamn beasts."

Red Squirrel hunched over to regain her balance. "That's . . . that's wonderful."

She poured the drink for her boss and then sat down in a dining-room chair, her back to the portrait. She needed to process this new information. What did it mean?

The Main Street Boarding House sheltered most of the city of Winthrop's black population, which had declined because so many had been arrested after the supreme leader's impulsive order to round up every dark-skinned person in Ohio. Not one of the prisoners ever stood trial.

Red Squirrel found her third-floor room much smaller than the Family House at Mount Vernon, though she didn't have to crawl over three other slaves to find a comfortable sleeping position. Ten square feet, four walls, and a mattress; a slight improvement compared to hiding out in the woods from slave catchers and National States soldiers. After hearing the latest news, she would never have to hide from anyone ever again.

Chasing Honey joined her with a few changes of clothes and some cooking utensils. He grabbed her by the waist and thrust his body toward her as they embraced. He kissed her and spoke at the same time. "I heard. Did you hear? I heard!"

Red Squirrel smiled and kissed him hard on the lips. "I heard. We been captured. We caught." He warmed her face with his deep breaths. "I think we safe," she whispered.

Honey agreed. "They must think these people are us. I think we really safe."

"You think they'll be killed?" Her voice grew sullen.

"They gonna be killed with savage brutality, like wicked traitors." He closed his eyes at the thought.

"It should be us," she whispered.

"It shouldn't be anyone, girl. Not us, not them. But we can't dwell on that. We safe now."

He pulled her close again, and they tumbled to the bed. It was the first time they'd made love in complete safety. A roof over their head, and no bloodhounds or soldiers on their tail. The sensations felt a little warmer, his embrace a little tighter, their movements more graceful. He cradled her body with a soothing touch. The evening began a new chapter of their love, an unfamiliar love.

John Jay barely recognized Philadelphia anymore. He remembered an ordinary town of a few taverns and civic halls that had hosted the first and second Constitutional Conventions. He remembered a younger version of himself and an even younger Alexander Hamilton getting drunk, debating politics late into the evenings. In just a few short years, Philadelphia had grown into a thriving capital city, almost reminiscent of London or Paris, and Jay, another cog in the wheel of the federal machine, locked in the chambers of the Supreme Court, arguing over the fine print of maritime law, original jurisdiction, and the most insipid clauses of the National States Constitution. He and Hamilton had created political success for themselves, though not quite as planned. Jay had begun to wonder if it had all been worth it.

The two old friends met in an empty courtyard of the Federal Palace, void of any flora in the brisk February climate. Jay always found Philadelphia's winter a welcome departure from the rotten stench of the warmer seasons. Hamilton paced with the posture of a king, though Jay could detect that his friend's mind was preoccupied elsewhere.

"I've come first and foremost as a friend, Alexander. How have you been? How are Elizabeth and the kids?" He always had a way of putting Hamilton's mind at ease, though it would be a much more difficult task these days.

"Elizabeth is with child. Our fifth. We haven't yet made that public, to spare her the national attention and stress. Neither of us can walk down Market Street without being mobbed by revering common folk." Hamilton grinned, reveling in the new inconvenience, though it was a serious problem for his family. "Americans are quite peculiar. They insist on not wanting a king, and they reject royalty. Yet they rush to treat their leaders in a fashion one step above royalty. A king is what they really want, for all their denial."

"Well, I can't say I know what that is like, Mr. Supreme Leader." Jay refused to address his old drinking buddy as "Your Majesty." "When I walk down Market Street, I have just as good a chance of being robbed by a pauper or propositioned by a prostitute as any other man. I was better-known in New York as a legislator. Here, I enjoy a greater sense of anonymity—invisibility, even. I could vanish tomorrow in the winds of the Schuylkill with little notice. But on the subject of a fifth child, I do have experience. After the fourth, it's a breeze. Sarah birthed our fifth two years ago now. A breeze, I tell you," he said with a sarcastic laugh.

They reminisced of family and friends, and of James Madison. What had ever happened to James Madison? He hadn't written either of them since returning to Columbia from his ambassadorship in France. Jay expressed deep concern for their old friend, in hopes of his well-being, even though Madison now pledged allegiance to a different country. Despite the political battles they'd fought, Jay always prioritized his friendships, with Madison and with Hamilton, too. He needed the supreme leader to understand this before firing a new shot on the current battlefield.

"Work has been steady these days on the bench. But these allegations. Allegations against you."

"Yes, of course. Allegations of me protecting our homeland," Hamilton scorned. "You and I have been the source of outrage to these blockheads for years. We actually govern, and simpleminded fools just can't handle it. Would they prefer an executive to just sit back and allow mob rule? No, sir. A majority of Americans support the policies of this government, I can guarantee you that."

"Yes, but I'm afraid the Supreme Court has little concern for how many Americans are on your side. Rather, we need to determine if the Constitution is."

Hamilton stopped in his tracks. "Ah ha! Ha, ha! You're joking, of course." After an awkward silence, he continued. "Mr. Jay, you and I constructed our Constitution from scratch. For heaven's sake, how could I violate it?"

"These allegations from publishers, Alex. Censoring free speech; accusations of reprisals on the press; brute force; arson, even. These are serious charges."

"Censorship of sedition?" Hamilton retorted. "The National States Congress passed the Sedition Act, and I am duty bound to enforce it. Now, if you have a problem with the legislation, you should pay a visit to the halls of Congress and leave me to rule my country as I see fit."

"I have not come here to debate. I am simply providing an update, as a courtesy from one statesman to another, and one friend to another. There are other accusations. Election fraud, violations of due process. Rounding up citizens? Citizens, Alex. Is this the America for which we fought, for which we devoted our sacred honor? Would Madison approve? Would you yourself approve, back at the Van Kleeck Tavern, just a few years ago? I think not, friend."

Hamilton's face turned red, despite the bitter cold. "For the sake of argument, suppose I have violated my own constitution. What on earth could the Supreme Court do about it? The National States Constitution does not establish equal branches of government, as the United States version did. The supreme leader possesses more power."

Jay inhaled another shot of frigid air that burned in his lungs. He cleared his throat and tasted a drop of blood before getting to the point. "Dickinson, Wilson, and I have considered declaring some executive actions unconstitutional."

Hamilton stared down his old friend as if on a dueling ground. Steam floated from each man's lips toward the other. "And under what authority would you commit such an overreach? How could three paltry judges—appointed by me, I might add, serving at the pleasure of my good grace—how could three ungrateful and unelected lawyers possess the power of which you speak?"

Jay ignored the challenge. "In all likelihood a violation of the right to a free press. The court is still reviewing evidence"—Hamilton tried to shout over him, but Jay continued with an inspired roar—"The court is still reviewing evidence of the other allegations. A ruling should be announced within days!" He chose not to reveal that he would have to cast the deciding vote. John Dickinson, a staunch nationalist, would defend the supreme leader on just about anything. On the other hand, James Wilson was prepared to strike down Hamilton's gross violations of the Constitution. John Jay possessed the mighty swing vote and, at least for the moment, was the most powerful man in the National States.

Hamilton stepped in closer to his opponent. "We are done here. But before you show yourself out, you should know this: if you dare to presume that a court can issue decrees to a supreme leader; if you neglect to acknowledge and respect the enormous power attached to this office, then sir, I will make those powers more obvious than the hairs that stand on your head, and you will rue the day that you walked on to these grounds, in my palace, with the misguided audacity to challenge my sovereignty."

The Supreme Court justice turned toward the back exit of the court-yard. "You'll give my best to Elizabeth, I trust."

Chapter 14

As the Columbian army pushed General Ricardos farther south, farmers and merchants flocked north to Standing Peachtree, the largest trading outpost in Georgia unscathed by warfare. Each morning, the tangerine sun peeked above the Chattahoochee River, casting shadows, like goblins chasing the native Creek Indians and traders through Standing Peachtree's marketplace. Between the shadows, small pockets of sunlight fell to the ground as if the dirt paths were paved with speckles of gold.

One hundred captured runaway slaves stood restless, awaiting their turn on the auction block, their bodies shivering in fear. Eager buyers eyed them up, like lions on the hunt, just before the bell rang to begin the sale. Rumors spread that a decent slave could be purchased at Standing Peachtree for under one hundred Columbian dollars. When the war ended and conditions returned to normal, these same slaves could be sold for five times that price—quite a risky investment in slaves who had already escaped once, but the potential profit margin was too tempting.

Before stepping up to the podium, the auctioneer glanced out at the crowd of greedy men, gray and too old for military service—just good for slave-driving these days. The young, guilt-ridden salesman could have borne the uniform of the Columbian army and taken up arms in defense of his country, but instead fled to Standing Peachtree upon learning of his conscription. With great shame, the tall, slender coward profited from the wartime economy while most men his age fought with valor. He turned to face the seething slave vultures with the warmest of smiles. His outstretched arm reached for the clapper of the bell, and just as he threw his weight into it, a single shot fired from beyond the river. The clang of the bell signaled every buyer in town to come closer and witness the bullet that had just pierced the young slave peddler's temple. Hunched over the auction block, he was the first casualty of the Standing Peachtree Massacre. The war had arrived.

It arrived from the West. Upon hearing news of the Spanish defeat at Augusta, a reluctant supreme leader ordered Mad Anthony Wayne and a large regiment of the National States army down the Mississippi River, where they would join Creek and Chickasaw Indians, and a small Spanish brigade from New Spain.

"Take no prisoners!" Wayne commanded as they approached Standing Peachtree. "These old-timers are armed with dueling pistols and hunting rifles, so don't go feelin' sorry for 'em." The general had nothing less than absolute slaughter on his mind, which is exactly what transpired. Wayne took sadistic pleasure in watching civilians scalped, women and children caught up in the crossfire, and the surrounding village burn like an offering to the salacious demon that had sent his army of fallen angels.

"Confiscate the goods, gentlemen. It's all contraband—food and supplies better used by us than our enemies. Take what's rightfully yours as victors," Wayne ordered.

It was all sport to him. National States soldiers competed with the Spanish to rob and pillage as much as they could. Armies needed food, and Standing Peachtree offered eggs, milk, bread, fresh meat, and whiskey— lots and lots of whiskey. The National States soldiers, including General Wayne and more than a few Indians of the war party, guzzled alcohol as the massacre played out.

The situation brought out the absolute worst in Mad Anthony, drunk and arrogant. His infamous exploits in Ohio had inflated the general's ego, already oversized, like the gut that hung over his belt and pushed out a few buttons from his military blues.

"Over there, wench! I'll take that bottle and the ham to go with it!" He shouted out orders to one of the female slaves about to be auctioned. Terrified, the young, bare-breasted woman complied. She wore only a thin linen cloth below her waist, revealing most of her smooth brown skin, oiled up for the auction.

The general sat atop his horse and watched the carnage ensue as he stuffed his mouth full of meat, stolen from the market. Halfway through the bottle of whiskey, an inebriated General Wayne shouted out, spraying his spittle, "Up here, girl!" He pet the hind of his warhorse, signaling for the young slave to jump up. She cried and fell to her knees. "Stand at attention!" Wayne shouted in a menacing, drunken slur. The woman, no older than twenty, crept up to her feet and then flew higher, pulled by the general's fat, muscular arm. "You obey your master. Didn't you learn that on a plantation?" Wayne mocked with an obnoxious Southern twang. The girl sobbed in terror.

Mad Anthony swung her fragile body around so she sat in front of him. He gnawed one last bite of ham straight off the bone and pitched the rest of it to the ground. He would need a spare hand with which to touch his new friend. Wayne holstered his sidearm and held the half-empty bottle of whiskey in one hand while reaching around to feel the girl's breasts with the other. Pig grease dripped from his filthy hands on to her chest and stomach.

"Ah, whiskey, war, and tits! What else does a man need in this world?" He reached down and tore off the skimpy linen from around her waist and wiped his mouth with it before tossing it, leaving the woman completely nude. He tossed away the bottle, too. She squealed and squawked, crying out for help, but Mad Anthony silenced her with a slap to the face and his relentless grip around her neck. He choked the oxygen out of her with one hand and slipped the other between her legs, inside of her. She gasped for air, only to inhale gusts of his whiskey, cigar, and pig breath.

In utter desperation, General Wayne's captive wrestled her neck free from his control and sank her front teeth into his hand, biting deep into the flesh around his thumb. She threw her naked, wilted body off of the horse, plunging to the ground hard and spraining her ankle. The young girl screamed out noises that could have been mistaken for a wild animal being hunted. She crawled away in the dirt, but to nowhere safe. Wayne used the girl's linen cloth again to wrap the wound on his hand, and then caught up to her with a few jogged steps.

"Stupid girl," he said in a calm voice.

"I'll have you arrested," she sobbed. "Sheriff here is a good man."

The general's laugh echoed across Standing Peachtree. "I'm the commanding general of the National States army. I believe that's a bit more authority than the sheriff of this shithole town. But go ahead and call for your sheriff—if you'd like to see a bullet between his eyes."

Wayne reached for his sidearm and shot the girl in her foot. He and his men had already grown immune to her shrieks. With his hostage immobile, Wayne pulled off his boots, unbuttoned his belt, and slid out of his breeches and trousers. He twisted his filthy pants and whipped the girl across her face as he stood over her, naked from the waist down.

The young slave's only hope was for some soldier with a conscience to intervene, to stand up to his general—maybe a Spanish officer. Most of the Indians and black soldiers were occupied in the work of terrorizing the fleshmongers of the slave market. Instead of assistance, she found more humiliation as the onlookers howled and cheered their general while he raped the young woman in plain sight.

It didn't take long for the commanding general's example to spread to his subordinates. Staff sergeants, corporals, and privates all began to participate in what would become known to survivors as the Rape of Standing Peachtree. No woman was safe. Old, young, black, white. No place was off limits. Mothers were raped in their own homes, young girls in the public square, and in many cases by more than one offender. Most of the perpetrators were NSA soldiers, but the Native Americans and former slaves did not always abstain.

On one occasion, an NSA private first class, disgusted by the debauchery, struck a Chickasaw Indian over the head with a bayonet and tackled him off of a pregnant woman who'd come to the market to buy some eggs. He held the Chickasaw down and threatened what he would do if the innocent woman was harmed, but another tribesman shot the young private in the back of the neck. The National States army didn't have the best reputation with Native Americans, so the decision by a fellow Chickasaw to protect his brother was an easy one. The woman did not escape sexual degradation—from either of the two Indians.

The tragedy at Standing Peachtree represented humanity at its worst and a natural consequence of the loose association of soldiers in an uneasy alliance. No single leader possessed the power to stop the madness. The NSA soldiers took orders from General Wayne, the natives from their chiefs, and everyone else, from their Spanish officers.

With National States soldiers on their side, the alliance outnumbered and outgunned the Columbian army that stood in their way, but their victories would not be pretty. Their triumphs would not come without shame.

—

The surprise attack on Standing Peachtree led to a change in strategy for Light Horse Harry Lee and his division of the Columbian army.

"Pinckney is all the way to Savannah by now, and we're all that's left to defend against Wayne—us and a spattering of militia. We must hold off the enemy to the west. Keep 'em out of Augusta," Lee insisted.

"Cedar Shoals, sir." Lee's aide de camp focused his eyes on the torn, coffee-stained map in front of him. "The path from Standing Peachtree follows a straight shot to the next town, about seventy miles away—Cedar Shoals. We can get there first if we move out quickly." The young aide grinned to congratulate himself on the suggestion.

"Cedar Shoals?" Lee pondered. "Another innocent village with no military value whatsoever." He sighed in disgust.

"No value, other than the fact that it's the only town standing between the enemy and a second attack on our capital. It seems that geography played a cruel trick on poor Cedar Shoals."

Lee rested his head back in deep thought for a moment. "We can't leave it undefended. We can't leave Cedar Shoals to the same fate as Peachtree. Our women and children must live without the fear of rape and plunder. We'll move out tonight. In the meantime, I'll be sending dispatches to the vice president, urging him to get his ass back to Augusta as fast as humanly possible. Should we fail to hold them off at Cedar Shoals, then the fall of the capital may be inevitable."

The aide stopped in his tracks; his beady eyes widened at the prospect of losing the war. He swallowed a thin trickle of drool and continued to strategize. "Sir, if they're lugging heavy artillery and the pathway from Standing Peachtree is as choppy and overgrown as the roads here, we should have plenty of time to alert President Henry as well."

Lee scoffed at the president's name. "Alert him of what? The man hasn't even acknowledged that there is a war going on."

"The president could send our agents to repossess property to Cedar Shoals. Hundreds of armed men that could be of great assistance. We'll need all the help we can get."

Impressed with his young advisor, Lee stood and began pacing the room again. "You're damn right about that, kid. ARPs and the South Carolina militia, too. They're of little use, just hanging out on the beach looking out for the Spanish navy."

General Lee began drafting the dispatches while his aide prepared the camp for departure. The Battle of Cedar Shoals awaited them.

Cedar Shoals sat beneath a labyrinth of mossy green hills and vast forestland. The Georgia and North Carolina militias arrived first and fortified the high ground, just after notifying a few merchants that there would be no trading taking place for a while, but that their services would be needed in defending the state of Georgia.

The militiamen sat on the hilltops, shaking in anxiety, waiting for the enemy to arrive. Every moment they were not joined by Lee's division was a moment closer to death. They began to consider the ramifications of defeat.

"I'll never submit to those dago bastards," an old farmer preached. "I'd sooner move my family to the Carolinas, or even the National States, before submitting to a king again."

As the scorching sun retreated and an evening breeze arrived, the major general of the Georgia militia stood up in a panic. "Quiet! Shut your holes!" he commanded. Three hundred petrified men all gave their full attention. "Listen, to the west." He pointed to the dipping sun. The sound of thunder came closer and closer, though no storm clouds colored the horizon. "That's the sound of horses," he confirmed. "Quite a few of 'em."

The men clutched their weapons tighter as the sounds grew louder, like a tornado making its way through the forest. "At ease, soldiers. Still at least a mile in the distance. But make no mistake. That's an army. Now don't be stupid and go giving away our position."

With all eyes fixed in the direction of the approaching menace, the major general continued his commands. "Look for the red and gold," he whispered. Spanish uniforms stick out like a sore thumb. That's how Vice President Pinckney whooped 'em in Augusta."

After the longest forty minutes of their lives, the men detected movement in the trees below. They could make out individual voices and neighs. The first horses emerged from the greenery carrying tattooed Indians, bald, bare-chested, in deerskin pants and boots.

"Now that's interesting," the old farmer whispered. "Cherokee," he affirmed. "Can tell by the tattoos and the feathers on the chief, there." He smiled, arrogant and foolish to think that perhaps they could defeat an army of uncivilized natives; the Cherokees continued to arrive in larger numbers, armed with iron weaponry.

Two hundred Cherokee Indians came into full view, several hundred yards away, with more sounds rumbling through the woods. Searching for red-and-gold uniforms, the Columbians in the hills remained still as the evening stars. The Spanish didn't appear. The incoming soldiers wore beige and blue, and their voices became crystal clear. The approaching army spoke English. They were Columbian! The crescent moon of the Columbian flag waved high above the last of the soldiers.

An untrained volunteer jumped for joy, yelling out, "Hoorah!" from high above the hills, startling the Columbian army and drawing gunfire from below.

"Shut the hell up, you dumb shit!" one of the militiamen shouted. "You wanna get us all killed?"

Orders to hold fire could be heard below. After an awkward standoff, the Georgian stood again, slowly with his hands up this time.

"Don't shoot!" His voice cracked. "Georgia and North Carolina, at your service!"

Now the hoorahs came from the Columbian regulars, led by Light

Horse Harry Lee and joined by a war party of Cherokee Indians.

⟋⟍

"The plan is quite simple," General Lee informed his colonels. "Stall, stall, stall. Now that Hamilton has sent an army to help fight against us, we'll be outnumbered for sure, even with the Cherokee alliance that we were fortunate enough to establish. Stall the shit out of them. If we're lucky, we'll be here for a month. Pinckney needs the time to get his ass back to Augusta. So, no surrender, no matter what. Casualties will be high, but this is war, gentlemen."

Lee's keen, young aide followed right behind like a puppy dog. "If we move fast, we should be able to fortify five or six of these hills. We'll be patient and fire from one hill at a time, sending the enemy on a wild goose chase, back and forth from one hill to another. As soon as they attack one, fire small cannons from an adjacent hill. We'd conserve ammunition and stall as long as you'd like, General."

"And suppose they take control of a hill or two. Then what?" a concerned Lee probed.

"Well, then the fight becomes our hills against theirs. Firing from hilltop to hilltop; no lines to break; no hand-to-hand combat, no dragoons, and very little artillery. It would delay the fight for days, or even weeks. A total stalemate, just as you've planned."

"I'd prefer not to lose control of any hills. Victory must be an option at Cedar Shoals. But, if not, we retreat to Augusta and join Vice President Pinckney. We can push the bastards back from there—for the second time."

"Sir, I do have one concern," the aide pleaded. "These Cherokees."

General Lee shook his head and waved his hands in front of the young aide's face. "Not to worry."

"Sir, they fought for the British against our revolution," he interrupted. "Chief Dragging Canoe has been very outspoken against Columbian encroachment on Cherokee land."

"I appreciate the concern. But has it occurred to you that Dragging Canoe despises the National States even more? He assured me of this.

Truth be told, he and I have much in common. And he hates the Chicka-saw the worst. There's no love lost between Cherokee and Chickasaw. I fig-ure, if our Indians neutralize their Indians, then we can focus our attention on the Spanish and NSA."

Lee put his aide's fears to rest, and the two got straight to work on earthworks to barricade the hilltops of Cedar Shoals. It would take another week for the Spanish to arrive with their NSA and native allies. The stage was set.

When the Spanish arrived with Mad Anthony, and the first shots fired, Light Horse Harry Lee discovered some obvious holes in his battle plan.

"We're even more outnumbered than I predicted," he bemoaned. "Two to one from the looks of it, and they're charging more than one hill at a time." He cursed his ambitious aide who'd suggested the strategy.

"Numbers should be of no consequence, so long as we maintain the high ground," the boy's voice crackled as he clutched the cross around his neck. "Our bigger dilemma is the cannons. Some good it was dragging them up four-hundred-foot slopes. The heavy foliage and oak trees have rendered them useless. We'll have to mow down the enemy with muskets, one by one."

Despite the obstacles, the Columbians mounted a heroic defense of the hills on the first day of fighting. General Lee's agitation turned to brag-gadocio.

"It's Bunker Hill all over again, I tell you. Except this time, we'll hold the hills and push the greedy bastards back to where they came from. They can send as many pawns up these hills as they want. It's like shooting fish in a barrel."

Even the inexperienced farmers plucked from their homes found it easy to pick off the slow charging soldiers from below the hilltops—a nice way to ease into battle for ordinary men who felt that they'd been thrown to the wolves of warfare. The Columbians inflicted heavy damage on their enemy on the first day of fighting, hundreds of casualties, mostly Spanish and black.

However, after a whole afternoon of being gunned down in humiliation, Mad Anthony Wayne convinced his Spanish counterparts of a tactical change. Wayne realized the greatest advantage they held was not in numbers, but instead, the Creek allies and their knowledge of the terrain.

"We'll choose one hill to create a distraction," Wayne asserted, "while at the same time sending companies led by the Creeks to surprise Lee's army from behind the hills. It will take another day, and increased casualties, but it's the best way to capitalize on our advantages." He wasn't asking. He was telling the Spanish officers.

They executed Wayne's plan with surgical precision. A combination of NSA and Spanish squads blitzed the one hill that contained the most trees for cover. Lee took the bait and concentrated all his forces on the target while six companies, led by the Creeks, reached the hilltops of Cedar Shoals from the rear of Lee's division.

Now face-to-face on the hilltops, the undisciplined Columbians didn't stand a chance. As casualties mounted, the final deathblow came from Chief Dragging Canoe of Lee's Cherokee allies. In a carefully coordinated betrayal, just as darkness fell over the gory scene, hundreds of Cherokee Indians turned their weapons against the Columbian army in unison. Nightfall concealed the treachery and caused great confusion. Planned well ahead of time, the conspirators struck on multiple hills. They targeted Columbian officers first.

Chief Dragging Canoe stood closest to General Light Horse Harry Lee. He raised his tomahawk and sounded a penetrating war cry that echoed in the darkness. The weapon swung down like lightning toward Lee's head. Much younger and stronger, Lee dodged the attack and grabbed hold of the tomahawk, pushing his former ally to the ground. The struggle for control of the weapon didn't last long. Lee wrestled the tomahawk from Dragging Canoe and, with one powerful blow to the head, ended the life of the great Cherokee chief.

In a panic, General Lee sounded retreat. What was left of his army fled the hills through pitch-black darkness and chaos. He hoped Vice President Pinckney and his men had reached Augusta. They would rendezvous at the capital to make one last stand in defense of Georgia.

———

"Goddamn Cherokees! Goddamn all these vulgar mobs of beasts! If you've got any, I mean any Indians in your ranks, I'd dismiss them at once. Hell, hold 'em prisoner until the end of the war," Lee barked out like a hungry dog denied a bone.

Vice President Pinckney scratched the sharp hairs on his chin as he listened, concerned for the fate of his men and his country. He would need General Lee in a focused state of mind if they were to stand any chance of defending Augusta again. "How many, General? How many troops, and how far behind you? What kind of time do we have?" Pinckney grew more alarmed by the minute. Augusta looked like a ghost town compared to the days when the proud residents of the capital city came together to drive out General Ricardos.

"Maybe a few thousand left, and not far off. A couple of days at most. Goddamn it, we had 'em beat! We may have ended up with just two men standing, but by God, we had them beat. That bastard Dragging Canoe may have just lost us the war. I sure don't regret smashing that creature's skull. But I must take responsibility for the defeat, Mr. Vice President. Why I ever trusted the rat, I'll never know."

"Well, our intelligence has relayed that Cherokees have been playing a game of sabotage for months now. Declared neutral, but in reality, anything but. They've burned crops, obstructed roads, and spread false information, all on behalf of the Spanish. They must be crazy if they think the Spanish will treat them any better than the Columbian government."

Lee lowered the volume of his voice. "Supreme Leader Hamilton didn't help much when he exterminated the Shawnee in the NSA. Indians don't trust Americans. But we are not Americans; we are Columbians, and the world needs to know the difference."

"They will soon enough. Mr. Hamilton's outrageous actions against us will sour the waters between our two nations for decades to come. If we'd been prepared for such calamity, we could be responding with an invasion of the NSA right now; but alas, all that remains of the Columbian army is right here in Augusta."

Lee shook his head with a sigh. Both men considered the unthinkable, the real possibility of surrender. The surrender of Georgia territory to the Spanish empire. And over what? A silly dispute over runaway slaves. Damn the whole institution of slavery along with the Native American tribes.

"Oh, and there's more disturbing news," Pinckney added. "General Ricardos's army is marching toward us from Savannah—again. We pushed them as far south as Sunbury, but had to evacuate in order to get back here. I expect Ricardos at our doorstep in maybe ten days."

"We have no choice but to fight," Lee stated the obvious.

The vice president returned to his quarters to exercise his best defense. He said a prayer.

As commander in chief of the Columbian army, Charles Cotesworth Pinckney accomplished all that could be expected of him. He'd successfully defended the capital of Georgia once, had the enemy on the run, and inspired tens of thousands of Columbians outside of Georgia to enlist and defend the confederation. Yet no amount of heroism or brilliant military strategy could match the might of the Spanish Empire allied with the National States, and every Indian tribe and escaped slave in Columbia.

⌁

Pinckney looked on as Mad Anthony Wayne ordered his men to shoot and kill anyone who stood in their way of sacking Augusta, Georgia, once and for all. In perfect timing, Ricardos's army arrived from the south. Blitzing through the Columbian lines, they left very few standing. Columbian soldiers deserted by the hundreds, unwilling to fight a hopeless battle.

From his horse, Pinckney watched the ruin as Georgia's state capital building went up in flames all around him. He gazed into the inferno and saw a young private, no more than eighteen years old, struggling to hold the Columbian flag above the salvo of gunfire. Twelve pounders came soaring overhead from National States artillery, and a thick fog of gunpowder concealed the shrapnel that pierced anyone close to the carnage.

A reflective Pinckney eyed the young man, just a boy with a whole life-time ahead of him, yet likely to die at any moment. He saw the Columbian crescent moon begin to waver through the black soot, and when the smoke cleared, Pinckney watched the boy drop the flag and sprint as fast as he could away from the army, away from the country he'd pledged to protect.

The vice president dismounted his horse and dove for the flag. The Columbian flag, created in the image of his beloved South Carolina's flag, lay tattered and frayed, about to catch fire. Pinckney held the emblem with pride even as it caught fire and turned into a torch. He rushed toward enemy fire, raising the burning flag as high as he could. The bullet entered the front of his neck and choked off his guttural cries. The commander in chief fell to his knees, hunched over, dead. The Columbian flag fell to the ground like a spear and stood erect in front of the vice president's corpse. General Light Horse Harry Lee surrendered before sunset.

⟡

In Philadelphia, hundreds of Blackshirts lined the front entrance to the Federal Palace. They stood as stiff as toy soldiers in front of thirteen Roman columns underneath an enormous golden dome that loomed over Chestnut Street. Construction of the palace was still years from being complete, but at least the supreme leader had an office from which to work. The massive structure was already the most recognizable symbol of American strength, perfect for national celebrations, such as the one on March 2, 1792, the second anniversary of Alexander Hamilton ascending to the office of supreme leader.

The National States army, still black and blue from their victory in Georgia, paraded down Walnut Street, Market Street, and then stopped on Chestnut in front of the palace. The mass of onlookers cheered their servicemen louder than anyone else that day, save for the supreme leader himself. General Anthony Wayne sobered up enough to lead the procession and bask in the military worship that had become commonplace among National States citizens.

Jonathan Dayton dressed for the occasion. The young attorney general flaunted a knee-length, copper-colored coat and his finest low-heeled, leather shoes with silk stockings that matched an imported tricorne hat with an enormous upturned brim. Underneath the hat, Dayton let the flowing locks of his wig dangle in the wind instead of tying it back. He inhaled a few deep breaths before turning to an audience of thousands, and then delivered one of the most important speeches of his career.

"He kept us safe from the Shawnee!" he shouted to thunderous applause, though much of the crowd could not make out a word.

"He has formed a strong alliance with Spain and crushed the Columbian traitors in Georgia!" Again, the crowd went berserk, and Dayton's nerves disappeared. This would be the easiest speech ever delivered. No matter what he said, as long as it praised the supreme leader, the audience loved it.

"He has created a homeland for the downtrodden in Montgomery. For the slave, for the red man, for the poor farmer in despair. To those who yearn, we say, despair no more. Our crops in Montgomery and our livestock in Pennsylvania feed the fires of industry from New York to Philadelphia, from Buffalo to Dover! And the expansion of our great nation will continue to the west, to Ohio, and beyond! Our economy could not be healthier." Dayton had the crowd in the palm of his hand as he reached the most important rhetoric of the address. "But there is a threat among us! An affront to our government that festers in our towns, in our villages—a menace among us that threatens to stop our steadfast progress dead in its tracks."

The people hushed in concern. The news was not all rosy.

"As attorney general of the National States, I have spent countless hours investigating and combating a factious Whig conspiracy that spans from the taverns of New York to the boarding houses of Pennsylvania. A danger that threatens to infect the halls of our Congress." The crowd booed with a brewing animosity that grew louder as Dayton elaborated.

"This dangerous Whig faction promotes treason and subversion. It promotes distrust in our glorious supreme leader!"

"No!" the citizens objected in angry unison.

"It would have us ignore the security of our people and disgrace the military! The Whigs would have us be more Columbian than American by disbanding our army. Just look how well that's worked for Patrick Henry!" His words created an uproar.

"And for as poisonous as this disease has become in our society, it continues to grow in popularity; it spreads in the hearts and minds of our innocent, unsuspecting people. It does this, in part, through the publication of trash. The publication of libelous, treasonous deception. The conspirators call it free press, but it is in fact phony, deceitful puffery. And we will crush this phony news! Under the leadership of the supreme leader, we will crush Whig treachery!

"Under my supervision, the Department of Justice has rounded up, and continues to round up, dangerous collaborators who engage in sabotage and subversive activities designed to antagonize and debase the basic values of the National States of America."

Worked up to pandemonium, the audience turned its attention to four prisoners, escorted toward the podium by Blackshirts.

"These conspirators have been rooted out from our government. They have been placed under arrest for treason, and will be transported to the federal prison in Pittsburgh without delay." People howled and threw rocks as the helpless men stumbled closer to the mob.

"Representative William Findley of Pennsylvania!" Hisses echoed through the capital. "Senators Albert Gallatin of Pennsylvania and William Floyd of Montgomery!" Pelted with a stone to the face, Gallatin fell to the ground, and the noise escalated in simmering anger.

The fourth prisoner inched forward in astonishment at the vitriol on display. He stared down Jonathan Dayton and shook his head, then marched toward the hateful rabble as his name was announced. "Supreme Court Justice John Jay of New York!"

Dayton did his best to hush the crowd, but had to bark over the commotion. "In response to such a conspiracy reaching the highest level of our judicial system, the supreme leader has ordered the temporary suspension of the Supreme Court until he can appoint new judges, free of intrigue or avarice, and whose ideals are consistent with those of the National States of America."

After the prisoners exited, the attorney general stepped aside and made way for Alexander Hamilton, who emerged from the Federal Palace wearing a crown of leaves and roses and a red, velvet robe embroidered in gold. He extended his arms to welcome the sea of people. There was no use trying to speak over the deafening applause. He directed the crowd's attention to the main event, the public execution of the most serious criminals.

The mob watched the gallows in the distance. Most believed that hanging would be too generous a death for the scum about to be put on display. Four prisoners approached the platform that held four sturdy guillotines, or as Hamilton referred to them, the French contraptions.

Dayton addressed the people again. "Enemies of the State!" Although the platform sat about one hundred yards from the palace, the prisoners could hear the malevolent screams from the masses.

Each prisoner coped with their last moment on earth differently. Chief Blue Jacket, quiet and calm as always, focused his tired eyes up to the sky. In deep meditation, he prayed to the Great Sprit, and when his fate arrived, he closed his eyes and let the executioner do his worst. Not a sound of protest from the great Shawnee warrior. Aaron Burr, on the other hand, demonstrated the exact opposite demeanor. Kicking, shouting, and even biting the Blackshirts that pushed him forward, Burr had to be gagged with cloth and a leather strap. He shouted his last audible words to the supreme leader, before the muzzle. "Fucking tyrant!"

Next to Burr stood two black prisoners, apprehended in Ohio, taken to prison in Pittsburgh, and then chosen for public execution. Marcus, an escaped slave from Virginia, stood at six feet one inch, two hundred and twenty pounds. It pained him to speak, on account of the pain that ripped through his gums since having a tooth removed against his will by a military doctor at Fort Pitt. Confused, he entered the French contraption in deep thought, questioning God and wondering how the world could be so unfair.

The second escaped slave was a young girl of seventeen, thin and freckled on the cheeks and forehead. Patsy was blessed with speed. She could run and jump like a rabbit; she outran every slave catcher in Columbia who'd hunted her and her family when they took flight from a Kentucky farm.

Patsy's mother never got past the bloodhounds that gnawed at her legs. Her father couldn't outlast the ARPs on horseback, and her seven-year-old brother had drowned in the Ohio River. When the National States army finally detained her and took her to Fort Pitt, she was relieved to have a roof over her head. But when Jonathan Dayton arrived in Pittsburgh to inspect the black prisoners, Patsy looked too much like the most-wanted woman in North America. Petrified, she stood next to the three other indicted criminals and the executioner that would end her life. Her first instinct was to run. With her arms still tied behind her back, Patsy jumped off of the five-foot platform and sprinted. Too fast for the executioners to catch, a soldier had to fire a bullet into her back. She died instantly, but her body was still needed for the public display.

The prisoners took their final positions, knelt down with their heads through the wooden lunettes. A Blackshirt forced Patsy's corpse into her assigned French contraption.

The crowd began to chant in the distance. "Death to traitors! Long live Hamilton! Death to traitors! Long live Hamilton!"

Jonathan Dayton hushed them one last time to give the final order. He shouted toward the gallows. "Blue Jacket, Aaron Burr, Ona Judge, Hercules. You have been sentenced to death. Commence with justice!"

The end came quick. Four angled blades rattled above the prisoners' heads. The wooden frames creaked in the wind. Four Blackshirts released their ropes in unison, sending the blades in a fatal freefall. Four heads rolled forward, off of the platform, Patsy's the farthest.

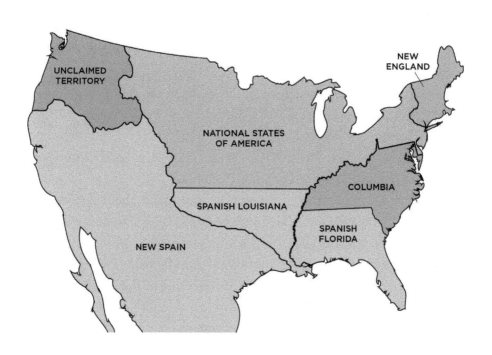

Chapter 15

1793

James Madison arrived in Hartford, Connecticut, to negotiate an end to the bloodshed in Georgia. A peace treaty could not come fast enough for Columbia, but Madison wondered why President Henry had assigned him such an indispensable position. Perhaps it was an apology for having shipped him off to France, or perhaps the beleaguered president finally acknowledged that no Columbian possessed more natural political instinct than his old nemesis. Madison received just one set of simple instructions: "Put an end to this catastrophe, however you need to do it. Just end the damn thing."

Madison's cheek twitched as he tightened his jaw muscles to hold a poker face. New England Prime Minister John Adams welcomed him toward the negotiating table, next to the Spanish ambassador Don Diego de Gardoqui and the National States Secretary of State Rufus King.

"Let us spill no more blood," Adams proclaimed. "This Treaty of Hartford will create a lasting peace among the nations of North America." In a friendly gesture, the prime minister grasped the arm of Rufus King, originally from Massachusetts. "You should have never left New England," Adams asserted. "We could use your talents in our Parliament, and you wouldn't find yourself bogged down in war, as you do now."

King offered a warm smile to accept the compliment. "That's quite kind of you, Mr. Prime Minister, but I'm afraid I can no longer tolerate these New England blizzards of yours. A fine capital city you have here in Hartford, even if it is frozen solid. I had to duck the falling icicles that came at me like daggers when I entered."

"Yes, but if my options are the stench of Philadelphia to the frigid air of Hartford, I prefer my current lot," Adams retorted. He inhaled a deep breath of fresh air to make the point.

It was obvious to James Madison that the cards were stacked against him. In addition to being old chums with John Adams, Rufus King had already conducted private negotiations with the Spanish ambassador. There was also the inconvenient truth that Columbia had lost the war, and badly. Still, Madison tried to project strength when meeting Ambassador Gardoqui face-to-face. Refusing to bow, the short little diplomat widened his shoulders in a poised stance and offered a firm handshake. He squeezed Gardoqui's hand like it was a sponge and held on when the Spaniard tried to pull away. The handshake ended on Madison's terms. But that was about the only moment in Hartford that Columbia would have the upper hand.

"Mr. Madison, it has been too long," King interjected as they sat at the table. "It has been years. Not since the First Constitutional Convention."

"Too long, indeed. But shameful that we must meet under such circumstances today." Madison displayed the proper decorum, but was in no mood to cozy up to the National States representative. How dare the sons of bitches provide military assistance to a European enemy of American states? And how dare his old friend Hamilton direct such atrocity?

Adams began the peace talks by outlining some of the more obvious components. "First and foremost, all military campaigns will cease, as I believe they already have. The Columbian army is to move north, to its forts outside of Georgia. Any remaining National States soldiers are to exit the disputed territory at once. The National States have no legitimate claim to Georgia. Spanish Florida will acquire all territories formerly under the jurisdiction of the state of Georgia."

Madison shook his head, biting his lower lip. "Reward the aggressors then? With all of Georgia?"

"Aggressors, you say?" Gardoqui would not ignore the accusation. "Spanish generals are not murdered without aggression. Juan de Courten was my friend, slain at the border. Murdered by aggressors in the business of slave catching."

"Murdered by a man who in no way represented the Columbian government. We cannot go starting treacherous wars over every criminal act that takes place on the continent. We have law enforcement for that. You should try it in Florida instead of martial law."

"Gentlemen, please," Adams interrupted. "The war ends here, on these terms, lest General Ricardos pushes his army into the Carolinas."

"Which he is eager to do," Gardoqui added in a direct threat to Madison.

"In return, Columbia will receive some concessions as well," Adams continued, "starting with a pledge from the Spanish crown that neither she nor her colonies, including Spanish Florida, will invade Columbia by land or by sea."

"And a similar pledge from the National States Government," Madison demanded.

Rufus King wasted no time in giving a stern rejection. "I am under no authority to make such a pledge. The National States simply aided an ally in this war. We have no territorial ambitions, nor have we ever had such ambitions, in the Confederation of Columbia."

"Then I trust it should be no inconvenience to pledge what you have stated, on paper."

"I'm afraid I cannot do that, Mr. Madison. Matters of war and peace are decided by the supreme leader of my nation."

"Then what in bloody hell are you doing here, King? Why do you even warrant a seat at this table?"

Gardoqui cleared his throat and nudged his head toward Adams.

The prime minister got straight to the point. "It is my understanding that the National States does in fact have regional interests in the Louisiana Territory."

"*Upper* Louisiana," Gardoqui corrected him.

"The sale of Upper Louisiana to the National States Government in a transaction in the amount of twenty million American dollars," Adams confirmed. King and Gardoqui nodded in agreement. "With the southern border to be at parallel thirty-six, thirty north," Gardoqui specified.

"Absolutely outrageous," Madison interrupted. At a huge disadvantage, he replayed President Henry's instructions in his head. *However you need to do it. Just end the damn thing.* But it was unlike James Madison to go down without a fight. "I have a demand of my own," he shot back. "The National States government has captured and detained Columbian property at Fort Pitt. Runaway slaves. Columbians would like their property returned to them, unharmed."

In deep thought, Secretary King pulled at a thin strand of curled hair on the side of his forehead. Fort Pitt did in fact house over a thousand prisoners rounded up in Ohio, though not all were Columbian runaways. Hercules and Ona Judge had already been executed, so the remaining prisoners just took up space.

Madison continued his argument. "You have already killed the Mount Vernon conspirators, whom you should have extradited to Columbia for trial. The suspects were executed before Martha Washington even knew they were apprehended. Regardless of your injudiciousness, the least you can do is return our property."

Rufus King's response surprised Madison as much as every other man in the room. "I think that sounds like a reasonable proposition. Arrangements can be made in Pittsburgh."

"However, there could be an alternate course, gentlemen." Now Adams surprised them. "We could sign an ordinary peace treaty here that ceases hostilities and redraws some borders, or we can add to it a bold statement in defense of humanity. Mr. Madison, I know your personal views on the institution of slavery well. It has been a necessary evil, but an evil you concede. At this precise moment in our history, gentlemen, we have an opportunity to eradicate that evil once and for all. Slavery is doomed, Madison. No matter what we say or sign here today, African slaves will take flight across borders in larger numbers. In the worst-case scenario, you're looking at a mass slave insurrection like what we've seen in Haiti. God forbid, they could overrun state capitals. We could prevent it here and now by adding to this peace treaty, at least some language to express a willingness to end Columbian slavery in the future."

Madison smiled and shook his head. "Mr. Prime Minister, I agree with your sentiments. But as Mr. King has stated, these are decisions to be made by a higher authority. These decisions will be made by the Columbian people. Now if I can guarantee you anything, it is that the Columbian people would have me crucified for assenting to any such language in this treaty."

In a rare moment of agreement, ambassador Gardoqui came to the defense of his adversary. "King Charles would also object. Though Spanish Florida recognizes liberty for fugitive slaves, our colonists in New Spain and southern Louisiana profit from the slave trade in New Orleans. Of course, this business in Haiti is troublesome, but there is no need to overreact."

A disappointed Adams continued the negotiations to a conclusion. The state of Georgia no longer existed. Georgians would face no repercussions if they chose to stay in Florida, though they would have to emancipate their slaves. Florida would grant safe passage to those Georgians who chose to migrate with their slaves north to Columbia or west to New Orleans, where they could contribute to the slave economy. The Treaty of Hartford established an official end to the war and redrew the map of North America. John Adams had failed in his mission to destroy the institution of slavery.

After signing his name to the Treaty of Hartford, James Madison returned to Richmond to find that President Henry had abandoned the capital city. Standing no chance of winning reelection, the president retired to his Red Hill Plantation in Virginia with his wife, Dorothea. He had no interest in waiting around to see who would be elected his successor.

Madison continued his journey south and found the vanquished statesman, once a political giant, his most formidable opponent, alone on the front porch, slouched on a squeaky rocking chair with a tobacco pipe dangling idly out of the side of his mouth. It took all the strength in his shaking hand to hold up a glass of whiskey.

Madison extended a sarcastic greeting. "Would you care for a debate, Mr. President? Perhaps a good old screaming match like we used to have in Richmond."

"What in God's name are you doing at my home, Madison? I left the capital to get away from politics. To get far away from men like you."

"Well, I suppose you'll have to put up with me just one last time."

Madison sat next to Henry and shared the news from Hartford. He accepted his host's offer of whiskey and a pipe full of homegrown tobacco. For the first time in over a year, Madison's stomach did not rage in a sea of acid. "We've had our share of disputes, Patrick, but there is one area where I cannot compete with you. You always grew the most delicious tobacco."

"I still do." Henry smirked. "I haven't retired from farming, and I may just take up practicing law again. But politics, good riddance. A profession for rotten men."

"And you were so good at it," Madison joked again. "You rotten man."

"You were damn good at it, too, sir. I can't tell you how many times I wanted to tackle you at that Godforsaken convention." Henry's laughter choked the smoke out of his mouth. "Are we both just rotten men? Is that what it comes down to?"

"Oh, I don't think so. Good men in a rotten world, maybe. If times were different, perhaps you and I would be heroes." Madison gazed out at Henry's slaves working the Red Hill tobacco fields.

"Heroes," Henry repeated. "Where have all the heroes gone? They're all dead, that's where. George Washington, dead. Charles Cotesworth Pinckney, dead. All the others, retired or disgraced like you and I, and Light Horse Harry Lee for surrendering. Disgraced. A damn shame."

"Well, you may not care to discuss it, but it seems that one man will be coming out of retirement. Coming back to serve as the second president of the Confederation of Columbia." Madison's voice softened. He treaded lightly with the topic, hoping not to anger the spurned president.

"Oh, I've heard the rumors. And you are correct, sir. I don't give a shit about any of it."

"Jefferson will be perfect for the job," Madison said with confidence. Madison also had high hopes for a cabinet position in a Jefferson administration, if his signature on the Treaty of Hartford hadn't tarnished his reputation too much.

"I'm not sure Thomas Jefferson is rotten enough," Henry said, swallowing the last drop of his whiskey.

"Or perhaps Jefferson is the one man left who can mend a broken world. His only serious opposition for the presidency is Pierce Butler from South Carolina. I'm not aware of anyone who defends the institution of slavery with more earnestness than Butler. Which makes Jefferson the anti-slavery candidate. The liberty candidate, at least in favor of gradual emancipation. There can be no doubt, Thomas Jefferson is at his best when he defends liberty. He has launched ruthless attacks on Hamilton in the press. He calls the Louisiana Purchase the most reckless, unconstitutional abuse of executive power imaginable."

"Well, he should take some advice from me. A lifetime spent defending liberty has not been worth it. Not one bit," Henry responded.

"Mr. Henry, you are a hero, no matter what popular opinion dictates at the moment. It is undisputable that you've made history, and history has a way of seeing long-term effects. Without your political contributions, Columbians would still be under the yoke of King George, or even worse, Supreme Leader Hamilton. You were correct to demand a people's republic. You didn't have to give me so many bloody ulcers in the process, but you're a fighter. A true warrior in the battle for liberty. You and I are not on opposite sides of that battle. Maybe different fighting units, different regiments, but of the same army for liberty and justice for all."

The two titans of American democracy buried the hatchet, a sincere reconciliation, with a handshake. It was the last time they would speak to each other.

⟿

In November of 1793, the Columbian Congress chose Thomas Jefferson to serve as their second president by a narrow margin of votes over Pierce Butler. Maryland's delegation nominated James McHenry with the sole purpose of electing him as vice president and commander in chief of the military. Due to his credentials from service in the American Revolution and the Georgia War, he was a shoo-in for the position. President Jefferson and Vice President McHenry took office in a time of desperation in Columbia, a nation desperate for heroes.

Nelson had grown accustomed to insecure leaders opening up their souls to him. First George Washington, then Chief Blue Jacket, and now Alexander Hamilton. The supreme leader walked Nelson through the small rectangular yard in back of the Federal Palace while consulting with the old warhorse. Nelson was a great listener, but indeed old. He shivered in the Philadelphia ice storm, a type of cold that only Hamilton enjoyed. The horse hunched over, unable to hold up his own weight. Through the explosive wind gusts, he rocked back forth in an erratic zigzag similar to Hamilton's stutter steps when he'd had too much to drink. Hamilton held on to Nelson's collar to help guide him over the icy patches of snow in the grass.

"Unbelievable, how far we've come in just a few years." Hamilton slowed his pace so the horse could keep up. "You and I have both bared witness to the creation of the National States, from revolution to the present." Nelson stopped and rested his head on Hamilton's shoulder. He hadn't purred since the supreme leader had recognized him at Fort Pitt. Instead, the horse groaned out a low pitch. Nelson was in pain.

Hamilton pulled his companion forward and continued his reflection. "Without question, I've been the beneficiary of good fortune. Rich, powerful, an entire city built in my image, and my son, God willing, will someday become supreme leader just like his father." A huge blast of wind almost knocked Nelson on to his side. Hamilton slipped on the ice but was able to keep his balance and hold up Nelson. "Still got my strength," he bragged, "but I was stronger in my youth. And idealistic—so damn idealistic." He laughed at the thought of his former self. "What in God's name were Madison and I thinking? I mean no offense to your former master, of course, but it just wasn't possible. All thirteen states united as one nation? Just think of it. A nation, half slave and half free. Half federalist, half Whig. Half agricultural, half industrial. No, it just wasn't possible. Had we been successful in realizing our dream of a United States Constitution, we would have only delayed an inevitable Civil War. It would have ripped us in half anyway." Nelson pulled his head away from Hamilton. He turned his face up to the freezing rain that fell from the sky and howled to the faint moon peeking through the daylight.

"I know you're in pain, buddy." Hamilton rubbed Nelson's ears and hugged his face, guarding him from the assaulting wind. Nelson found enough strength to pull his body away from the supreme leader again.

"Do you not approve?" Hamilton laughed. "We avoided civil war by going our separate ways. Believe me, Nelson, union was not the best option. The nations of North America can no more unite than England, France, and Spain. North America will be no different than Europe. It is our destiny. The people of the National States are better off for it, and I'm proud to serve them. I give them protection. Protection from Indians, protection from the lying press, protection from French extremists."

Nelson limped a few more steps away from the supreme leader until he could move no more. His knees buckled like he would fall over at any moment. "It's okay now, buddy. I'm gonna take that pain away for good. Put you out of that misery." Hamilton adjusted the leafy crown on his head and sucked in the bitter chill. He reached for his flintlock pistol, then aimed it between Nelson's eyes. "An honorable American," Hamilton said has he pulled the trigger.

Nelson died instantly. A loud thud erupted when he fell, and steam rose from his warm blood that stained the ground. To Hamilton's astonishment, Nelson still made sounds after the shot. For a full ten seconds after he'd fallen, Nelson purred.

Jonathan Taylor's stomach turned upside down at the thought of Aaron Burr's execution. He'd contributed to it, earned money off of it. Just like his former master, politics had chewed Jonathan up and spit him out. Government work was not for him, and he expressed as much in his final meeting with Alexander Hamilton. He demonstrated proper etiquette and respect for the supreme leader, even wearing a ridiculous powdered wig for the appointment. He expressed gratitude for the job in New York but, in no uncertain terms, declined the offer for similar work in Buffalo, Montgomery. His future was in the burgeoning town of Winthrop, Ohio.

Benjamin Winthrop kept his word and pulled the necessary strings for Jonathan to have a few acres of land and a log cabin. After giving Winthrop a grand tour of the two-room cabin, Jonathan gave thanks.

"A gift for you, sir," he said while handing Winthrop the powdered wig he'd worn in Philadelphia. "For more formal occasions."

"A kind gesture of you, Taylor. I've never been one to wear a fancy wig, but perhaps my new lot in life may require it from time to time. My balding head requires it for sure."

Jonathan held back laughter at how comical the alabaster wig looked overtop Winthrop's thin, greasy bangs; uneven sideburns; and handlebar mustache. A ludicrous look for a ludicrous man who lived in a purple-and-yellow mansion.

"That'll do just fine," Winthrop smiled, "but I think you'll find life more easygoing here in my town. A coonskin hat is far more appropriate than a wig."

Jonathan shrugged and shook his head. "I'm no Benjamin Franklin, sir."

"No, you won't get off that easy. I'm sure a coonskin offends your advanced sense of fashion, but it will suit you well here. You're the finest-dressed Negro I've ever known, that's a fact. But your new life in Winthrop demands more simplicity. I trust you'll come to appreciate that."

Jonathan still choked at the thought of donning wild animal fur, although maybe the tubby millionaire was correct. If a man with such terrible style as Winthrop could be the most powerful man in town, then maybe Jonathan would benefit from a wardrobe change.

"At any rate, you'll need some furs for Ohio weather," Winthrop continued. "Ain't nothing like New York, I'll tell you that much."

On their way to the market, they discussed clothing and the weather, and arrangements for Jonathan's employment in keeping financial records for Benjamin.

"Despite the town's name, I actually don't know too many people here. Not well, at least. Truth is, I can't trust anybody, not since I've made my money. Everybody wants to know me, and everybody's got a motive. You and I were never the best of friends, Jonathan, but you knew me before the money, and you were kind. Those New York sons of bitches made a clown out of me. My weight, my odor, my weakness for pretty ladies. You refrained from the ridicule, sir, and your employment now is a token of my appreciation."

Jonathan puffed up with pride. He'd always believed that determination and kindheartedness would pay off. It always had in the past. "Much obliged, Mr. Winthrop. You have my full commitment. I helped manage a farm in Virginia before my time in New York. Though your wealth is much greater than my former master's, I shall conduct my work with the same earnestness."

"Earnestness indeed. But keep the damn politics out of it, huh? No more Whig shit." Winthrop winked a playful eye.

"None whatsoever. I've taken your advice on the matter, sir, and I thank you for that." Jonathan laughed at himself and his old political passions as the two men approached the center of town.

Although miniscule compared to the heart of New York City, Winthrop had already built itself up to a respectable trading post. Native Americans and merchants traveled from Detroit, Cincinnati, Pittsburgh, and even from towns in Kentucky and Virginia, across the Columbian border. Most of the traders dealt in fur or guns, but lumber, nails, foodstuff, and National States banknotes had become more common. Benjamin, of course, rushed to buy a few jugs of whiskey. Jonathan conceded and carried his cash to the Seneca traders for some buffalo furs and beaver skin.

What hideous-looking garments, he thought. How could anyone prefer the carcass of a rotted beast to the fine silks of Europe? Unable to bring himself to wear a dead animal on his head, he settled on a shirt and boots. In addition to skins, the Seneca Indians sold the meat to take home for supper.

Jonathan distracted himself from the ugly garb by examining the salted meats. Buffalo, pig, squirrel, fish, chicken.

"These chops, here, as tender as they come," a voice echoed from above. "Clean, fresh, and a good price for ya today."

Jonathan peered up at the massive body beside him. The man was clearly not a Seneca Indian—heavy, muscular, and dark-brown skin.

"Also got a few jars of honey left. Last ones until spring and summer.

Better buy now 'cause them honeybees don't come back for a while."

Jonathan shifted his focus away from the food. He stared into the man's shiny emerald eyes. "Your face is familiar, sir. Have we met before?"

The merchant took a step back and squinted at Jonathan below him. He hesitated. "No, suh. Not to my recollection," his voiced tapered off. "No, suh," he insisted with more confidence.

"Jonathan Taylor, from Virginia." He offered his hand to shake. His eyes began to interrogate the suspicious man. So curious, a single black man alongside a tribe of Seneca Indians. Jonathan never forgot a face, and the voice sounded even more familiar.

"Honey Johnson, suh. Like that honey straight out the comb. From right here in Ohio. Don't reckon I know any free black men from Virginia."

"You're not a former slave? A house slave?" Jonathan pressed. "Escaped from Columbia?" His heart raced. He was getting closer.

"No, suh. I'm a free man. You must have me confused with someone else." Honey slipped his tongue through the empty space on his bottom gums, where a tooth once sat.

Jonathan noticed the nervous habit. His eyes widened. George Washington's cook. Hercules, was it? His heart sped up even faster. It was surely the man who served him delicious hoecakes and honey at Mount Vernon on the morning after James Madison fell ill. The cook without a sweet tooth. Jonathan scratched his temple, pretending to ponder the man's identity, even though no doubt remained. He needed to buy time, to understand the situation and how to respond. Before him stood a dead man. Supreme Leader Hamilton had executed Hercules, or at least someone who'd matched his description.

He looked up at Honey Johnson again and shook his head. "Perhaps in a former life."

"Yes, suh. In a former life," Honey affirmed. The conversation paused for a brief, awkward moment until the sun peeked through the clouds to warm their faces. "Now 'bout that honey. Last of the season, and all yours for two dollars a jar."

Still speechless, Jonathan reflected on Mount Vernon before coming out of the spell.

"Yes, of course. Who couldn't use a little honey in their life? I'll take the last two jars off your hands."

Red and Honey Johnson married on the pristine landscape of Whetstone Manor, Benjamin Winthrop's Ohio mansion. A black preacher joined the two in matrimony in the presence of Jonathan Taylor; Winthrop; and Winthrop's dog, Smokey. Winthrop donated the wedding dress, an ivory petticoat with a rolling, floral frock of greens and yellows, along with a matching bonnet. He'd purchased the gown in New York for Lydia just days before she'd broken his heart.

Even through the layers of fabric blanketed Red's figure, she could not conceal the bump in her belly. In just a few weeks, she would bring Chasing Honey's child into this strange new world.

"Born free," Honey stated with pride. "We'll raise this child our own. Not on some plantation, not to serve some mastuh." He pushed back the moisture underneath his eyelid.

Red wiped her husband's eyes and kissed his lips. "Our baby will be so strong and good-lookin', like her daddy," she smiled.

"Smart and courageous, like *his* mamma." He kissed her again. "How you know it's a girl?"

"I jus' know, Honey. Some things you jus' know."

Jonathan approached the altar and hugged the bride in a delicate embrace to congratulate her. "The most stunning bride, Mrs. Johnson. And not too shabby a groom, I might add." He winked and patted Honey on the back of his blue silk vest.

"Oh, but not quite as dapper as the esteemed Mr. Taylor," Honey conceded to his new friend. Both men knew of the other's past in Virginia but chose never to acknowledge it. Honey's true identity was all too obvious once he'd found work cooking in local taverns.

"The two best-dressed men in Winthrop! No offense, Benji," Jonathan joked.

Benjamin wrestled with Smokey in the yard, painting his wrinkled suit with grass stains and dog slobber. "None taken, sir. None at all."

The wedding party moved inside the mansion, where Chasing Honey prepared a feast for their guests. Hazelnuts, grapes and cheese, an enormous bass caught from the Scioto River, chicken, and pheasant. Benjamin provided an exquisite bottle of sparkling French wine, which he claimed was a gift from the Marquis de Lafayette, but nobody believed him. After the main course, Smokey enjoyed his own feast of chicken bones while the party drank tea with their honey-dipped apples.

They discussed the future of Winthrop, its industry and infrastructure. Jonathan had been saving money to open a school for black children in the heart of the city.

"School was never my sort of thing. I'm sure you're shocked," Benjamin slurred. "But the children here wouldn't suffer from a little education. It's a grand idea."

"God willing," Jonathan prayed. "A school for the children, and Red and Honey's child will be among the first to attend. Reading and mathematics. Natural science and philosophy. The possibilities are endless."

Red shook her head, amazed at the thought of her child learning to read. She flashed back to her having to spy on George Washington as he read the newspapers aloud to Martha.

At the meal's conclusion, Smokey cozied up by the fireplace while Benjamin escorted his guests on a stroll down Main Street as the sun began its retreat. Three blocks off the road, they reached a desolate, wooded area near a small creek.

"One acre," Winthrop said as he reached in his pocket for a crumbled parchment. He handed it to Chasing Honey. "Now it's just one acre, and not exactly fertile. You've got access to the creek and the river just over yonder," Benjamin pointed.

Confused, Honey Johnson looked down at the land deed in his hands. "One acre?"

"Your wedding gift. Like I said, it's not much, and you'll have to build. But Jonathan here will help you out. Construct a sturdy cabin, just like he's got." Jonathan nodded his head in agreement. "I won't have you raise a child in that boarding house. It wouldn't be right."

Benjamin Winthrop never ceased to stun them all. So generous for such a flawed man to whom the world had been so cruel. The newlyweds thanked him and cried tears of joy.

A fiery sun sank below the horizon and released a surge of color that shone through the trees and lit up the small patch of earth that now belonged to Red and Honey Johnson. They stayed behind to gaze at the stars when their guests walked back to Whetstone Manor. Lying flat across the high grass, Chasing Honey held his wife in his arms, an unborn child in her womb, and they listened to the sounds of their new life. It was dead silent, a cloudless sky, but Hercules and Ona Judge could still hear the songs of field slaves marching off to work at Mount Vernon.

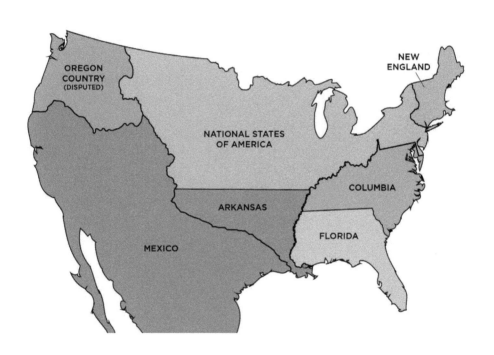

Epilogue

1820

President James Madison did his best to conceal his awe and wonder at Philadelphia's Federal Palace, its Coliseum, the immaculate bank building, and the construction of railroad tracks in and out of the famed capital city. He did not come to reminisce with Alexander Hamilton about the good old days of federalism and the First Constitutional Convention. Their friendship had fractured long ago with the deconstruction of the United States. Madison would not insult his old friend's sensibilities with empty small talk. He had official state business to conduct with the supreme leader, a man whom, in Madison's mind, had grown more powerful and more tyrannical than any European monarch.

Madison did not age with grace. Already sixty-two when he'd taken office as Columbia's third president, Madison appeared more wrinkled than a bulldog. Underneath his pale skin, veins crawled up and down his arms, and of course, his perpetual upset stomach still plagued him. He reclined in an uncomfortable wooden chair and fiddled with his silver-knobbed cane as he spoke.

"It's the worst economic crisis Columbia has ever experienced—and on my watch." Madison had begun to regret even running for president. The rough-and-tumble world of politics had beaten him down before, but he'd never learned his lesson.

"On your watch, but in no way your fault," Hamilton replied. "It's President Jefferson's policies that have led to this. And you know, James, years ago, I was the one person warning you and everyone else that Thomas Jefferson is a ruthless, rebellious, Jacobin. He's a madman."

"Thomas is a brilliant statesman and a patriot."

Hamilton sighed. "Come now. Do you really believe he retired from politics for pure and noble reasons? Giving up the presidency, not running for another term because he no longer wanted power? Horseshit! He knew what was about to happen. He initiated gradual emancipation, declared slavery over by 1820, and then got the hell out of the way before 1820 arrived. He threw it all on your lap! He's the 'great emancipator,' and you take blame for the consequences. Quite genius, actually."

Madison grunted in disgust. "Regardless of the history, it is now my problem to solve. On the one hand, Columbians are happy that our country has just about rid itself of Africans. Most moved to Florida, very few to Africa, and the ones who remain are farming for their former masters anyway. The larger dilemma is this movement in Arkansas. We've seen a mass exodus of slave owners taking their property to Arkansas for the past ten years, and they take with them productivity and commerce, the agricultural backbone of our economy."

Hamilton smiled at the chaos ensuing south of the border. The National States dominated economic activity of North America, especially since the fall of Spain's American empire. "I blame the Mexicans," he gloated. "Mexico should have never allowed an independent Arkansas in their backyard. They should have whipped those rebels into submission. Now they've got an enemy on the doorstep, as do you."

All hell had broken loose in the Spanish colonies after Napoleon invaded Spain in 1808. By 1820, Mexico and Florida had both declared independence and had both abolished slavery. Refusing to accept emancipation in lower Louisiana, Columbian expatriates declared their own independent Arkansas, the one remaining slave power in North America.

The supreme leader continued crowing from his high horse. "From what I can gather, this new president of Arkansas is the most ruthless of them all. What do you know of him?"

Madison shrugged. "Not much. He's from Tennessee—renounced his Columbian citizenship on the day Jefferson signed the Gradual Emancipation Act. Also, God in heaven could never in a million years create a human being more opposite to Alexander Hamilton than President Andrew

Jackson. Slave driver, hates banks, hates the British, and adores the poor middling class of society."

"Well, if that is the case, then he won't find much success. I've done quite well for myself and my empire. As for yours, I'm not sure I can solve Columbia's problems. You want a thriving economy again? Bring back slavery. Go ahead, ship 'em in from Africa again. Invade Arkansas, take control of it. I won't stand in your way."

Madison shook his head. "No, thank you, but there is indeed a way that you can assist—cotton. A trade agreement for the NSA to purchase cotton exclusively from Columbia. Boycott Arkansas cotton in protest of the archaic practice of slavery. The prime minister of New England is willing to do the same."

Hamilton's laughter interrupted the aging idealist. "Mr. Madison, why on earth would the National States buy Columbian cotton for three times the price? That archaic institution you refer to produces cheap cotton that fuels our textile industry. Indeed, the backbone of *our* economy. Even with the highest tariffs on Arkansas, you cannot compete with slave labor."

"Which is precisely why I am asking you to take a moral stance. Like we took a moral stance against the British, against anti-federalists in Poughkeepsie. What has happened to you, Alex?! You used to stand up for your principles. Do you have any principles left, man? I don't even recognize you anymore in that ridiculous crown."

The supreme leader rose from his throne and spoke in a low-pitched voice before showing his old friend the door. "You and your principles, James. Where have they gotten you? A failed Untied States. A faltering Columbia. And all you can do is come begging me for help. Begging like a pathetic, helpless pauper, because for all of your principles, James, you've forgotten the most important one, and the one that I've valued the most. Survival. You've failed to survive in this new world, old friend. I've won."

Benjamin Winthrop died of a heart attack, alone, with no family. None. He willed most of his vast fortune to charitable causes in the city of Winthrop to secure his legacy, the benevolent founder. Red and Honey Johnson inherited a generous amount, as did Jonathan Taylor. Benjamin also sent Jonathan back to New York City on a fool's errand to locate his beloved Lydia and present her with a large sum. The old Merchant's Coffee House had long since burned to the ground. Open political debate was not as common in the National States of America after the supreme leader had outlawed dissenting political parties and disbanded the Congress. No one in the area had ever heard of Winthrop's harlot, so Jonathan donated the bequest to the New York Society Library instead.

Winthrop passed down the largest endowment of his estate to Jonathan for his endeavors in education. Jonathan turned the giant land grant on High Street into Winthrop-Taylor University, the first Negro college in the National States of America.

On a brisk autumn morning, a guest speaker arrived at the main lecture hall on the Winthrop-Taylor campus. She was thirty-two years old, Canadian, and nervous, even though she had over-prepared her remarks on the history of slavery in America. Eliza Hale gnawed at her fingernails and raised her chin to see the small gathering of young black scholars, most of whom were born free citizens. She gripped the podium hard as she began her speech in a deep, raspy voice.

"Most people don't believe me when I say that I grew up on George Washington's plantation at Mount Vernon in Virginia. I lived there for the first fifteen years of my life, before my escape. I was a young infant, too young to remember when Washington was murdered by his stableman, Peter Hardiman." The crowd hushed as she described the hideous murder. "All I know of my mother is that she was a skilled seamstress, but she fell out of favor with the new master after Washington's death. He sold her to a Georgia trader before I grew old enough to know her. Today, she could be free in Florida or a slave in Arkansas. She could be dead from the war, or perhaps a runaway like me. I'll never know. It was rumored that my father was a white man, although my dark skin would suggest otherwise."

This brought a slight laugh from the audience, but one of very few throughout her solemn talk. She described slave life at the mansion and labor in the fields with gruesome detail. Work, expectations, and punishment.

She explained her yearning for belonging in an environment that discouraged family bonds. Eliza's tale of escape captivated her audience the most.

"By 1800, the population of runaways outnumbered those of us still in bondage. Slavery had become unsustainable. The only means left to manage a plantation was the use of extreme violence, brute force, and the overseers at Mount Vernon did just that, especially after Lady Washington died in 1802. At the same time, the abolitionist movement reached the height of its popularity in New England and Canada. Boats roamed the Potomac River, many of them full of escapees and other abolitionists looking to rescue us. This was very risky business, though. Slave catchers often posed as freedom fighters to lure you into a boat and then punish you for attempting to escape."

She horrified the students with a grim account of a father and son tied up, face-to-face, and whipped to shreds, together, by two different overseers.

"Later, I learned how to interpret the coded language used to identify a legitimate northern vessel. On the evening of my exodus, three men dressed in black rowed close to the riverbank. They offered protection and escape. I replied, 'But my master is wealthy and provides me clothing and shelter,' to which they gave the correct response, a bible verse: 'Set your mind on things above, not on earthly things.' I recognized the code and didn't look back. They took me to Nova Scotia, where today I live in freedom and work in a clothing factory, a seamstress like my mother. It seems that New England will soon annex Nova Scotia and New Brunswick, so I guess that will make me a New Englander. Oh, how men like to draw imaginary lines and then fight over them. It is imaginary lines that divide us. Imaginary lines between slavery and freedom, and between the nations of North America."

An attentive young pupil sat in the cold lecture hall that morning, one of the few females in the class, and by far the most intelligent student at Winthrop-Taylor University. She stood almost six feet tall, her face heavily freckled. The speech brought tears to her eyes. Charlotte Johnson thought about her parents and their struggles. She thought about boundaries, imaginary lines, and the threads of humanity that connect the past to the present. Across those imaginary lines, Americans draw warmth from the same rising sun, their lives held in orbit by the same blue-sky moon.

Appendix

CONFEDERATION OF COLUMBIA: HEADS OF STATE THROUGH 1850

Term	President	Political Party	Vice President
1789 – 1793 (1 term)	Patrick Henry (VA)	None	Charles Cotesworth Pinckney* (SC)
1793 – 1813 (5 terms)	Thomas Jefferson (VA)	Democratic-Republican	James McHenry (MD) Robert Smith (MD)
1813 – 1821 (2 terms)	James Madison (VA)	Democratic-Republican	Robert Smith (MD)
1821 – 1829 (2 terms)	William Wirt (MD)	Democratic-Republican	James Monroe (VA)
1829 – 1845 (4 terms)	Henry Clay (KY)	Whig	John Forsyth (SC) Winfield Scott (VA)
1845 – 1853 (2 terms)	John Tyler (VA)	Whig	John Branch (NC)

*Died in office

NATIONAL STATES OF AMERICA:
HEADS OF STATE THROUGH 1850

Term (Life term)	Supreme Leader
1790 – 1823	Alexander Hamilton* (NY)
1823 – 1841	William Henry Harrison* (OH)
1841 – 1866	Lewis Cass* (MI)

*Died in office

REPUBLIC OF NEW ENGLAND:
HEADS OF STATE THROUGH 1850

Term	Prime Minister	Political Party
1790 – 1810 (4 terms)	John Adams (MA)	Federalist
1810 – 1812 (1 term)	George Clinton (SA)*	Anti-Federalist
1812 – 1825 (2 terms)	John Quincy Adams (MA)	Federalist
1825 – 1830 (1 term)	Dewitt Clinton (SA)	Anti-Federalist
1830 – 1840 (2 terms)	Daniel Webster (MA)	Whig
1840 – 1850 (2 terms)	Martin Van Buren (SA)	Democrat

Died in office

ARKANSAS:
HEADS OF STATE THROUGH 1850

Term (1 term limit)	President	Vice President
1820 – 1828	Andrew Jackson	Roger Taney
1828 – 1836	William Crawford	John Calhoun
1836 – 1844	John Calhoun	Richard Call
1844 – 1852	Sam Houston	James K. Polk *

*Died in office

FLORIDA:
HEADS OF STATE THROUGH 1850

Term	Executive Council
1820 – 1832	Juan Jose de Estrada Sequoyah John Berrien
1832 – 1836	Jose Masot Micanopy Wilson Lumpkin
1836 – 1842	Jose Maria Coppinger Osceola William Schley
1842 – 1854	Joseph Jenkins Roberts John Ross William Dunn Moseley

MEXICO:
HEADS OF STATE THROUGH 1850

Term	Emperor		
1820 – 1824	Augustin de Iturbide		
Term	**President**	**Political Party**	**Vice President**
1824 – 1829	Guadalupe Victoria	None	Nicolas Bravo
1829	Vincente Guerrero	Liberal Party	Anastasio Bustamante
1830 – 1832	Anastasio Bustamante	Conservative Party	--
1832 – 1833	Manuel Gomez Pedraza	Liberal Party	--
1833 – 1835	Antonio Lopez de Santa Anna	Liberal Party	Valentin Gomez Farias
1835 – 1836	Miguel Barragan*	Liberal Party	--
1836 – 1837	Jose Justo Corro	Conservative Party	--
1837 – 1841	Anastasio Bustamante	Conservative Party	--
1841 – 1847	Antonio Lopez de Santa Anna	Liberal Party	Valentin Gomez Farias
1847 – 1851	Jose Joaquin de Herrera	Liberal Party	--

Died in office

OREGON:
HEADS OF STATE THROUGH 1850

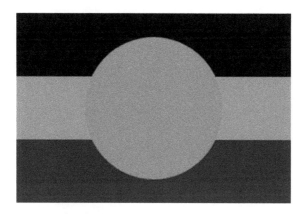

Term	President	Vice President
1848 – 1856	Abraham Lincoln	Thaddeus Stevens

About the Author

Adam Sivitz teaches early US history, American civics, and psychology at Chartiers Valley High School in Bridgeville, Pennsylvania. Also an accomplished musician, he has toured throughout the United States, composed and recorded music for the Weather Channel, and performed on national television. He currently lives in Pittsburgh with his wife and cats.

CPSIA information can be obtained
at www.ICGtesting.com
Printed in the USA
LVHW05s1756021018
592155LV00012B/1134/P